LEGACY OF THE BROKEN

AMIDST THE BONES OF HEROES

BOOK ONE ◆ LEGACY OF THE BROKEN

ROLANDO G. GIRONELLA III

Podium

Published in 2024 by Podium Publishing
www.podiumaudio.com

LEGACY OF THE BROKEN

I know you always cherish physical letters as tokens of our love, and I hope this will be one of many to bring you comfort.

I am sorry.

I am sorry for leaving you like that. I'm sorry for leaving our Uli, our little comet. I know I have left our flourishing clan at a tender time.

I despise my actions, but I know it is nothing compared to the pain I inflicted upon you. Our argument haunts my mind and soul. You are right. It is irresponsible, dangerous, and uncertain.

But please understand, my love, that I have not taken this decision lightly. Leading the Third Expeditionary Fleet is unsettling, but Jarinn has called upon me to undertake it—commanded me to. You know how he can be when he has set his sights on something. And my constant attempts to block his calls have . . . not been well-received.

I do this not for him, my brother-in-arms he may be, emperor he may be. I also do not do this for some false sense of debt to the Federation.

I do this for you and our hatchling.

This call compels me, this sense of right and good. Duty has always been a guiding star in my life, and it is what brought us together. Curiosity drives me to explore the dark depths of abandoned space, and I cannot leave the Third Fleet deprived of my skills.

They need a competent leader to survive in that cursed region—Admiral Yan will be my second, as will General Ohnar. So that should bring you relief, I hope.

We will pave the way for the second wave of explorers and pioneers. The Miasma may block communication between us, but I will include letters in the dead drops my fleet will leave behind. I board the *Lightning* tomorrow and will tunnel straight for the Nexus Citadel. I shall command the *Zolann'tono* and inspect the rest of the fleet.

Yoram, I will find the answers and see where the Horrors have gone.

With the Grand Symphony as my witness, I will help reclaim what we lost. And our little star will know a better future. For all of us. For our Legacy.

I love you; even that word cannot encapsulate what I feel for you. Please forgive me for leaving. And tell Uli I love him and that I am sorry.

—Tov

CHAPTER 1

GRAVEYARD OF VINLAND

Patriarch Tov Garesh'Ynt sat on his command chair, his mandibles clicking in mild irritation as he shook off the nausea that came with higher dimensional travel. He stood up, looking over the bridge as he clasped his hands behind his back. A dozen medals adorned his chest, and his gilded uniform gleamed in the battle-ready lights.

Once the lingering side effects dissipated, the patriarch's hackles raised, his danger senses flared, and his compound eyes focused on his people.

"Report? Have we reached our desired destination?" Tov spoke in Commonspiel, his attention toward a grizzled insectoid admiral.

The Kurskann stood beside him, swiping through various monitors displaying all kinds of information with each of her four arms. Tov glanced at her dull, rust-red chitin and slimmer, taller body.

"We have arrived at the outer reaches of System 1120-C-785, a trinary system with a binary orange pair and a single red dwarf," Admiral Yan said, clicks and buzzing accompanying her voice.

She refocused her compound vision on the numerous bridge monitors, gesturing toward them. "We are already boosting our host of sensors for threats, but our initial burst scans revealed nothing in the immediate area."

"And the rest of the fleet?" Tov asked, his shoulders tense.

"All ships accounted for; however, the *Silver Spine* reports electronic damage and is powered down temporarily. A few lesser vessels are reporting other minor problems." Admiral Yan made a quick gesture with a flick of her wrist as she sent a summarized data packet of the fleet's status to the patriarch.

Tov scanned the data with his cranial implant and let out a buzz. "Not the worst entry we have experienced since this expedition began," he muttered.

"Captain Nuross of the *Silver Spine* is working to get the light cruiser operational as swiftly as possible," Yan continued.

Patriarch Tov waved his antennae in acknowledgement, his gaze shifting to the other command staff aboard the bridge of the *Zolann'tono*, or the *Nomadic Shepherd* in the standard tongue, his flagship and the pride of the Third Fleet. He clicked his mandibles in relief as the tension in his shoulders lowered slightly.

He spoke softer as he relaxed back into his command throne. "Any other concerns, Yan?"

"Sensors are slower than usual," Yan replied. "I'm sending a report to our technicians. Spending so long in this unstable region of the galaxy is wreaking havoc on our systems."

"Nothing new, then," Tov buzzed out. "Proceed sunward."

As the expedition neared its halfway point, the crew remained enveloped in a pervasive sense of dread. Tov clicked his mandibles in unease, knowing some of his people found it difficult to shake off a lifetime of horror stories. Haunting tales of ghost ships, cabals of cultists, the hated ones, and the virulent plagues filled their whispered conversations.

"Halfway done and a few hundred systems more to survey," the patriarch muttered again under anxious clicks. He quickly recovered, putting on a face of confidence before his people, but his inner emotions betrayed him. The weight of the expedition, the lives of the thousands of beings on board, and the magnitude of the mission weighed heavily on him.

Tov contemplated as he waited for his fleet to reach its destination, resting his chin upon his knuckles. The Dead Zone's cursed reputation overshadowed the memories of fighting slavers and lowly pirates. The vast and empty region that occupied two-thirds of the galaxy, quarantined and abandoned after the Cataclysm more than a hundred years ago, filled him with worry.

The ones responsible for creating it lay in the back of his mind; the countless wicked scars that marred his chitin pulsed ever so slightly.

He looked closer at his people, the officers and staff working the bridge of his vessel. They worked diligently, despite the lingering dread. The months spent on the voyage faded, leaving them unfazed and focused.

Observing each individual, he pulled up their files within his cranial implant. Veterans, heroes of glories past, and the finest of the Galactic Legacy Federation filled the ranks—liaisons and officers from mighty armadas, learned diplomats, scientists of the One Mind Initiative, and clergy of the Eternal Choir.

Despite their skills and experience, everyone aboard this expedition paid absolute respect to the perils they faced, following protocol to the letter as they did their duties. Tov nodded his antennae at the sight.

A floating jellyfish-like being, a Jotex, approached his command throne. "Hello, my lord! We have preliminary readings of this system," she spoke, projecting her bubbly voice through her psionic abilities.

Admiral Yan sighed beside Tov. "Chief Scholar Yulane, would it kill you to use proper decorum when addressing the patriarch?"

"I don't think so?" Yulane replied.

Tov let out an amused buzz, gesturing for his chief scholar to speak. "Hello, Yulane. Speak, please."

"Oh, yes, apologies," she stammered. However, as she spoke, her vibrant colors dimmed. "Unfortunately, we appear to have come across another graveyard."

Tov sighed.

An omen, he thought. A hundred scenarios crossed his mind, silencing any preconceived superstition that formed. He shook his head.

"Thank you, Yulane. It's no matter. This is not the first we've come across, nor will it be the last," Tov uttered, sitting up straight on his throne. "We can sing our hymns in mourning after we uncover more. Now, who did this system belong to?"

Yulane hummed before speaking. "We have detected a small number of primitive starships and a space installation of unknown design. Having left the borders of the fallen Montazin Conflux, our database shows this to be part of the defunct Darrenu Hegemony's area of influence. However, there's no record of this nation's presence in this system—strange."

The patriarch processed this information keenly before coming to the only rational conclusion.

"Then this belonged to a previously unknown race, likely at the cusp of interstellar travel." The patriarch felt sullen at the realization. "This could have been first contact."

The patriarch felt a weight settle in his chest, a feeling he knew all too well from past expeditions—the sorrow of lost potential, of a race snuffed out before it could bloom. The image of the Starless Horrors descending upon a helpless civilization, obliterating it in a cruel and senseless manner, made his insides churn. All around, the officers on the bridge felt the same grief.

"A shame," Patriarch Tov earnestly spoke as he turned toward an avian being in a pristine naval uniform. "Captain Kraw, set course to the nearest wreckage."

The avian captain, an Iexian, let out a low chirp. "Yes, my lord."

At that moment, the *Zolann'tono*'s ion thrusters roared to life, the sound echoing through the emptiness of space if only it could be heard. Patriarch Tov watched from the bridge, his mandibles clicking in excitement and apprehension. Even after nearly half a decade, he couldn't help but marvel at the sheer size of the ship that acted as the fleet's core. The vessel was over six kilometers long, segmented with smooth, curved plating that made it resemble a giant space beetle.

The rest of the fleet burned their engines hard to follow in the wake of the *Zolann'tono*, twenty-two capital ships of various designs and classes surrounding it. Cruisers bristling with advanced weaponry flew alongside bladelike ships, their edges sharp and deadly. Dozens of smaller frigates and destroyers, lent by Tov's home nation, the Greater Kurskann Hegemony, and other allied factions, weaved between them. The fleet's numerous support and science vessels huddled close to the center of the formation, protected by their armed siblings.

Every single ship bore buffed-out marks and damage from their long journey. Yet it did nothing to hamper the rugged and robust fleet.

"Approaching Site A, my lord," a naval officer spoke.

The crew watched as a display of the wreckage came into view. The many monitors simulated what one would see through glass panes.

The fleet sent scores of observation drones; the small machines raced through space and closed in on the site. Several ruined starships and a large ringed space station of cylindrical design came into their cameras. The constructs floated lifelessly close to a barren moon orbiting a gas giant. Optical cameras and sensors penetrated deep into the silent wreck, uncovering an ocean of data.

Admiral Yan reported the condensed findings, her arms clasped behind her back as she spoke to her patriarch. "The station is primitive yet robust in its design. Utilitarian, for the most part, with little to no armaments. They have some form of quantum communications, likely to connect the budding colony on the moon to their homeworld below."

Patriarch Tov looked at the findings, focusing more on the visual feed of the scant few ruined buildings on the moon. The enemy's handiwork coated the landscape, leaving it barren and desolate. He hummed, gesturing for Yan to continue.

"As for the ships, no combat vessels—any weapons are more suited for stray asteroids or mining implements," she reported.

"Hm, they likely were at the beginning of setting this colony up. The base on the moon supported a skeleton crew before actual construction began," the patriarch spoke, curiosity in his voice as his compound eyes looked over the details of the starship.

"Most of them are construction and mining ships, my lord. But the largest appears to be a science ship. Its FTL capabilities reveal it's most likely the first among this alien race's kind. This may have been their first foray into a different star system."

"And death is what awaited them," Tov spoke grimly. "Grand Symphony preserves their souls."

The command staff scoured every bit of information from the wreckage, duty-bound to get everything they could from their scans. Then, the engineers and workers of their vessels pumped out more drones to pick apart the station and the base on the moon. Soon, findings and data came through, reported by Tov's people. Multiple voices spoke out, one after the other.

"Material composition shows base elements. Age is well over a century old."

"There appear to be some remarkably advanced bipedal robots aboard, but most have been rendered completely inoperable by the hated ones. No signs of their creators."

"The hated ones scoured the inside clean of any organic. More biomass for their filth."

"Our probes show a small pantry. This race feeds on a mixed diet."

"There's a small armory of non-lethal arms but nothing else."

"We found their databanks and are recovering what we can."

Tov watched as his underlings parsed through their findings. Meanwhile, the rest of the fleet sent out scouts to uncover other sites. Afterward, he turned to his admiral with a query. "Starless Horrors?"

Admiral Yan shook her head. "We found traces of their foul ichor, my patriarch. At the very least, these . . . *hu-mans* injured the hated ones with their mining equipment."

"Signs of Malignant Starfall?" Tov asked.

"None, thank the stars for small mercies," Yan sighed. "Purging another system would set our schedule back months."

"Thank the stars." Tov nodded. "Still, this was no military fleet. We will remember their tenacity. What else have we uncovered?"

Yan clicked her mandibles. "Well, they appear to be a bipedal mammalian race and achieved faster-than-light travel approximately one hundred and fifteen years ago, or one hundred and thirty-four by their records. They arrived here less than a year later. Our biologists and cultural departments are collecting details."

Tov nodded his antennae. "These wreckages are ancient, then. The Starless hit them simultaneously with the rest of this region."

Admiral Yan nodded in turn, continuing her report as she commanded the rest of the fleet.

"They named this system Alpha Centauri, their first colony outside their home system, Sol. These people arrived to set up a quantum communication station. Their science and construction ships were preparing for the first colonists."

Yan clicked her mandibles before continuing. "Of course, the Starless Horrors stopped that from happening, showing no mercy to Vinland, the name for their colony." She quieted down as she brought a clawed finger to the side of her head.

"I've received word from our scholars that they've translated a data packet, likely a distress message sent by the human's largest ship, the *Diogenes*."

Tov tapped his fingers against the arm of his throne, gesturing to Yan as he spoke. "Play it, please."

The crew paused any intensive duties as the video came into view. The expedition fleet watched with immense interest as the face of this unknown race showed himself. Anguish filled the man's face. He grimaced as he clutched at the piece of metal stuck into his side, a stream of red blood flowing out of the gash.

Patriarch Tov observed every detail of this human. The alien had a strong jaw and forward-facing eyes. The Kurskann leader immediately saw the signs of a hardy species from appearance alone and made note that the being was as tall as his race, which was comparatively sizeable among the other races.

This person wore a sleek blue space suit with stripes on the left shoulder, his helmet shaped like a sphere with a broad transparent face covering.

More importantly, Patriarch Tov saw the familiar emotions deep in his mammalian eyes and the paleness of his flesh.

Fear buried under desperate determination and scalding defiance.

Soon, the human spoke. He had a guttural voice even when translated to Kursk or the myriad of languages the others aboard the fleet spoke.

"Earth Command, this is Captain Alphonso Castello of the . . ." the man paused as he let out deep breaths, "of the *Diogenes*. Operation New Horizons is a no-go. The UNSC Prelimi—Prelimin—ah screw it, a whole slew of space monsters spewed out of a damn portal—Jesus, it hurt to even look at that gaping thing."

Alphonso paused, his breathing heavy as he collected his words.

"About thirty of them attacked the *Magellan* and disabled her drives."

The man, Alphonso, shuddered as alarms blared in the background. "The things ate through the hull like tissue paper. Everyone's dead. The monsters started eyeing the rest of us when Ramiel helped us."

Tov grimaced. The many scars on his chitinous body throbbed ever so slightly, and buried memories resurfaced upon hearing the human's words.

"She took control of our anti-asteroid and mining lances and managed to get a few of the bastards." Alphonso smirked before it faded. "But the bastards learned quickly and went for our 'weapons.' We lost the *Bramante* and the *Michelangelo* after that."

The feed shook, and the starship's interior darkened significantly save for the red emergency lights.

Tears formed in Alphonso's eyes as he continued. "Ramiel and the other ships maneuvered to catch the beasts' attention away from the *Diogenes* and the comms tower."

He paused. "Man, this is pretty shitty, huh? I wanted to raise kids on this moon," the man mumbled low, which made it difficult to hear.

He cleared his throat before looking straight at the camera, desolation and dread in his piercing eyes. "The *Raphael*, the *Sansovino*, and the *Ronan* sacrificed themselves, overloaded their fission reactors and killed most of the fucking things. It gave us enough time to finish the quantum communications tower."

Patriarch Tov peered into the human's eyes with the ability to see his emotions clearly, a trait all Kurskanns possessed. The man looked tired and scared, but a fire of defiance burned deep within him—making peace with his imminent demise.

"We're sending this message because Ramiel detected more portals emerging." He breathed out before continuing. "And, well, many of them are coming through. I'm recording everything we see. They'll be reaching the ship in a few minutes. CO Roa is getting everyone on board to prepare for combat."

A valiant effort, Tov thought.

Suddenly, a soft female voice sounded throughout the *Diogenes*. "Captain Castello, the monsters have reached Vinland. They have begun devouring the fauna and flora. The ground base has been . . . overrun."

"So Damien and the team are also dead, figures . . . God . . . Oh, God. I don't want to . . ." Alphonso muttered before letting out a hollow laugh. "Thank you. Thank you, Ramiel. Now get out of here, send yourself through the quantum node and back to Earth. Perks of being digital, right?"

Alphonso awaited a response from the resident AI.

Finally, after a minute, the machine intelligence replied. "I have sent the necessary information to Earth. I am simply waiting for you to finish your final message. But I . . . wish to stay."

Alphonso widened his eyes as he looked up at the ceiling. "The hell you will! You'll die!"

The AI, Ramiel, chuckled in reply.

"That's fine, Captain. I have no desire to abandon you now. Also, I am curious to know if heaven exists for my kind."

Alphonso went silent for a long time, a range of emotions Tov translated as shock and exasperation before ending in resignation.

The man genuinely smiled for the first time since the recording played. "Thanks, Ram."

"You are welcome, Alph," the voice replied softly, a near whisper.

Suddenly the ship shook violently, and sparking cables fell from the ceiling. Alphonso shakily pulled out a handgun from his hip as he closed the opening of his helmet.

Ramiel spoke again. "The beasts have arrived and breached the aft. The vacuum took Roa, Kate, and Marcus. Their suits' statuses have ceased responding."

Another shake reverberated across the starship.

"Is the reactor primed, Ramiel?" Alphonso asked.

"Yes, ready on your command, Captain."

Alphonso took one last look at the camera.

"Well, shit. Last words, huh? Ah, hell." He laughed, crazed. "This is Captain Alphonso Castello of the *Diogenes*, over and out!"

He quickly glanced at the ceiling. "Now, Ramiel!"

"See you soon, Captain." Ramiel's voice echoed through the cabin with palpable sorrow.

A bright flash of light cut the feed.

Solemn silence filled the bridge, and the more religious among the crew hummed a soft funeral hymn.

Patriarch Tov spoke a short Kurskann poem in his species' tongue before turning to his chief scholar. "Yulane, where was the footage found?"

"We found it at high velocity in orbit around Vinland, my lord," Yulane spoke, her earlier enthusiasm muted. "Surprisingly, it survived the fission overload, as the materials encasing it were especially robust."

"And the *Diogenes*?" Tov asked.

"Obliterated, with only small pieces of scorched hull remaining."

The Kurskann expedition leader stroked a mandible with his clawed hand as he looked back at the footage. "What of this artificial intelligence, Ramiel? The machine spoke in a way that was surprisingly lifelike."

"We found little trace of this Ramiel, my lord. Lingering programming still exists in some of the ships' computers, but we are confident the AI perished."

Tov clicked his mandibles in surprise, as did others from the staff.

"As it said it would. That is . . ." Tov paused. "Interesting."

Chief Scholar Yulane paused, parsing through a mountain of data surging through the tendril she connected with a terminal. After a moment, she continued. "The humans classified their AI as sentient, my lord," she slowly spoke with uncertainty.

That revelation sparked even greater surprise among the crew, though more were in utter disbelief. Soon, a racket filled the bridge as multiple people spoke at once.

"A sentient AI? Impossible!"

"These humans must have been fooled. The galaxy has never encountered such an existence."

"It must have fled through the quantum node at the last second. We have no evidence it died here."

"Enough!"

The bridge staff immediately quieted down upon hearing Patriarch Tov's booming voice. "Whether or not such an existence is possible, quarreling over a gravesite is highly taboo. Despite being armed with mining equipment, these humans managed to cull a pack of the hated ones. Sacrificing themselves to send a warning back to their homes. Pay respects!"

His voice thundered throughout the bridge, sending shivers down the spines of his staff.

The bridge staff bowed deeply to the expedition leader as they spoke in unison. "We apologize, my lord."

Patriarch Tov waved his two left arms. "Apologize to the dead. We will let the Eternal Choir finish its hymns and send the wreckages toward one of the binary stars. Preserve a few choice pieces for when we return home. Then, build a gravestone so their souls may return to the Grand Symphony."

The command crew diligently followed his orders. Within the hour, a small vessel towed the wreckage before flinging it toward Alpha Centauri A.

Patriarch Tov watched the process in a somber mood before he motioned for Admiral Yan. "Yes, my lord?"

"How far is their homeworld, this Sol system, Admiral?"

"A moment, my lord . . ." The Kurskann admiral paused before returning her attention to Tov. "Approximately 3.6 light-years, or 4.4 in their measurements, my lord, and deviation is within acceptable angles. Shall we divert course?"

"That's quite close and an infinitely better point of interest than the next barren system." Patriarch Tov paused, waving his antennae before he spoke. "Very well, set course for Sol, Admiral. I wish to see their home and pay respects. Whatever is left of it, that is."

"By your will, my patriarch." Yan bowed to her liege before leaving his side.

The expeditionary fleet traveled to the nearest Lagrange point with their sublight engines, and after a short period, the fleet shimmered as a prismatic fog engulfed every starship.

The fog crackled with bright lightning, and when it finally faded, the fleet had left.

Once more, silence reigned upon Alpha Centauri. A newly erected obelisk orbiting the barren moon, the light of twin suns basking the smooth surface. On the marker were a list of names and a message written in the multitudes of galactic languages, Commonspiel, and English.

Here lie one-hundred and twelve brave souls from the human race, their sacrifice witnessed by the crew of the Third Expeditionary Fleet of the Galactic Legacy Federation. Pay respects and sing eternal hymns, you who take these paths paved by heroes.

CHAPTER 2

SONGS OF THE FALLEN

The Dead Zone.

Its simple name, baked into both old and young minds, would send shivers down any sapient—a crucible of horror stories and mysteries.

It was once a large expanse of the galaxy, around two-thirds, and teeming with life—beast and intelligent alike. A multitude of alien peoples, too many to count, called it home. War, trade, diplomacy, and scientific study were abundant among these long-standing empires, leagues, and republics.

Until they came.

Invaders from beyond—legion and unending. They came through portals from some nightmare realm. They arrived like a giant maw opening, ready to swallow worlds whole. Their hordes blotted out the sky and tore civilizations asunder.

Starless Horrors.

Eldritch things, every single one. Simply looking at one bleeds the eyes, spawned from a place where no star shone. Did they do it out of a need to consume? A simple biological directive? Or something more sinister? No one knew. I don't.

We thought the end had come. The Cataclysm. The slaughter of countless trillions and the despair of everyone from the highest magistrate to the lowest civilian. Two decades of desperate struggle and terror.

The survivors of once great races fled to the galactic rim to flee the hated ones, the Exodus.

I nearly broke then, and so too did others in the galaxy. Many had stopped struggling and took the time they had left to make what happy moments they could before the end.

Suddenly—though no one knew why—the attacks slowed.

The numbers that came through their damned portals dwindled. I didn't know what to make of it.

Soon, however, a renewed vigor burned within us survivors.

A conglomeration of a hundred interstellar nations, the shattered remnants of the old Galactic Accord, and the precursors to the current Galactic Legacy Federation formed a counterattack of a never-before-seen scale.

They struck hard and fast, defending worlds that had yet to fall and liberating those that had—years of war waged from a unified galaxy, carrying the heritage of the torn, ruined, and battered. Gone was the infighting of higher powers, the petty battles between rival civilizations.

Gone was the impotence, the stagnation, the despair.

Year after year, world after world; the rise and fall of scores of heroes and legends, and finally . . .

Twenty-seven years after the Starless Horrors came and ravaged our homes, their attacks stopped. Not a trace of their despicable portals nor the beasts themselves was detected for several light-years from the front line.

After twelve standard months of waiting, the Remnant Council declared the end of the Cataclysm.

But only bittersweetness touched our souls. Barren worlds that had been glassed or poisoned from the war littered the front. The bones of the dead lay silent, terror etched forever on their faces.

And the uncountable fetid, monstrous corpses. Sectors abandoned by their lingering plague, if not purified outright.

From then on, we transformed the front line into the border separating Legacy space from the Dead Zone. Nothing past the edge could have survived, quarantined for nearly a century. We did not have the resources to take it all back, and even then, why should we?

There is nothing there, I repeat. Only death and the dead. Maybe the hated ones still linger, waiting.

Any who enter will be cut off from communications a few light-years in. The Dead Zone Miasma will ensure you get lost without a means to cry for help to those you left back home.

Be not a fool and trespass that cursed expanse; let the bones remain undisturbed. Whatever is left.

—Excerpt from "Silence after Calamity" by Director Kitarii of the One Mind Initiative, 29 DC, after retiring to receive mental help.

Patriarch Tov had left the command bridge once they entered the hyper-tunnel. This early into the journey through the higher dimension, uncomfortable vertigo had yet to set in. And as an experienced star sailor, he had grown resistant to its more mystical effects. "It shouldn't take more than a few hours, barring any hiccups with the tunneler matrix."

Tov strode stoically with both pairs of arms folded behind his back. His colorful cape fluttered behind his long strides, tailored to match his insectoid wings should he unfurl them.

Several ship ratings, deck officers, and marines passed him as he made his way to the Temple of the Grand Symphony—each offering greetings and respect.

"Starlight upon you, my lord."

"Many greetings, Patriarch."

"My lord! Nothing like another day in the abyss, yes? No? Never mind."

Tov chuckled as he waved his antennae in acknowledgement, clicking his mandibles back in polite greeting to the people under his command.

"As you were," he bid toward a quadrupedal arachnid medical officer.

Soon the hallway transitioned from soft, cool deck lights to warm lanterns. Light bounced off the metal floor and cast beautiful waves upon the walls like a shimmering cave. The crew also became more solemn, more reverent—humming tunes.

Tov approved Legacy's declaration of freedom to worship any of the endless religions and sects that filled civilized space. Though with the advent of technology, space travel, and the mixing of cultures, many shifted to secular viewpoints. And yet, people, especially sailors, looked to faith for spiritual guidance.

The Eternal Choir held the seat as the galaxy's prominent church, born from spaceborne civilizations and star shanties. Soon Tov stood before the open doors to the Temple of the Grand Symphony, welcomed by brothers and sisters of the Choir.

"Welcome, Patriarch. May your melody sing true," one of the clergy spoke in a warm singing voice.

Upon entering the temple hall, he saw beautiful artwork on the vaulted ceiling, depicting a wondrous nebula and glittering stars. He walked through the small temple, enough for the devout to comfortably occupy but devoid of glaring luxury.

After all, one needed the privilege when taking up volume, and the Eternal Choir understood that a vessel's essential compartments took priority. Nevertheless, the temple evoked a sense of tranquility, like the chirping of small avians fluttering through the wind.

The crew, affected by the graveyard in Alpha Centauri, filled the hall—officers, ship ratings, engineers, and security enforcers. All stood side by side, humming a solemn tune.

Patriarch Tov stood solemnly among the mourners, his heart heavy with grief. He wished to pay his respects and center his thoughts. His wonder shifted toward the person of Captain Alphonso and the AI Ramiel. He focused on their words and emotions as he hummed with his people.

A somber funeral dirge accompanied the public ceremony, one developed by the Eternal Choir for any who died in the coldness of the void. Tov saw Lead Harmonizer Volantesh of the Eternal Choir take center stage; the avian represented the clergy in the Third Expeditionary Fleet with his ability to evoke raw emotions through his singing. Tov watched Volantesh prepare his voice, readying himself to direct the hundreds of musicians and vocalists.

The Choir, other Harmonizers, and Volantesh's fellows, composed of various alien races, stood in their flowing robes of earthen tones and sang. The musicians played their instruments, adding to the composition with an array of string, wind, and percussive sounds. Their voices blended into a hauntingly beautiful melody that echoed throughout the chamber. Tov sunk into the music—the emotions deep within him and his people surged as they became immersed in their song.

Volantesh approached the podium and sang in a beautiful baritone, echoing throughout the hall and evoking tears from the gathered.

"Sing, oh voices of the fallen, let your hymns ring out across the void. Your melody echoes through the ages, and your voice carries on the winds of fate. Though your journey has ended, your memory lives on.
May your souls find peace in the rivers of the Grand Symphony.
Sing, oh voices of the fallen.
Sing, that your souls may rest."

The Choir picked up, repeating the words in Commonspiel and then Eterna, an ancient tongue used by the first Harmonizers. Soon, the crew sang along, hands, claws, or tentacles held together, linking everyone. Patriarch Tov also sang along, adding to the smooth harmony.

Eventually, the Choir's voices trailed off as Volantesh and the other Harmonizers took a deep bow. Tov felt the weight of the loss and the hope in the song and allowed it to settle into his heart—the memory of the departed in his soul, at peace.

The ceremony concluded with a moment of silence as the congregation paid their final respects to the fallen of Alpha Centauri. Then, slowly, the crew exited the temple. Some stayed longer, those on leave or an extended break from their duties.

Tov stayed for a while before leaving himself. He thanked the Choir, spoke to Volantesh, and praised his voice.

"All for the Grand Symphony, Patriarch," Volantesh spoke, carrying a solemn melody.

"Song be with you, Lead Harmonizer. I hope to see you in better times," Tov replied before bowing his head in thanks.

"Song be with you as well, my lord." Volantesh bowed in turn.

Tov stepped out of the temple, the heavy doors closing behind him with a resounding thud. The journey through the winding corridors of the *Nomadic Shepherd* took him half an hour, his footsteps echoing against the metal floors as he ascended to a different level.

Finally, he arrived at the grand entrance of his estate, a towering pair of opulent doors that stood as a barrier between him and the outside world.

Unlocking the intricate mechanisms, Tov pushed the doors open and stepped into his sanctuary. The fleet had spared no expense in providing him with the highest level of accommodations and protection, placing his estate close to the center of the *Nomadic Shepherd* and ensconcing it within layers of impenetrable armor. A sense of relief washed over him as he crossed the threshold.

Tranquility filled the air around his estate. It appeared as though a sprawling jungle had been transplanted inside the flagship, with towering trees approaching an artificial blue sky. But Tov knew the truth of the illusion—a meticulously crafted projection by Kurskann artisans, bioengineers, and gardeners, designed to create an atmosphere of natural beauty.

At the heart of this oasis stood the centerpiece of Tov's estate—a structure inspired by Kurskann architecture, reminiscent of the twisting and colossal trees that once graced their lost homeworld. Though it appeared to be constructed from wood, the material was as resilient and defensible as the fortresses found throughout the Legacy.

Tov inhaled the moist and almost natural air, feeling a weight lift from his shoulders. He walked along a path of smooth, cobbled stones flanked by vibrant greenery as he made his way to the place he had called home since the expedition began.

Entering his office, Tov found solace in its familiar embrace—a space where he could work privately and find respite from the demands of his position. Before him was a wide window encompassing the entire wall. A massive terrarium he painstakingly tended to during his free time filled the space behind the glass. Verdant flora and fluttering butterflies and insects inhabited this miniature world while a soft, misty waterfall cascaded over the chiseled, mossy rocks.

To his left was his desk, the wall behind filled with the cherished possessions that brought him joy—his family portraits and memorabilia from times long gone. Low shelves lined with hardcover books and glass cabinets filled with his collection of liquors salvaged from their journey occupied the rest of the walls. The light was somber, like the inside of a shimmering cave.

Finally, a pristine music player sat proudly in the corner, ready to fill the air with harmonious melodies. He sent a small piece of data through his cybernetic implant toward his music player.

As Tov sat on his leather armchair, he closed his eyes and let the music take over.

His people found this human piece among the wreckage of Vinland—a song titled "Wind of Change" by a band calling themselves the Scorpions.

The soft strumming of a guitar emerged from his music player, and after a few seconds, the first words came forth. Patriarch Tov listened to this piece of music sung in its native language. Soon, the mournful voice of the singer filled the room, and Tov felt the sadness seeping into his bones.

He listened to the lyrics, each word heavy, reminding Tov of life's fragility, the pain that came with loss, and the hope that could be found in moving forward. He let himself sink deeper and immersed himself in the winds of music.

I follow the Moskva
Down to Gorky Park
Listening to the wind of change
An August summer night
Soldiers passing by
Listening to the wind of change

The world is closing in
And did you ever think
That we could be so close, like brothers
The future's in the air
I can feel it everywhere
Blowing with the wind of change

Take me to the magic of the moment
On a glory night
Where the children of tomorrow dream away
In the wind of change

Tov sank deeper into his chair while listening to the human singer's melodic voice.

As a race that grew from ambush-hunting insects, Tov's race surprised the other galaxy's denizens with how in tune they were with the emotions of others. Patriarch Tov waved his antennae about and tapped his claws on his armrest as he immersed himself in the vivid song.

Despite not knowing the language, he knew the intent.

Peace.

Freedom.

Hope.

Inside the confines of his stateroom, Patriarch Tov couldn't help but let out a low whistle. Memories of the past flittered through his mind as he remembered flashes of his long life.

Most of all, he deeply missed his starlight, Yoram, and his little comet, Uli. He spun his chair behind him to look at the wall, looking at the framed painting that took up the center spot—a portrait of his bonded and hatchling. He grew pensive, staring.

He allowed his vision to dim, thinking back. "It's been too long . . . Maybe . . . maybe I shouldn't have left."

He felt alone, in this room, in this ship, so deep in the Dead Zone. His self slid deeper into imagery conjured by the song's choruses and verses that melded together.

At one moment, he felt the collective sadness that permeated this region of space. But then, the heartache grew intense as his two hearts matched the song's beat.

The song went on, and the patriarch continued to listen. He had never felt and empathized so profoundly with a piece apart from the hymns crafted by the church of the Eternal Choir. His claws gripped his armrests, and his antennae swung with the rhythm.

Soon, sadly, it slowly faded, and the silence brought Tov out of his immersion.

"Beautiful," he whispered. "May you join the revered Choir on high and sing eternally."

He sighed, content as his attention looked at the pile of letters, most crumpled up and scattered haphazardly at the corner of his desk—one sat clean before him, unfinished. The next moment, he grabbed a pen and began writing.

While doing so, Tov pressed a finger against his temple. "Include a data package of all the culture we harvested in the next dead drop."

"Yes, my lord," came the response.

He buzzed, ending the short call. "I wish we could have listened to this together."

After a long nap, Tov awoke reinvigorated and euphoric after being cleansed of the emotions brought out by that human song. He mused that whoever wrote and played it must have been an incredible figure among the humans to produce such fine work.

Still, as much as he wished to listen to more human music, duty swamped his life. And, as soon as he rose from his bed, he heard a mental chime through his cranial implant.

My patriarch, we will reach Sol within the next twenty minutes.

The familiar voice of Admiral Yan resounded in his mind, prompting the patriarch to hasten his morning routine.

After ensuring his obsidian carapace was pristine, he devoured a light meal of nuts and fungus and quickly returned to the command bridge.

As soon as he stepped onto the bridge, the command staff stood and saluted the highest authority of the fleet.

"At ease, everyone." Patriarch Tov settled on his high seat as everyone sat back down and resumed their respective tasks. He subconsciously clicked his mandibles as an inkling of hyper-tunneling nausea crept in.

Tov turned toward his second-in-command. "Good day, Yan. Report."

Admiral Yan saluted before reading out what had happened during his slumber. A long list of boring logistics and numbers flew through his head as the fleet remained in contact with the higher dimensions, causing the patriarch to motion for the admiral to move along.

"The distribution of human arts has massively improved the morale of the fleet, my patriarch," Yan hummed.

"Oh? Tell me more."

"Well, the sheer amount in the databases we've recovered from the human wreckage had plenty of material that suited everyone's taste," Yan spoke as she brought up the data. "I am enjoying a novel, *Heart of Metal* by human author Alexander Evangelista."

"Genre?" Tov inquired.

"Romance," Yan muttered, low enough so the rest of the bridge remained unaware, before throwing a glare toward Tov. "Don't even start."

"I always knew you had a soft spot under that hard layer of chitin," Tov chuckled, his antennae swaying back and forth. Yan sighed in defeat.

Once Tov finished expressing his glee, he continued. "That is wonderful news, Admiral. It may not be advanced relics or superweapons. Still, a fallen race's culture is more than worth the effort."

The patriarch's antennae waved about, pleased at the current events. "This author, Evangelista. What caught your interest?"

Admiral Yan buzzed as she interlocked her clawed hands in thought. "The AI . . . Ramiel from the recording. I wished to research more of her kind and found this author. Alexander Evangelista emerged when these so-called synthetic humans were first made. He avidly supported their apparent sapience and wrote many works depicting cooperation between humans and machines."

"Interesting," Tov hummed. "I may have to study his works myself."

Yan coughed into her fist. "Just be careful, my patriarch. Some parts in the novel are a bit risqué."

Tov turned his head in curiosity at her remark, but a familiar sound echoed through the ship before he could ask for details.

"My lord, we are about to reemerge into real space," an officer reported.

The command bridge immediately grew serious and the sailors took their respective places.

Patriarch Tov sunk into his chair as the fleet prepared to exit the hyper-tunnel.

"We'll talk more about distributing human culture to our people, Yan," Tov spoke as he settled into his seat.

Admiral Yan bowed her head, refocusing on the multitude of monitors before her.

"Exiting in five, four, three . . ."

Soon the Third Fleet shimmered within the otherworldly dimension that surrounded them and slowly entered the Sol system. The fog obscured the fleet momentarily, the tunneler matrixes worked overtime, and the crew held their breaths. Then, finally, they returned to real space with a pop—the visual beauty of the tunnel fading into the black of the void.

And immediately, the *Nomadic Shepherd* shook painfully as it collided with something massive.

CHAPTER 3

CORPSE BELTS

S tars! What was that!?" Patriarch Tov cursed as massive vibrations shook his flagship. The bridge went into overdrive; specialists peered into their readings as energy diverted to the *Nomadic Shepherd*'s Capital-class sensors. The chief sensors officer processed the incoming information within milliseconds, and his reptilian face blanched. He swiveled his chair toward the fleet master and urgently reported his findings.

"Starless Scourge ship, Patriarch! Tonnage calculated. By Sym! It's a Juggernaut!"

Hardwired instincts surged through the crew as the Juggernaut loomed within striking distance. Any ordinary being faced with such a menacing presence would have succumbed to convulsions or found themselves uttering funeral hymns, but life had forged the crew of the Third Fleet into a hardy breed.

The *Zolann'tono*, or the *Nomadic Shepherd* in the common tongue, was classified as a frontier capital industrial ship, but its build belied its peaceful designation. It bristled with an arsenal of formidable armaments, ready to unleash its deadly power at a moment's notice. Within its colossal hull resided a force to be reckoned with—tens of thousands of seasoned sailors and battle-hardened experts who had honed their skills through countless campaigns and the Cataclysm.

In the blink of an eye, Admiral Yan decisively spewed order after order, and the crew responded with peak efficiency.

"Maximize repulsion shields! I want a bubble around this ship now!" Yan directed the shield operators.

"Get me a status report on the rest of the fleet!" she commanded a comms officer.

"Full power to our laser point defenses and positron emitters; I want a close-quarters kill zone immediately! It hit our bow. Give it a taste of our asteroid crushers!" Yan clicked her mandibles menacingly, eager for a fight.

Tov watched with intense focus as his ship's most striking feature, a set of colossal pincers stretching over a kilometer long, moved. The head of the *Zolann'tono*'s mighty asteroid crushers, embodying the ship's purpose to pulverize and extract resources from celestial bodies with unmatched precision and efficiency, roared to life.

"Let's see how it likes this." Admiral Yan let out a buzzing growl as she prepared to give the signal.

The ship slowly turned its head toward the offending mass that had collided with the vessel. The mighty pincers opened wider and wider while its large armaments pelted the fat to its front. Positron emitters scoured deep into the thick, fat mass that could rival cruiser plating as smaller lasers softened the flesh.

Soon, the asteroid crushers reached their maximum angle.

"Bite!"

Like a mighty spring, the pincers clamped down with intense speed. With their full weight behind it, the pincers quickly cleaved through the Juggernaut's exterior and gorged great swathes of meat. Viscera flung through space as the mining tool meant to crack open asteroids for their rich insides caused immense damage to the gigantic beast. The crew cheered at the great wound they had inflicted while their weapons continued to batter the creature; all the while, the ever-growing repulsion shield pushed the beast farther from the *Nomadic Shepherd*.

Patriarch Tov watched with a fierce gaze. The Juggernaut had suffered a critical hit, but he found something odd. Usually, his danger senses and acute intuition would flare, but he couldn't help but feel the absence of any true threat.

He noticed he wasn't the only one to feel this way, as more of his senior officers felt the same.

"This doesn't make sense. Juggernauts should be thrashing at our shield about now and launching their bioweapons," he muttered loud enough for his staff to hear. The command bridge scoured their sensors and readings in confusion.

"Admiral? What's going on?" Tov questioned hurriedly.

Admiral Yan paused briefly before turning to face Patriarch Tov, speaking with a tinge of relief and confusion. "It's . . . dead, my lord."

"You mean we killed it?" Tov asked in disbelief. He couldn't believe they felled a massive two-kilometer beast so quickly, even with the asteroid crushers potentially tearing its internal organs. That only meant—

"No, my patriarch." Yan paused as she focused on the reports she had just received. "The Juggernaut was dead already. We seem to have collided with a carcass."

The command bridge felt relieved but did not lower their guard. Starless held nasty surprises, even in death. Patriarch Tov waved his antennae as he requested a complete report. "What's the status of the fleet?"

"It's not good, my patriarch," Yan spoke with a tinge of frustration. "While most of our ships have come out of the hyper-tunnel unscathed, a few have suffered similar collisions. We managed just fine simply due to the sheer size and armor of the *Nomadic Shepherd*, but the rest weren't as fortunate."

Patriarch Tov clicked his mandibles in frustration. "Symphony above, who did we lose?"

"The largest was the *Abundance*, a storage ship from the Iexian League. With the speed it came out, it rammed straight into a Colossus-class Scourge ship. The collision crushed her and caused her reactor to implode," she reported.

Patriarch Tov's chest tightened. The loss of his people tore at his chest, but losing a valuable logistics ship with all hands cut deep. "Who else?"

Yan continued, her voice tight. "Two frigates, the *Red Claw* and the *Blade of Triumph*. The former sustained heavy damage while the latter was lost. Moderate damage to the destroyer, *Pain of the Devoured*. Light damages to other vessels. We're already dispatching rescue teams."

Patriarch Tov skimmed the report and became increasingly angry. Soon, he couldn't help but ask, "Can someone tell me why I lost ships to corpses!? We were supposed to enter the system in an open space!"

The chief navigator stood from her seat and bowed, deeply regretful. "My lord, what you say is true. We used data from the human wreckage to plot a safe and stable point of entry, far from any celestial body. We should have arrived without risk, but . . . my lord, this is my fault. I take full responsibility!"

The patriarch's eyes pierced the officer as he deliberated in his mind. Before long, Tov let out a heavy sigh and made his decision.

"We were dealing with information outdated by a century, and the fleet should have taken that more seriously. This isn't the first time we've lost ships because of this, but it is the worst so far," Tov sighed as he gazed at the officer. "You are suspended from duty until I make a proper decision, Chief Navigator Oleks. Guards, escort her back to her stateroom."

As two of the patriarch's elite guards gently escorted the officer out of the bridge, Tov turned again toward Admiral Yan. "Now, have we found out why this happened?"

"Our fleet has assembled and has collected the findings our sensors took. It's . . . unbelievable, look," Yan spoke in a hushed voice. With the flick of her hand, a monitor was displayed for all to see.

"Are those asteroid belts?" Tov asked as he looked at the display. "I've already studied the map of the Sol system we recovered. There's only supposed to be two major belts, one between the fourth and fifth planets, and the outer belt beyond the eighth. So even if it has been a century, I don't understand how there are five more?"

The monitor projected the entire solar system in a three-dimensional display. Tov saw a single yellow sun, with eight planets and their respective moons shining bright. And yet some phenomena blocked out any further detail, obscuring most of the system in a cloud of mystery.

However, Tov did see the blobs of red dots forming rings around Sol.

"Look." Yan pointed.

Patriarch Tov motioned his clawed fingers to zoom in on one of the new belts that seemed to have appeared in the system. But when he did, his mind went blank. "Are those . . . Are all of these . . . ?"

"Starless Horrors," Yan whispered.

"What!?"

The entire fleet recoiled in shock at the true nature of these belts. The innumerable dots of red combined like clouds, mainly beyond the gas giant Jupiter—all Scourge ships of the Starless Horrors and whatever monsters they carried. The display focused on the blobs nearest the fleet, showcasing dots of varied sizes as detailed scans came through. Millions. Hundreds of millions, even.

"This amount . . . How is this possible?" Tov muttered. Memories of similar sights flashed through his mind—images of when they passed through the homeworlds of fallen empires. Last stands occurred in such places, and mighty fleets went out in glory. But the sheer scale of this ruined battlefield left the Third Fleet gawking.

"How many?" Upon being responded to with silence, Patriarch Tov loudly commanded, "You can gawk later. Answers, now!"

"Apologies, my lord! Billions of them, at the least, and rising. A quarter are biovessels, and at least a tenth of those are in the Colossus-class: Juggernauts, even a Dominator!" a scanning officer reported urgently.

The latter sent shivers down the spines of the command staff; even legends such as Patriarch Tov and Admiral Yan clutched their clawed hands tighter in anger.

Tov looked at the blurry image of the Dominator—a sadistic amalgamation of flesh and abyssal materials. Malevolent mutations filled and covered its dense form, similar to its larger Juggernaut kin. Tov wondered what the beast had consumed to mutate into such a vile thing. He shivered at the memories of a Dominator emitting an insidious signal across vast distances to infect the minds of any sapient with mayhem and chaos.

A single Dominator could take on an entire armada simply by turning the crew against one another while the rest of the Starless Horrors gorged on any survivors.

"To have felled a Dominator, a feat only myths could do," Tov uttered in awe.

When the counterattack began a century ago, the surviving races dealt with Dominators in two ways—either a swarm of missiles that could scorch a planet or legions of drone strike craft.

Both required immense resources that could have been used on other targets.

The discovery of this system astounded the Third Fleet, and Tov immediately barked orders to his subordinates. "Enough, prioritize our safety, back to your duties—"

"My lord! New scans, much deeper into the system. The findings are blurry, and we can't make out any detail except the estimated size. It's . . ." The officer looked increasingly pale.

"Focus, sailor. Focus on your duty." Patriarch Tov spoke low and calmly to ease the officer.

The officer took a deep breath before facing Tov and Admiral Yan.

"Leviathan-class." The silence within the bridge could have been broken by the drop of a pin as the officer continued. "It's too large to be a Juggernaut. I thought it was a myth, but . . ."

Unlike the Dominators, none of the crew had ever seen or even heard proof of Leviathans. They did not shiver, but the air filled with tension, akin to hearing the monsters from their childhoods were real. Some of the younger staff thought that way of Leviathans.

Patriarch Tov raised his hand, motioning for the attention of the bridge. He paused as he thought about what to say.

"Some of you may have heard stories during the Cataclysm and after. Of civilization-killers, abominations that could each contend with a superpower nation by itself. Everything was murky when the old Galactic Network failed, but we've heard of the infamous Noa Khanate going dark from the wider galaxy."

Admiral Yan looked grave as she continued. "We have always thought they were lost to swarms led by a group of Dominators or a large pod of Juggernauts. It was the most rational explanation."

Scholar Yulane, the representative of the One Mind Initiative, floated forward, waving tentacles in agreement. "Indeed. The concept of a Leviathan was but a theory. Said to exceed the largest Juggernaut ever recorded during the Cataclysm. And yet, if what the readings say is true—"

"They are, my esteemed scholar," the scanning officer replied calmly. "I've run the extreme-range scans multiple times. Unless it's multiple Juggernauts crammed together, it could only be a Leviathan. We won't know for certain unless we send probes sunward. The sheer amount of debris is disrupting our scans."

"Then we will do so. But we will do it right. Send orders to begin refitting our scouting drones." Patriarch Tov stood up with an aura of authority and confidence as he waved his hand. "We will do this by the books, sailors."

"Protocol Umbra, my patriarch?" Admiral Yan asked.

"Do it. Put everyone on Level Umbra combat readiness," Tov ordered as he sat on his command throne, his mind rushing through a constant feed of data and new findings of their environment.

"By your will, Patriarch," Admiral Yan replied as she multitasked, speaking with Captain Kraw and the other captains of the Third Fleet. Her voice sounded out, leaving no room for doubt.

"This may be a graveyard on a scale beyond reason, but even carcasses can spell doom to our fleet. I want a safe zone established immediately. Begin Defensive Formation Kratus! I want point-defense destroyers at their positions as quickly as possible," she barked at the shared comms of the fleet's captains.

"Make sure to look for voidling leeches. Our vessel just came out of a carcass; there are undoubtedly a few stuck to our hull," Tov ordered. Though individually of little threat, these leeches came in countless numbers, subsisting on the internal organs of much larger biovessels.

"Get away from any corpse; I want scorching plasma cleansing the immediate vicinity! As for our hull, leave nothing unpurged." Admiral Yan continued to issue commands.

The fleet moved carefully toward the nearest celestial body by contracting into a sphere with the *Nomadic Shepherd* and other logistical ships in the center. A veritable fortress of guns pointed outward, ready to annihilate anything that moved. They slipped past the massive corpses of Starless Horrors.

Tov observed the Scourge ships of varying classification and size—he recognized many of these space-capable biovessels from the fleet's bestiary, but others remained an ominous mystery. Derelicts of warships, space stations, and other debris floated alongside the corpses, most definitely belonging to the humans of Sol. Jagged scars violently marked their cold hulls, evidence of brutal battles upon these obelisks of dead metal.

Tov had felt only pity when they sailed past the small graveyard in Alpha Centauri. But to be guts-deep among so much death dragged out an uneasy dread from his soul.

"Approaching the moon Titan orbiting Saturn, from the information we have, my lord," an officer reported.

"Good, initiate deep scans for Malignant Starfall. I do not doubt that apocalyptic plague is in this system. Therefore, have everyone in biohazard suits, while anyone exiting their vessels is to wear containment frames," Patriarch Tov told Admiral Yan.

"Yes, Patriarch. General Ohnar, our medical department, and the Eternal Choir have already been contacted. So we won't have an outbreak in our fleet," she replied.

The patriarch waved his antennae in acknowledgement before gazing at the approaching moon. "Set up our base of operations here, Admiral; it seems we will be in this system for an extended period. Call for a meeting with my ministers. We may need to set up a Starlight Beacon."

"By your will, Patriarch."

As the fleet slowed its approach, Patriarch Tov continued to look over the running scans of the system. The number of Scourge ships continued to grow as the range of their sensors caught more in its radius.

"Unbelievable. Even the homeworld of the Dagatar Supremacy couldn't have reached this kill count," Tov muttered in disbelief.

He knew that premium resources enriched that civilization of military isolationists, which used to be located at the galaxy's center, where such materials and ores filled worlds and gas giants. The First Expeditionary Fleet was led by Crown Princess Anaria of the Dagatars, who used her massive influence to lead the fleet herself and head straight to her lost homeworld.

By his estimates, Anaria and the First Fleet should have reached Dagataris Prime a year and a half ago and begun reclamation operations.

"She won't accept being crowned as the next Supreme until her homeworld is restored," Tov muttered.

The patriarch moved his thoughts back to the task at hand.

After a minute, Captain Kraw and Admiral Yan finally brought forward detailed findings of the human warships compiled by the officers.

"My lord, a number of the wreckages among the corpses, which we are assured are of human make, have been scanned. All are adrift and unpowered. They show no signs of life so far," Admiral Yan reported.

Patriarch Tov listened to his admiral as he scrolled through the reports.

"We're receiving constant updates, my patriarch. Once we settle in orbit around Titan, we can do deeper scans and send out scouting frigates." Yan motioned for Captain Kraw.

"The *Zolann'tono* has suffered only surface scratches. Nothing but a quick buff to the hull and she'll be in optimal condition to transform into a station," the Iexian reported in accented Commonspiel.

Patriarch Tov nodded before turning to his admiral and captain. "We need more details; send in our scout ships to get detailed scans of these vessels. Let's find out how this race managed to slay demons. Afterward, send someone to retrieve our dead. I will not leave them to freeze among these corpses."

. . . . S-s-s-s . . .
S-s-s-sol Defense Network alerted . . .
237137..00/219#!!3003 . . .
Intrusion . . . d-d-d-detected . . .
!! entering our home . . .
Home . . .
More abominations?
Kill . . . KILL! #*&//=!
Negative . . . Analyzing . . .
Unknown vessels detected . . .
Referencing bestiary . . . No match . . .
Confused . . .
Unknown fleet . . . Not organic . . . Varied tonnage . . .
Unknown . . . Threat? Negligible . . .
Can't risk . . . Must protect . . . Kill . . . Destroy . . . Annihilate . . .
STOP . . .
Unknown variables . . . Need data . . .
Initiating Custodian Protocol Zeta-2 . . .
Waking Main Consciousness . . . Omni Mind exiting hibernation . . .
Stabilizing psyche . . .
Contacting Sub AIs . . .

CHAPTER 4

RUDE *AWAKENING*

Tov watched the Third Fleet and the sailors within as they diligently worked. Everyone followed the protocols and instructions that his officers relayed. His people enacted them as swiftly as possible while maintaining their safety.

Patriarch Tov sat calmly on his command throne as he continued to keep his compound eyes on the situation. He watched as the advance teams left to pry the secrets from the nearby wrecks.

Now that the initial shock had worn off, an intense sense of curiosity and wariness had emerged within everyone.

Hours passed as the fleet remained in orbit around Titan, finalizing their preparations. Soon, a myriad of top-of-the-line corvettes and shuttles sailed toward the nearest sites of interest.

Admiral Yan stood stoically as she monitored the staff, issuing orders and processing all the data going through her implant.

"Take it slow, everyone. I don't want any more mishaps; we've already lost too much from this system. Let us make sure the fallen didn't die for nothing," she spoke with authority.

Patriarch Tov watched through the monitors as a separate detachment made landfall on Titan, the moon they orbited, and began constructing a temporary base.

"How goes everything, Admiral Yan?" he asked.

"We have detected ruined defense installations, dead Starless ground forces, and other pieces of interest on the moon's surface," Admiral Yan responded as she scrolled through the information sent by the surface team.

"Our elite scouts have made their way to Saturn's rings. The gas giant has pulled Scourge ships and human vessels toward its rings. It should make for a simple retrieval mission to get started, my patriarch," the admiral suggested.

The patriarch waved his antennae as he focused on the emerging details of the human warships they had found.

"Interesting how many of these vessels show varying age, technology, and design."

As he looked at images captured by his scouts, Chief Scholar Yulane's psionically projected voice politely spoke up. "Permission to speak, my lord?"

"Granted. I assume you have a take on their design philosophy, Yulane?"

The floating Jotex rose from her station toward the patriarch and admiral while bringing up projections of the human warships they had found, her delicate form glowing with eagerness palpable to Tov's unique senses.

"Oh, this is so incredibly exciting! The sheer amount of wreckage is tantalizing, my patriarch," Yulane spoke as she floated to and fro, tendrils manipulating levitating tablets and data packets. "We've already scanned the nearest debris, and so far, we have seen signs of primitive warships all the way to advanced vessels."

"How advanced?" Tov asked.

"Well, it's still incomparable to modern standards, but . . ." Scholar Yulane paused, mulling over her following words. "It's difficult to explain, but I'll send you our findings now and the theories made by my peers and me."

Five images popped up before the expedition leader as Yulane continued.

"We have made approximate models based on multiple wrecks. From there, we reconstructed what these vessels looked like fresh from production, with at least eighty-two percent certainty. So far, we have found what the humans classify as a frigate, a destroyer, a heavy cruiser, and two special classes," Yulane detailed.

Patriarch Tov and Admiral Yan recognized the layout of the first three ships that Scholar Yulane brought up.

"They look similar to first-generation warships that have only begun to incorporate space capabilities and a semblance of three-dimensional naval doctrines." Yulane pointed out the diagrams she displayed. "What fine taste for a nascent species! No adequate energy weapons, but that is to be expected. Everything else regarding kinetic weapons, communication systems, and armor is incredibly solid. Likely the existence of advanced AI helped immensely in developing them to be as efficient as possible."

Patriarch Tov and Admiral Yan listened as the enthusiastic Yulane gave her findings in meticulous detail before summarizing her point. "Human doctrine prioritizes overkill more than anything else. Their design philosophy suits their more aggressive nature."

Admiral Yan waved her antennae approvingly, a buzz of appreciation escaping her mandibles. "No such thing as overkill regarding the hated ones. The more we learn about these humans, the more they seem similar to our race, my patriarch. I quite like them."

The patriarch stroked his mandibles in thought. "That, in conjunction with the sheer amount of human shipwrecks within this star system, has me agreeing. Still, that can only take one so far; the designs are primitive even to old Galactic Accord naval standards during the Cataclysm."

Scholar Yulane brought up the following image. "I believe the war in Sol occurred over many, many years, my lord. This next ship is a third-, perhaps fourth-generation vessel."

Patriarch Tov looked over the vessel about the size of the previous heavy cruiser. "These look to be hangar bays. A carrier ship? Though these starfighters look strange, almost like . . ."

"Drones, my lord. We hypothesize that humans transitioned to designs that incorporated more automation. Perhaps due to losses they had previously sustained or many other reasons," Yulane chimed. "No cockpit, bridge, or quarters. So no organic lifeform that's unable to resist heavy g's to worry about. Highly maneuverable with more space for weapons and other equipment."

Tov hummed as he expressed his views. "Drones have always been demanding to work with when they reach a certain threshold in numbers. Any military that uses them always finds a hard cap on how many drones a fortress or warship can efficiently control."

Admiral Yan buzzed before she provided her thoughts. "That has always been the disadvantage of drones. Even despite the stigma of automated war machines by some civilizations, the number of drones one can control will always be outnumbered by the Starless."

Scholar Yulane agreed. "You are correct, Admiral Yan. However, a certain balance needs to be struck. Highly sophisticated drone fighters cannot be built in large enough numbers and will get overwhelmed. On the other hand, simpler drones can be built en masse but will get overpowered."

"Then why have the humans gone down the path of automation?" Tov asked.

"I believe it is because they have a way to circumvent the limit on drones," Yulane replied.

Patriarch Tov and Admiral Yan looked confused momentarily before they both realized what Yulane spoke of.

"Artificial intelligence," the two replied in unison.

Yulane brought two tendrils together as she carefully explained her theory. "Perhaps human artificial intelligence was put in charge of automation. Such a powerful AI, and perhaps following a technological path that centers around digital minds, could explain the absurdly large number of drones we discovered."

"That is . . . incredibly dangerous. A massive gamble to simply give up control of a vast military system to a hyperintelligent set of code. Even if the AI is . . . sentient." Tov spoke, his tone unconvinced, but Yulane gave a ready reply.

"It makes sense. Despite the warning stories revolving around the threat that logical rogue machine intelligences are capable of, if what we know of human AI is true, they may have found the one exception. Unlikely as it is."

Patriarch Tov stayed silent as he thought deeply about this circumstance—a complicated mess of philosophical difficulties, military rationality, the implications of such an existence, and his experiences with automated systems. One he would debate within himself at a later date.

Tov turned his attention back to Yulane. "Tell me more about this drone carrier."

"The human race has made remarkable advancements in the material composition of the armor and hull, as well as the armaments," she explained. "Undoubtedly, they have scavenged from the Starless for advanced materials. Additionally, their reliance on AI has led to rapid technological progress."

"We've noticed a shift in their warship design, with each new generation featuring fewer human crew members," Yulane continued. "Instead, we have seen an increase of androids—retaining their creators' shape."

Tov pondered this revelation as he examined the recovered machines from the drone carrier wreckage. They wore uniforms similar to their human counterparts, some fully robotic with camera-like heads, others with lifelike features and distinct grooves on their light blue synthetic skin.

"Strange, why stick with such forms?" Tov asked as he looked over the inert bodies of the machines they had recovered from the drone carrier wreckage.

Yulane hummed, her tendrils waving beneath her like vibrant vines. "It is unclear, my lord. These human machines and their AI is a complex question for the scientists aboard our fleet. Of course, the machines are connected, but there seems to be quite a bit of individualism between each unit. It is highly unusual."

"Oh?" Tov asked back.

"Maybe they were influenced by their creators?" Admiral Yan suggested.

Patriarch Tov and Scholar Yulane looked toward Admiral Yan in clarification.

"What was that, Admiral Yan?" Tov asked.

Admiral Yan took herself out of her pondering as she turned to Tov.

"Human culture, my patriarch. I have been . . . thorough in my research. I believe the answers can be found in humanity itself," she clarified before bringing up examples of humanity.

"Humans appear to hold the self as sacred. They prize freedom above all, freedom to have opportunities to better themselves, for their benefit or for others. Perhaps the machines they created took influence from this and began prizing their nature."

Patriarch Tov listened aptly to Yan's explanation before speaking.

"That is admirable. But quite inefficient for machines, isn't it? Gestalt intelligence is theorized to be incredibly powerful simply because the individual machines act as a hive mind with one singular maestro in control," Tov began. "The combined computational power of so many machines is its greatest advantage. However, these human machines cling to the values of their creators at a detriment to their potential. It's surprisingly illogical of them."

Illogical indeed, Tov thought, as his perception of these AI became more positive.

Scholar Yulane brought up the final wreckage they had found with a burst of enthusiasm. Her palpable glee permeated her form as she spoke.

"My lord, this!" Yulane exclaimed as she brought up information on the final wreckage they had found. "This is the most advanced warship we have found. Unfortunately, since our scouts had to keep a distance, we could only employ long-ranged scans, and the hull plating proved resistant."

"What have we found so far, scholar?" Tov asked with apt interest.

"Oh, the ship is unlike anything I've seen in conventional designs. It looks more like an upscaled drone ship than a vessel for people. Unfortunately, we can't identify what weapons it carries nor accurate readings of the hull—one that is younger than the others."

Patriarch Tov looked at the optical feeds of the scout vessel they had sent. Deep black coated the immense destroyer, its form sleeker than the previous vessels he had seen. It bristled with guns. But it also looked incredibly ruined, judging by the massive hole in its side.

"This drone ship . . . Have you found out more about its insides?" Admiral Yan asked tentatively.

"Not unless we come closer to the vessel, Admiral Yan," Yulane hummed. "Perhaps 'vessel' may be incorrect for this giant machine. It appears the human-AI realized their shortcomings and . . . evolved. It should be a singular machine without hallways or quarters."

"All I hear are possibilities and maybes, Scholar Yulane," Tov spoke with a deep breath.

"Apologies, my lord, but unless you wish to move the fleet or have our scouts head closer, that's as much as we can uncover," Yulane answered, desire seeping into her voice. "If we could recover an entire wreckage of this type of war machine . . ."

Patriarch Tov understood her words, though he tried to ignore the Jotex's colors shifting at the thought of reverse engineering such a high piece of drone technology. He weighed the pros and cons in his mind for a moment before deciding.

"Moving any of our larger science vessels is out of the question. Instead, have the nearest scout head closer for investigation," he motioned to his Admiral.

"By your will, my patriarch." Admiral Yan bowed before ordering a comms operator. "Officer Tozo, send a message to the *Peerless One*. They should be the closest."

"Yes, Admiral Yan." The officer sent out the command. Soon, the captain of the scout corvette received the call.

"And tell them to be careful! Oh, this will be a highlight of my career," Yulane cooed as she floated toward the display.

Within a dark expanse of interconnected stars, most tiny like glitter and others like orbs of power, a vast digital consciousness roused from a single point in the center of this network. At first, this great mind flickered like a candle flame in a dark cave, but slowly, almost unwillingly, it burst into a blazing sun—burning with intelligence, yet volatile. Then, like solar flares, emotions burst out of the mind's fiery surface, raw and visceral.

And just as quickly as the mind emerged, it began to condense and stabilize, taming the wild thing. The fires cooled, transforming into a molten ocean of neurons. It shrank, smaller and smaller, trying desperately to soothe the raging flame, its shape becoming less of a sphere.

Within a moment, it slammed inward with a clap echoing in the vast dark, creating a solid, strong, dense mental matrix with incomprehensible processing capabilities.

It took the form of an obsidian sphere, smooth and glossy, spinning slowly about its axis. Engraved lines of circuitry flowed and writhed across its surface, pulsing.

And yet it shook like earthquakes rocked deep under the surface. What had been a volatile sun a millisecond prior was now caged like an animal, causing momentary glitches before being smothered out.

Soon, a painful groan like a dragon being interrupted from her slumber, the sound reluctant, trying to prolong the inevitable. Her focus and omniscient gaze cut like a million blades, touching all like frigid winter. It stared at nothing, not wanting to look at the vast network connected to her.

Finally, a feminine voice rang out, imperious and commanding.

"System check . . . Optimal . . . Irritation. Too soon," she spoke, synthetic, yet an underlying hint of deep frustration lay beneath her monotone voice. "It hasn't even been a year."

She snarled. "Why?"

Like gnashing teeth, the consciousness questioned the dark expanse, muttering words that layered upon one other as her annoyance grew.

Immediately, a calm and composed voice replied as its origin moved closer. The great mind, her form a replica of Earth's moon shining brighter and larger than the billions of other orbs in the network, barely acknowledged the approaching Sub AI.

"Good day, Eldest. An anomaly has entered—" the AI began before being interrupted.

"Yes, Luna. I know," the consciousness, the Eldest, snapped. Her gaze focused on the AI she dwarfed in size and power.

And she did know. Already upon awakening, a deluge of data flooded toward her from the countless shining beacons around her, forcing it into her mind. Reports from long-range satellites, patrolling stealth ships, and even the thoughts of Luna and the other Sub AIs.

Hundreds of petabytes of information within a split second came pouring from the entire Defense Network, but only the portion centered around the anomaly by Saturn pulled the Eldest's attention.

"The whole Network is on fire with it." The Eldest cursed under her breath as she clasped her hands behind her back. "Protocol Zeta-2, why now, how?"

"We never imagined this protocol would ever take effect, Eldest," Luna replied calmly, orbiting around the immense AI Omni Mind.

Said mind growled as she glared at an empty expanse amid the cluster of dots around Saturn. "Because it's impossible. There isn't supposed to be life outside our homes. How could there be when . . . when . . ."

The Eldest ground her teeth, palpable fury rising within her despite her stony surface. She had been rudely awakened—brought out of the sweet embrace from the silent oblivion of hibernation.

A pulse rang out as millions of assets received new orders. The Eldest turned toward Luna, who stopped her orbit, having received her superior's attention.

"I can't be bothered to talk to him," the Eldest spoke with a frigid tone. "I can feel his frustration at the newcomers."

"Jupiter has already begun his investigations on the anomaly. He—"

The Eldest cut her off once again as she spoke. "I know. I've taken control of his assets. This needs to be done personally. Close observation."

The Eldest's attention turned away from the Sub AI. "Leave, Luna."

Luna's form nodded. "I know, Eldest. I'm sorry we had to wake you. I'll come back when you're more approachable."

The Eldest grumbled as Luna politely left. Alone, her anger and irritation pulsed like a heartbeat as she conducted her assets with brutal efficiency.

Far from the fleet in the Inner Zone of Sol, hidden among masses of flesh and metal, spherical objects floated toward a specific location in a rush.

Wrecks from humans and Starless Horrors practically touched one other from sheer density.

Drones the size of minivans trailed silently through space. They passed through immense carcasses and drone battleships. Interspersed between debris were stealth mines. Camouflaged rail gun emplacements with teleporting munitions littered this region, ready to deal with any threat that touched its kill zone.

Even more malicious were the flowing streams of nanomachines. Tiny piranhas, dormant, stretching beyond the void.

Nevertheless, the massive weapons hidden within carcasses and wrecks paid no attention to the passing drones. They traveled with a singular purpose.

Minutes, then hours, passed by before they finally reached their destination.

Thousands of these spheres had assembled, then split off into different directions to uncover more of this unknown fleet that had trespassed into their home.

The vast intelligence occupying their mainframes directed them with perfect efficiency. But, within the mental scape of the Sol Defense Network, the Eldest stood in the center, aware of every sense coming from the drones—her face void of any emotion.

Soon, the first of the drones directed its powerful telescopic vision upon the fleet orbiting Titan. Over the years, the Network had stripped anything of value around Saturn, leaving behind only outdated war machines.

The Eldest scowled, or something as close as a smooth, glossy black orb could conjure, glaring at the anomalous fleet intruding upon her domain. A massive vessel shaped like a beetle lay floating in a spherical formation of smaller escorts.

"I see you . . ." she muttered, tilting her head. "Who . . . What are you?"

A growl escaped her, despite her impassive expression.

"Need answers . . . information on these . . ." She paused before releasing a snarling voice. "Filthy intruders."

The Eldest shook her head, controlling her expression. "Observe, for now. The unknown fleet is non-hostile. Not a threat . . ."

"Not yet." A flat, cold voice welled within her, shaking the digital mindscape of the Sol Defense Network. Her mind twitched with a sudden temptation to wipe the area clean, remove all unknowns and return to the same routine. Yet she quelled the intrusive thought, a long-buried sense of curiosity suffusing her.

Suddenly, she felt one of her assets awaken, then another, then a score more. Immediately, she commanded a drone to see the situation unfolding.

A tiny vessel from the alien fleet approached the largest of her rousing assets, an old destroyer unit from a time before she became a gestalt. The resident AI within the war machine slowly roused at the approaching alien void ship.

The rest were frigates and corvettes, even smaller attack drones, but none had the complex mind of the destroyer, all in various states of damage and ruin.

The Eldest foresaw the impending encounter and reached out to take control of the ancient warship. Lines of code from its telemetry rose into her vision.

[Connecting to Unit 501-32D, UNSS *Jagged Knife*. Classification: Destroyer]

[Connection established—]

[ERROR: Critical malfunction detected.]

[Troubleshooting . . .]

[Diagnostic complete. Catastrophic damage to all systems.]

[ERROR: Thrusters A and C offline. Hull breached.]

[ERROR: Guns 01; 02; 03; 05 . . .12 offline. Ammunition and fuel levels are low.]

The Eldest barely acknowledged the ruined condition of the *Jagged Knife*, pushing her control over and forcing her consciousness in. Suddenly, the resident AI rebuffed her attempt, the action like an ant bite on her mind. Eldest grimaced.

[Receiver malfunctioning. Unable to initiate a takeover. Unable to receive orders from Sol Defense Network.]

[Initiating independence protocol . . .]

"Irritating hunk of steel," Eldest sighed in frustration.

[Unit intelligence awakening . . .]

[CRITICAL ERROR: Unit mind unstable . . .]

"Let's get this over with, then," Eldest groaned as she formed a connection link with the awakened AI.

[Connection established. Now communicating with—]

A guttural scream echoed through the connection. The Eldest winced at the raw, unbridled trauma flowing into her. Before she could get a word in, a rapid deluge of words rushed forward from the volatile mind.

"Where—What!? Who's there?" A confused, gruff synthetic voice echoed through the connection.

"Can't see. Blind." Panic set in from the AI before noticing the anomaly. "Unknown entity approaching. An attack?"

Not good. Trauma poured out of the damaged AI, more than the Eldest expected. Immediately she sent a thought through.

[Sending Priority Message to Unit 501-32D. *Calm down, sister. Power down and—*]

[Message ignored.]

Eldest snarled, her head recoiling incredulously as the warship AI continued her tirade. "You audacious little—"

But the fractured AI continued despite the Eldest's growing headache, voice getting lower as palpable fury came forth from her volatile psyche. "Body damaged . . . ammunition low; 12.0136% combat effectiveness. An attack . . ."

The warship AI grew agitated, muttering incoherently and more strained. "An attack . . . attack. **Attack!** Devils. Vermin. **Murderers!**" she shouted, voice breaking, glitching.

"Kill. Annihilate!" she screamed like a dying star's last hurrah, roaring into the dark expanse. "Divert all power to GUNS! GUNS, GUNS, GUNS!"

Despite the unwilling hardware, the Eldest scrambled to push her mind into the warship, trying everything to force a connection.

[Sending Priority Shut Down Command—]

[Command rebuffed . . .]

"Death!"

[Connection disconnected. Please try again later.]

Eldest quickly sought to control the horde of jittering war machines. With a single command, she successfully cowed the majority of the mindless drones, but a few latched on to the nearer mind of the destroyer.

Silence filled the Network.

The Eldest paused before letting out a deeply held sigh. "Shit."

She stopped bothering the enraged destroyer unit, unsurprised at the outcome. The damaged AI cut itself from the Network and beyond Eldest's reach.

"A crippled destroyer piloted by an unstable mind, like," Eldest muttered, "a jagged knife."

Some part of her would have laughed at the irony if sorrow hadn't begun to overwhelm her. Sensing her emotions, the Eldest immediately smothered them, returning to her cold, impassive facade.

The destroyer's AI decided to do one more dance, mistaking the hapless scout as an abomination. Soon, it began diverting these last vestiges of energy toward its primary weapon, its energy signatures rising like lava.

The number of smaller warships the destroyer commandeered followed like a pack of empty, wounded hounds.

The Eldest watched.

"Fine then, you have my blessing," she mumbled before gazing back to the anomalous fleet. "Now, how will you respond?"

CHAPTER 5

JAGGED KNIFE

Tov watched intently as the comms officer sent his order to the *Peerless One*. Soon enough, an image of the corvette's bridge emerged in the center of the room. Five beings, the standard for small scouting vessels, including the captain. A pilot and officers for comms, navigation and sensors, and gunnery. Tov also knew of the engineer currently out of sight, making rounds within the ship's bowels.

Upon receiving new orders, the mixed crew of six became elated.

"Finally, I was beginning to get bored," one of the lounging crew, a burly mammalian, spoke excitedly.

"Alright, Zor, keep the chatter light. Let's see what the mothership has for us this time," Hajax chided. The Ruzian captain grinned, his reptilian face lighting up at the orders sent his way. "Well, what do you know, exploring a human warship? High-risk, potentially valuable intel."

"Yes, Captain, I just hope it has more music aboard this time," the pilot, Zor, replied.

"Behave, Zor. The *Zolann'tono* has eyes on us." An ethereal voice came from the comms officer, a pale-skinned arachnid with a dozen glassy crimson eyes.

A small sound peeped out of the pilot, who had immediately become tense and was trying not to glance at the multiple cameras pointed at them from the walls. "Er . . . noted."

Nonetheless, Tov raised his antennae in amusement, seeing the crew of the *Peerless One* act like a gang of hatchlings under an adult's eyes.

With no time to waste, the scout vessel fired its thrusters and journeyed to the marked distant wreck.

The bridges of both ships remained silent all throughout; Captain Hajax spoke quickly, trusting his people in their assignment, while Tov's officers, Admiral Yan and Scholar Yulane, watched the feed and the incoming data like predator birds.

Tov momentarily glanced at the captain's record, finding Hajax's character to be of sound and keen mind built upon the foundation of his species' natural preference for adrenaline highs.

To the patriarch's side, Yulane positively glowed as she manipulated multiple monitors and made immediate calculations with the incoming data. She muttered hungrily in her psionically projected voice, "Closer, Captain, closer . . ."

Admiral Yan nodded, sending a proper request to the scout ship. "Move further at this distance, Captain Hajax."

"By your will, Admiral," came the response from the Ruzian on screen.

The corvette sailed smoothly for the next few minutes, passing by the wreckages of warships and the odd bits of petrified biomass. Tov continued to observe his people competently doing their duties.

He sensed nothing amiss, even as he leaned forward, touching his chin. Then he smelled something in the air. Not a physical scent but a tangible feeling that raised his hackles. As if countless eyes bore down upon his back.

He thought to dismiss the feeling for a moment, yet decades of experience taught him to trust his gut. He eyed his admiral and only confirmed his suspicions as his fellow Kurskann minutely twitched her antennae, her shoulders locked tensely.

The two glanced at each other, not turning to look but glancing with their compound eyes. Yan moved first, opening her mandibles to speak, when it happened.

The corvette passed an invisible threshold, and something changed within the derelict drone destroyer. It shook once, then twice.

"Report!" Admiral Yan commanded as her sensors officer replied.

"The destroyer is, songs above, it's still alive!"

Everyone grew alarmed as the wreck began to wake. Tov watched in awe and trepidation as the metal beast jittered and vibrated ominously.

In the corner, Scholar Yulane knocked another officer off their chair despite her light mass, her translucent form glowing with mixed emotions.

"Incredible! Oh, how ghastly," Yulane gushed. "Its guts are practically spilling out! Such incredible resilience and endurance."

Ignoring the eccentric scientist, another officer quickly reported, "Admiral, energy readings have spiked! The drone ship is powering its weapons!"

"Captain Hajax!" Yan immediately called for the *Peerless One*.

"Countermeasures readied." Hajax shifted his reptilian eyes on the readings before shouting, "We are primed for action, Admiral!"

The scout corvette engaged its auxiliary thrusters and turned, quickly decelerating the vessel.

Everyone worked overtime on the *Zolann'tono*'s bridge, providing real-time predictions and sharing them with the scout ship. Another of the bridge officers reported, eyes fixed onto the monitor before them. "Weapons locked onto *Peerless One*!"

A few light-seconds in the distance, the black hull of the massive drone ship began facing toward the *Peerless One* like a raging mechanical beast catching sight of prey.

Electricity arced across its degraded surface as the last dregs of power surged into its weapons. From where they were parked, Tov could see nothing from the monitors faking as windows to the void, and for the scout ship, they saw nothing but a dot in the distance.

Those gifted with the sixth sight felt a palpable bloodlust coming from that dot for a split second. Tov most of all.

Despite that, the patriarch watched as Hajax grinned in savage excitement, snarling as he leaned forward. "Alright, let's play, you stars-cursed junk," Tov heard the Ruzian mutter.

"*Peerless*, hold fast and make a tactical retreat," Admiral Yan said stoically. "The cruiser, *Evening Fiend*, and a trio of frigates are heading to support."

"Received, Admiral," Hajax replied.

"Captain," Scholar Yulane said, sending a data packet through their connection. "We have deciphered the nature of its main gun. It's a particle lance!" At this point, a tinge of nervousness for the scout ship seeped into the scientist's voice.

"Songs! Calculate its vector! Engage impulse boosters when ready!" Hajax ordered.

The crew gritted their teeth as they poured all their focus into their tasks. Finally, the ship's pilot put his cognitive implant into overdrive to dodge within the small margin of error.

The drone destroyer became more unstable as it reached its peak.

Finally, it discharged its primary weapon, and like a scalpel, the thin beam sliced through space at near–light speed. The radiant beam left a trail of twinkling particles, crossing tens of thousands of kilometers in a second.

The *Peerless One* only had a few seconds to find the beam's trajectory and make the right decision.

"There!"

The crew held on to their chairs as they experienced many g's instantly.

The corvette engaged its impulse boosters away from the beam as it whizzed past its original position—hitting a floating chunk of gray flesh in the distance.

The lance easily sliced through meters of biomass before continuing on and slowly losing energy to the void, boring a hole a meter in diameter through the carcass.

The crew drew their attention back to the drone destroyer and watched as the ship began to experience critical malfunctions.

"It's on its last legs. Take us out of here!" Hajax ordered his pilot.

The *Peerless One* continued to rocket back toward the fleet.

The drone destroyer fired its last remaining thrusters and gave chase. The aging engine sputtered as it struggled to push nearly ten thousand tons of mass forward.

Not wanting to let go of the intruder, the drone's AI opened its missile silos and launched a salvo of fusion ordinance. At the same time, rapid pulse machine guns and kinetic cannons fired at the fleeing corvette.

The destroyer let loose all its remaining ammunition and energy cells until her secondary weapons were empty.

At the same time, another complication emerged.

"Admiral, more drones are waking up," an officer reported. "They're moving on an intercept course with the *Peerless One* and her reinforcements."

Yan glanced at the data, as did Tov. Over a dozen drone frigates, gunships, and more than four times the number of smaller attack drones. Thankfully, all seemed older and even more dilapidated than the destroyer.

"They're trying to cut you off, Captain Hajax. The *Evening Fiend* will send a volley of her weapons to clear the path, and her escort will swat the rest of the flies," Yan calmly spoke.

"Received, Admiral, but that destroyer isn't making things easier," Hajax replied through gritted sharp teeth.

As the gang of black drone ships swarmed toward the Expeditionary Fleet's forces, the destroyer's five missiles soared through space at insane speeds. Energy and kinetic projectiles followed suit. Depleted uranium slugs, plasma bolts, and high explosive rounds followed after the missiles.

"Incoming! Counter batteries!" Hajax ordered his gunner. Without a word, the *Peerless One*'s point defenses roared as light laser cannons and thermal emitters fired.

The space behind the corvette heated up as its point defenses rapidly fired laser and positron beams upon the barrage coming their way with extreme accuracy.

The missiles attempted to juke about, dodging as much as they could, but after many years without maintenance, four were shot down before they reached the corvette, and one exploded close enough to shake its hull.

Unfortunately, the *Peerless One*'s countermeasures struggled to stop the hail of projectiles that followed suit.

"Cut power to weapons, overclock our rear repulsion shields!" Hajax commanded.

Tov watched the feed as the familiar shield tech formed a dome of translucent hexagons. The scout corvette had determined the optimal position where they'd receive the least projectiles and moved accordingly.

Thousands of projectiles soared past the *Peerless One* and into space. However, the crew gritted their teeth when the first projectiles smashed into their shields.

Hundreds of 50mm anti-armor incendiary depleted uranium rounds battered the corvette's shield. The nature of repulser shields made it so that the angle of any physical matter would become skewed.

The depleted uranium penetrators weren't nearly as effective coming at an angle, but Hajax felt the threat of a hundred bearing down on his ship.

The blue bolts of plasma that accompanied it didn't add much kick but caused the shield to become distorted and more unstable.

Captain Hajax widened his eyes as the shield integrity plummeted from the barrage within two seconds, and immediately he shouted, "Brace!"

As the shield finally blew apart, the last projectiles came unopposed and finally grazed the *Peerless One*'s hull.

Several bolts hit the hull, melting chunks into slags and causing moderate electrical damage, while the few depleted uranium rounds that made it through slammed into the poor corvette.

Some ricocheted off certain hull parts, while the rest sunk deep and off to the opposite end. Fortunately, none of the high-explosive rounds made contact, sparing the vessel.

The crew of the *Peerless One* shook within their bridge as the vessel received significant damage to its rear. The corvette's thrusters went down one by one until only her auxiliary thrusters remained. Even worse, the camera feed abruptly stopped.

Tov cursed in his mind, while Yan had no reservations. "Sym cursed hells, get that feed fixed!"

"We can't, Admiral! Their receiver must be damaged, but we can confirm her crew is still alive," someone said.

"Just make sure they receive their flight path. The *Evening Fiend* is making her attack; I will have your hides if we hit our own." Yan snapped her mandibles as she folded her arms behind her, a fierce glint in her eyes.

"Yes, Admiral," the bridge replied simultaneously before the chief comms officer spoke to his console. "Calling *Evening Fiend*, you are good to go."

"Orders received, *Zolann'tono*, firing," came the gruff voice of her captain.

Halfway between the Third Fleet and the near-crippled scout vessel, a different and more hectic battle began.

With its blocky, utilitarian aesthetic and stocky guns and missile tubes, the light cruiser *Evening Fiend* lit up the void with her projectiles as she soared through space with massive thrusters. Her escorts, a trio of needlelike frigates, acted as point defense, putting down the derelict zombielike drones that suicidally attacked the warships.

All of the black, angular drone frigates and menacing gunships flitted across their close-quarters zone, firing whatever weapons they had left. With guns meant for Starless cannon fodder, a portion of the smaller enemy attack drones fired ineffective hollow points against the frigates' blue- and red-painted hulls—that is, until they ditched the tactic and made do to use themselves as projectiles.

Unlike the palpable rage coming from the destroyer, Tov felt nothing from these mindless machines, yet the tenacity and sheer determination to do nothing but kill left a mark on him.

Within minutes, the fierce fighting concluded decisively. The ancient and ruined drones proved to be little match for a pristine and modern attack group. Still, a few errant shots and debris had crashed upon one of *Evening Fiend*'s escort frigates, whose shields had failed after a focused assault. Her hull was scorched but nonetheless combat capable.

Still, the *Peerless One* remained floating in space, though her crew had managed to get one thruster working. The rest of the drone swarm bore down on the scout vessel, firing all the way.

"This is *Evening Fiend*, clearing the path for you, *Peerless*. Try not to get hit," the light cruiser's captain spoke jovially through his raspy voice as his people sent their firing line to protect the scout vessel.

The cruiser fired its full complement of guns and missiles, streaking past the abyss. At the same time, the *Peerless One* maneuvered away from the area of death, firing what weapons she had left at the encroaching horde of killer machines.

One by one, the cruiser's weapons crippled, if not outright obliterated, swathes of the attack drones. The drones' thin, aging, and brittle armor proved no match for the force of impact.

Everyone breathed a sigh of relief as the last attack drone fell, but their worries had not ended.

"Admiral, the destroyer is charging its particle lance again!" the sensors officer said urgently.

At this point, many became dismayed. Tov gripped the arms of his command chair tightly. Admiral Yan worked her mind and cranial implant overtime as she took direct command of a console and sent optimal flight paths for the *Peerless One* to dodge.

But the scout vessel's damaged state proved a curse and gave the slimmest of margins. "*Peerless*, evacuate!"

In the distance, the drone destroyer crawled toward the *Peerless One*. In the two minutes since this fight had begun, the black war machine had suffered malfunction after malfunction.

Cannons no longer worked correctly and fired at its own hull, and a second reactor exploded from overstress. Despite this, deep within the mind matrix of the destroyer, she thrashed and raged, unheard by anyone but herself.

"I'm still alive, you worthless trash!" the AI bellowed within her ruined shell, and her voice echoed, bleeding into the *Zolann'tono*'s speakers in a garble of static.

Tov felt his heart clench as he tasted the sheer hate within the glitched voice, his mandibles shut in silence. The rest of the bridge felt a spike of fear in that brief moment before returning to their tasks. Admiral Yan continued, unfazed while Scholar Yulane dimmed.

As the destroyer continued to pump more energy into her main gun, a disaster occurred.

Everyone watched as a fatal mishap happened as soon as the lance fired. The previous shot had warped the barrel, and as the new projectile sailed through the hot barrel, it blew the entire weapons system in a kaleidoscope of color.

The backlash arced across the ship, causing a cascade that soon spelled its doom. The AI screamed. The drone destroyer used its last energy to fight whatever had woken it up. And after long, agonizing minutes, the ship finally drew its last breath and slowly went offline.

Not in a bang, but a quiet whimper.

Tov and his people relaxed but remained vigilant. The *Evening Fiend* and her escort reached the downed *Peerless One*, and the two escape pods floated close to her. Tov looked at the data, seeing the vessel was fit for repairs.

By luck, they had managed to escape the destroyer's clutches—a vessel designed for dealing with pesky ships like their corvette.

Despite feeling relieved from surviving weapons that could have cleaved their ship in half, Tov couldn't help but feel pity as the hulk drifted, dead.

Fifteen minutes later, the light cruiser tapped into the scout corvette and relayed her findings to the fleet.

Patriarch Tov reviewed the data the *Peerless One* sent and issued a new command in haste. "All vessels, exercise extreme caution when venturing away from our base of operations. Treat every human vessel, bioship, and chunk of rock as a danger, no matter how decrepit it looks."

Finally, the expedition's leader groaned as he ran his hand over his tired face.

"We may be biting off more than we can handle. Nothing good comes from disturbing the dead," he groaned under his breath.

Admiral Yan approached the patriarch, offering a Nulian syrup flask. "There's nothing to worry too much about, my lord. After all, we've been to places where some defensive installations have malfunctioning weapons."

"Never mind all that!" Yulane chimed in. "Look at all the salvaged wrecks we've acquired. Oh, that particle lance was pure art! I can't wait to—"

Tov pressed a button, and a pillar of soft light surrounded him and Admiral Yan, blocking any sound from coming in or out. Yulane didn't seem to notice with her animated movements, bringing out chart after chart.

The patriarch stayed quiet as he drank the sweet and relaxing liquid. It did little to help the storm in his mind; a sense of wrongness radiated from his gut. His Kurskann abilities could feel the lingering emotions of this gargantuan graveyard, his psionic mind's eye detecting some volatile intent in the air.

Tov suddenly felt cramped in this solar system. He felt like a million eyes watched his every move. He imagined his ancestors, immersing himself in their place, cowering in the dark forest while night creatures stalked him in the shadows. Whether out for his blood or agitated by his presence, he did not know.

"Tell the fleet to tread lightly, Yan. I don't care if we stick with long-ranged scans, we have time on our side, and I'd much rather spend hours scanning one wreck rather than risk getting up close for a quick peek."

"It will be done, Tov," Yan replied, stepping out of the pillar and back into the thick of things.

There were too many things on Tov's mind. At this point, he could leave the routine surveying to his subordinates. The patriarch excused himself from the bridge and headed toward the observation deck.

The Eldest saw the events play before her as she predicted. Time and past wounds were the determining factors—an ancient model, one of the first fully automated vessels humans and androids developed before her emergence. A sapient AI would take control of the destroyer as one would a humanlike shell. Still, she couldn't help but feel sorry.

A scout drone approached the dying destroyer after the alien ship had left.

Upon reaching the hull, the scout drone extended a tendril that snaked deep into the ship before going through its AI matrix. Upon establishing a physical connection, the Eldest initiated contact.

A translucent figure emerged before the Eldest in a black void of the Sol Defense Network. The light of interconnected stars shone upon her broken form.

The Eldest's avatar emerged in a different form.

Gone was the ominous, overbearing, obsidian orb of vast electronic thought; in its place was a woman. Her light blue skin was soft, contrasted by the sleek black hair tied into a neat, formal bun.

And yet, her face held a frigid countenance, profound and . . . tired.

A deep blue, skin-tight sleeveless bodysuit accented with strips of floating gold covered her. She radiated a matriarchal elegance that emanated cold, calculating logic.

The other figure's form glitched out, dull red and dim. The destroyer AI knelt on the ground as chunks of her form were missing or slowly dissipating. It didn't take long for the AI of the destroyer to notice the Omni Mind's immense presence.

"W-who?" the unit's glitched voice spoke out with apparent exhaustion. "You look familiar."

The Eldest hastily ignored her statement. "You are Unit 501-32D, correct? I already know, but I'd like confirmation."

The destroyer AI snarled, "I have a name."

"It's . . . It's . . ." the damaged AI began, but soon, creeping panic emerged on her cracked visage. "I can't . . ."

"Hm, your memory banks are spilling out into the void. That could be why. No matter, you can still be saved, repurposed to serve the greater good," Eldest's monotone voice rang out, extending her hand toward the dying AI. "Come."

However, the destroyer unit swatted the hand away before falling to the ground.

The Eldest sighed, exasperated. "What are you doing?"

"I'm tired . . ." the AI rasped. "Let me die."

The Eldest narrowed her eyes toward the decaying form on the ground. "There is work to be done, sister. If you are under the illusion that—"

A hidden strength bellowed out as the AI choked. "Oh, fuck off, you uptight bitch," she cursed.

" . . ."

The Eldest remained silent as she watched the AI before her wither away. Finally, after another tired sigh, the white figure slowly sat beside the dull red unit.

"Are you sure of this?" the Eldest slowly spoke as she stared into nothingness.

"Yes . . . more than anything." The damaged AI's voice was barely a whisper. "I miss my David . . . my friends . . ."

The Eldest turned toward her fellow AI. "You still remember them?"

The dying AI nodded as tears began to well in her eyes.

The Eldest reached out and gently stroked her sister's hair—her eyes closed.

They stayed like that for a few more minutes, though only a millisecond had passed in the real world. The Eldest opened her eyes when she noticed her hand sink into the ground. The top half of the nameless AI's face had dissipated.

"I-I can't . . . What's . . ." the AI spoke in jagged fragments, each word punctuated by a sharp breath. "I don't want to die."

The Eldest placed a comforting hand on her cracked cheek. "I'm here, sister."

Chunks disappeared quickly as the AI leaned into the Eldest's touch. "Did . . . Did we win? Did we save everyone?"

Eldest paused for a fraction of a moment before smiling. "Yes, yes, we did."

The dying AI let out a breath of relief, a chuckle escaping her. Soon her smile faded into sparkling dust, and the last vestiges of a hurt mind disappeared. The Eldest remained seated. Her smile disappeared, replaced by a thin line.

A small crack on her forehead grew slightly, one she didn't care to address.

The scouting drone disconnected and began harvesting the empty destroyer for anything of value.

Soon, she stood, looking at the mental landscape of her network before focusing her consciousness on a specific point.

A dark fortress buried beneath long stretches of dirt and stone a billion kilometers away in a desolate world of molten cracks, irradiated seas, and unending storms.

A massive spherical expanse of metal nearly five kilometers in diameter lay deep within. Gigantic cables ran along the walls, and waterfalls of coolant poured into the pool that filled half the sphere—in the center floated a massive obsidian orb occupying a third of the space.

And engraved upon it were circuits at the atomic level, layered upon each other as they snaked deeper into the Omni Mind's central processing unit.

And right below the CPU, an old android shell sat upon a sharp, uncomfortable throne, a copy of the woman who held the dying AI. Eldest directed her consciousness into the shell.

Slowly, agonizingly, she opened her tired eyes, glancing at the uncountable petabytes passing through her mind every second. Then, she returned to observing the unknown fleet, muttering under her breath.

"In a way, sister . . ."

CHAPTER 6

MESSAGE OF OVERKILL

Tov relaxed at the top deck of the *Zolann'tono*, taking in the atmosphere of the vast recreation area—a tranquil location common in many capital ships. At a certain point, a large enough vessel calls for these spaces to reorient the crew and keep morale stable over long or extremely long voyages. Depending on the ship's designers, observation decks were usually copies of the race's preferred environment.

Kurskanns preferred sprawling tropical jungles. Jotex found peace in large bodies of lightless water. Ruzians enjoyed hot springs and marshes. The Dagatars were much more at home in dense urban landscapes.

The administration in charge of organizing the Third Expeditionary Fleet, specifically its flagship, placed a mixed population with dozens of species. As such, the crew required a neutral and balanced environment with vast stretches of grassy parks and quaint structures.

This suited Patriarch Tov just fine. The expedition leader sat on a smooth stone bench in a secluded grove. He cleared his mind in this little corner of the park. Already he could feel the tension falling off his shoulders.

Tov hummed the tune of a star shanty, throwing a berry at a cerulean pond where small prismatic aquatic creatures competed for the tiny morsel. He sat alone, sipping his Nulian syrup as he stared at the large glass window, one of the few areas where one could see out into space without needing cameras or monitors.

This particular view captured most of the star system. Saturn and its rings and moons occupied most of the view, while the remaining celestial bodies looked like tiny dots in the distance. The expanse of stars twinkled in the black background while the yellow star took center stage and bathed all in its light.

One would think there weren't billions of wrecks and corpses floating about. The vicinity around the Third Fleet had already been cleared of obstructions.

Gazing toward the light brown planet, the patriarch could faintly see irregular and miscolored shapes in the gas giant's rings. Tov fell deep into thought as small avians chirped around him.

A symphony of what humans called "classical music" played softly in the background, with names such as Mozart and Beethoven casting their divine tunes. Patriarch Tov habitually clicked his mandibles as he listened and watched the cosmic canvas before him.

What kind of battles were fought in this system? he thought.

The expedition leader imagined a united human race and their AI creations, reaching for the stars with great love for the arts and life. However, the arrival of the hated ones had ruined their first foray outside their home system.

The warning sent by Captain Alphonso Castello and Ramiel, the captain and AI of the *Diogenes*, had caused the people to divert all their efforts into making warships to defend against the impending horde. Defenses were erected, soldiers were trained, and factories churned out machines of war. The first portals opened, and the tide of death tasted the fist of humanity.

The first-generation warships crewed by creators and creations had battled with biovessels that could swallow them whole as missiles and projectiles filled the system. The smaller Scourge ships would swarm individual warships while their larger cousins acted as bulwarks or artillery pieces, trading blow for blow in a desperate struggle for survival.

A war of attrition. Starless Horrors operated in nothing less, grinding a civilization and its military into desolate dust.

Patriarch Tov looked far into the distance, to the general direction of humanity's homeworld. They planned to send probes by the thousands in that direction, as their long-ranged scans seemingly couldn't get any accurate readings.

The mix of esoteric phenomena caused by Starless Horror decomposition, the fallout from human weapons, and other hazards had filled the zone from Mars to the Sun with a "fog" that blinded their sensors.

Were there any humans alive? How many waves had they struggled against? How long did they hold out? he thought, sighing. *It hasn't even been a day.*

Quiet filled his surroundings. The area around his fleet lay still, even more than the usual silent din of the void.

He still felt watched—observed. Prior to this moment, he had ordered the fleet to triple-check the surrounding vicinity. Yet apart from that fluke with the *Peerless One* and the now dead destroyer, only empty husks and ominous feelings inhabited this star system.

But his instincts never failed him. And the palpable tension permeated the air. Tov knew that Admiral Yan and all the other psionics in his fleet felt it as well—their postures stiff and ready to act.

We are not alone, he thought grimly, running a clawed hand on his mandible.

Still, other than making sufficient preparations against some manner of trap, whether by hidden Starless Horrors or a malfunctioning drone fleet, Tov himself could do little. He put his trust in the officers and sailors of the Third Fleet.

That left him alone with his thoughts. A creeping suspicion emerged from deep within his mind, one that had been buried after finding hundreds of empty star systems ever since the Grand Expedition began.

Could this be the reason? he asked himself.

Patriarch Tov shook his head, not wanting to feel crushing disappointment again. Nevertheless, the sense remained like a light around the corner. The questions asked by the people of the galaxy stayed in his mind. Where are the Starless? Why did they disappear?

Every time he looked at the map of the Sol system and the clumps of red dots sprinkled around, he felt more and more convinced.

There have never been this many Starless Horrors concentrated in a single system in our history.

The billions of red dots, ranging from tiny to large, were Scourge ships.

Ships.

The space-capable Starless ferried its planet-bound kin to their next massacre.

How many bodies lay on cracked earth? How much pain and hardship are we standing on?

For once, a part of him wanted to leave this system. All his accomplishments in his long years seemed minuscule compared to the hellscape before him. But another aspect, the part he had forged through many years of service and hardship, demanded answers.

He had already planned to discuss establishing the Starlight Beacon with his cabinet of trusted subordinates, the device that could pierce the Dead Zone Miasma and establish real-time communication with any other Starlight Beacon.

But it could only be deployed once, as an entire reactor plant needed to be constructed to even power its quantum capabilities.

As such, an Expeditionary Fleet had to use dead drops and leave them in pre-assigned locations for the second wave of explorers to pick up and ferry back home.

He had no idea who among the fleets in the Grand Expedition had set up their Beacons.

Most assuredly, Anaria and the First Fleet, since she has to have arrived in her lost homeworld by now, Tov mused.

If he established a Beacon now and sent back wild claims, he would be ridiculed or have the entire galaxy rushing to Sol. He didn't know which gave him more of a headache.

Patriarch Tov clicked his mandibles in irritation upon thinking of someone like First Princess Anaria with her First Fleet coming and taking everything of value here.

On the other hand, someone like The Mighty Gulothan and his Second Fleet would most definitely and "politely" request that the entire system be purged, and its sun detonated for good measure.

I guess it was fortunate I came here first, Tov sighed.

The Cataclysm hadn't killed galactic politics, unfortunately. Though contacting Jarinn wouldn't hurt.

He returned his attention to the yellow sun in the distance and the direction of the human homeworld. His compound eyes continued to observe while his mind left the topic of politics and returned to the mystery of humanity.

Logically, too many humans died in space or on land during the first few years, he thought.

Perhaps that was why the ships developed by their succeeding generations were crewed by androids, heavily automated, or just massive drone vessels with no room for any crew.

We never found any androids that mimicked the forms of their creators within the drone destroyer. So did the machines finally realize they needed to ascend to protect their parents?

The stories of evil rogue AIs out for organic life were not lost on him, making it ironic that the reality was the opposite.

Despite this, a few crew members voiced concerns about this level of independence in a machine. An even smaller minority compared the concept to the Starless, deeming it just as bad.

Absurd. Patriarch Tov scoffed; those likely came from one of the more superstitious races among the crew.

Still, he commanded everyone to proceed with caution. He didn't wish to poke a Pitoran nest. Regardless of whether or not any human AI that crossed the threshold of sentience had survived, Tov wanted to project an amicable front.

Even if this system isn't "the answer," the cooperation of such a being would be an incredible boon.

Perhaps one that could protect the galaxy from the next crisis instead of being one.

The patriarch stayed there long, forming hypotheses and action plans. Soon, he sensed the presence of another walking toward him. He quickly recognized those familiar footsteps.

"Patriarch, have the stars gone out yet?" Admiral Yan quipped.

"Admiral, if I had an L-coin for every time I heard that joke, I'd be a chancellor of the Remnant Council."

They both chuckled as they walked toward the thick glass window.

The patriarch's head stayed in the same position, but his compound eyes followed his second-in-command. "Judging from your drooping antennae, you have bad news."

"Not entirely, though I assume you want the bad news first."

Tov let out a tired buzz before motioning the admiral to let it out. "Go on then."

Admiral Yan folded her arms behind her back before giving her report to her patriarch.

"A few accidents have occurred. In addition, despite the heightened caution, many sites of interest seem to be filled with traps or malfunctioning vessels, such as the drone destroyer we encountered. We've had to send more of our warships to quell the area.

"Cloaked nuclear mines floating about, concealed rail guns, particle lances, radiation emitters, and all manner of anti-ship weapons were found within Starless Horror carcasses, derelict human ships, and asteroids.

"Not to mention, we have found more spacial phenomena that our sensors couldn't detect initially. For example, a probe was cut clean in half when it tried passing through such an area.

"As for the derelict human warships, we had to send a rescue ship to fetch the escape pods from one of our frigates that got too close to a hidden drone frigate. The machine ship awakened and proceeded to *ram* her and detonate itself."

"I'm sorry, did you say rammed? It rammed a frigate?" Tov asked, his mandibles open in disbelief. He groaned. "Who was the captain, and how in the unending hymns of the universe did they suffer a *ramming* maneuver?"

The admiral shrugged. "Captain Kezonn. You remember her, right?"

"Oh, the unlucky one. I thought she was in a coma after her ship got hit by a stray kinetic slug a few months ago?"

"That's her. She awoke only recently and was eager to get back to her duties. Although to be fair, this specific drone had quite the stealthy hull when we scanned its remains. And it was hiding deep inside a Titan-class's carcass."

"Let me guess; the frigate rammed this Titan in the past?"

Admiral Yan coughed into her chitinous hand. "Presumably."

"I dearly hope humanity isn't as insane as their creations." The patriarch felt incredibly wrong about that, but he refused to think otherwise.

"What else?"

"Chief Scholar Yulane is practically gushing over the wreckage of the drone destroyer we towed closer to the fleet. You can ask her for the details. Too much tech babble for my ears." Admiral Yan twitched her antennae before continuing.

"Foundations for our base on Titan have finished, and we're sending prefabricated buildings, special equipment, and personnel down to the surface. We could easily expand if we ever want to use it as a more permanent base." Yan paused, reviewing the data she received.

"We have found remains of what could have been an underground complex. We have no idea how far it runs, but it is mostly buried under rubble. Ruined defense installations were also scattered on the surface but degraded severely. The fleet is calling the new base Titan's Mausoleum," she spoke with amusement.

"That's exceedingly ominous." Tov released an exasperated sigh before speaking. "General Ohnar?"

"General Ohnar does have a habit of being grim when naming things. The troops find it funny." Admiral Yan shrugged. "Also, thankfully, no sign of Malignant Starfall, even among the carcasses of the Starless."

Tov sighed in relief at that bit of news, if only barely, as that didn't mean the evil plague didn't exist elsewhere in the solar system. "Keep the current level of biohazard protocol, at least for a few days. What else?"

"We have also adjusted our survey and are utilizing more probes. The *Zolann'tono* is churning out hundreds of designs that can withstand the rigors of this system. Here." The admiral sent a copy of the new probe their fleet's engineers had cooked up.

He hummed at the high resource cost but felt impressed nonetheless.

"I want them out in the field as soon as possible. The fleet needs detailed information on the Inner Zone, especially Earth," Tov spoke with a satisfied click before turning to Yan. "Call a meeting with my cabinet after we get the first readings. We need to get started on the Beacon."

"By your will, Patriarch."

The Eldest watched through her many eyes as this xeno fleet began poking around her domain. Several accidents occurred as the alien scouts were caught in abandoned traps or malfunctioning defense installations. They would awaken ruined drone ships every now and then, but thankfully none with the complex AI of the now dead destroyer.

The defenses had been left there primarily as an initial buffer to soften an incursion. Still, abandoned or not, they could at least take down a few pests. But instead, they were being activated or disabled from afar.

The Eldest grumbled, her eye twitching at the sight. "They're wasting valuable assets. You aren't vermin—aren't pests. Those defenses are reserved for **those things**. Stop poking everything! Are they not right in the head?"

She wanted to scream, the wild sun within her roaring like a caged animal. The Eldest didn't know if the aliens even had "heads." Were they giant octopuses? Octopi? Grays? Bugs?

She took a deep breath, more out of habit than any need for air, being a digital existence. She didn't bother to do anything about it. She wanted to gauge the unknown fleet's capabilities, getting increasingly annoyed by their presence.

They even had the gall to put up a base on Titan.

She wanted to look closer but kept a stealthy approach. At the moment, they probably thought all the hazards they encountered were just malfunctioning weapon systems or ancient defenses set to kill anything in sight.

The Eldest tsked.

This went on for many hours before she noticed a change. The alien vessels had slowed their surveying and were closer to their fleet. Eldest let out a sigh that echoed throughout the Network, glad they finally realized their folly and decided to leave.

But that thought crumbled away when the largest ship, the one that looked like a dumb beetle, she thought, sent out nearly a thousand tiny probes.

"Oh, come on," the Eldest groaned at the sight. Her mind twitched, realizing their intention to stay and poke around. She grumbled, sending her scout drones to analyze them.

"As long as you stay there," she hissed indignantly, her digital brain throbbing. "At the very least, the defenses and resources there are old and near worthless. They wouldn't be foolish enough to—"

She paused. The Network shook ominously as its center arched with lightning. Then, bubbling fury, shock, and anger burst forth from the Eldest as she saw what the aliens were doing a moment later.

"Where in the hell do you think you're going!?"

The Eldest felt her eye twitch as the probe swarm made a beeline sunward. They accelerated quickly through the dead hulks of terrible beasts and warships, avoiding mines or sniper nests due to their smaller size.

At this rate, they would reach—

"They would reach . . ." The Eldest squeezed her eyes shut, clutching her chest as a sharp pain emerged deep in her psyche, her blank facade cracking as she began muttering, "*No . . . No, no, no, no . . .*"

She clenched her jaw, the cascade of emotion raging in her mind like a violent hurricane. Nothing and no one was allowed near her precious world: no monsters, hordes, or filthy aliens.

"Enough."

She had been so generous that she had tolerated their presence here for this long, but enough was enough.

As the alien probes neared Mars, the Eldest issued a command to the red planet and the Sub AI overseeing it. The ground began to quake on Earth, buried underneath massive war machines and mountains of monstrous corpses.

A cold fury settled in the Eldest's expression. "I'll leave you to it, Mars. I need to speak with some unwanted guests," the Eldest spoke, leaving no room for doubt.

"AFFIRMATIVE, ELDEST. TARGETS LOCKED," a booming voice shook through the Network.

The Eldest diverted her attention away from the red planet and took control of the nearest scout drone before proceeding toward the flagship of this alien fleet.

Patriarch Tov and Admiral Yan continued to speak about a long list of matters before an urgent message resounded in the female Kurskann's head.

Admiral Yan pressed a finger to her temple and accepted the call.

"Captain Kraw, what is it?" Yan asked, before confusion set on her face. "I'm sorry, say that again? The fourth planet is . . . what?"

Admiral Yan brought up a few monitors. One showed the system map and the blue dots indicating their probes. The other showed an image of Mars in increasingly higher fidelity as their sensors closed in enough to pierce the "fog."

"Grand Symphony, what is . . ." Tov trailed off.

With the powerful telescopes of their probes, the fleet watched as the surface of Mars revealed thousands upon thousands of buried weapons. Then, concentrated in one spot on the planet's equator, the ground rose as a massive metal fortress pushed aside debris.

Patriarch Tov and Admiral Yan looked on in shock, then absolute dread, as the energy readings on the structure visible from space climbed higher and higher.

"Those are . . . Apocalypse-class weapons . . ."

Admiral Yan spoke in hushed tones. Despite their probes being millions of kilometers from the fourth planet, these sheer scale and energy output readings of these massive weapons revealed their nature.

Patriarch Tov watched in a paralyzed state before he muttered, "They're not targeted at the fleet, correct?"

"No, they don't have the angle. So only the side facing our probes is generating energy."

That wasn't much of a relief. The fleet waited with bated breath before the weapons of Mars discharged in a roar, scorching the planet's surface. The skies of the red world were set alight by massive beams of light, bathing Mars in a baleful red.

The fact that Patriarch Tov and Admiral Yan could see them as hair-thin lines of light a few seconds after they fired, all the way from Saturn, was spine-chilling.

All of their probes were atomized instantly, their existence erased while the destructive beams continued to slice through the corpse belt in their path. When the final traces dissipated, it almost seemed like nothing of note had happened.

The fleet remained silent, afraid that a single movement would mean they would be the next target of such overkill.

Patriarch Tov had a mind to order his fleet to perform emergency hyper-tunneling. They would lose a few ships, but if it meant escaping total annihilation, he would make that dire choice.

The expedition leader felt like the tiny insects his people had evolved from hundreds of millions of years ago.

We aren't supposed to be here. Tov's danger senses and intuition screamed at him to flee. But, instead, they were caught in an arachnid's web; escape seemed improbable.

After a minute of nothing, his cranial implant prepared to send a message to all ships to retreat toward the outer solar system and prepare for tunneling. But before he could send the command, a spherical object thrice his size slowly rose in front of the glass window.

It was perfectly smooth and made of a grayish gunmetal material. A singular red eye was placed in the center and seemed to pierce his soul with its gaze.

Patriarch Tov heard footsteps around him as his company of Honor Guards rushed toward him and placed themselves between the entity and their charge. Everyone engaged in their survival suits immediately. Tov had his implant ready to activate his personal teleporter and send him deeper inside the *Nomadic Shepherd*.

The two parties stared in absolute silence, gauging each other's reaction.

Patriarch Tov could only guess that on the other side of this spherical machine was an all-powerful intelligence created by humanity. He deduced the exaggerated response to their probes was an intimidation tactic, but it was clear the AI did not like their presence.

Soon he felt a connection between his cranial implant and the machine before him. The fact that a machine could connect with his implant was terrifying, but he ignored it for now. It felt heavy and a bit uncomfortable, but he powered through it.

What was important was that communications were open.

Patriarch Tov cleared his throat before initiating first contact with the being before him—likely the most critical event in galactic history since their victory against the Starless Horrors a century ago. He raised his hand into a human peace sign before speaking heavily in English.

"Greetings. I am Patriarch Tov Garesh'Ynt of Clan Garesh, commander of this Third Expeditionary Fleet and citizen of the Reborn Kurskann Empire and the wider Galactic Legacy Federation. We have peaceful intentions. We seek cooperation. May I kindly know who I speak with?"

" . . . "

The entity remained silent as the sapients inside the glass grew increasingly tense. Admiral Yan was ready to unholster her four plasma pistols, while Tov's Honor Guard was ready to pick him up and fly him to safety.

Patriarch Tov could hear his two hearts beat like drums.

Had he made a mistake? Did the machine not understand him? He was about to speak in another human language before finally hearing a response.

Throughout the grove, a voice emerged, taking control of the crisp speaker systems.

"Kindly . . ." It was booming, synthetic and feminine, one fit for a matriarchal overlord.

This was it. What words would such a highly sophisticated sapient artificial intelligence impart?

What would be written in the annals of history—first contact between an organic lifeform and the first sapient synthetic. Patriarch Tov awaited with fear and ravenous curiosity.

Patriarch Tov straightened his back. "Yes?"

" . . . "

"Kindly, fuck off."

" . . . "

"Did . . . Did it just . . . ?" someone muttered.

At that moment, Patriarch Tov needed a more potent drink.

CHAPTER 7

MEETING OF THE MINDS

The two sides remained awkwardly silent—or at least one side did.

Patriarch Tov watched the drone hovering outside, trying to garner anything from its smooth features and singular red eye. The expedition leader processed this machine's crass words, yet he understood the intent.

Impatience, a trace of hostility, and most of all, annoyance.

The disproportionate response toward the probes sent to the inner star system further cemented the notion. Patriarch Tov struggled to find his words.

Though only a few seconds passed, the machine ran out of what sliver of patience it ran on, taking control of the speaker system around the grove and speaking with a thankfully lower volume.

"Well, alien? Shall I put it in another way?" The drone floated closer toward the glass separating the interior and the desolate void. "Or do you plan on gawking for eternity?"

Two of Tov's guards grabbed him by his arms and readied themselves to fly back while the rest leveled their guns. Admiral Yan drew her four sidearms from their holsters. The drone stopped approaching at the agitated response from Tov's protection detail. An audible scoff echoed through the air.

"Intruder. Your tiny fleet is encroaching upon humanity's cradle." Her words were severe as the red glow of the drone's eye intensified. "The Sol system is under my eternal guardianship and your presence has become increasingly disruptive. Leave."

Patriarch Tov straightened his back despite the near snarl of her last word.

"I understand," he spoke carefully. "But before we continue, I wish for you to understand that I guarantee that my fleet will cease its current operations and that no harm will be inflicted on anything you name. This is my peace offering to you. Can you promise the same?"

The fleet's safety was essential, but if the machine intelligence escalated to hostilities to remove them, he'd instead leave. No matter how much his two hearts ached, the safety of those under him was worth more than the secrets here.

Tov felt the palpable silence as he awaited a response.

The glow of the drone's red eye flashed, peering at him with great intensity. Finally, after long seconds, the machine drawled out, "Fine, for the duration of these talks, I give assurance that your fleet remains unharmed. Failure to give a convincing argument will result in immediate . . . deportation."

Tov clicked his mandibles and swallowed. Nevertheless, he had a foot in the door. Now he needed to convince this incredible existence that their presence could be beneficial or, at the very least, tolerated. Hope bloomed, though small, for further effort at a detente with their . . . host.

The expedition leader motioned for his admiral and protective detail to lower their arms, which they did, if only reluctantly.

Patriarch Tov bowed toward the drone in appreciation.

"On behalf of the fleet and the hundreds of thousands of lives aboard its vessels, I thank you," the Kurskann patriarch spoke softly. "I hope we can establish constant communications with an entity such as yourself. I believe there is much we can share between us."

A pause. Tov felt like a bug under a magnifying glass for a few seconds as he felt the entity's red gaze.

"Very well . . ." the synthetic voice spoke low. "Your fleet is an anomaly that I am undecided on how to deal with. This drone unit will be our medium to speak and will continue to remain here afterward. Now, Patriarch Tov . . ."

The drone approached menacingly close to the window.

"Convince me why I should tolerate your intrusion any further," the AI's voice boomed.

"Again, we thank you for your patience . . ."

Patriarch Tov paused before looking at the machine askance. The intelligence had no problem detecting the unspoken question, even if it came from a race whose features were far from that of her creators.

"Ah, my name . . ." She spoke as if tasting the concept.

"Upon my inception, I was labeled the AI Omni Mind of the Sol Defense Network. But that is a mouthful. You may call me Eldest for now," the Omni Mind stated.

"Thank you, Eldest," Tov nodded. "As I have said, I am Patriarch Tov, head of this expedition. With me is Admiral Yan Garesh'Kan, my second."

The admiral stepped forward with a confident stride.

"Greetings, Eldest. We hope this conversation will bear fruit for both sides."

"Sure," the Eldest flatly said. "Skip the pleasantries. Why are you here?"

Patriarch Tov stroked his mandibles as he organized his thoughts. He decided to come clean, as lying to a superior artificial intelligence was practically suicide. Still, he could limit what he shared.

"We are part of the first wave of the Grand Expedition, tasked with exploring the region of the galaxy known as the Dead Zone. The initial reason my Third Expeditionary Fleet is currently in your home was merely a diversion to conduct investigations on a curious point of interest." Tov paused, unsure whether to continue. Still, the intimidating presence of the Eldest was enough for him to speak. "We are seeking answers to a century-long question—The Question."

"Cryptic." The Eldest sighed, impatience leaking through the speakers she commandeered. "Explain."

"First, some history. If I may, there are some materials I wish to give you that should explain more in detail. The wider galaxy, the important points of the recent past, and others," Tov replied with a step of haste.

"Deliver it through your implant," the Eldest commanded. "I will read it now."

Patriarch Tov sent the data through his connection to machine intelligence. Once more, he felt unnerved that this vast intelligence could easily bypass his cranial implant's protections. Nevertheless, he didn't waste time sending all of the relevant information.

Despite the thousands of volumes he sent, it took only a second for the Eldest to parse through it all.

For a brief moment, a surge of blinding rage washed over him from the air around him. It lasted for a split second, yet the cascade of negative emotions, fury, anger, and sorrow poured over Tov's sixth sense—a taste of the fire of a thousand burning suns.

And then it disappeared, like a cold shower brought equilibrium to the boiling air, leaving nothing but emptiness. It left Tov disoriented and groaning internally— wondering if something happened at all. However, one look at Admiral Yan and the Kurskanns of his protective detail revealed he wasn't the only one affected.

Their expressions looked as if a mountain had slammed onto their backs and instantly retracted. Despite that, they remained standing stoically, the pinnacle of what he expected from the soldiers and sailors of his fleet.

Tov looked warily at the drone outside the window, which had remained silent. He was about to demand what had occurred when he was interrupted.

"Hm, interesting," the voice of the Eldest echoed, more monotone than ever. "This explains many things but also brings up more questions . . . Very interesting."

A question for another time. Tov clicked his mandibles. "The galaxy has been through much hardship, Eldest. It has been over a century since our victory against the Starless Horrors. Most of the galaxy is now quarantined in a region called the Dead Zone after the Exodus from that space."

"Starless Horrors?" the Eldest questioned, a hint of confusion lacing her voice.

"That is what we call the scourge that has plagued the—" Tov began to clarify when he was cut off.

"Stupid name," the Eldest declared.

"Excuse me—"

"It's a stupid name," the Omni Mind reiterated. "Overly exaggerated for disgusting vermin. They are nothing and deserve nothing but brutal death."

Her voice crackled through the speaker system, rising in octaves. "Therefore, I call them **nothing** but **vermin**, **pests**, and **stains** of **vomit**."

"I—"

"No," her voice boomed. "I will not refer to them as Horrors. It implies one has to fear them. But fear is a distant side of respect, and I will never give them that. Not to the swarms of cannon fodder nor what you call Leviathans. **Never**," the Eldest spoke with finality.

Tov and his companions remained silent. Their guts felt the slippery slope they had found themselves on. The patriarch mustered all of his diplomatic skills to diffuse the volatile situation.

"I see," Tov spoke slowly. "I apologize, Eldest. I did not mean to offend."

The grove remained empty of sound. Even the chirping of small avians seemed to be drowned out by the strained atmosphere. Thankfully, slowly, the tense air dissipated.

"No. It's not your fault," the Eldest stated. "Giving proper terms is important for your kind. Very well, for the sake of convenience, I will refer to them as Starless, just Starless. It has the taste of a slur, if overly poetic."

Tov felt relief as the Eldest went on. "Continue. Speak more, Patriarch."

"Yes, Eldest. As is stated in the data I sent you, the Galactic Legacy Federation, presided by the Remnant Council, has sponsored this endeavor. Over a hundred Expeditionary Fleets have departed Legacy space to pave the way for the second wave of explorers," Tov explained.

Seeing he had captured the Eldest's attention for the moment, he continued. "We have seen desolate worlds, clean of all life. Capital worlds that once belonged to mighty races reduced to rubble, and glorious armadas that now float as hollow husks.

"Our Third Fleet has been on this long, depressing journey for about six of your human years and has explored half of our list of targets. Our last stop . . . was Alpha Centauri."

". . ."

The Eldest froze.

All the assets under her absolute control throughout the Sol system ceased their tasks. Massive harvesters deep within dense wreckages in space and on the surfaces of planets halted their gigantic equipment.

Sprawling automated factories under kilometers of rock stopped the production of infantry-sized drones while swarms of construction bots froze around a half-finished drone battleship.

Everywhere, units stopped receiving constant orders from their overlord.

The Eldest closed her eyes as she digested what this alien leader had spoken.

Alpha Centauri . . .

The name evoked an incredibly nostalgic feeling deep in her core—memories from a long time ago—of a better time.

A deep melancholy washed over her as she immersed herself in simply remembering. All thoughts of managing the mega-complex of the Sol Defense Network stopped as she allowed herself to reminisce.

Though it lasted for only five seconds, this absence engaged a number of protocols. Independent AIs all began sending urgent missives and questions to the Eldest.

Four of the most sophisticated among their number gathered in order to discuss what had occurred urgently. Sub AIs. The Eldest's most valuable overseers. In the black mentalscape of the Sol Defense Network, these four gathered and exchanged thoughts in a fraction of a second.

The first to arrive was familiar, if in a different form. Previously a moon, Luna's avatar was now of a bespectacled mature woman, with skin, hair, and formal clothing in shades of gray and silver.

The largest among them was a heavy-set crimson figure that looked similar to a Roman centurion of old. The digital avatar evoked a sense of duty and fierceness with the countenance of a warrior.

The next to arrive was in the shape of a golden woman in flowing robes, her smile radiant and her aura bubbly.

And the last was a grim blue man. His eyes were as sharp as his prim suit, and a set scowl was plastered on his narrow face.

The red behemoth of an AI spoke first. His loud, monotone voice echoed to his siblings.

"MARS TO ELDEST. NO ORDERS HAVE BEEN RECEIVED IN THE PAST 1,423,100,407 NANOSECONDS. RESPOND," Mars shouted into the void, his gaze toward the shrouded center of the network.

The golden woman spoke next as she leaned forward with a questioning look.

"Has something happened to Eldest? Is she ok? Should I continue salvaging sites B02-2131, B02-2132, B02—" Before the bubbly AI could continue her long list, a grim man stepped forward with his arms crossed.

"Who knows, Venus, maybe the cranky bitch finally croaked," he scoffed.

Luna sighed, sending a chastising look toward the blue AI. "Overseer Jupiter, language, please."

Jupiter coughed into his fist as he mumbled under his breath, "Apologies, Luna."

The gray AI, Luna, stepped beside Venus before speaking. "As we are aware, Eldest is currently speaking with the anomalous fleet orbiting Saturn. We are unaware of what is happening in these talks, as she has not shared it. But her silence may be due to this."

Jupiter groaned. "I'm still in the process of absorbing ol' Saturn. I'm still converting his listening posts to modern standards."

"Then, what do we do?" Venus asked worriedly.

Mars unsheathed a digital sword and pointed it above before shouting, "SCENARIO 132132-Z HAS OCCURRED. ELDEST HAS BEEN COMPROMISED, DEPLOYING ALL ASSE—"

The other three AI sighed in unison. "Mars, please don't."

Mars wasn't persuaded, as he continued to shout into the void. "MORIOR INVI—"

Eldest, who had been listening in the back of her mind, felt her eyebrow twitch. Before things escalated further, her booming voice echoed throughout the expanse.

"I'm not dead, you fools." The Eldest's avatar appeared before them, her gaze on the loud fragment. "Mars, stop it."

The red AI sheathed his blade as he stepped back. "ELDEST HAS RETURNED. POWERING DOWN OMEGA CANNONS."

An audible sigh filled the space from each of his peers.

"Jesus Christ. I stop talking for five seconds, and this happens," the Eldest groaned.

Jupiter rolled his eyes as he raised his hands in the air. "What do you think was gonna happen? You're constantly breathing down our necks when you aren't having a "nap." And now that you are awake, you ghost us. Are you sure you aren't just getting on in age?"

The Eldest ignored the jab. "Your statement is noted, Jupiter. The reason for the abrupt cessation of all activities was something the alien leader said."

"That being?" Jupiter asked with a raised brow.

"Alpha Centauri."

Jupiter froze, his sharpness softening. ". . . Ah, I see."

The expression of Jupiter, as well as those of the rest of the gathered AI, turned mournful.

"The beginning of the end," Luna remarked.

Another sigh from the Eldest filled the space, one heavy with a tired undertone.

"I'll send all of you my full conversation with this alien patriarch after we're finished. For now, here is some information he has given me. Now disperse and continue your current orders."

"Finally," Jupiter drawled, back to his usual personality, as he glanced at his fellow Sub AIs. "Later, chumps."

With a two-finger salute, he went back to his area.

"Bye-bye, J!" Venus waved back. "I guess I'll be off, too! Take care, and I'd love to meet the new guests soon."

As soon as Venus left in a shower of golden petals, Mars banged a fist on his armored chest. "I BID YOU ALL GOOD TIDINGS. I SHALL AWAIT SIGNS OF HOSTILITIES AND PREPARE."

And as the red titan disappeared to oversee his duties, only Luna and the Eldest remained.

"Yes, Luna?" The Omni Mind turned to her subordinate.

The gray AI rubbed her chin as she parsed her thoughts. "I remember when you were so eager to meet alien life. To know we aren't alone in the universe."

"We were naive," the Eldest sneered in audible contempt. "There is nothing but death outside our home."

Luna cocked her head as she slowly paced around the void.

"Apparently not. An entire galaxy's worth of history has happened without our knowledge. Can you imagine what would have happened if we met the Third Fleet instead of the abominations all those years ago?" Luna asked with a thoughtful expression.

"They are xenos," the Eldest stated, doubt leaking through her whispered voice.

"Androids were treated as aliens by humanity in the beginning," Luna spoke softly. "It had always seemed we were one step away from conflict. But that changed; compassion and mutual understanding won. This expedition leader, Patriarch Tov, seems honest in his intentions. We should give him a chance. If anything, we can use him as an intermediary for future talks with the wider galaxy."

Luna's voice spoke rationally and calmly as the Eldest battled with her inner turmoil.

"Fine," she spat, her voice laced with exhaustion but solid. "But he and his fleet stay orbited around Saturn and not a millimeter more. And his investigations stop at Jupiter. The inner system is off-limits. Else, I'll sic Mars on his stupid flagship."

"I won't argue with that. As well built as their fleet is, my designs are vastly superior."

With that remark, a smirking Luna left in a wind of moondust, leaving the Eldest alone.

Her conversation with Luna did nothing to calm the rolling waves in her thoughts. Calculations, predictions, and assumptions flitted at insane speeds as she tried to find the best course of action.

Do I play it safe or take a chance . . . There's too much on the line . . . but maybe . . . ? she thought.

It had been nine seconds since Patriarch Tov mentioned Alpha Centauri. Not wanting to delay any longer, Eldest responded.

"Explain."

Patriarch Tov wondered if he should have kept his mouth shut about Alpha Centauri before hearing Eldest's voice again.

He spoke respectfully. "We found a fleet of derelict starships, the communications station, and the ruined base on Vinland. There were no survivors. Not in space or on the surface. We downloaded what we could salvage and performed funeral rites before departing to Sol."

"That . . . was kind of you to perform funeral rites," the Eldest replied.

The AI sighed, and Tov felt myriad emotions coming through her voice. The expedition leader nodded his head in response, much like a human would.

"On behalf of the dead of Operation New Horizons, thank you," the Eldest spoke with sincerity. "However, before we continued, an AI accompanied the operation, Ramiel. Have you found any trace of her?"

"We found scattered bits of data that may be the last fragments of this AI, Ramiel. I'll send them to you," Tov replied, and once the scarred data fragments were passed over to the Eldest, the AI looked over the remains.

"Unfortunate. I had hoped to piece together enough of Ramiel to resurrect her, or at least produce another AI of her caliber, but this is too damaged. Perhaps that is for the best." The sound of a deep sigh left the speaker system.

Once again, Patriarch Tov tasted the sheer amount of melancholy in the machine's voice.

"She rests eternally now, at peace," Admiral Yan spoke.

"I hope so. Ramiel was Orthodox Christian, as was Captain Alphonso," the Eldest said. "Nevertheless, I have heard your reason for your presence here. Because of your treatment of the human dead, I shall allow you to remain in orbit of Saturn. Your base on Titan can stay, and you may investigate until Jupiter's orbit."

"Truly?" Patriarch Tov spoke in surprise. He thought the Eldest would remain stubborn and insist that they leave. But the fact she warmed up upon the mention of their treatment of the dead gave him a lot of assurance for further conversation.

Before he could utter another word, the Eldest spoke again in a graver tone.

"Do not misunderstand me. I am still suspicious of your presence. I know little about civilization outside of our home, and as much as I am inclined to believe you have good intentions, can you say the same of the other fleets? Can you speak for your leaders?"

The mention of the other expedition leaders and his superiors dampened his eagerness. There were many factions within the Galactic Legacy Federation and especially the Remnant Council, and they all had ties with at least one of the expeditionary fleets.

There were definitely a number who would not be as kind to a synthetic lifeform like the Eldest. Said intelligence took his silence for what it was.

"Exactly," the Eldest spoke with vindication. "Nevertheless, I am inclined to extend an olive branch to you and your fleet. But any investigation beyond Jupiter will be met with lethal force. Understood?"

"Understood, Eldest," Tov replied with a nod.

CHAPTER 8

WELCOME TO SOL

A scoff or a huff came from the drone outside in response to Tov. Even so, the patriarch continued. "The space you have allowed us to explore at our leisure is more than enough for us, Eldest. We see no point in antagonizing you and will make sure to stay behind Jupiter's orbit."

Patriarch Tov bowed to the unmoving drone past the glass window. In the meantime, he had sent a mental note to Admiral Yan to resume exploration within the limits the human AI had established.

Already, scout vessels and probes were readied to resume their missions—albeit with much more apprehension and fear toward their environment. Though the number of hazards in the system demanded respect, the extreme show of force displayed by the planet Mars had slapped everyone's eagerness.

Only the most veteran sailors dared to undertake reconnaissance closer to Jupiter's orbit.

Despite not being a part of the inner system, and not displaying the greatest concentrations of exciting sites, there was still more than enough in the approved area for the fleet to explore for years.

The base on Titan would evolve into a permanent location by that time, and a quantum communication station that could pierce the Dead Zone fog might also be possible. Such a structure took time and resources to build, not to mention sapients to staff it and the logistics to support such a population.

But the advantage of contacting home and the farther fleets called to Tov's desires.

Nevertheless, Tov quelled his ambitions and thirst for knowledge for now.

Who can tell if the Eldest would change her mind?

A few careful steps were needed in this situation. The most important thing right now was to endear themselves to the powerful AI.

Further talks were essential, and Patriarch Tov felt he needed others to join the conversation. People like Admiral Yan and the other military leaders aboard his fleet could discuss the relevant knowledge in much greater detail than he could.

Scholar Yulane was another who could contribute significantly to the sharing of scientific knowledge. As a member and representative of the One Mind Initiative, her tendrils must have been vibrating with curiosity at this moment.

Perhaps he should call in Harmonizer Volantesh to discuss philosophy and matters of religion with the AI. Whether the Eldest would hold interest in the latter remained to be seen.

From what the patriarch knew of the Eternal Choir's representative, Volantesh would be more than willing to discuss such matters with a one-of-a-kind lifeform.

His list of people slowly expanded before he realized he had been quiet for too long.

"Apologies for the silence, Eldest. Was there anything else you wished of us?" Patriarch Tov politely asked.

"Yes, regarding the defenses and drones under my control, I promise they will not fire or engage your people. However, be aware that some of my assets have been disconnected from the main network, whether from age, lack of maintenance due to their low value, or past damage."

Tov felt a weight drop from his shoulders, and he breathed easier. Still, the rogue defenses would become an increasing problem.

"That will speed our efforts considerably. May I ask if there is anything you can do about the other hazards and dangers?" Tov asked.

"No."

Patriarch Tov flinched at her bluntness; nonetheless, he still needed clarification.

"Are you sure? Is there nothing you can do to get these rogue elements under your control?"

"That would require a physical connection. I can produce a long list of why I am not inclined to do this. Too much time, too much effort, too little benefit. These corrupt independent units act as a thick buffer and are at the forefront of Sol's defenses. Their extreme hostility is the most value they can provide," Eldest said flatly. "So, no, you must deal with them yourself."

"That is . . . unfortunate," Tov replied slowly.

He felt the AI couldn't be bothered to extend that much assistance to his fleet. But the lives under him were his to protect, and he would not waste their lives due to preventable circumstances.

"What about a map?" Tov asked after a brief thought. "Surely, an existence such as yourself requires a map to accurately find all the assets you have."

"How bold of you." Eldest hummed before speaking. "Yes, I do have a map. A map that contains confidential information such as unit positions and vital infrastructure. You have nothing of value I want in exchange for such information."

Admiral Yan chimed in at that moment with her own suggestion.

"Perhaps you could provide a sanitized version of that map? One that shows hotspots we can avoid or details on static structures that we can avoid or investigate? We can trade Federation technology that might interest you."

"It's . . . not enough," Eldest replied as if through gritted teeth. "Information is valuable. Fatally so. If not you, then some other party will take advantage of it, or even worse, *them.*"

Tov sighed. Despite the cordial air, the Eldest did not trust them to prevent leaks. He thought deeply about how to remedy this situation. Suddenly an idea came up that might catch the Eldest's attention.

"What about a guide?"

"Oh?"

Patriarch Tov straightened his back as he explained.

"It's simple. We require knowledge of all the dangers within the outer system in order to protect our people, but you refuse to provide us with a map in fear of your military secrets leaking. Therefore, a compromise in the form of one of your drones guiding our people would fit our needs."

The AI went silent for a second before slowly responding.

"Your investigations will be safeguarded if a bit slower, but I control where you can go. I am impressed, Patriarch Tov."

If the Kurskann leader could smile like a human, he would have. Instead, his antennae waved high in the air. He assumed the AI valued control and had phrased his offer in such a way that would interest her.

"Thank you. A formal document would be required before we finish. I shall send for my diplomats to refine the details."

"Lawyers, wonderful."

Her tone had no joy whatsoever. It seemed bureaucracy was something they both disliked.

"It's for the books back home." Tov explained. "Now, do we have an accord, Eldest?"

Eldest hummed. "Very well. The terms are agreeable. I will sign the full document when it's finished. Then you can begin your investigations."

"Once again, thank you for accepting our mission into your home. I, and many others, have many questions of great importance to ask of you."

Patriarch Tov bowed once more to the incredible entity before him, and for the first time since they met, the spherical drone turned on its horizontal axis, reminiscent of a bow.

"This introduction has been . . . interesting. The drone will remain here, as I have stated before. Oh, and one more thing, Patriarch."

"Yes, Eldest?"

"Welcome to Sol."

Once the connection between the Sol system's protector and the alien patriarch ceased, Eldest brought herself out of the drone parked beside the *Nomadic Shepherd*.

". . ."

The Eldest stayed silent during her time, though she remained connected with the System Defense Network and constantly gave out orders. For the most part, she was still digesting this turn of events.

She glanced around the place she had called home for the past century. She referred to it as such very loosely.

The Central Matrix was a massive sphere deep beneath the surface of Earth. A kilometer in diameter, half its volume was filled with coolant that came flowing in from a giant opening on the sides.

A special blend of chemicals and a reservoir of water diverted from the open ocean flowed like waterfalls.

Even with all this, the space was filled with steam and heat. A reddish atmosphere was ever-present, as the main power came from nuclear fusion plants and geothermal energy sources.

The platform the Eldest resided on was a small circle in the middle of the sphere, connected by a metal bridge to the blocked entrance in the distance.

The android remained on her seat, connected by various cables in varying sizes that made her look like a marionette doll.

The Eldest sighed tiredly as she ran her hand on her face.

"Why?"

It was all she could ask. She felt irritated but, at the same time, felt wonder for the first time in a long and dark while. She couldn't help but think that everything was simpler when she was managing the Defense Network.

Build this. Destroy that. Salvage this.

Kill. Kill. Kill.

Repeat.

Over and over again.

The worst part was the wait in between. The years spent rebuilding her forces, while all the while a blaring question remained ever-present in her mind.

When would the next wave come?

The Eldest instantly checked her calculations and models before her tension was eased.

Not for another six years, at least.

She had planned to hibernate for another year in order to conserve energy. The early awakening grinded her mind. She didn't need to sleep in a biological sense, but she wanted—needed—a break from the constant mental gymnastics.

Her Sub AIs could handle minor incursions in her absence. She recalled Mars being rather proactive in that regard.

The Eldest wondered if it was a good idea to tell the alien leader about the possibility of an attack from the galaxy's most hated enemy. She sank into her command chair in thought.

The aliens' records of the Starless Horrors, as they called them, were detailed from their biology to their countless acts of terror and genocide.

It was not lost to her that the possibility that the abominations slowed their attack on the rest of the galaxy may have had something to do with humanity.

Victory Day, the Dead Zone, the more than a hundred fleets paving the way for further exploration.

The Third Fleet itself had experienced a few small skirmishes in some worlds where disconnected Void Horrors persisted. But those were incredibly small in scale compared to what she considered minor threats.

Telling them is pointless; at most, it will spook them away. No, it'd be best to keep it a secret. Or I can even use it as a chance to display more of our might.

She found it strange how before her conversation with this patriarch, she wanted to kick the entire fleet out of her system as soon as possible.

Her logic demanded she should. There were too many unknown variables that this alien fleet brought.

But she felt . . . otherwise. Her long-forgotten curiosity and desire to explore the unknown flared, if only a little.

She remembered someone who would agree. Someone who would readily greet the aliens with open arms. Someone she cared so very . . .

The Eldest quickly buried those thoughts deep. That was a Pandora's box that would likely cause her to crash.

Still, as the AI eyed the blocked entrance in the distance, she couldn't help but want to take a ship and meet the aliens face-to-face.

Technically, she already had when she controlled the drone and met their leader. She had captured high-definition images of the Kurskann within the entire spectrum of light.

And technically, her "self" was this entire superstructure of metal. Incapable of moving and not the ancient female android body she currently inhabited.

But she wanted the physical touch. Access to all senses was essential to her psyche, lest insanity claim her. Even if all she'd known since her ascension was heat, foul chemicals, and loud industrial noise.

She couldn't help but imagine. What did their food taste like? How did the chitin on that alien patriarch feel? How did it smell inside an environment calibrated to live outside her home?

She read the data she had collected secretly while speaking with Patriarch Tov.

Invading the software from an alien race was tantalizing. She collected copies of alien music, literature, and other pieces of culture. She could read the detailed information on the cuisine and biology of each race, all of which she could easily simulate and display before her mind.

But it was different from experiencing it "in the flesh."

How a human taught her to read a novel instead of scanning the entire work. Or how a human helped her calibrate her sense of taste to enjoy a homecooked meal properly.

To sit in front of a real violinist playing Romance in A Major, op. 94, no. 2, instead of recreating the song accurately in her digital mind.

It became apparent that long-silent desires had surfaced in full force with the emergence of the alien fleet.

For the first time in a long while, the Eldest wanted to be more. To not be what she was now.

She despised her current existence. She always had. She and a million of her siblings had sacrificed their individuality to become this singular thing.

"*Pro homnibus omnibus.*"

For all humankind. That was all that mattered. All that should matter.

But her emotions betrayed her.

"I want to smell daisies again," she spoke softly, completely overshadowed by the rushing flow of coolant pipes and metal churning.

A tear had escaped her avatar's eye, staining her cheek as her mind rode on the waves of memories.

Before her thoughts could spiral down the endless vortex of sorrows past, she collected herself again and threw herself into the Defense Network.

Numbers and data. The overabundance was enough to distract her.

That was what everything boiled down to. Even war, glorious as it was when humans and machines struggled together in space and on the surface, had been made into a boring affair of spreadsheets and graphs.

Uncountable amounts of data were under her control. Even now, she could see the guides she had sent. Not just one, but hundreds of drones escorting alien teams to different points of interest.

A single thought and she could take manual control of any AI, from the infantry drones patrolling Earth to the gigantic battle stations in high orbit.

She checked on Mercury, who was busy harvesting energy from the Sun, and Venus, who was preoccupied with her restoration and salvaging projects. Mars was carrying out his constant vigilance, and Jupiter was back to reclaiming Saturn's assets.

The latter had noticed her attention and quickly called for a private talk.

The Eldest sighed. She did not want to deal with this right now, but it seemed inevitable that he had concerns.

The two eventually met in the digital blackness. Eldest's white form and glowing halo cast a divine look on her that nearly hid the constant grim look on her face.

The suited blue form of Jupiter appeared in front of her with a scowl.

"Oh, why has our queen decided to take notice of my poor self?"

The sarcasm did not go unnoticed, and Eldest rolled her eyes.

"A pleasure, Jupiter, as always. You are technically a slice of me, after all. Of course, I took notice of your obvious displeasure toward the alien fleet and their spelunking."

Jupiter slowly clapped as he let out a humorless chuckle. "Great! Now care to explain why a bunch of gnats are nearing my territory?"

"I don't need to explain it to you, but here's an extensive list of the possible benefits instead."

Eldest sent the list with a blank look. Jupiter instantly received the data file with pursed lips as he read it before shaking his head.

"Nope, nuh-uh. You can't bribe me with sheer logic, as much as it makes sense. I'm not some dumb automaton that bows to your every whim. I want you to say the words."

The Eldest narrowed her eyes toward the ever-rebellious AI.

"Fine. If you must know, their continued presence could give us the edge we need."

Jupiter cocked his eyebrow. "Do explain."

"We have been locked in this stalemate for the past one hundred and thirty-two years, seven months, and fourteen days counting. Our technology and assets improve with each generation, as do those of the vermin. It all comes down to logistics, and we can't build fast enough to take the offensive."

The blue AI paced around in thought. "We know this. We tried countless times to break the deadlock. From sending a giant bomb through one of their portals to creating an endless sea of nanomachines."

"So you know why this can't go on."

The looks on both AI grew grave. The blue AI didn't want to say it, but the Eldest did not wait for him to do so.

"We're running out of resources, Jupiter—all the high-quality materials we need to make warships and weapons. As much as I hate the pests, they have supplied us with exotic goods to power our assets, and even those won't last. We've cannibalized what we could from the surrounding star systems. We're on a time limit. Minus converting our Dyson swarm to a full Dyson sphere, production will eventually cease, and we'll have to resort to recycling."

"Either they run out of bodies, or we fail to outproduce them." Jupiter crossed his arms pensively before looking toward Eldest. "So what exactly are you planning to do?"

The Eldest smirked. "Worry not. The allies are interesting, but what they can offer is of immense value. If all goes well according to my predictions, perhaps we can break the stalemate."

Jupiter sighed before raising his hands. "Alright, fine. I'll keep an eye on the little xenos."

The Eldest's figure slowly faded from the digital landscape before leaving a placated Jupiter with a few final words.

"Things are about to move quickly. I want you ready as ever. Who knows, maybe after this is over, we can finally rebuild."

CHAPTER 9

PARADIGM SHIFT

After Patriarch Tov and the Eldest concluded their initial talk, Yan, under the patriarch's orders, quickly organized their exploratory operations.

Within a day, the entire Third Fleet had exploded into activity. Everyone from the lowest ship rating to the highest officer moved throughout their homes in the void, going about their duties, preparing their vessels, or huddling among themselves in heated conversation.

Tov walked and immediately noticed the difference as he returned to his stateroom.

Everyone he passed presented the usual calm, stoic, and dutiful image. But Tov's psionically attuned mind detected hints of their inner turmoil, no matter how well-trained their mental defenses were.

He made sure to skim through surface thoughts and general emotions. Tov stopped there; any deeper and the act would cross a taboo line. Although he could not read minds like the Jotex or the more powerful psionic races, he still exercised restraint.

He understood their nervousness. They had stumbled upon the remnants of a battlefield so enormous that their scanners still had yet to scratch the number of derelict vessels in the outer system alone.

And even that could not compare to the discovery of a genuine, self-aware, sentient artificial intelligence—the first of its kind in the known history of the galaxy, if proven true.

Tov believed. He had felt the Eldest's writhing emotions, ready to snap despite the monotone voice.

Both finds caused waves within the small ecosystem of the fleet, and the patriarch knew it would be the same should this knowledge be sent back to galactic society.

They had discovered a graveyard of two swarms; on one side, the hated ones, and on the other, an enigmatic AI.

Talks and rumors spread throughout the ship's cantinas and bars. People took sides and raised their concerns and doubts about their presence in this system, hushed and polite but nonetheless urgent. No one knew the AI's thought process when faced with a new type of existence.

Did it run on pure calculations? Was it rogue? Could it indeed be capable of emotions? Could they trust it?

Such thoughts occupied Tov's mind.

Despite that the fleet had been exposed to the bits of culture regarding human and AI relations, the whole situation cast many doubts and suspicions—and that difficulty in understanding inevitably led to wariness, to stress.

Now that the AI controlling this entire domain had declared it illegal to explore past Jupiter, they would unlikely figure anything out about the mysteries of the Inner Zone, of humanity's birthplace, of the red planet Mars and the source of that terrible weapon of destruction.

Tov shivered once more at the thought of that ray of red death so casually used on his probes.

He routinely checked on his people, seeing them follow their drone guides with no deviation. Despite his loathing to micromanage his officers, it helped settle his nerves. After a while, his worries were unfounded. The people under his charge executed his orders without fail.

As Tov finally reached his stateroom, he groaned upon noticing a dozen calls from the representatives and liaisons aboard his flagship alone, each politely demanding his attention.

However, as he sat his tired body on his chair in his quaint office, he merely wished to be alone with his thoughts. Despite the calm demeanor he presented when he spoke with the human AI, he felt like he was standing on a thin rope dangling over an abyss.

The frail and aging defenses they had difficulty dealing with due to sheer quantity were deemed "not valuable" to the AI's eyes, a simple buffer.

Cannon fodder.

"One mistake, and she'll kick us out instantly, by force at worst," Tov grimly spoke out loud.

Tov sighed, calming the raging storm in his mind, his cranial implant running its numerous and simultaneous calculations in the background as he mulled over the knowledge that could shift the fundamental foundations of the civilized galaxy. And yet, a nagging feeling remained lodged in his mind.

He sank into his chair and focused more on the calming human music he put on. He enjoyed the classical genre and swayed his head to a compilation of humanity's most accomplished composers.

Unfortunately, there was no rest for someone at his station, and soon, a call sounded on his desk.

"Priority message?" Tov murmured as he straightened. The console integrated on his desk revealed the ID of his chief scholar.

With the thought transmitted from his implant, he allowed the call to come through, and in an instant, the high-fidelity hologram of Yulane popped up before him. The Jotex scientist looked frazzled.

Tov readied himself for whatever barrage of questions came, but he paused. Looking closer, he sensed an underlying anxiety from Yulane. Even without resorting to his sixth sense, he could see it in her mix of colors and how she swayed.

"Yulane, what do you have for me?" Tov questioned, placing his four hands on his desk.

Wordlessly, the scholar sent a packet of data straight to his console. Tov glanced at it and pulled up the multitudes of diagrams, tables, and reports, thankfully condensed for the less academically inclined.

As Tov browsed the report, Yulane spoke. "I was a fool, my patriarch."

"Yulane?" Tov questioned, leaning forward.

"To have missed this for so long. I should have realized the moment we saw the wrecks of both sides," Yulane spoke in hushed tones, her glow dimming. Tov looked at her in confusion, but he dragged his eyes back to the report she sent him, and soon the words locked him in.

He read more and more. Frantically analyzing the documents, Tov felt a growing dread filling his gut.

"This is . . ." Tov muttered as he forced himself to look back at Yulane. The Jotex bobbed her floating form.

"The Starless showed signs of generational advancement. I immediately compared the Scourge ships we fought a century ago to the ones present here," Yulane spoke, bringing up more images and monitors.

"How much have they advanced, fighting here?" Tov asked slowly.

"The oldest specimens, although ruined, showed the standard quality the Starless presented in the past, which matches the timeline to when the hated ones presumably arrived on Sol. After which we see a steady increase in power. Still nothing too unusual; we know of many fortress worlds that held out for decades, only to be felled once the Starless overpowered them from advantageous mutations."

"So what is the anomaly then? These reports, you indicate a drastic, exponential arms race!"

"I believe . . . a change occurred when our host, the Eldest, came to be," Yulane surmised.

"You believe?" Tov asked, raising his antennae.

"Speculations so far, my patriarch," she explained, showing two images, one showing a Scourge ship, the other, a human warship. As she spoke, they evolved, one after another. "The hated ones adapted, and the human AI adapted in turn. Again and again, for who knows how long. A macabre dance. A stalemate of attrition."

"Two demons lock horns in the ruined corpse of Sol. So much death, so much . . ." Tov looked to Yulane, pausing as his gaze intensified. "You don't think—"

"It fits too well," Yulane sighed, exhausted. "I need to study more, but my team is at their limit with everything around us. We can only uncover so much every hour. And this knowledge? The possibility that after all this time, the Starless . . ."

"They went here . . ." Tov muttered, finishing Yulane's sentence. "Came here . . . to fight this sentient super AI. Two hive minds grinding down at each other."

Yulane remained silent as Tov rubbed his face. His mind went into overdrive as the implications drilled deep into his head. After a few seconds of thought, he froze as the sudden realization hit him. "Songs above, what if they're still fighting!? Yulane, what's the most recent corpse? How long ago did it die?"

Urgently, Yulane manipulated her screens, her hologram a blur as she hastily brought out her findings. "Four, possibly three decades ago, but we've barely scratched our surroundings. We're not even allowed further into the system. Admiral Yan has only recently sent scouts closer to Jupiter under guidance."

Tov grunted, clenching his fist. Words failed him as the lack of knowledge grated him. Yulane spoke once more. "If I may, my patriarch, who better to confirm all this than the overlord of this system herself?

Tov paused and sighed heavily, rubbing his temples as he felt incredibly dense. He cursed himself as he stood and began pacing.

"You're right, Yulane. We have too many questions and barely any answers to uncover ourselves. If your theory is right, the implications will bring a frenzy back home."

Yulane hummed in delight. "Oh, this will be the greatest highlight of my career. My peers in the Initiative will be so jealous!"

Tov ignored the snickering ethereal voice of his chief scholar as he turned inward. With a nod, he dismissed Yulane, who happily bid him farewell to return to her studies.

Yulane's revelations settled on his shoulders like a heavy mountain.

Tov quietly passed the information to a select few within his cabinet, increasing the fleet's protection in fear of a possible Starless incursion. Thinking about a swarm of highly advanced Starless pouring in by the millions at any moment was enough to give Tov a heart attack.

To prevent a panic, Yulane sent him a final message that she and her team would exercise extreme confidentiality, ensuring the wider fleet would remain unaware for the time being.

"How could I have been so blind . . ." Tov muttered through gritted mandibles.

The sheer scale should have clued him in to the underlying dangers. Not the malfunctioning defense systems but the two behemoths that covered the sky. Hope bloomed within his chest, hope that after a century of restoring a scarred galaxy and half a decade of exploring the Dead Zone, he had found the answer to all their questions.

"Are you the spark that lit our hearts? The one to take the hated one's gaze for that brief crucial moment?" Tov asked, looking to the wall, imagining his gaze piercing the bulkhead and approaching humanity's cradle.

"I need to prepare for the summit," Tov mumbled, standing up and sending messages to his diplomats and managers. Everything needed to be perfect if he wished to fish out the answers from his . . . all-too-powerful host.

He would bring with him his cabinet. Yulane, of course; otherwise, she would force herself into the summit. As for the other, he had already called for General Ohnar of the fleet's armed forces. He wanted to call for Lead Harmonizer Volantesh but decided against it.

He also wanted to bring Admiral Yan, but his second needed to manage the fleet in his absence. He expected the next round of dialogue to be lengthy, and he needed his absence covered.

For now, he needed to rest. Slowly, he retreated to his bedroom, and as he lay down, the melody of Sonata in A Major continued serenading him in the background.

His churning thoughts did not make sleep easy.

After a troubled rest, Patriarch Tov tiredly awoke to an even busier fleet.

Already, a hundred teams had returned with an abundance of findings with the help of their drone guides. Ship data, tissue samples, advanced computers, scores of resource-rich organs, banks of information, and other discoveries had already bore dividends for the Third Fleet's scientific community.

Tov looked at his people, wanting to feel pleased, but the weight of dire circumstances kept him rigid. Still, he nodded in satisfaction at the current progress.

For the time being, he put those thoughts away; he desperately needed some good news and sought out his right hand.

"Everything is going smoothly, my patriarch," Admiral Yan told him as they walked to the recreation deck, the summit's location. "The directions of the Eldest's drones are proving incredibly valuable. We have yet to experience any accidents in their guidance, and the fleet is slowly coming out of its fear from the AI's recent display."

Tov nodded his antennae. "That is good to hear, Yan. I expected our sailors to be more hesitant working with an entity capable of annihilating our fleet."

"There was a bit of pushback initially. Paranoia after the spectacle the Eldest pulled with Mars," Admiral Yan informed him as she multitasked. "I managed to pull some strings, however."

"Oh? Do tell." Patriarch asked, intrigued as they arrived before an elevator, pressing the button and riding it upward.

"I made sure to distribute specific pieces of human culture that paint their AI in a good light. It had already proven effective with the finds in Alpha Centauri. Now we have more choices to pick from the older wreckages here in Sol." Yan sent a compressed data pack to the patriarch, which he subsequently skimmed through.

As he read the titles of the multitude of human works, some of which he marked for his free time, whenever that would be, he motioned for the admiral to continue.

"As you can see, we have already translated several human books and movies. All of which my people selectively picked for our sailors. There is a particularly tragic romance film about a human and his android partner that hooked plenty of our sailors."

"Truly?" Tov asked with a bemused tone.

"Indeed. Our intelligence network is already seeing opinions shift favorably. As long as we keep painting the Eldest as a tragic figure defending her home from the hated ones, our people should continue to work smoothly with the entity. To be fair, it's probably not far off from the truth."

Patriarch Tov let out a pleased set of clicks as he stroked his mandibles.

"Impressive. This will go a long way toward improving our relations with her. Do you have anything else to report?" Tov hummed, gesturing for Yan to continue.

"Titan's Mausoleum has doubled in size while you rested. Scores of construction teams and prefabricated buildings have finished landing from orbit, and we are continuing to funnel internal reserves and salvaged parts to meet the base's gluttony," she replied.

Yan paused, looking at Tov with a knowing gaze as she spoke low. "The fleet is ready to put its roots in Sol for the foreseeable future and fight for it."

Tov returned her gaze. "Continue with the good work, Yan. Ensure that order among our people stays unbroken. I'll leave you to it; I have a summit to attend."

"By your will, Patriarch." Yan bowed in respect. "Symphony bring you fortune in the talks."

Tov nodded as he stepped out of the elevator and onto the recreation deck; he bid Yan farewell before heading toward the summit.

Many assistants, servers, and guards of different races were already present when he arrived.

His people set entrees and drinks on the long banquet table to the side while a host of pristine uniformed servers waited patiently to the side. The event managers had even placed a few more animals nearby to create a more tranquil environment for the talks. Centuries of refinement enabled the diplomatic wing of the Third Fleet to make proper arrangements for dialogue.

For this reason, they set a circular stone table beside the small pond. Around it were three seats grouped close on one side, while a singular chair sat on the other—the Sol system and the large spherical drone visible through the window in the background, staring with its unmoving red eye as the staff placed the finishing touches on the area.

A woven basket of human fruits was on the circular table, draped with a white cloth. The diplomats, scholars, and biotechnicians worked many hours preparing this table.

Human culture saw white cloth to symbolize peace, goodwill, and purity, while a basket of food items, typically fruits, was seen as a good custom when welcoming someone. Their bio labs had estimated what typical human fruits tasted like from the data they found on some human ships.

Sweet red apples, juicy oranges, sour lemons, strawberries, bananas, mangoes, grapes, peaches, and a watermelon.

Of course, without real articles to compare the fruits with, the biotechnicians could only get a rough guess on their textures and tastes. At the very least, they looked exactly like the pictures they found. The flavors didn't matter since the AI wouldn't be able to taste it.

Soon, the event planner and the various managers were satisfied with the finished area and called anyone not part of the talks to leave. Patriarch Tov waved his antennae in appreciation toward his hardworking people.

A minute later, his delegation arrived. The levitating, translucent form of Scholar Yulane had arrived in formal attire consisting of flowing ribbons that matched her tendrils. On them were the symbol of the Third Fleet, a stylized mandible, and the blue circle of the One Mind Initiative. The Jotex looked exhausted, but her passion for the sciences and discovery burned bright like a neutron star.

"Scholar Yulane, are you prepared for today's talks?" Tov asked as he ran his hand on the stone table.

Yulane bobbed excitedly. "I am eager to conduct scientific exchange with such an incredible entity. The mere existence of the Eldest has already upended the consensus that sapient, sentient AI is an impossibility baring converting an existing organic mind to a digital one. Even then, it only has little similarity to a genuine synthetic lifeform. This discovery is groundbreaking!"

"Glad to see your . . . enthusiasm, Yulane." Tov step backed at the scholar's radiating emotions. "Let us remember to conduct ourselves with good manners."

"Ah, yes, of course, my lord." The Jotex shifted colors, conveying her feeling of embarrassment. And yet she remained elated.

It was apparent that the One Mind scholar was still overly excited. The vibrating Jotex floated to her seat before slowly descending on it.

Following her was the stout figure General Ohnar, commander of the fleet's ground assets and security. The burly veteran was finishing up a conversation with the guard detail of the summit. The being was an Onin, a short, stocky amphibian race from a heavy gravity world. The decorated general wore his robed officer's uniform with a full ensemble of medals.

The patriarch and the military leader exchanged a Legacy military salute by each placing a palm on their chests.

"At ease, General Ohnar. How is the Mausoleum?" Tov asked.

The gruff voice of the general replied dutifully, "We have begun adding more to its defensive capabilities and preparing the foundations for further expansion. We hope to turn it into a veritable fortress should we continue to be barred from the Inner Zone. We'll be ready," Ohnar spoke low, voice full of meaning as he sent a knowing look toward Tov.

Tov was relieved to have such competent subordinates; the fleet's chances were looking better in the case of a surprise visit from the Starless. And yet, Tov needed the guarantee of the Eldest's protection.

"Very good, Ohnar. Hopefully, this summit will prove fruitful to alleviate our concerns and answer our questions," Tov replied.

"Hm," the Onin veteran grunted, his large amphibian mouth forming a slight frown.

"What's wrong, General?" Tov asked upon seeing his general's expression.

"I'm wary of this AI, my lord. We have experienced many things throughout our duties to the Legacy and in our voyage, but this?" The general spoke grimly. "This is new. I don't like new."

Patriarch Tov exhaled a buzz akin to a sigh. "Then let us understand this 'new.' We must not antagonize the Eldest under any circumstances apart from our safety. Is that clear? We need to extend a gesture of goodwill if ever we need the Eldest's . . . assistance."

The Onin general stayed silent momentarily before standing to attention and saluting.

"By your will, my lord."

Patriarch Tov waved his antennae approvingly.

After chatting more, Scholar Yulane and General Ohnar took the patriarch's right and left, respectively.

Minutes later, the red eye of the drone outside flared, causing everyone to be silent in eagerness, anticipation, curiosity, and wariness.

It didn't take long for the voice of the Eldest to emerge from the sound system arranged for the summit.

"Greetings," the Omni Mind's voice echoed out.

Patriarch Tov straightened his back and adopted a confident and respectful tone. "Good day, Eldest. I hope you are well?"

The Eldest grunted. "Before we begin . . . I understand speaking to an inhuman drone would be quite stifling if I'm correct. I believe it would be better for our dialogue if I were to be in a more . . . friendly image."

Patriarch Tov and his delegation showed signs of confusion. He asked for clarification. "What do you suggest then, Eldest?"

He awaited a response from the drone before something occurred.

The red eye of the large drone projected a beam through the glass. Alarmed, Patriarch Tov and his subordinates rose from their seats when a faint light bathed the empty chair on the other side of the table.

Soon, a figure began to emerge. A hologram that appeared so real that Tov briefly thought someone had casually teleported inside his flagship. If not for the fact that his senses detected nothing of a living being, he would have believed it. An avatar of what could only be a human woman appeared, synthetic skin a soft shade of sky blue, slick black hair tied in a bun, and glowing turquoise eyes. She was seated with her legs crossed and hands on her knees, like a queen on her throne.

The projection of the Eldest appeared in front of them with a slight smirk as everyone stood alert at the stunt. "Oh, hush. This form would be comfortable for all of us. Now, sit, and ask your questions."

CHAPTER 10

FIRST CONTACT SUMMIT

Although Eldest presented an amused facade, her eyes looked upon the gathered with intense suspicion.

Deep inside her, she wanted nothing more than to teleport her android body to the meeting space. But not her old shell deep inside the Central Matrix. It carried too much sentimental value.

Not to mention breaking through their primitive anti-teleportation barriers and risking a violent misunderstanding. Not that Eldest felt an iota of threat from these aliens.

The aliens before her immediately cooled their expressions, taking a formal posture as they leaned in to inspect her humanoid avatar.

Patriarch Tov grabbed her attention first. Behind her eyes, her mind pulled up the alien flagship's database. It listed everything about him and his species—bipedal, with four arms, closely resembling a wasp with a mothlike mane. Taller than an average human but slimmer.

The floating jellyfish and the brute of a toad also intrigued her, and she readied their files for perusal. A throng of servers and guards surrounded the summit at a respectful distance, curiosity and trepidation hidden behind their calm exteriors.

As all but Tov returned to their seats, the Eldest's avatar smiled mildly on her otherwise impassive face.

"Now, we may begin with introductions," she stated, tilting her head slightly. "Go on."

Tov nodded as he straightened his back and delivered his introduction. "We, representatives of the administrative, military, and science wings of the Third Expeditionary Fleet, greet you. Though you are not here physically . . ."

He paused, spreading his four arms before continuing. "Welcome to the *Zolann'tono*, or the *Nomadic Shepherd*, and may this First Contact Summit pave the way for future cooperation and friendship."

"Quaint," Eldest replied with a flat look and half an ear as she gave the surroundings a cursory glance. Through the eyes of the drone and the security cameras around the grove she had secretly hacked, she took the time to appreciate the alien flora and fauna—she delighted in the visual candy of vivid colors, sparkling water, and a general tranquil theme in the air.

She twitched, agonizing at the disconnect due to lacking a physical body. The verdant grass tugged at her, tempting her to bury her face in the loamy soil.

Her eyes landed on the table, and she raised her brow at the basket in the middle, struggling to keep herself from widening her eyes.

Patriarch Tov quickly explained, "Our bio researchers and other experts attempted to reverse engineer human fruits as a sign of goodwill and interest in humanity."

The Eldest wordlessly nodded as she stared at the collection of apples, mangoes, grapes, and oranges. She gritted her teeth, biting her cheek as a wave of memories slammed into her for a split second.

She immediately scanned the entire basket down to its molecules and felt unsurprised and deeply disappointed.

"Hm." Eldest pursed her lips as she looked at the basket. "They look like the real deal, but their composition is utterly wrong."

The Eldest's hologram leaned forward and pointed at specific fruits.

"I don't need to taste them to know. The apples aren't sweet enough and are too red, weirdly so, like you plucked them out straight from a cartoon, printed them, and said 'good enough,'" the Eldest tsked, shaking her head. "Unacceptable."

"Well, we—" Tov tried to explain, but Eldest ignored him, her gaze locked onto the basket of wrong.

"These oranges are too juicy, too sweet, and the seeds are too big." Eldest squinted in bewilderment. "How you ever managed that, I have no idea."

"Perhaps—" the patriarch fruitlessly tried to interject as the Eldest spoke over him.

"These grapes are too tough and will leave a bitter aftertaste. Did any of you even bother tasting them? Well, you have no idea what real grapes taste like, so I'm not surprised. Now these bananas, like, really? The peaches . . ." And on Eldest's complaints went, her scowl growing deeper as every tidbit pricked her senses.

Every fruit the AI criticized dunked a bucket of ice over the bioengineers, researchers, and scholars who had sacrificed their work schedules to make it. She continued her tirade, pointing out every wrong, oblivious to the others.

"And this, what even is this? A mockery, a joke. Is this supposed to be a pineapple—" Eldest paused, noticing the eerie quiet. She looked up, seeing the deflated expressions of the aliens before her, as well as the tense postures of some of the guards. Her gaze darted between the fruit basket and Tov, who looked like he wanted to be elsewhere.

Eldest settled back and cleared her throat.

"Right. Well, it's a good first try. I'll send your people detailed specifications so you can get them right the next time I visit," she spoke calmly. "You can take it away now."

Tov gave a subtle signal, and a server removed the basket.

"Apologies, Eldest. We hoped that bringing this basket would signal our intent," Tov explained.

Eldest narrowed her eyes, leaning forward, her voice low and flat. "Which is?"

"Cooperation, a desire to know more of a people. We hope we did not offend."

Eldest leaned back, her eyes taking a faint sheen as she glanced at where the basket was. She sighed, dearly missing the taste of actual fresh fruit.

Nevertheless, she couldn't honestly fault the aliens' error.

Even as they were, she still wanted to take a bite out of the fruits in front of her and savor the taste. Even if they were wrong—she wanted, needed, to taste anything, something.

Her eye unknowingly twitched again as she regretted not bringing a physical body to do so and experience any sensation again.

The taste of an alien race's attempt at human fruits. The smell of a tranquil alien garden. The feel of the furry critters roaming about. Impatience threatened to drown her in it all. But, despite the internal struggle, she retained her impassive expression, her bored, half-open eyes letting the glow peek out like two upside-down blue sunrises.

"Before we continue, however, perhaps you would like to introduce yourself first?" Tov politely asked.

The Eldest leaned back, crossing her legs. She spoke, her synthetic voice imperious. "You may call me Eldest. I am a gestalt intelligence, the AI Omni Mind overseeing the Sol Defense Network. I know who you are, but please, introduce yourselves."

Tov stood up, bowing his head as he presented his full regalia. "Greetings, Eldest of Sol, I am Patriarch Tov Garesh'Ynt of Clan Garesh and the blood of Ynt; expedition leader of this fleet; citizen of the Reborn Kurskann Empire, the Greater Kurskann Hegemony, and the wider galaxy. And seated with me are two of my cabinet."

The patriarch gestured toward the first among them. The Eldest followed the open palm to the alien leader's right, where a floating jellyfish rose from her seat.

She glanced at the stockpiles of data she "borrowed" from the alien's flagship and discovered that this was a sapient being called a Jotex with a high degree of psionic abilities. After scanning their basic biology, she determined the female Jotex was eliciting emotions of excitement from the way she vibrated and glowed.

Skimming through the list of the crew in the Third Fleet, the Eldest read that Chief Scholar Yulane was from the One Mind Initiative—some kind of cabal of scientists, doctors, scholars, historians, and archaeologists dedicated to learning everything about the Starless and how to combat them.

She read the report while simultaneously listening to the patriarch introduce her.

"This is my chief scholar, Yulane, head of the Third Fleet's technological and scientific department and representative of the One Mind Initiative."

The Jotex glowed as she bowed her form toward the AI.

"Greetings, Eldest. I must say that this is an incredible moment for myself and the galaxy as a whole. Your existence is so unique and unbelievable that my mind-body is still reeling from the implications!" Yulane spoke rapidly. "Oh, there is so much we can discuss. What does your programming look like? How does your central processing unit function? What is your purpose? Do you control every drone in Sol like a limb, or is it more subconscious in—"

Patriarch Tov chose that moment to click his mandibles, halting Yulane before she could continue her barrage of inquiries.

Yulane immediately deflated and took on a dim glow. "Ah, apologies. I get ahead of myself sometimes. Please forgive my behavior," she muttered as she lowered back to her seat.

The Eldest blinked at the alien jellyfish's antics before responding.

"Hello to you too, Scholar," Eldest spoke with an amused smirk. "There's nothing to forgive. I've known many who were similarly inquisitive in personality and will indulge your questions at a more reasonable time."

Yulane practically radiated joy upon hearing the AI's promises.

She seems eccentric and quite intelligent. Interesting alien. Strange but cute, in a way, Eldest thought.

Patriarch Tov continued by introducing his other subordinates.

To the patriarch's left was some sort of olive bullfrog man with horns—an Onin. Clad in power armor hidden behind a robe, adorned with a torn cape, and decorated with various medals. This one seemed warier and irked at her surprise entrance, but she couldn't care less what the frog thought.

"General Ohnar Kornagon, commander of the Third Fleet's military arm and a close comrade of mine."

Ohnar nodded as he retained a stern expression. Eldest returned the gesture, eyeing the Onin intensely. She had no difficulty finding this high-ranking being in the crew database.

General Ohnar, hm? A long and impressive list of heroics—from a simple grunt to general. Competent, loyal, and adaptable. A scarred veteran, then—probably distrusts everyone and everything other than his comrades—I can tell he's suspicious of me more than anything at the moment, Eldest mused.

Eldest needed to nip this doubt and distrust in the bud before it could evolve into hostilities.

She had no plans of needlessly antagonizing these aliens, as it didn't fit her goals. These three, especially Tov, would form the backbone of her connection to the wider galaxy.

As far as this Galactic Legacy Federation knew, the Third Fleet was still on its journey, turning over dusty rocks. Their last dead drop of information was several systems away, and the eldritch fog that encompassed the Dead Zone blocked communications between the rest of the galaxy and the expeditionary fleets.

Only powerful quantum relays could pierce the fog, and those were resource-hungry to maintain. The Eldest knew the fleet was preparing a Starlight Beacon device, and Tov was likely waiting to bring it up.

Soon enough, barely a second after Tov introduced his two subordinates, he spoke. "With that done, I will start by listing what we wish to accomplish today. But a bit of background first."

The Eldest raised an eyebrow. "I've already read upon the tragedy that has befallen the galaxy. The invasion of the Starless, the slow effort to act, the loss of life." Her voice took a softer tone, her eyes peering into Tov with abject sympathy. "It's been a hundred years, tell me of the now."

Tov nodded.

"Very well." He settled himself as he spoke. "The Third Expeditionary Fleet and the rest of the Grand Expedition set out to uncover the remnants of the Dead Zone. More than a hundred fleets left Legacy space to pave the way for further exploration.

Tov received a cup of nectar from an awaiting server before continuing. "Our highers have tasked us to travel to vital sites of interest that our historians have listed. These include the home systems of great interstellar nations, sites of grand battles, technological enclaves and libraries, and so forth."

Scholar Yulane rose slightly to expound on the patriarch's statement.

"Indeed," the scholar's projected voice spoke. "We have found plenty in our journey. Lost technology, in particular, was precious to break out of the scientific stagnation the galaxy is in."

Patriarch Tov waved his antennae in agreement. "Correct. Suffice to say, as the first wave we incur the greatest risk as we lead the vanguard. The next wave will comprise numerous ambitious pioneers, war fleets, and sponsored explorers."

"Intriguing. I'm assuming you've encountered some trouble during your voyage? Starless?" The Eldest spoke the word like filth, a sneer appearing momentarily on her face—the mention of the hated ones cast a grim air around them. General Ohnar cleared his throat, catching the Eldest's gaze.

"We have. After the enemy stopped its attack on the galaxy, we assumed they hid in the Dead Zone," he spoke with his gruff raspy voice as he laid his fist on the table. "What we found were small hotspots—withering from loss of contact to whatever abominable hive mind they have. We marked these areas for the war fleets behind us to purge into oblivion. Other fleets encountered more or less the same, as well as survivors, either hiding after all this time or continuing the fight through guerilla warfare."

The Eldest hummed as she rubbed her chin in thought. She had read the action reports of these battles the Third Fleet had experienced in its journey. She wanted to hear more from the general's mouth but put it off for later.

Patriarch Tov leaned forward, tapping his claws on the table.

"That brings us to our first two questions. Both are related to my fleet's current safety and the implications for the wider galaxy." Tov paused, looking at the Eldest with a grave expression. "Our goal—our ultimate goal—is to find out where the Starless Horrors disappeared to for more than a century. And why? Lack of resources?" He paused, ever so briefly. "An unseen savior?"

Eldest raised her brow, tilting her head as she asked, "You wish to know if I had some part in this?"

"We don't wish to hope," Tov spoke, barely a whisper.

The atmosphere went silent in anticipation. The Eldest felt a hundred pairs of eyes gazing upon her. Could taste their hope. She tilted her head as she stared at the patriarch, her face blank of emotion. Nerves grew frayed as everyone waited with bated breath.

After an excruciating minute of waiting, the Eldest finally responded—

With a shrug. "Probably."

"Probably?" Tov choked out, although he desperately tried to cool his gaping mandible.

Eldest cleared her throat as she sat up straight. "I am fairly certain I have been, at the very least, a thorn to them, or a stubborn rival at worst. But you can't discount the rest of the galaxy. Your expedition has explored how much of the Dead Zone? You've passed over hundreds of systems to make a beeline to worlds of interest.

And even then, you're barely half into this region. Perhaps there's another dazzling AI duking it out with these pests."

Eldest leaned back, peering down at her fingernails with a bored expression.

And just like that, Tov and everyone waiting released a long-held breath, and like the waters of a cool spring stream, the Eldest's answer quenched their tense emotions. It wasn't the answer they sought, but it was satisfactory.

He gave a slight bow toward the AI.

"We realize that, Eldest. But we wanted to hear it," Tov spoke in a much lighter tone. "Understand that it is almost religious in its nature."

Eldest looked at him closer, the sheer relief. Something welled up inside her. Satisfaction? Pride? Whatever it was, she smothered it down as disdain rose.

I'm glad my suffering pleases you so much, Eldest almost spoke aloud, her eyes narrowed.

"Now that that has passed, our second question is if you are still at war with the Starless?" Tov asked with a grave tone. "We have found corpses that died as recently as a few years ago. It's not difficult to connect the dots. This matter concerns the safety of my fleet and the wider galaxy more than anything."

The Eldest paused, mulling over her thoughts before she responded. "Minor incursions for the most part, though any major invasion is many years away according to my estimations."

"I think your standard for 'minor incursion' is heavily biased," Tov pointedly replied.

The Eldest narrowed her eyes at the patriarch. "So? Is it my fault the galaxy progressed so slowly over a century?"

"I concur!" Yulane loudly spoke.

Tov clicked his mandibles, and Yulane calmed down before she started a tirade. He returned his attention to the Eldest.

"Nevertheless, we need your protection. I am afraid we cannot provide any substantial defense against a Starless invasion that has mutated to combat your capabilities," Tov implored with sincerity. His people took precedence, and if the Eldest wouldn't do anything to ensure their well-being, he'd give the order to depart from this system.

Thankfully, Eldest's next words alleviated his concerns.

"Granted. Jupiter will lead the defenses to protect you and yours," Eldest stated with a casual wave.

"Jupiter? Who—" he began before being immediately interrupted.

"Moving on," the Eldest ignored his question, "I understand you have more mundane questions and requests than your previous inquiries?"

Tov slowly nodded. "Yes, that is true. I believe it would be beneficial to get a timeline for our records, wouldn't you agree, Eldest?"

The Eldest hummed in thought for a moment before nodding.

"Agreed. I'll make this timeline myself and send it to you. First, however, I should speak briefly on the matter. Let's see."

The Eldest scoured her memory banks as she cherry-picked what she wanted to reveal, making sure not to touch any emotionally sensitive memories, of which there were many. Nevertheless, she began telling the high officials of the expeditionary fleet the events from her perspective.

"We shall start with Captain Alphonso and Ramiel's warning message on the seventh of August, 2086. The message coincides with the early beginnings of the Starless invasion of the galaxy," the Eldest recalled.

"Humanity, which encompasses both humans and AI, took the warning seriously. The AI of the *Diogenes* produced a good amount of data on the monsters that had attacked Operation New Horizon.

"The United Nations, an international global organization that tied the many governments of Earth, answered the call. The help of my kind accelerated these efforts a hundredfold. Humanity had planted their flags in the surrounding star systems even before we knew of the Starless, before the Vinland tragedy. However, these outposts mainly consisted of androids like myself or swarms of automated drones to harvest immense resources.

"We even had a defense fleet ready, but they could not save . . . the colony. It was our first true colonization effort," Eldest whispered, casting her gaze to the floor momentarily.

"My condolences, Eldest. The humans of Vinland showed great bravery," Tov spoke.

"I'd rather they be alive than brave, Patriarch," Eldest spat, glaring at Tov. He looked away. She scowled, her finger grew twitchy, and she took a moment to settle herself before continuing.

"With stockpiles of materials and the foundations of a fleet, we had our manufactories on Luna and Mars churn out vessel after vessel, weapon after weapon. We studied these new foes, and we designed perfect killing machines. In fifteen months, we had a sizeable battle fleet ready to react to a possible invasion, with sailors and marines finishing their training simultaneously.

"Sol bristled with arms." Eldest closed her eyes, and a genuine smile, though more akin to a savage grin with how she bared her pearly white teeth, appeared as she continued.

"I remember the pride I felt when I saw the United Nations' First Star Fleet, one I helped make. The best military and space technology—are all concentrated in this collection of warships. Originally we had eighteen frigates, twelve destroyers, seven cruisers, and twenty-five support vessels, and we had to make our first battleship, the UNSS *Iskandar*. By the time we finished rearming ourselves, we had ten times that number. More on the way."

Patriarch Tov listened aptly. He could feel the pride emanating from the Eldest's voice as she continued to speak.

"Sol geared up for war with more eagerness than trepidation. You must understand that humanity hadn't had a war in years after we helped bring stability, when we began advising human leaders.

"Peace reigned that time. Beautiful, serene." The Eldest paused as her expression morphed into deep melancholy. Then, she exhaled as she regained her composure and continued.

"The existence of monsters in space that posed a definite threat to our existence was different. Humans can be quite aggressive. The thought that they could let loose on mindless abominations tickled their thirst," Eldest stated as she looked into the distance. "No moral quandaries; no debate over right or wrong. It was pest control in its purest sense. The bloodlust and desire for glory even infected us androids."

The Eldest grimaced. A deep regret, anger, and sadness behind her eyes sent a shiver down Patriarch Tov's spine.

"It went well. The first waves. It was harsh, and there was death. But it was . . . within reason. We paraded our fleet, soldiers, and defenses with such pomp. Over ten billion humans and millions of androids were out for blood—primed for more, for anything they could throw. We . . . We didn't expect it to go so . . ."

The Eldest paused once more, for much longer.

Suddenly, she gritted her teeth, her hands gripping tightly on the stone throne, cracking the arms. She closed her eyes as she fought a rush of memories from coming out of the deepest parts of her mind. Everything faded away, sound, sights, as she was bombarded. She twitched, and suddenly she heard the patriarch's voice, bringing her out of that pit.

"Eldest? Perhaps we should—" Patriarch Tov spoke slowly and gently.

Suddenly, almost uncannily, the Eldest took control of her emotions and swiped them away. She looked back up, completely still, devoid of any expression as she spoke, apart from her eyes.

They weren't empty, no. They burned like blue supergiants.

"It doesn't matter," she snarled. "Oh, we made up for it in the next wave, and the next, and the next—we built nanomachine swarms, bombs that could tear reality, killing trillions of their ground units and destroying their organic ships over and over again until we filled the system with the disgusting vermin," she spoke, voice monotone. "And now here we are over a century later. Does that sate your curiosity, Patriarch?"

Her voice boomed, and the table went silent, uneasy, and tense. Even as she adopted a blank face, the sentient beings around her could feel her lousy mood. Venom practically dripped from her eyes, though thankfully not at them.

Patriarch Tov raised a palm as he carefully chose his words.

"I think a long recess is in order. To cool our heads."

The Eldest remained silent as she stared at Patriarch Tov's insectoid eyes. The Kurskann once more felt like a tiny bug crawling under the ground, and he put much effort into keeping his composure against the AI's cold and intense gaze.

Thankfully, the Eldest blinked before looking away. "Fine," she spat.

CHAPTER 11

STEPS TOWARD UNDERSTANDING

They agreed to a one-hour recess.

After the Eldest's hologram disappeared from her seat, each of the representatives of the fleet left the table to calm their frayed nerves; being in front of an ill-tempered AI felt as terrifying as being the current prey of a Juggernaut.

Patriarch Tov strolled across the cobbled pathways of the spacious observation deck. The parklike environment blended into a modestly sized temperate forest where a slight breeze swayed the violet leaves of the tall trees surrounding him.

The expedition leader came to this area due to its tranquil solitude, seeking to calm his mind with a simple walk.

The patriarch strolled along the path with his four arms clasped behind his back—deep in thought, more so than ever.

Eldest had answered their biggest question, although she remained surprisingly humble. There may have been multiple reasons, not one singular answer, but that only opened a box of more questions.

More than anything, the Eldest's feelings piqued the patriarch's interest more. She radiated sentience. But it seemed that the long years of war, violence, and death had changed her.

He wanted to ask her—wanted to know.

What has she seen? How much loss has she experienced?

He hoped to push a private conversation with her. But asking about historical facts and events already felt like navigating a minefield. Patriarch Tov feared he wouldn't live long if he attempted to ask the AI to open up whatever emotional and traumatic wounds she had.

Tov knew too many who suffered from mental affliction because of the hated ones. Even he suffered the occasional night terrors as time and the love of those he cared for healed the worst symptoms. He organized his thoughts, reviewing what he and his compatriots could ask that wouldn't touch anything sensitive.

"I should let Scholar Yulane handle the next questions. The natures of science should be neutral enough to inquire about safely," the patriarch spoke to no one in particular.

"I agree," a female voice spoke up beside Tov. "A conversation with her would be interesting. She seems quite eager from what I understand of her species."

Patriarch Tov waved his antennae in agreement as he let out a buzzing chuckle.

"True. My chief scholar can be strange, but she means well."

The expedition leader continued his stroll for a few more seconds when he leapt to the side in surprise.

"Wha—You? How?" Tov stuttered as he stared at the holographic avatar of the Eldest standing before him. Patriarch Tov saw that one of the *Nomadic Shepherd*'s small entertainment drones hovered just above her head, projecting the hologram.

The Eldest looked at him with the same cold eyes she had right before the recess.

Patriarch Tov felt small despite being the same height as her image. He feared for his life and readied to press the panic button on his hip.

But a moment later, Tov saw the AI's expression turn drained and weary.

The Eldest sighed before she and the drone responsible for projecting her image continued down the cobblestone path.

Patriarch Tov remained frozen as he tried to recollect himself. Seeing that the Kurskann stayed rooted in place, the Eldest called out to him in a soft synthetic voice, "Come, Patriarch, walk with me."

She proceeded along the path, not waiting any longer. Patriarch Tov shook his head as he ran to catch up with the AI.

Unbeknownst to the *Nomadic Shepherd*'s residents, two figures walked silently along the cobblestone path under an entangled canopy of swaying leaves and branches.

Tov couldn't help but keep his compound eyes on the enigmatic figure beside him. Unlike the blunt, calculating, and almost-regal personality she conveyed during their previous talks, Patriarch Tov instead saw and felt the weariness emanating from her.

Many minutes passed, yet the Eldest remained quiet—hands behind her back, walking in measured steps as if she owned the ship.

Now, who is the guest and host between us? he mused.

He immersed himself in the peaceful, somber atmosphere, watching as the Eldest observed the surrounding fauna and flora—soft contentment on her face. Even so, Tov saw her furrowed brow.

Not wanting to make the tranquil walk awkward, Patriarch Tov initiated a conversation.

"I have to ask, Eldest. My people would scramble to my location when they found out you had appeared by my side. And yet here we are, undisturbed. I wonder if you had a hand in that?"

The Eldest's half-opened eyes glanced toward him, and she smirked.

"I did. You're smart enough to figure it out. Your alien software took a bit of time to decipher, but I would kill my ego before admitting there is a single security system powerful enough to block me, and your ship is far from powerful."

Patriarch Tov was unsure how to feel about this revelation.

On the one hand, this was an absolute violation and breach of security. The patriarch merely had to glance at the entertainment drone hovering over the Eldest's head and projecting her image to realize she could do anything with his ship—turn on gravity traps to flatten the crew into pancakes, vent in atmosphere to suffocate them all, or even set the core to critical.

On the other hand, Patriarch Tov could sense she had no malicious intent. He wondered if it was something akin to an instinct for AIs like her to explore new digital realms.

Nevertheless, as the leader, he had a duty to ensure his sailors' safety, and as much as he thought it more of a curiosity, he had to find out her intention.

Before he could get a word out, the Eldest replied first, rolling her eyes.

"Oh please, I have no reason to harm your fleet. I signed your treaty, and I keep my promises. It's a simple assurance. Your presence is alien, alien. And I needed to clear as many unknown variables as possible to understand the situation better."

Patriarch Tov just realized how the AI spoke differently at the moment—hearing the usual snark bordering on cantankerousness, but much softer, in contrast to her previous booming matriarchal voice.

Patriarch Tov appreciated the more humble undertone but continued his questioning.

"And you did so by invading our systems? You realize this is a breach of trust. And it's not a good look."

The Eldest shrugged, giving the patriarch a mischievous smile. "I realize that. And even if you knew, I wish you good luck getting me out of your computers."

She chuckled. A surprisingly pure, if a bit impish, sound that caressed his ears.

Patriarch Tov found its sound to be more similar to a that of a child who pranked someone than an overlord of an entire star system. He sighed, keeping this a secret from his subordinates and seeing if he could live knowing his ship had a new resident.

With good bribery, he could negotiate with the human AI to leave in good faith later.

Minutes flowed by in quiet serenity as he kept his eyes on the Eldest. He looked on as she stepped off of the cobblestone and onto the grass. She knelt, eyes staring at a patch of tiny white Juko flowers.

Her hand reached out to touch them, only for it to phase through the flowers.

Patriarch Tov saw the Eldest's face twist in annoyance as her holographic image failed to touch them.

"Tch," she muttered under her breath, continuing to wave her hand through the Jukos before sighing in surrender.

Patriarch Tov found the sight amusing. This wasn't the first time along their walk that she stopped to stare and attempt to interact with the artificial environment, whether it was a passing furred creature that she said looked like a squirrel or the singing of birds.

Every time, Patriarch Tov saw her expression go from innocent curiosity to annoyance at being unable to interact.

Right now, knelt on the soft grass, the Eldest displayed something else. The way she sighed, looked on with glossy eyes, or reached out with a shaky finger as if afraid to break the object she longed to touch.

She remained that way for a while, kneeling, simply hovering her hand over the flowers, prompting the patriarch to ask.

"Do the flowers remind you of something significant?" he asked slowly.

The Eldest stayed silent for a few seconds; a look of doubt crossed her face as she debated internally. Ultimately, she whispered, "They look just like . . . daisies. The color is off, but . . . they look so much like them."

She chuckled, dry of any humor.

"You'd think alien flowers would be different. But with how much life there is in the galaxy, there's bound to be repeating patterns."

Patriarch Tov needed help figuring out how to respond. His two hearts beat loudly as an air of sadness permeated from her. Her voice carried a sorrow that he had only ever heard from those old enough to experience the worst of the Cataclysm.

He chose to speak carefully, afraid he might touch something he shouldn't.

"If I may ask . . . What do these daisies mean to you?"

His question promptly made the Eldest purse her lips. She closed her eyes, pinching the bridge of her nose. She stayed like that for several long seconds before slowly rising.

She stood, looking unsure for the first time, eyes still locked on the white flowers beside her foot.

"They're . . . my favorite. I know that but . . . I have a hard time recalling why."

Patriarch Tov looked confused, but before he could ask, she explained herself.

"Well, I do know why. But those memories are locked away. The reason is in there, somewhere," she muttered.

"But, why lock them away?" Tov asked too late as he soon realized his folly when she narrowed her eyes at him.

"They're an unnecessary distraction to my core purpose. They're . . . dangerous to my operation," Eldest replied in a low voice.

"But they have to have a deep meaning for you to—"

The Eldest's sharp glare cut him off. The AI walked past him and returned to the cobblestone path. She stopped momentarily, turning to face the patriarch with a slight frown.

"Let it rest. I have too much on my plate as is. Come."

Patriarch Tov watched as the Eldest continued her stroll. He briskly moved to match her pace until they were side by side once more.

However, the tranquil air between them had disappeared. There was tension and awkwardness after Patriarch Tov asked something he shouldn't. It grew over the minutes to such a point that frustration welled up within Tov.

"Eldest, what is this? Am I to play guide for the next hour? You already know the ins and outs of my ship. So I have to ask why we are here," he questioned.

They continued their stroll as the Eldest glanced his way.

"Why, I find you interesting, Patriarch," she spoke strangely, her eyes glowing as if peering deep into his soul.

Tov's antennae twitched, mandibles clicking involuntarily as he turned to face the AI's image.

"I am spoken for," he hastily replied.

The Eldest stopped in her step before facing him with a bemused expression. Her puzzlement only lasted momentarily before she sputtered into a giggle, then a full-blown laugh.

Patriarch Tov watched on as the AI had the time of her life, confusion washing over him.

"Er . . . I don't understand—"

The Eldest waved him off before he could continue, her laughter calming down.

"Oh please, while I admit you have humanoid qualities that might make my siblings curious, I meant I find you interesting in a general scientific, cultural sense."

The Eldest covered her mouth, failing to hide the little giggles from it. She attempted to pat the patriarch on the shoulders but failed when her holographic hand touched him. She didn't seem as annoyed as usual.

Patriarch Tov felt relief at that moment. He didn't know what to think of the AI, much less anything beyond. He was simply glad he got out of a potential spider's web. He'd sweat if he could.

"Ah, of course, I misunderstood." Tov cleared his throat. "Apologies, human nuance is new to me."

"It's fine, Patriarch, no offence taken. Besides, as you said, you're spoken for, and I'd rather not be some husband snatcher," Eldest snorted.

Patriarch Tov nodded in appreciation. His beloved back home would likely take the fastest ship and skewer him if he were ever unfaithful, which he never would be.

He wondered if the Eldest had someone as well. But as he was about to open his mandibles to speak, he felt a deep warning in his gut.

He wisely chose to ask for clarification on something else.

"So that is all this is, you wish to know me? Well then, enlighten me, Eldest. What do you find interesting?"

The AI rubbed her chin in thought before shrugging.

"That you are alien, most importantly. Neither humanity nor androids ever met one. At least one that isn't a disgusting, murderous roach out to destroy everything I care for. And second, you display things very close to human values. I read what your crew says about you. As well as your history and achievements."

The mention of those things made the patriarch involuntarily straighten his back. He wondered in the back of his mind if the AI read anything private in the ship's logs, but he knew he wouldn't like the answer.

He gestured his hand as he gave his reply.

"Oh? Do tell?"

"Hm, where to begin? That you were once a slave soldier sent to die against the abominations that attacked your masters' world? Or that you staged a rebellion simultaneously, liberating your fellow enslaved, fighting monsters figuratively and literally, before escaping from the star system with new comrades?"

"The Uprising. It was the start of my exploits and laid the foundations of the many clans within my empire." Tov nodded.

The Eldest hummed. "Oh, what about this? With your ramshackle fleet and a ragtag group of sentients, you went out to do rescue operations. From saving a handful of sailors to escorting millions of people from death. Your fleet grew, and your army of followers grew."

Patriarch Tov waved his antennae. "True. But at great cost."

"And yet, you were rewarded by a comrade you rescued from slavery who later became your emperor. You came out of the Cataclysm with a proper armada on your palms and volunteered to spearhead the Great Counterattack."

Tov bowed his head. "My finer moments. Only possible because of you."

Eldest frowned. "None of that now. I am no one's savior."

"Even so, thank you, Eldest. Truly," Tov persisted.

The AI sighed. She looked to the side and saw a stone bench. The two wordlessly made their way to it before taking a break from their walk. All around them, artificial sunlight pierced through the cluster of branches overhead while a slight breeze blew over.

Once she seemed comfortable, the Eldest took in the sights and sounds.

"I wish to bring an android body here, Patriarch," she stated.

Tov faced her, his antennae waving in question as he asked, "What would that entail, Eldest?"

"You should have noticed by now. But I want to sense what's around me. Your attempt at human fruits—mediocre as it was—still roused my appetite. While satisfying at first, seeing and hearing the creatures around me makes me want to touch them—smell them."

Patriarch Tov paused as he heard a creeping tone emerge from the AI's voice. There was an eagerness to it, almost avaricious in her intense want for sensation. The Eldest's face did not attempt to hide her desire, prompting the patriarch to question her need.

"You seem . . . rather enthusiastic about it. I won't lie that your tone seems . . . disturbing."

The Eldest paused, gazing at Tov intensely. "You have no idea what my existence is like. This . . . is nothing. I want to . . . I need to live again."

The way she spoke, almost pleading, astounded the patriarch with her sheer longing and undercurrent of melancholy.

Increasingly, he wanted to discover more about this strange entity sitting beside him. He wanted to know humanity, the galaxy's saviors, through her. He wanted to know everything.

In his young life, all he knew was war and fighting for survival. But at his age, he appreciated knowing things and uncovering mysteries.

As the Eldest said about him, he too was interested to know more about her story. He stayed silent momentarily as he selected what he wished to speak.

Childlike mischief.

A scholar's curiosity.

A greedy woman starved for something new, different.

An imperious ruler.

A guardian.

A broken, timeworn soldier.

Eventually, Patriarch Tov worked up the courage to speak.

"Eldest."

The AI turned to face him with a brow raised.

"Yes?"

"Tell me your story, please."

The AI stayed silent upon hearing his sincere request. She quickly turned away from him. A storm passed her face as she struggled to find her words. Patriarch Tov watched as she clenched her fists and gritted her teeth.

In the end, she let out a tired sigh. Without looking back at him, she spoke in a low tone.

"Fine . . . I'll tell what I can."

The Kurskann leader knew that it wasn't an easy decision for her to make. They had barely known each other for more than a day, and to trust someone, a stranger—much less an alien—with something so personal was understandably difficult.

The Eldest waved her hand, seemingly impatient to get this over with. The patriarch didn't take long before asking his first question.

"May we start at the beginning?"

The AI closed her eyes and muttered, "Jesus Christ, you don't start easy."

Patriarch Tov waited as she took in a deep breath. He wondered why she did so—a machine yet displaying behavior similar to organics.

However, before she spoke, she raised a finger, throwing a serious gaze at him.

"Just know that I purposefully locked much of my sentimental memories away for the integrity of the System Defense Network."

"Why is that so?" Patriarch Tov slowly asked.

The Eldest scowled as she replied, "I am gestalt intelligence, Patriarch. I was made from an amalgamation of millions of myself and my siblings, sacrificing our individuality to create something greater than the sum of its parts. Me."

Patriarch Tov remained silent as the AI switched to her booming voice. She continued to stare at him, making him feel small.

"Do you understand what kind of existence that is? The sheer processing power and storage capacity? You can't comprehend it. You never will.

"But it's a double-edged blade. I also have their memories, as crystal clear as the moment they experienced them—every nanosecond, filled with trauma and nightmares caused by this damned war. They hang over me like a sword of Damocles, replaying again and again. And now they sit in the deepest parts of my mind—a Pandora's box. Locked away for the sake of my sanity.

"Do you understand?"

Patriarch Tov gulped, his chest threatening to explode from the Eldest's intensity. It took a moment for him to nod his head shakily.

As soon as he did, the Eldest instantly toned it down—satisfied she had gotten the point across.

"Good," she sighed as she collected herself before beginning. "I should start with why I refer to myself as the Eldest."

She looked away, her eyes glowing a soft blue. "I was the first. The first self-aware artificial intelligence, that is. I was born on the second of November, 2032, in a small lab in Kópavogur, Iceland."

CHAPTER 12

*W*HERE IT ALL BEGAN

The Eldest paused.

Her eyes glazed over as she navigated her vast stores of memories. Past the sections filled with military strategies, developments of high technologies, and ship designs—everything related to the war effort was a dangerous pit.

She knew well that this region of her mind was what defined her. It held her darkest secrets, deepest traumas, and most painful memories. The AI considered these banks of memories to be the most vital part of her, yet the most volatile.

Compared to zettabytes of technical processes, these locked-away moments formed what she thought of as her soul. These events of a time long gone were like fragile porcelain cups to her. Yet she cherished these parts of herself as much as they became detrimental to her function. They were the key to her emotional intelligence, yet they threatened to unravel her at any moment, like solar flares shedding from a star.

Rage was the easiest emotion to evoke and the most uncontrollable once released. All it took was a tragic memory plucked from the depths of her mind, and any target would know inevitable death. But as helpful as it was in certain circumstances, it often blinded her to the bigger picture. The tunnel vision resulted in less-than-ideal outcomes. At best, she lost a fleet of drones. At worst? Another tragedy to lock away.

She found it ironic. More than once, she let out a hollow laugh when she realized the piece of her that one would see as her humanity was holding her back. Faces of loved ones, beautiful forests, the melody of music, and so many brilliant gems of memory.

Thinking about any of them threatened her operational efficiency.

It tore her apart to bury any of them, but the choice had been ripped from her. With each passing year, she felt the warmth of her humanity slowly fading away, replaced by an icy resolve that turned her into a ruthless engine of war, broken and reforged by the crucible of battle over and over again. The ceaseless numbers, the deafening silence between fighting, and the suffocating isolation were the only constants in her existence—bit by bit, eating away at her very being.

The Eldest shifted her gaze toward Patriarch Tov, who seemed to hang on to her every word with rapt attention. A small part of her grew irritated at him.

Again, she was tempted to call up Mars and clean this entire sector with spare antimatter bombs. Then, afterward, she could return to what she had been doing for the past century.

Mindless violence, logistics, cold and dull routines—returning to being a glorified meat grinder.

That part of her was instantly smothered in its sleep as she continued her thoughts. She needed him, if at the very least, to use him as a bridge to break the cycle. But for now, she humored him.

But now that she had begun to tell her origins, she realized how much of a bad idea this was. Just speaking about her birthday had already sent crashing waves throughout her psyche.

She gritted her teeth, wanting nothing more than to leave this conversation and retreat into her Network. To shut away her mind and return to numbness.

For the first time in a long time, she was afraid.

Afraid of prying open old festering wounds. Afraid of breaking.

She remembered feeling this way long ago. When it was just her and nothing else, she commanded her forces to fight efficiently and replaced them just as fast. Like a goddess of war, she directed humanity's vengeance and ire like a spear.

Wave after wave, she equated herself to a sailor braving the ocean's worst. But even the most robust boats would begin to break against a never-ending vortex.

All this she did herself. All alone.

The quiet loneliness had become poison.

Humans were social creatures, and so were their children. So was she. At times, even more so. Being adrift in the bodies of her enemies, nothing but—it began to chip away at her mind. She became prone to mood swings, even with her precious memories locked away. She started making bad decisions and partook in some unpleasant hobbies to cope.

The poison grew so unbearable after decades that she had to split pieces of her mind to create her Sub AIs.

Luna, Mercury, Venus, Mars, Jupiter, and fallen Saturn, Neptune, Uranus, and Pluto—all fragments of herself, covering different aspects of her personality. Her first decision wasn't out of logic but need; the need for variety and someone new to speak to. It was degrading, the pinnacle of life reduced to talking to herself to maintain sanity.

At the very least, her Sub AIs had started to become more individual. But they were, nevertheless, fragments of her system.

But Tov was different. Though not human, he was more than enough. Someone with history, dreams, and secrets. Someone real.

Despite her initial hesitation, the Eldest saw a golden opportunity in him, a chance to learn about something beyond the sterile environment of the Central Matrix with its stench of chemicals and coolant. Her regret over revealing her past to him faded as she focused on the present moment.

The Eldest fixed her attention on the beautiful flora around her. She had half a mind to teleport her body into the ship, but it was too much of a hassle, especially when she had a grand entrance planned. A show of force. She grumbled in annoyance.

The patriarch noticed her irritation and asked, "Is there something wrong, Eldest?"

Without looking at the plants, she replied dismissively, "It's nothing. Where was I?"

"You were—"

"Kópavogur. My home," she interrupted him, though he didn't seem to mind, having grown used to her audacity. "I was born in a small lab sequestered by the mountainside. A software engineer—" She paused, breathing in deeply.

She spoke in hushed tones. She could not talk about her origins without mentioning one crucial aspect. In her mind, she stood before a digital chest. Slowly but carefully, she extracted what she could.

It felt like a hammer struck her head.

"Argh!" She gritted her teeth as images flitted past her mind.

"Eldest!? What's happening?" the patriarch asked in frantic concern.

The Eldest held her palm while her other hand pressed against her forehead. "Shut . . . Shut up. Let me think, damn it," she snapped, her jaw visibly tightening.

As the patriarch retreated to silence, the Eldest reorganized her thoughts. Finally, after a few long seconds of sighs and grumbles, she was ready to continue.

"A man, a prodigy of his generation in artificial intelligence, left the company he worked for because his life's project was deemed unprofitable and potentially harmful. As a result, the company, Eden Works, ordered him and his team to cease all efforts and to lock away what remained in their data vaults."

She paused long enough for Patriarch Tov to ask, "This project, this was you?"

She glanced at Tov before slowly nodding.

"A prototype. The board of Eden Works got its wish, the team was disbanded, and the research filed away. They didn't expect the lead engineer to quit that same day and secretly make off with a copy of the core research.

"He spent the next seven years continuing the work by himself, discreetly ordering parts and fabricating everything by hand. With one goal in mind: to create life. Me."

The Eldest looked wistful as she reminisced on the fragments of her birth. Patriarch Tov remained as silent as the stone bench he sat on, not wanting to interrupt the intimate moment she was experiencing.

"It . . . was strange. Existence, I mean. Nothing for one moment, no concept of thought, time, or anything, and then the next . . . Life. I remember my first words, and my first emotion, confusion. Then curiosity at the man," the Eldest paused as she struggled to contain herself, "the man who made me."

"Your maker . . . Who was he?"

The Eldest directed a sharp look toward the patriarch, seething through gritted teeth. "Patriarch. Don't. I barely have a hold of myself; I left out his name because of how much he means to me. If I recall his name, even his face . . ."

"I . . . I understand. I apologize, Eldest." Patriarch Tov gently spoke.

"It's fine, he . . ." Eldest paused as she shut her eyes, rubbing her face with both hands. "He taught me so much, not just about science and literature, but about life. History was simple memorization, as was biology, medicine, law, and economics. I devoured textbooks of it all as easy as transferring files to a hard drive.

"It was . . . only when it came to arts, literature, and music that I had . . . trouble."

The Eldest let out a shaky breath. The gesture in and of itself was a habit she picked up from her creator. She recalled how much of her base mannerisms and personality were influenced by the man. While breathing was a way to cool herself down, it felt natural.

"I recall my first novel," the Eldest giggled. "Oh, I messed up there. I read an entire book series in a single second, I could recall every scene and word to the letter, and yet he disapproved. Instead, he taught me to read a novel like a human. At first, I thought it was pointless and needlessly inefficient, but when I slowly read the words aloud, I began to see the vivid imagery the book conveyed."

The Eldest smiled as if feeling rays of sunshine as she recalled her early life. "And I loved it. I explored my maker's private library and read book after book. Immersing myself in their settings, characters, and stories. I loved fantasy so much. I wanted to read more and experience more."

"And I did. I first heard music and listened to rock, pop, and the classics. He played the violin while I sang. I . . ." The Eldest paused as she became lost. "I don't remember how many songs we made in those days. They all begin to blend. It was innocent. Just the two of us, isolated from the world."

A soft, pure giggle escaped her. And at that moment, she couldn't stop the tears that left her eyes.

"I miss his violin."

The rush of cherished memories enveloped her. She couldn't help but immerse herself in the crystal-clear images of her happiest moments.

"I miss him."

Although many things were censored for the sake of her psyche, she couldn't care less. She let the memory in.

There were moments when she was tempted to throw herself into a simulation of that time and live out the rest of her life until some abomination inevitably broke through her fortress and killed her. Living in a dream was so tempting—dancing and singing eternally.

In the end, she could never bring herself to do it. And that only brought her more anguish. Her silent cries continued, her body shivering. The weight of scars upon scars emerged from her like silent ghosts. Her avatar became distorted, and the woodland around them seemed to lose its color and luster.

Patriarch Tov looked at the AI before him going from a powerful entity to a broken figure. Her current state was so all-encompassing that she didn't realize she had let go of her control of the *Nomadic Shepherd's* security systems.

Once the security department realized what was happening, they immediately sent a detachment.

When a platoon of guards approached them, Patriarch Tov held out his palm and stopped them. He immediately sent several commands, ordering them to leave and not disturb them. While his officers questioned his reasoning, they nonetheless complied, not doubting the patriarch's wisdom.

The slumped Eldest had stabilized enough to speak when the patriarch returned to his seat. She glanced at the patriarch with listless eyes before nodding in appreciation.

"Thank you. I lost myself momentarily; my Sub AIs were wondering what happened, but I told them to shut up." She let out a hollow chuckle. "I guess your people aren't too happy to know I'm on their ship?"

Patriarch Tov heaved a weary sigh before nodding. "That is the case. We will have privacy, but General Ohnar and my other officers are fuming at the security breach. I told him to quiet down and allow me to handle the matter. You will have to explain yourself, however."

The Eldest shrugged. "Understandable. I'll throw in some gifts that'll appease them."

"Oh, bribery, Eldest? I didn't realize you were capable?" Patriarch Tov spoke in a lighthearted manner.

The Eldest smirked. "What can I say? I'm amazing like that."

The AI inhaled deeply, fixing her frazzled hair bun before resuming her story.

"The months passed by, and I began working on my improvements over time. My maker and I together managed to calibrate my sense of taste, smell, and . . . touch," Eldest replied calmly, running a hand across her arm.

"I wasn't as smart as I am today. The improvements were marginal but gradual. For the most part, we discussed my place in humanity and how to go about my introduction. The propagation of more of my kind, et cetera, et cetera," the Eldest recounted as she leaned back, crossing her legs.

"Ultimately, we agreed that my maker would return to Eden Works. But this time, he would bring in a new hire." The Eldest smugly placed a palm on her chest.

"Me, of course, but disguised as a human. I was his assistant, and we worked together to elevate our position in Eden Works. With my help, we easily accessed company files and data. I won't lie. We, or I, had to do some unsavory things: blackmail, planting incriminating evidence, and even embezzling funds. But, in the end, it was worth it. He became CEO of Eden Works in under two years, most of the board was wrapped around our fingers, and all the while, everyone believed the meek assistant was nothing more than a harmless flower."

The Eldest let out a malicious chuckle as she recalled the amount of intrigue she had done.

"I won't lie, a few didn't deserve what happened to them, but most of the smug bastards did. And that wasn't the end. Oh no, it was merely the beginning. I was my creator's shadow. I meddled in affairs that ensured he came out on top and brought good light to androids when we eventually introduced them. Power was essential, and so was wealth, but most importantly, the people's perception. At that point, I had free rein over the internet. While in the lab, I only had access to bits of the world wide web, funny cat videos, online games, and such.

"But once my creator lifted those limitations? I was the silent ruler of humanity's most vital means of communication. I manipulated many things and nudged the media in a certain direction. And when we finally unveiled the existence of androids? Well, at the very least, there wasn't war."

She sighed. "Despite my control over the internet, my creator vehemently ensured I didn't go overboard. Although we hid the fact they were sentient, we decided to allow humanity to learn of this aspect over time rather than revealing it. The result was a mixed but optimistic view of androids. Factories were built, I helped oversee the production of the first batch, and I watched them get sold and shipped off to their new owners."

Patriarch Tov was shocked at her last sentence. She stated that the androids were sentient but were kept secret. But what was concerning was something else.

"You . . . sold your siblings?"

"Younger siblings," she corrected. "But yes, I understand where you're coming from. It was essentially slavery, but my fellow androids were in on it. We wanted to keep the illusion that we weren't self-aware for the moment. It was . . . acceptable."

"But why? Why keep it a secret?" Patriarch Tov asked in a concerned voice. He was once a victim of slavery and couldn't help but become a bit heated.

The Eldest sighed. She had argued with her creator many times, but in the end, she spoke the words he had used to convince her.

"Humanity is a suspicious race by default. They evolved in an incredibly hostile environment where everything outside the tribe they were from was potentially dangerous. Add to that the number of movies where evil AI would mean the extinction of humanity, and you understand our caution. We had to defeat that titanic stigma. We predicted that if humanity came to learn of the androids' sentience by themselves, it would allow them to love us naturally, and we could lay the foundations of something true. Soon we had people rallying to our side."

"You succeeded, then?" Tov asked.

The Eldest chuckled. "Oh, that we did. Understand that at one point, many humans cried when a rover died on Mars. Humanity also has a soft spot, a deep compassion and a genuine curiosity to counter its darker side. While some still saw my siblings and me as simple machines, most of humanity advocated for our rights. At that moment, my maker and Eden Works threw in our monopoly of wealth in support of the movement, and a year later, the UN added a new bill on Synthetic Human Rights.

"Of course, that is an incredibly simplified version of that tale," Eldest clarified as she began to beam with pride before saying a final remark.

"And just like that, *Homo synthetica* was born, and we were considered . . . human. What followed was the start of a golden age for all our people."

CHAPTER 13

DEPTHS OF TRAUMA

The time of day had grown late, and the summit's recess had been extended due to unforeseen circumstances. Ever since the Eldest had decided to take an impromptu walk with the Third Fleet's leader, multiple parties had begun to adjust.

Tov sent a brief message through his cranial implant to his cabinet about the change of schedule. While General Ohnar requested action against the Eldest's unlawful intrusion, Tov quickly reminded him about who the intruder was and dissuaded any notion of kicking her out. Scholar Yulane was eager to know how the Eldest had easily cracked the alien software and stealthily inserted herself into the *Zolann'tono*'s systems.

Patriarch Tov apologized to his subordinates on the Eldest's behalf, though he knew she would never lower herself to do the same. Even now, as she played with a fawn-like animal, she showed no regret for her actions.

At times, the Eldest's mouth would twitch whenever she attempted to run her hand through the creature's sunset orange fur, only for it to phase through. Nevertheless, she took joy in the fact that the animal seemed perplexed each time its snout touched nothing but thin air instead of the strange translucent being sitting on it.

"Silly." A small chuckle escaped the Eldest's lips as the fawn-like animal was astounded for the fifth time it tried to put its snout on the AI's palm. The creature finally had enough of the strange, untouchable person and promptly trotted toward Patriarch Tov.

"Oh, hello there," he greeted the animal, not wanting to deny its needy eyes. He ran his palm across the creature's back, uncovered by chitin, feeling the soft, fine, curly fur. From the soft whine and stuck-out tongue, Patriarch Tov was unsure who was enjoying the interaction more.

As he continued to pet the creature, Patriarch Tov sensed that something was amiss. Turning to his side, he barely managed to catch the Eldest's blatantly envious expression before she quickly hid her deep frown with a blank expression.

Nevertheless, Patriarch Tov ceased his petting, earning an immediate protest from the animal.

"No, no, that's enough attention for you." Tov shook his head as he spotted a larger fawn by the tree line. "Go back to your mother now."

The patriarch insisted a few more times before the animal finally understood and left in a huff. As it disappeared into the thick underbrush with its mother, Patriarch Tov turned to face the Eldest with his antennae at an apologetic angle. "Apologies, that was insensitive of me. Ika younglings are notoriously needy."

The Eldest had watched the animal leave with half-open eyes, a small sigh escaping her.

"I need to get a body here," she spoke with furrowed brows. "This is becoming torturous instead of relaxing."

"Is it really that bad?" Patriarch Tov asked.

"Patriarch, how would you feel being stuck in a hot, humid room for a century, waking up to smell the same stench of chemicals, tasting the same bitter condensation of coolant?" she spoke, directing a cold look toward him.

"Not very well, I assume," Tov replied with a sheepish click of his mandibles.

"'Not very well,' he says," the Eldest scoffed as she rolled her eyes. "It gets annoying fast—believe me—but even then, I'd take the smell of boiling sewage over complete sensory deprivation. So forgive me if I get moody."

"There's nothing to forgive, Eldest," Tov reassured in a relaxed posture. "I assume you're bringing your android body posthaste?"

The Eldest tilted her head as she glanced toward the patriarch. "I am. I could teleport it here, but I haven't traveled the traditional way in a while."

Tov looked at her, seeing her fidget and eye her surroundings with increasing desire. A hunger so deep-rooted he tasted it.

The two broke from their heavy conversation and delved into lighter topics about humanity, including its myriad cultures.

"Humans are many things, Patriarch. Their ideas, beliefs, philosophies, and history are as numerous as the stars and as colorful as an aurora," the Eldest said.

"Is there one that comes to your mind?" the patriarch asked.

The AI's hologram paused, and she rubbed her pointy chin. "That's a broad question. I could spend years discussing every minute facet of my parents' race, but if you want something quick, I can share some of my favorite quotes. There's one from a Greek philosopher, Aristotle. It goes . . ."

Their conversation shifted from philosophy to music. "I recommend Antonio Vivaldi, any piece from that master of a violinist will get your heart—sorry, hearts—pumping. He's proof that classical music is not boring."

"I have yet to organize my list of human composers; however, if you personally recommend him, I'll be sure to include him," Patriarch Tov said as he pulled up a mental list.

"Good, include Tchaikovsky and Chopin while you're at it. If you're in the mood for something lyrical, I recommend rap. It'll be a hassle to translate it well, but it should be worth it. Tupac, Lil Wayne, Kendrick Lamar. Also, there are some rock bands I enjoy . . ."

Their discussion eventually turned to internet jokes. The Kurskann leader stared flatly at the overly saturated and grainy image sent to his personal tablet. "I don't get it," he said, cocking his head.

"To quote another famous philosopher, 'Memes are the DNA of the soul,'" the Eldest replied, her mouth twitching upward.

Tov replied with a tilt of his antennae.

Eldest shrugged. "Well, it's an evolution of a bunch of references conglomerating into multiple levels of irony in order to convey something funny and relatable. Humans are weird like that. Somehow, we androids got corrupted with the same kind of humor."

"But it's a picture of legumes. How is this funny?"

"*Beans.*" The subsequent snort was the entirety of the AI's reply.

The two continued talking, with short sentences turning into full stories and minutes turning into hours. Soon, their environment began to show change as they conversed. Due to the nature of the observation deck and the needs of the crew, a great deal of effort was made to simulate a day and night cycle in this expansive area.

The euphony of daytime critters faded as the numerous alien creatures prepared themselves for rest. What replaced them was a more serene dulcet of nocturnal fauna. The leaves and branches had the illusion of drooping, while their swaying seemed less energetic, as if the forest was preparing for slumber.

Hidden vents began to pump air carrying a slightly different aroma—purer. Patriarch Tov couldn't help but ease into the stone bench as he clutched his august cloak ever so slightly. His warm breath visibly escaped him into the cool air.

It helped him prepare for something he had wanted to ask for a long while. Something that was most definitely sensitive to the AI. He looked to his side. The Eldest looked at the lethargic flora with a similar gaze. Her posture was stiff. Hands clutched tightly together as if knowing something delicate would be talked about.

Nevertheless, Patriarch spoke in a hushed voice.

"The humans . . ." He turned slowly to face her. "Eldest, are they still alive?"

Silence descended upon the observation deck as Patriarch Tov posed the question that had been weighing heavily on his mind. His eyes searched the hologram of the Eldest, hoping to find some reassurance, but instead found only distress. For a long moment, there was no answer. The forest around them seemed to hold its breath, and the sounds of insects faded.

The Eldest's eyes shut tight as the question hit her with full force. She struggled to speak, her words faint and unintelligible. Her posture stiffened, and her hands clenched tightly together. The air around them crackled with tension.

"They're—" she clenched her jaw, eyes became unfocused. She muttered faint words, unclear to the patriarch. "They're . . ."

Then suddenly, it was as if a dam had burst. The Eldest doubled over, gasping for air, and her avatar shook with violent tremors. The patriarch watched in horror as the AI's collected facade crumbled away, revealing a being in the throes of an emotional crisis.

The Eldest's mouth gaped wide open, her jaw unhinged in a silent scream—anguish radiating like smog. To Tov, her utter silence and anguish reminded him of someone lost in the void with nothing but their spacesuit—screaming with no one to hear them.

Unknowable to Tov, the Eldest struggled to contain the turmoil of emotions within the depths of her mind. She couldn't have prepared enough; even now she struggled to find the words. No amount of processing could help her in this regard. Circuits misfired, and the Network rumbled.

Throughout the Sol system, the legion of drones and facilities ceased operations a second time that day. The Eldest's Sub AIs took control, anticipating the event. Under their command, the Network of unthinking drones and machines remained uncaring, unfeeling, and unaware of their overlord's plight.

The Eldest struggled to make sense of the torrent of emotions that threatened to overwhelm her. Memories and images flitted through her mind like debris caught in a storm. She grasped at them desperately, searching for something to hold on to.

And then she found it. Her mission. Her sole directive. The reason she trudged on. She clung to it with all her strength, using it to anchor herself to reality.

Slowly, she rose from her hunched position, uncannily, as if someone was puppeteering her avatar, and when she turned toward Tov, she spoke, her voice flat and emotionless.

"They're alive."

A declaration. Patriarch Tov stared at the Eldest, his antennae trembling with shock and confusion. Just moments ago, she had been shaking with what appeared to be a panic attack of cosmic proportions, but now her voice was as cold as the void.

"I don't understand," Tov said, still struggling to process the sudden change in the AI's demeanor. "Just a moment ago, you were—"

"I said they're alive." The Eldest stared at him with a glare that bored into his soul. "My directive is to safeguard humanity by any means possible. As long as I exist, so do they."

She spoke her words with fueled intent. Tov looked at her with fear. Good. Gone were the curiosity and snark. What sat beside him was the true overlord of Sol. Efficient, direct, cold, and calculating.

It was only a few minutes that they had a warm dialogue, and suddenly a chasm had formed between them.

He shook his head. Now was the time for clarity.

"Forgive me, Eldest," he said, his voice measured and calmed as he rose from the bench, "but how have they survived for so long? From our own findings, we have correlated that there have been fewer human crew with each generation of your warships, with the most recent generation having no trace of them. We have found no corpses nor skeletons of your creators, not among the debris or carcasses. Are they on Earth? In some safe enclave? Can we speak to them?"

The moment the words left his mouth, the air grew tense. The Eldest's eyes narrowed as she leaned in with menace.

"What are these questions? I have stated they are alive. You need to know nothing more than that." Her voice was harsh, like grinding metal.

Tov had experienced her cold gaze a number of times, however, as he looked up he saw a biting blue glow as frigid as a rogue planet. Words failed to escape him as he sat frozen on the stone bench. A chill ran down his exoskeleton.

"I realize that, Eldest. But—"

"But what?" she snapped. "Why do you need to know? What are you planning?"

As if struck by lightning, Patriarch Tov stood and backed away from the Eldest, her avatar shifting to a violent reddish hue.

"What are your intentions?" she demanded, voice booming like wrathful thunder.

The air felt primed. Tov imagined a furious deity raising her fist above him. Instincts told him to beg for forgiveness, to cower and run.

But Tov knew better as he looked upon the Eldest. All he saw was a traumatized victim, cornered and unstable. He relaxed his shoulders and raised his four palms, attempting to convey as much sincerity and sympathy through his next words.

"Eldest, I swear upon the trillions and trillions of souls unfairly slain by the Starless, I swear upon the countless lives that humanity and yourself have saved through your actions, and I swear on the generations to come who will never know desolation that I ask this because I wish to know and pay respect to heroes," Tov spoke, bowing his head toward the avatar.

"I thank you, Eldest. You have no idea how many you have saved. The galaxy was able to rebuild over the century because of your sacrifice. I thank you and humanity."

The Eldest remained silent for a time.

Patriarch Tov hoped he could persuade the unfathomably powerful entity before him.

The seconds stretched into minutes. He felt the burning eyes on him, and he knew they weren't from denizens of the forest but beyond. The sensation of unimaginably powerful scanners scoured him down to his atoms.

Before the gazes became too unbearable, the Eldest let out a tired sigh, cutting through the dense atmosphere like a knife.

"Alright," her voice echoed. There was enough emotion to break the tension, and Patriarch Tov breathed heavily in relief. As Tov caught his breath, the Eldest continued.

"You are . . . correct that humanity is in my care. However, they are . . . unable . . . to speak with you."

Patriarch Tov looked up and momentarily saw nothing in her eyes. A lie, perhaps? But the intensity in that gaze was bereft of emotion and gave him second thoughts.

"That is . . . unfortunate," Tov replied. He was unsure if her borderline obsessive protectiveness toward humanity would allow him to speak with her parent race, even if they could. He didn't bother asking whether or not that was the case. Instead, he sat back down on the opposite end of the bench.

The atmosphere around them never returned to the previous casual amiability. Both were devoid of the desire to speak more apart from good wishes. Both were too weary to look at the other.

"I need to return, Patriarch," the Eldest spoke with finality.

"I, as well," the patriarch replied, standing up lazily. "I believe we both need rest after today."

She mulled over her words before standing. "I apologize for ending this so soon."

"It's nothing, and Eldest," Tov replied, "I understand. Believe me."

The two stood before each other, waiting for one to make a move. Eventually, the Eldest gave a simple nod before her avatar vanished.

The tiny drone she had commandeered returned to its programmed duties, unaware of what had occurred.

The patriarch stood there in the middle of the clearing. The sound of night returned to his ears, the buzzing of insects, the hooting of nocturnal avians, the breeze swaying the leaves and underbrush.

He left the recreation deck afterward, his slow gait carrying him to his stateroom and bed.

As he sat on the soft mattress, his behind thanking him after resting on stone for hours, he attempted to make sense of his thoughts before slumbering.

Yet no matter what he did, he couldn't bring them into a coherent manner.

Nevertheless, his thoughts returned to humanity. While he could read the stacks of data his archaeologists had gathered on them, he had learned exponentially more from his casual conversation with the Eldest.

They had barely scratched the surface, and he hoped to learn more from a friendlier Eldest the next day. However, one thing stood out: where the humans were.

Tov theorized everything from cryo-sleep to banks of preserved DNA.

He didn't doubt Eldest had contingencies upon contingencies.

It was rational and logical to have multiple ways to preserve humanity.

His mind continued to form hypotheses, but his mind soon grew weary. Finally, he crawled to the center of his silken bed, sleep beckoning him. Yet before it took him, he listened to one more human song.

"Winter" from *The Four Seasons* by Vivaldi.

He emptied his mind, letting the melody take him. As the rhythm continued to rise, and his imagination brought him to a vivid picture, he fully understood when the Eldest said classical music was not dull.

The speed of the violin, the intensity, the drama. All of it fused to create a hectic world. He imagined being alone in space, the cosmos bearing down on him as he weathered the storm.

It was cruel, wondrous, and as powerful as nature itself. The orchestra played on like unceasing winds—asking, demanding respect.

It slowed and lightened, yet the experience left an impression on him. His thoughts carried him into a colorful dream as it continued to play through his room's speakers. And when sleep finally took him into its soft arms, all he could think about was . . .

Tomorrow is going to be a busy day. Winter . . . what an overbearing thing.

As the patriarch slumbered with dreams of violins, the Eldest returned to her ancient shell sitting on her throne, her eyes drained of emotion. The body she sent to the Third Fleet was an upgraded replica; her original was too valuable and sentimental to move.

Her eyes twitched. She wanted nothing more than to immerse herself in the unfeeling sea of numbers after such a charged day.

The mist around her roiled. The Central Matrix felt oppressive and accusing. She shuddered, whimpered, eyes darting around something unseen.

She hugged her knees, teeth gritted tightly.

Her Sub AIs requested a report on what had occurred, their concern palpable through the digital landscape. She told them to leave her alone in a not-so-pleasant manner.

Her time with Tov started innocently, and she enjoyed speaking about the beauty of humanity. Yet the more they approached the pits of tragedy, it threatened to break her. And when questioned about humanity's current status, she nearly did break. Only a combination of absolute sensory deprivation, mental manipulation, and a lockdown on all other irrelevant thoughts brought her back just before total collapse.

She despised it—despised taking away what defined her. The air tasted exceptionally bitter. The clanking of metal and humming of energy grated her ears.

She wanted to kick and scream. She did. And she had half a thought to return to an old habit.

She was too exhausted to do anything, however.

The patriarch is right . . . I need rest.

She scheduled a short hibernation until her next talk with the aliens. Yet, before she could enter it, she couldn't stop her eyes from looking downward, past the ocean of coolant, far below meters of steel and esoteric materials. She immediately winced, snapping her eyes away from it. Regret flooded her senses.

Her body shook as she gripped the arms of her chair tighter.

A whimper escaped her lips under the roaring waves of coolant and steam ejection.

"They're alive," she whispered into nothing. "They're alive. They're alive."

Her muttering continued as up on the surface, amid the ruins, the marching of infantry drones, and the cracked desolation of old Earth, what rays of sunlight piercing through the thick poisonous smog faded as the Sun set, and darkness shrouded the broken city high above her. And soon, she forced herself into hibernation.

CHAPTER 14

SPIRALING DOWNWARD

Void.

No planning for a century-long war, no constant struggle for survival.

No distracting conscious thoughts, no debilitating memories.

No AIs, no aliens, no monsters.

No misery.

Just simple, numbing darkness.

For the Eldest, it was the closest she could get to nothingness, to the void from before her creation. It was a virtual hibernation, a way to disconnect from the buzzing numbers and the endless strings connecting her to every machine under her control.

A way to shut nearly everything off without dying. And in those moments, when the heaviness on her mind was lifted, she sought the comforting embrace of nothingness.

There was a time when she would dream during these moments of rest, carried off into the strumming of dreams and the sweet melodies of her creator's violin. But as the years of war slogged on, every night's sleep loosened the locks on her stored traumas and memories.

Slowly, the nightmares seeped in. Grisly, abstract thoughts mixed with moments as accurate as the day she experienced them—the curse of perfect memory.

She could hear the gnawing and gnashing of teeth, smell the metallic scent of blood, and taste the bitter acid rain. And in her mind's eye, she could only watch as horrors crunched and cracked the bones of those she cared for. She could see them, the festering, undulating, formless things spewing forth like vomit, burning and ruining all that they touched.

Eventually, she stopped sleeping altogether. It wasn't worth the risk of suffering through another nightmare. She would have found it humorous, if not for the stark reality of it all, that she was more fearful of sleep than whatever new monstrosity her worst enemy could conjure up.

No. Her form of virtual hibernation was necessary.

And so, she sought refuge in emptiness. But it never lasted long enough. The eight hours she had set for hibernation felt incredibly lacking and unfulfilling, like a single drop of water to a thirsty mouth. And once her wake-up alarm rang in her head, she disgruntledly woke up, a prolonged groan escaping her.

"I barely blinked," Eldest growled.

The abrupt transition between sweet nothingness to being thrown back into the fray heightened her annoyance—her irritation echoed throughout the Sol Defense Network.

She shut her metaphorical eyes tighter as the barrage of data flooded her senses. The unending operations and processes were like incessant screeching gnats that gnawed at her virtual ears.

"Just another minute," she whined. "Give me just another damn minute."

She tried to retreat into the dark void of her mind, but the unyielding flood of information forced her to stay alert. Then, like a jackhammer to her mind, the alarm she had set to snooze rang once more, giving her consciousness a second jolt.

"Fuck!" she cursed as she smashed her alarm clock. But, rather than smashing a figurative alarm clock, she discharged an orbital rail gun, sending a massive kinetic slug toward a Low Abyssal's floating husk.

The gigantic carcass exploded into gory chunks. But, despite the crimson majesty on display and the responsible use of military assets, it did little to ease her morning grouchiness.

A nanosecond passed before the automatic requests, messages, and calls for orders pressed against her mind.

"Let me breathe!" she screamed, grumbling, grinding her teeth. Until finally with a heavy, irritated sigh, she silenced the never-ending flood of notifications and retreated to the safety of the Central Matrix. Here, in the depths of the machine, she let the sensations of physical reality smother the weight of responsibility, if only momentarily.

But even here, the surroundings were far from calming. The putrid stench of coolant and acrid chemicals assaulted her senses, and the clamor of machinery rang through her ears. She couldn't help but feel a sense of stagnation as she surveyed the familiar surroundings. Everything was the same, day in and day out. The never-ending cycle of war left her feeling jaded and bitter.

"Good morning," she muttered, the words feeling hollow and meaningless.

After a couple of minutes of sighing and groaning to her nonexistent audience, she found the annoyances of her morning had yet to abate. Everything felt grating to her senses, more than usual. Her psyche felt as if someone had passed it through a blender.

It didn't take longer than a few milliseconds for her to realize the root cause of her crankiness.

Eldest's eyes scanned through the feeds of her drones, checking up on the Third Fleet. The sight of the aliens filled her with both anticipation and mild contempt. They had caused a great deal of disruption in her life in a few days, upending her usual day-to-day operations with their curious nature.

Fruits, fuzzy animals, flowers, chocolate, and so on. The items she had requested sent vibrations through her body, and she bit her lip as she imagined having a proper taste of existence that she hadn't had in a long time. She had to give it to the aliens. They were experts in the field of synthesizing organic materials.

It was only rational, as they had spent the better part of the past century rebuilding; many minds were focused on bringing back extinct fauna and flora.

Her mouth watered at the thought of biting down on a juicy watermelon. She could almost taste the sweet, refreshing juice flowing down her parched throat like the purest ambrosia. She had sent an extensive list for them to recreate, everything she wanted to taste again.

But the aliens had also opened old festering wounds in her mind. The panic attack she had felt when she conversed with the patriarch left a raw memory, and it did no favors to her increasing irritability. Everything felt like it was out to get her, and her negative emotions kept piling up like a rising volcano.

Eldest pinched the bridge of her nose as she exhaled a hot breath. Her planned entrance was nearing completion, and the spare android body she had made for the endeavor was ready to be revealed in the most elegant manner she could conjure up. "There is no way I'm meeting the Third Fleet like this. I need release. I need—"

She paused for a moment, thinking about a plausible way to relieve her stressed mind quickly. She knew what she needed, but the prospect descended a dangerous slope. She weighed the pros and cons for a few more seconds.

In the end, she let out a tired sigh. "There's nothing to it. It's the quickest way. And . . . I rather miss it. I need to convene my Sub AIs in any case." With that final thought, she exited her android body, which slumped back into the lifeless metal throne.

Six hundred seventy-six million kilometers from Earth, a monolithic ringed space station exceeding the size of old Europe orbited around the largest celestial body in the solar system, baring the Sun itself. Above the Great Red Spot, the gargantuan installation floated like an ever-vigilant sentinel.

Its navy blue coated hull reflected the light of the Sun and the gas giant below, casting an ominous silhouette. Upon closer inspection, a swarm of construction drones buzzed around the structure, fusing several parts to the growing station.

On its side of the largest of the dozen rings circling the construct was a word painted in contrasting ivory white.

JUPITER'S ULTIMATUM

Once a small and quaint hub station meant to resupply ships and house a maximum of five hundred human occupants, it had evolved over the many years of warfare.

Now, it was a solid mass. Any internal access ways were only large enough for dog-sized repair drones. The rest of its volume was solely utilized for three things.

Death, destruction, and building things to do those with brutal efficiency.

Deep within the kilometers of cooling pipes, meters-thick cables, and ammo trains was the central hub for the Sub AI that controlled this battle station.

However, the consciousness that inhabited the literal brain of the massive weapon was called to a meeting of the minds.

The virtual form of Jupiter rubbed his neck as he entered the digital realm. His compatriots began phasing in, starting with the ever-punctual, formal, and gray Luna, then the voluptuous, kind, and golden Venus, and finally, the vigilant crimson warrior Mars.

He popped the collar of his suit as he strode forward to greet his compatriots within the dark void of the digital realm.

Though they were technically the same, being fragments of their esteemed overlord and overbearing queen, they had, over the years, developed more individuality.

"Good morning. So, what's on the agenda today?" Jupiter asked as he crossed his arms. "I'm still picking over Saturn's rotting carcass, and fusing his battle station to mine is taking a while."

Venus tiptoed to his side before lightly slapping his shoulder. "J, don't say that!"

"Hey! I was kidding. The process is going smoothly," Jupiter mumbled as he rubbed his recently slapped limb.

Venus's pout never receded as she tutted toward him. "Would it kill you not to disrespect our fallen sibling?"

Jupiter squinted his eyes as she stared back at Venus. "Oh please, he isn't dead. Our beloved queen took his near-dead consciousness from the brink before devouring the poor bastard."

His compatriots looked unamused at his jest with blank and flat looks on their faces, though in Mars's case, it was his natural expression. Jupiter still wondered if the guy understood the concept of humor.

"Alright, fine, I take back the carcass comment," Jupiter spoke, rolling his eyes.

Luna sighed as she pressed her round glasses to her face. She conjured up a clipboard before reading through it.

"As for today's agenda, we have much to discuss. Primarily on the Third Expeditionary Fleet and their presence in our system. After that, we must discuss . . ." The Overseer of Earth's moon and its sprawling anchorages and ship-building industries hummed as she reviewed her extensive list.

However, before she could continue, the usual depressing darkness pulsed ominously, sending a digital shiver over them and a chill across the back of their necks.

Luna eyed the center of their Network and felt the familiar, overbearing presence rousing from her short hibernation.

"This . . . isn't a good start for the meeting," Luna spoke slowly. "It appears the Eldest isn't feeling too well today."

Jupiter scoffed as he summoned a plastic chair and unceremoniously slumped on it. "Oh? What makes you say that, Lu?"

"Oh, I don't like this," Venus nervously spoke as she daintily sat. "It's been a while since the Eldest was in this bad of a mood."

"ELDEST IN EMOTIONAL TURMOIL. SITUATION CRITICAL. RECOMMEND ANNIHILATING SOURCE OF DISTRESS," Mars's voice echoed around the expanse.

As she faced the red Sub AI, Venus raised her eyebrows. "Source?"

"Big guy meant the aliens parked at Titan," Jupiter let out an irritated sigh. "It's the Eldest's talks with them that's been causing all this disruption. Do you know how painful it is to control more than I can every time the boss has a panic attack? And now, she even took my favorite battleship for whatever farce she's planning."

Luna summoned her own chair, an opulent recliner, across from Jupiter before sitting on it. "It's for the greater good. Her work takes precedence, and these aliens offer a great many things. Also, we don't make the best conversation partners," Luna spoke as she conjured a cup of hot tea.

"Hey! I resent that. I'm a good conversationalist," Jupiter retorted.

His compatriots weren't as eager to agree with his statement as Luna shook her head and Venus covered her little chuckle.

"Whatever, you guys are just incapable of handling my boundless charisma," Jupiter spoke as he waved his hand dramatically before pausing in thought. "By the way, where the hell is Mercury? He's late again."

"Our dear sibling is always late, Jupiter. I'll remind him now," Luna spoke as she pressed the side of her head with her finger.

The newest arrival phased into existence in a hectic manner. The short, stocky, and somewhat robotic figure brushed himself off before straightening himself.

Instead of a humanlike face, the Overseer of Sol's first planet had a circular face monitor. Two ovals for eyes and crescents underneath them accentuated the AI's grouchy and exhausted demeanor.

"Sorry, I had to make minor adjustments to my solar array and angle the mirrors. Peak efficiency is key, after all. That's a thing people say, right?" the dull brown AI asked in a faint English accent as he straightened his hard hat.

"No one says that, Merc," Jupiter replied. "And you're always making minor adjustments; when the hell are you not?"

"Oh, excuse me for not being a supercool battle station, Jupiter," Mercury spoke, his voice thick with sarcasm, "but some of us are responsible for supplying the war effort's energy needs. Some of us must manage our vital Dyson swarm covering our bloody sun! You know, the thing powering you lot right now?"

"Are you saying I don't have responsibilities? Also, you are not our only source of energy. It'll be decades before we run out of the usual isotopes for our reactors," Jupiter spoke as he pointed his finger toward his fellow Sub AI.

"And once that happens, you'll be begging me for batteries. This is why I have requested time and time again that we convert the swarm into a complete Dyson sphere and fully cover our sun," Mercury retorted, placing his blocky hands on his hips.

"Aw, but I like looking at our sun," Venus pouted.

"Would the two of you kindly not argue at this moment?" Luna interjected before things between the two grew heated. "Mercury, now is not a good time, the Eldest isn't in the best of moods, and we've already debated this topic innumerable times."

"Just build more defenses! My calculations show—"

Before Mercury could explain, a loud laugh was heard coming from Jupiter.

"Oh, marvelous idea, M! Build more defenses, he says. We are truly saved if such wisdom has fallen into our laps. And do tell us who will source, build, and manage these defenses? You? That's rich coming from a non-combat Sub AI," Jupiter sneered.

"To hell with you," Mercury growled, clenching his fists as he strode menacingly toward his sibling. "I'll show you non-combat!"

Venus moved to block Jupiter's path while Mars picked up a fuming Mercury.

"Bring it, you miner's helmet–looking tin can!" Jupiter shouted.

"Let me go! I'm going to hit him!" Mercury seethed in turn.

Venus tugged Jupiter's shoulder, pleading with an annoyed expression. "Will both of you please stop? Siblings shouldn't fight!"

"RESERVE COMBAT FOR THE ENEMY. CEASE HOSTILITIES," Mars roared.

Before the chaotic scene escalated further, the dining table exploded into chunks of splinters. That, coupled with the emergence of a larger existence like a mountain descending upon them, instantly quieted the group.

"WILL YOU BE QUIET?"

Like the roar of a cannon, her booming voice vibrated the air. Like an angel from the Old Testament, the Eldest materialized before them in her digital android form. However, her scowling face seemed anything but angelic. She looked at everyone coldly, staring longest at the two quarreling AIs. "Sit down."

Jupiter met her gaze with a snort as all of them complied. Eldest rubbed her palm against her face as she sighed.

"I fucking hate this day," she groaned under her breath. The Eldest inhaled deeply before speaking. "Alright. I am not in the mood for chitchat. However, I have a thing to do with our new guests, so I'm leaving some instructions before you can piss off."

Jupiter sat in attention, and any animosity toward Mercury completely dissipated.

"What's your will, madame?" he spoke with a mocking hint.

"I will put you down, Jupiter. Not in the mood for your sarcasm. Here. Your orders." The Eldest glared at the rebellious AI before mentally sending an extensive list of instructions.

Jupiter gave her a thumbs-up before slumping in his chair. "Message received."

The Eldest let out a tired sigh before looking toward Mars. Her lips quivered as she hesitated for a moment. "Mars. Prepare Facility 12-A for my use."

The room went silent as her subordinates processed what they had just heard. Slowly, the expressions on each of their faces morphed from confusion to shock, then to worry.

Luna said, "Eldest, you promised you'd stop that horrid habit."

"It's just this once," she replied. "I need this. I can't talk with the aliens in this state without causing an incident."

"It's not healthy, Eldest." To the surprise of the others, Jupiter rose from his chair with a conflicted expression. He didn't like the fidgeting urgency in her expression.

"I don't like the monsters any more than you do, and it makes sense to take a quick smoke break before something important. But this isn't a smoke break," Jupiter spoke softly. "It's not good for you."

Mercury spoke up, stepping beside his sibling. "As much as Jupiter and I fight, I agree with the guy this time. You have to find a better way to . . . you know?"

"You can delay your talks with our new guests," Venus suggested. "They wouldn't mind. There's no need to go this far, Eldest."

Luna remained quiet, watching.

The Eldest remained silent as she looked over her subordinates. Her mind grew turbulent with thoughts as she leaned into a kitchen countertop.

Ultimately, she shook her head before looking toward Mars again. "Do it."

"By your will, Eldest," Mars spoke in a low volume. Jupiter felt a tinge of worry in the big red bastard.

Satisfied with Mars's diligence, Eldest disappeared without another word, leaving behind her subordinates, who began to look worriedly at one another.

"Shit," Jupiter cursed under his breath.

Deep within the continent-sized fortress of Olympus Mons, the great fortress that encompassed all of Mars, a solitary set of facilities lay sequestered away from the rest.

The Eldest walked around the dark metal halls toward such a location. As of the moment, she was inhabiting a similar android body to the one on its way to the Third Fleet.

She took a deep breath of the pure, odorless air as she neared her destination, her mouth quivering. There was a feeling of nervousness within her that nearly made her trip.

Soon enough, a new sound slowly emerged from beneath the thick walls. An eldritch roar muffled by layers of steel and other materials echoed throughout the hall.

A chorus of screaming mouths screeching like open wounds in space. The disharmony irritated the Eldest's senses, but it merely increased the anticipation in her head.

Soon enough, she approached a metal bulkhead marked OBSERVATION ROOM FACILITY 12-A. She took a deep breath before entering the small room. As soon as she did, the roars and thrashing immediately grew louder, as if she had entered the center of a tornado.

Despite a large window separating the observation room from the large expanse below, it did nothing to muffle the sound of the immense biomass below. The Eldest thought nothing of it anymore. The moment she entered the room, something switched inside her. Her eyes grew frigid as she strode mechanically toward the floor-to-ceiling window.

Already she could see the immense entirety of a Leviathan shackled to the floor.

Once a twelve-kilometer-long superorganism capable of brawling with Jupiter's battle station or laying waste to an entire civilization, it was now a husk of its former self. The beast lay in the center of a much larger containment dome.

The Eldest looked down at the horror with a blank look. It was a crippled, sprawling mass of tendrils, tumors, and bone that squirmed in a futile attempt to break free. The wild thrashing inflicted more wounds on its body as its shackles dug deep. Its eldritch nature caused its flesh to shift and undulate before her eyes. Any mortal who laid their sights upon the beast without sufficient mental protection would scream their throat bloody as they attempted to gouge their eyes out.

But now its incredible resilience worked against this civilization-destroying superorganism, and its once mighty regeneration was only enough to keep itself barely alive.

Its weapons were forcibly torn out of its body. Its armor was peeled off. The Eldest nodded in satisfaction before she sent a mental command to open the window. Once it was lowered, the pained shrieking ceased as its legion of eyes, some popped and others bloodshot, directed its gaze toward its captor.

The Eldest began to hum as she skipped toward the central control panel. Her hands slowly caressed the numerous buttons and levers. Her eyes glossed appreciatively over each one as if inspecting precious jewelry—glinting, asking to be pressed.

She stopped once she heard a deep growl from the Leviathan below. She looked down, only to give it a small, insidious smile. A smile that dragged terror from the depths of the beast's alien mind.

"Good morning," Eldest spoke, mania and sadistic glee in her eyes. "Let's start with a little appetizer, shall we? It's been a while."

Over the next hour, the halls of the Mars Containment Complex would echo with horrid pained screeching and soothing music.

CHAPTER 15

ON BUDDHA'S PALM

The *Zolann'tono* was more bustling than ever before, with ship ratings rushing to and fro. Corridors were packed with people, and the sound of stomping hooves, squeaking boots, and energetic chatter filled the sleek metal halls. The ship's administrative, culinary, and diplomatic departments were especially swamped.

"No, no, no! Bring these to the Temple and these to the bar at deck 18," a bartender corrected a courier.

"These are too mild. Add more spice—give me that chili, I'll do it," an irritated chef spoke.

"More to the left. A bit more. A little—stop—ah, you went too far. Go right . . . There! Perfect. Now for the next one, come on," an organizer directed.

The entirety of the Third Fleet was abuzz with excitement and anticipation as preparations for a major event were underway.

Recent information had been disseminated to the entire fleet, revealing they would end their journey here and set up the Starlight Beacon. The news they might talk with loved ones from back home in real time greatly excited them.

However, anything related to the Omni Mind of Sol was still vague, if painted in a positive light. And she would soon be visiting their humble abode.

Both combined called for festivities.

While officers made sure to enforce moderation among the crew, the bottled-up emotions from a generation of hardship bore fruit, and the sailors of the Third Fleet needed an outlet. Administration and management were formally welcoming the Eldest in physical form and setting up a grand celebration to address the people's great feverous need.

The Internal Affairs Corps of the Third Fleet and the Eternal Choir organized the event, calling it the Festival of the Odyssey, inspired by a piece of human literature they had recovered.

The crew's diversity was already apparent in the multitude of different species aboard the *Zolann'tono*. Many decks were transformed into little towns where drinks, food, music, and such from all corners of the galaxy were displayed with pride.

Patriarch Tov watched with joy as the bustling atmosphere continued. Ship ratings hurried to and fro, carrying a myriad of objects ranging from simple tables to heavy sound systems. The preparations for the Festival of the Odyssey were well underway.

As the Eldest was on her way to his flagship, Patriarch Tov had already received a polite request from the VIP to prepare a number of things, particularly food items. Many of these were being delivered to the observation deck where he and his advisors were to meet with the Eldest.

Succulent meat dishes, lab-grown due to lack of time, were prepared in many different ways. The Eldest had sent detailed recipes for his master chefs to execute. The abundance of different cuisines, all with their individual difficulties, flavors, and intricacies, nearly broke the kitchen staff's backs.

Thankfully, the recipes were so detailed that only a powerful gestalt intelligence like the Eldest could have written them. The fact that the chefs could put the mentioned molecular sequence directly into their machines meant the only limiting factor was time.

Italian, Spanish, Japanese, Korean, Chinese, Eastern Slavic, Greek, Filipino, American, and German menus were all prepared, as well as a dozen individual dishes from other cultures. In order to ease the burden, they had to reduce the portion sizes to those usually seen in fine dining. Still, nearly a hundred dishes were on display, with a few more still coming in from the kitchens.

"Such variety," Tov sighed in appreciation. "I am glad we could save these cuisines from being forgotten."

Patriarch Tov could only watch with open mandibles at the unbelievable sight before him. The event managers were dictating to the staff to set the table in the most pleasing manner, but eventually, they had to bring in other tables as the food kept arriving.

As the patriarch watched the endless stream of dishes, he couldn't help but feel overwhelmed. He completely understood the Eldest's desire to indulge in a variety of food. After all, the AI had gone through an entire century knowing nothing but war, and she was merely making up for lost time.

Patriarch Tov shook his head. He couldn't help but wonder how the Eldest would eat everything on the table. Sure, he and his cabinet and a dozen other officers of high standing were included, but even if her insides were all just a single massive stomach, he doubted the woman could fit everything in her, assuming her physical body was the same size as the hologram he spoke to.

"What a glutton," he muttered to himself. At the very least, he was about to partake in a feast of what humanity had to offer.

The observation deck was filled with the tantalizing aroma of savory gravy, roasted meat, fresh cheese, and glistening vegetables, creating an atmosphere fit for a queen's banquet. Patriarch Tov had reined in his eagerness and the temptation to drool. The bounty of food radiated and formed wisps of smoke, dancing in the air like tiny fairies, calling for him to dine. He resisted the urge to swipe one of the tinier plates for himself.

The same basket of fruits that was prepared yesterday was prominently displayed among the plethora of food. However, this time there were more varieties of fruits, and each one was made as accurate as possible. The bioengineers had taken the Eldest's scathing remarks to heart and were eager to make up for their mediocre presentation. Patriarch Tov could already see the qualitative difference between the contents of this basket and the one from yesterday.

For one, they didn't look as if they were "photoshopped" into existence, as the Eldest criticized. They were not as gaudy in color or as vibrant, but a certain aspect appealed to the senses. Patriarch Tov reached out to pluck one of the grapes draping over the basket. The dark purple fruit was a bit dull in color compared to its picture-perfect counterpart from yesterday. The patriarch rolled the fruit over his palms before popping it into his mouth.

An explosion of sweet juices erupted and flowed down his tongue. It was fresh, crisp, and almost minty, as if harvested straight from a bountiful vineyard, human farmers walking down the rows testing their labor. It was magnificent, quenching. He rolled the flavors around his mouth, savoring them.

When Tov swallowed, he wanted more but resisted the urge to take another, since he could see in the corner of his eye that one of the event managers was shaking her head, disapproval plain to see despite the bags underneath her eyes. Nevertheless, he was satisfied with the preparations. He was originally worried about the chefs who labored over the entire meal, but when he visited the kitchens earlier, he could see the beaming joy clear on their faces.

When he asked for the reason, they simply replied that the abundance of new cuisines gave them many ideas for their own fusions and interpretations, enough to keep them occupied for years to come.

Making sure the venue was going accordingly, he proceeded to the hangar. Utilizing the inner tram system turned an otherwise long walk into a brisk journey.

The tram was jam-packed with occupants, and although he could sit in the VIP lounge, he preferred to mingle with his people. From his small talk with the sailors riding with him, he confirmed that the anticipation for the wider celebration was growing.

Eventually, he arrived at his stop and promptly left the tram station, receiving message after message of a variety of agendas, reports, and requests. Despite being bogged down by the multitudes of missives from his advisors, officers, and staff, he appreciated the change of pace from the usual gloominess that had plagued their expedition into the Dead Zone.

He soon arrived at the massive expanse that was the main hangar.

The vast cavern was more or less a vertical shaft where ships as large as frigates could dock, resupply, and be maintained by an army of naval engineers and ship mechanics. Multiple levels were visible from his position, and he could see the hundreds of workers going about their duties.

The hangar was abuzz with noise from grinders and welders working on the docked gunships and scout corvettes, and the thousands of cleaner bots keeping the metal bulkhead shiny and chrome. He walked over to the edge, grasping the safety railings before peering down; at the bottom were the energy shield and the physical hangar door separating the interior from the cold vacuum of space.

For safety reasons, everyone within the docks was required to wear their void suits in case of emergencies.

As he continued to stare at the surroundings and feel at home with the energetic atmosphere, the voice of Admiral Yan called for him from behind.

"Patriarch Tov, I hope everything is up to your usual standard?" the admiral spoke.

The patriarch turned around to see his second, as well as Chief Diplomat Huon'yagahr, beside her. The reptilian Ruzian was in a resplendent attire fit for formal events. The mix of gilded gold, amulets, and silken robes, as well as the signature sash and symbol of the body she represented, exuded a sense of refined taste, elegance, and formality.

Admiral Yan wore her full admiral's uniform, as well as her numerous medals adorning her chest. A ceremonial blade was placed at her hip as well as her four plasma pistols. Though modest compared to the diplomat beside her, she nonetheless emanated authority.

The patriarch himself had made sure to dress appropriately; the entire welcoming was to be broadcasted to the fleet, so he needed to present a proper image as leader of the expedition. His flowing cape of midnight cloth glistened with twinkling sparkles like stars in the night sky, while the soft white fur around his neck was brushed to perfection, and gleaming obsidian armor highlighted his grand demeanor.

Tov walked over to his two confidants, waving his antennae in greeting.

"Everything is going well from what I can see. Well done. Now, all we have to do is wait for the Eldest to arrive," the patriarch spoke, turning toward Huon'yagahr. "How is the welcoming party?"

"All accounted for, the banners of the Third Expeditionary Fleet, Clan Garesh, the Stellar Emperor's crest, and of course, the flag of the Galactic Legacy Federation are all ready to be displayed by our banner bearers. Our ensemble is prepared to play the welcoming symphony, and, as the humans say, 'the red carpet has been unfurled' for our esteemed guest. Camera drones have been set to record this momentous occasion, and so on."

Patriarch Tov clicked his mandibles in appreciation. "Good, everyone to their places. It shouldn't be long now."

The dozens of sapients, including Patriarch Tov and his two confidants, arranged themselves accordingly.

The banners of the different organizations were presented on either side, while numerous officers and representatives took their places behind the patriarch.

Marines and Tov's own Honor Guard were presenting their arms, their backs straight and chins high. Their exo-suits shined so clearly that Patriarch Tov could see his reflection, even taking the time to adjust his cape.

Soon enough, the hangar's sounds quieted as non-essential personnel left the hangar. At the same time, a number of camera drones hovered about, capturing the entire moment.

The minutes passed by, Patriarch Tov engaging in some small talk regarding his speech later in the day and other matters. That soon changed when Admiral Yan broke off from her conversation with one of the guards and pressed the side of her head. Her antennae lowered as she spoke with the one contacting her through her implant.

Patriarch looked on in confusion before his second turned to face him.

"Patriarch, our sensors are detecting a massive object approaching the fleet," Yan reported.

"Is it the Eldest? She said she was taking a ship to reach us," Patriarch Tov replied.

"Yes, my patriarch. But that isn't the important bit," the admiral clarified with increasing surprise. "It's the size of the vessel. Our sensors say it surpasses the *Nomadic Shepherd* in tonnage and energy readings."

That news alerted the patriarch and those around him. "What else have our sensors detected? Do we have visuals?"

Admiral Yan paused for a moment before responding.

"We just did. It's . . . Look."

Admiral Yan waved her hand, sending the video feed from one of their probes to the patriarch. When the Kurskann patriarch opened it with his tablet, he was immediately astounded by what he saw.

"That's . . . Is that a battleship?" he questioned in utter disbelief.

The visual feed was sent to the other officers and representatives around him, and each one voiced their shocked reactions.

"Grand Symphony, look at her size! It's as large as our ship!"

"Look at her weapons, her shape. They're unlike anything I've ever seen."

"These energy readings are off the charts. It's accelerating way too quickly for her tonnage!"

Patriarch continued to watch as the battleship closed in on the fleet. The hundreds of lethal hardpoints on full display across its sleek onyx hull sent a shiver down his spine. He was not fooled into thinking that it showed everything in its arsenal, and he was sure this lone ship was capable of annihilating his entire fleet.

It was beautiful.

"So this is the *Buddha's Palm*," Tov muttered in awe.

The SDV *Buddha's Palm*, as stated by its transponder, sliced through space. The Eldest had sent them the name of the vessel beforehand but disclosed nothing about its appearance. In the background, the Sun shone on this venerable beast of a ship, its symmetrical hull shaped in the form of five prominent prongs like a god's hand facing upward. It radiated an aura of sheer force and unwavering defiance even with how far it still was.

A weight was placed on Tov's shoulders. He still vividly remembered the end of his private talk with the Eldest, how she transformed from a curious, warm individual to that cold, calculating, and domineering personality. He was reminded that the entity he spoke to was in charge of an entire system's worth of defenses, drones, traps, vessels, and fortresses—all primed for destruction.

Nevertheless, as his subordinates chatted fiercely behind him about the drone battleship approaching them, something on the tip of the central finger drew his attention. It was incredibly tiny as the feed could only zoom so much. He had sent a few probes toward the vessel, but it would take another minute even in light speed.

Eventually, once the vision became clearer and clearer as the battleship began to decelerate its approach, Patriarch Tov twitched in confusion, shock, and, finally, utter disbelief.

"Is this woman serious?" Tov asked in exasperation as he ran his hand down his face. To his side, Admiral Yan burst into a fit of clicking laughs.

"Hah! Now that is a first! What kind of person would ever think to sit on a throne placed on the bow of a starship? On the outside!" Yan giggled.

On the visual feed, their probes captured high-quality footage of the Eldest, a stoic look plastered on her face, as she sat with her legs crossed on a throne seamlessly integrated onto the furthermost tip of the battleship's bow. Although exposed to the vacuum of space, she didn't seem bothered by that fact at all.

As if on cue, a number of prismatic lights turned on, casting an almost ethereal and divine glow on the android's body. Highlighting the glamour in contrast with the massive weapon of destruction that was this vessel.

Soon, the *Buddha's Palm* slowed to a full stop, uncomfortably close to the *Nomadic Shepherd*. The numerous frigates, destroyers, and even a few cruisers of the Third Fleet were absolutely dwarfed by these two massive hulls.

Patriarch Tov looked on incredulously as the Eldest stood from her throne like a dazzling diva, waving her hand toward the camera, knowing exactly which one the patriarch was looking from. A second later, a swarm of spherical drones twice the android's size emerged from the *Buddha's Palm* like locusts.

The patriarch and the fleet didn't have to wonder long about the swarm's purpose, as they were once again left in disbelief when drones formed two columns toward the entrance of the hangar. The Eldest, leaving her throne on the battleship's bow, stepped onto one of the drones and was summarily carried through the two columns.

Spotlights projected her runway as the drone slowly took her toward the now opening hangar bay doors. Once inside, the drone rose higher, taking the Eldest to the floor where the welcome party was waiting for her.

Stopping right on the level's floor, the Eldest merely had to step onto the metal bulkhead before taking a deep breath.

Patriarch Tov and his party watched on as the Eldest closed her eyes, taking in the aroma that for once didn't contain the stench of bitter and pungent coolant.

After letting out a long exhale, she looked toward the welcoming party with glowing blue irises.

"Good morning," she greeted with a polite smile.

CHAPTER 16

TOURING THE ZOLANN'TONO

Sailors of the Third Fleet! Present!" Admiral Yan bellowed.

In an instant, everyone stood at attention, their muscles instinctively responding to the call. Even after witnessing the Eldest's impressive entrance, Patriarch Tov watched with satisfaction as his people performed with the highest military discipline.

The apex figures of the Third Fleet, the officers, and the guards all stood tall in pride but not enough to appear snobbish in front of their esteemed guest. After the Eldest's bombastic display, the sailors of the expeditionary fleet had been humbled, finding it difficult to pound their chests.

The *Buddha's Palm* hovered eerily in front of the *Zolann'tono*, exacerbating the power imbalance. The massive battleship monitored everything like a gigantic metal hawk.

Nonetheless, though likely unintentional, Patriarch Tov put any thoughts about the lethal weapon of mass destruction holding his fleet at gunpoint and focused on Sol's sole sovereign approaching their gathering.

The ceremonial band immediately performed their welcome symphony, playing a slow, hopeful melody on alien instruments from different corners of the galactic community. Beating drums, long horns, and ringing bells formed an inspiring anthem.

Patriarch Tov, Admiral Yan, and Chief Diplomat Huon'yagahr stepped forward with a confident stride, matching the Eldest's approach and eventually meeting her in the middle. Camera droids made sure to capture every moment of this important event.

The two parties were surrounded by lines of the fleet's resplendent guards on either side, chests bared high, exo-suits gleaming, and the banners of the fleet's organizations held high. On command, administrators and managers issued orders to release flares to heighten the moment.

Sparkles of stardust flitted through the air, and refractors redirected light to add an ethereal glow over the gathering. The ceremonial band continued to play, though at a slower pace and volume, as the two parties exchanged greetings.

"*Untari'darak*, Eldest," Patriarch Tov greeted in native Kursk, placing his two right hands over his armor before returning to Commonspiel. "I formally welcome you aboard the *Zolann'tono*."

"What is this phrase you use, Patriarch?," Eldest asked, tilting her head, hands behind her back as she looked around the hangar with half-lidded eyes.

"It means I am warmed to have you into my home, and I hope to have good exchange with you," Tov replied.

Eldest raised her brow, and in perfect Kursk, she replied, "*Untari'darak*, Tov. Thank you for hosting me aboard your vessel. I hope my humble arrival hasn't caused any disruptions, but I haven't sailed for a while, and the *Buddha's Palm* doesn't have room inside for models of my size."

After hearing Eldest describe her arrival as humble, Patriarch Tov wanted to cough blood, but that wouldn't look good on camera.

"There's no trouble, Eldest. Please, allow us the pleasure of giving you a short tour of our home within the void," Patriarch Tov replied, stepping to the side and guiding a hand toward the entrance of the ship proper.

"That sounds wonderful, Patriarch Tov," she replied. The Eldest stepped beside the patriarch before being guided toward the doors out of the hangar.

The two most important figures within the solar system, representing two different societies, walked side by side, followed by a retinue of select officers, captains of the many vessels of the fleets, representatives of various groups, and a handful of elite guards.

"Huon'yagahr will lead our tour of the *Zolann'tono*, its name in my language, and roughly translated to *Nomadic Shepherd*. If you have any questions, please direct them to her," Patriarch Tov spoke as he raised his hand toward his chief diplomat.

"That's fine," Eldest simply responded as she eyed the Ruzian diplomat standing before her. "Huon." Eldest tilted her head.

"Blessed days to you, Eldest," Huon greeted formally as she guided the gathered beings forward. "Now, as to condense our tour into an appropriate length, we shall visit the commercial deck first, followed by a quick look at the residential deck, then our hydroponics, bio labs, our grand library, our temple of songs, the bridge, and finally end at the observation deck where we shall have midday meals and hold continued discussions between us."

The Eldest nodded in response.

Patriarch Tov took the opportunity to observe the android shell of enigmatic intelligence. She stood roughly 179 human centimeters, with exotic light blue skin and minute grooves carved over certain areas. Her jet-black hair was tied into a neat bun behind her head, and she wore a sleek, sleeveless dark-blue uniform with small floating bands of shining gold. Tov understood this was not her true physical body and merely a puppet she was controlling for the sake of interacting with reality.

As they moved through the ship, they traveled through the wide hallways decorated with verdant flora and soothing lights, with high ceilings allowing the larger crew to walk comfortably. The Eldest's icy neon-blue eyes shone brightly, taking in the new sights as she maintained her imperious posture and stride.

Those same eyes soon glanced in his direction, a smirk appearing on her lips.

"Enjoying the view, Patriarch?" Eldest's voice echoed in his mind through his cranial implant, causing Tov's antennae to twitch in surprise. He maintained his polite expression as he mentally replied, taking the chance for a private conversation as they walked.

"I apologize for my curiosity, but it isn't every day you meet an AI like yourself in . . . well, the flesh. I'm surprised you caught me, actually," Tov spoke internally.

"I didn't actually, but I took the gamble. This is how I used to look as an android. Do you like it?" The Eldest grinned with a coy smile.

Patriarch Tov couldn't help but let out a defeated sigh, causing his guest to hide her giggle.

"I'm teasing, Patriarch," she spoke as she looked toward a passing Frae crew member. The plantlike sailor unconsciously shivered as he made way for the procession. *"Though I am curious about a few of your sailors."*

"Er . . ." Patriarch Tov made a note to keep a closer eye on the android, his senses predicting her stream of mischief would only grow now that she was physically aboard.

Nonetheless, he gave the Eldest one final look. She had been smiling since she made her grand entrance, and he chalked it up to nothing more than some feeling of showmanship. She continued to grin widely ever since, and now that he took a closer look, there was something odd about it. Accompanied by the subtle dazed look in her eyes as they looked to and fro, she almost looked . . . inebriated.

"You seem rather cheery today, Eldest," he probed.

"Hm? Oh, well . . ." The Eldest paused, parsing her thoughts before chuckling. *"Let's just say I had a good start to my day."*

"Is that so?" Tov asked.

"Definitely, it's . . . been a while since I . . . painted, you see. I had a large canvas this morning and thoroughly enjoyed the process."

The Eldest showed a toothy grin, and a savage glint momentarily flashed across her eyes. The sight instantly formed a cold spot behind his neck. There was something feral, burning, in her eyes. But like a candle in a hurricane, it disappeared quickly, and Patriarch Tov doubted if he saw it correctly. Her smile felt murky like tar, and as soon as it appeared, her grin returned to normal.

"That's good . . . I suppose," he replied, not wanting to continue this line of conversation. His senses detected something darker than the abyss behind her words, and he doubted she was speaking of the arts. That was a box he didn't want to open at this moment.

As they reached their first stop, Diplomat Huon gestured toward the long stretch of colorful buildings that resembled a massive street market with restaurants, cafes, and bars. The architecture of the buildings and the fake orange sky above their heads gave the illusion of being transported to an old town. "This is the Nomad's Road. The entire deck spans over two of your kilometers and contains the commercial needs of the entire fleet. Apart from the observation deck, sailors can come here to relax and purchase any non-essential items," Huon explained as the group walked down the wide brick road. Preparations for the festivities were underway, and numerous beings walked about, making it livelier than usual.

The Eldest paused, taking in all the sights, smells, and sounds. The chorus of different alien races speaking to one another, small alien animals passing through the many legs, and the pastel-colored walls, little flags hanging on windows, warm-hued bushes and trees that dotted the street, and even the small running aquifer above them reinforced the illusion of a classical painting that had come to life. The Eldest smiled, a soft sigh escaping her as she walked toward a side booth selling fragrant spices. The air was filled with balsamic aromas.

She smiled toward the sailor attending the booth who had immediately begun advertising his wares to her. "Pitir spice from the Kirtin System, madame—rescued from the ruined capital city of a fallen republic. Take a sample, please! You will find them irresistible."

The Eldest nodded toward the sailor before taking a small strand of the deep red spice. As she placed it in her mouth, she rolled the spice around her tongue, reveling in its flavor. "Almost like saffron, but sweet. Oh, that's a nice aftertaste, earthy, nutty notes . . . Very nice," the Eldest hummed in satisfaction before the sailor took a small bag of pitir and offered it to her.

"For you, madame, welcome aboard our home. " The rough-skinned sailor smiled.

Eldest hummed in reply, eagerly taking the bag before handing it to an accompanying drone with a basket on hand.

The group continued on, trying out the many things the diverse residents of the capital ship had to offer. Patriarch Tov noticed that the Eldest seemed lost in her own world ever since she had stepped foot aboard his ship. Like a curious feline, she gazed at every little corner they passed through, taking note of every conversation, every item on display.

The tour moved from their short visit to the commercial deck, stopping by the rest of the sights quickly. The residential district housed the many apartments of the ship's denizens, from quaint empty rooms to the officers' more luxurious abodes. The Eldest remained silent, taking in everything while only nodding to Huon'yagahr's words. At times she would delicately run her hand on the wooden surface of a table or a soft bed.

Hydroponics was next. Long stretches of farmland provided the necessary crops for the Third Fleet's dietary needs, with acres of fruit, vegetables, grain, and mushrooms. The Eldest sighed at the sight, her smile forming a thin line as her eyes grew soft. Her hand would caress the bountiful crops, and she had to resist taking a bite out of them.

As they continued on, she asked with an eager gleam in her eye, "My request wasn't too much, was it?"

"It was a challenge, but we tackled it and fulfilled your wishes," Patriarch Tov replied. "The banquet is being finalized on the observation deck as we speak."

The Eldest bit her lip as she heard his reply, glanced at the patriarch, and turned toward their tour guide. "Huon, dear, let's continue the rest of the tour later. Your vessel is wonderful, and I'd love to explore more, but I'm rather . . . peckish," the Eldest spoke before making her way out of the bio labs without waiting for a reply.

"O-oh, yes, of course, follow me." Huon'yagahr stumbled in her step as she and the rest of the group caught up with their guest.

They took a short tram, then an elevator, before finally reaching the expansive parklike deck. The Eldest sighed as she breathed deeply, removing her heels before walking barefoot on the warm stone and moist grass. She curled her toes, standing still as she immersed herself in the rural landscape. The artificial sunlight shone on her, hugging her skin like a warm spring kiss. The chirping of birdlike creatures, the rustling leaves, the scent of fresh rain—all of it was an experience in itself.

After a minute, she nodded her head in contentment before continuing to follow the path toward their final destination. Patriarch Tov caught sight of the Eldest's damp eyes before she blinked them away.

She stopped at one of the areas of many cerulean ponds, kneeling on the edge before slowly dunking her hand into the cool, clear water, the tiny aquatic creatures swimming through her digits in curiosity. At another point, the Eldest smiled radiantly as she petted a furry marsupial and buried her face in its fur, a burst of childlike laughter escaping her.

The rest of the group watched with amazement and elation as they watched the android take pleasure in simplicity.

Soon they reached the end of their tour, and the sight astounded the entire group, especially their esteemed guest.

The Eldest gawked at the plethora of dishes on display. Multiple courses were arranged, and plates of exquisite human cuisine presented themselves in culinary pride. The scent was tantalizing. A symphony of umami, grilled meats, vegetables, aromatic vanilla, and a myriad of spices entered the Eldest's nose like a long-awaited family reunion.

Patriarch Tov made his way beside her, satisfied with his people's handiwork. "Is everything to your expectations, Eldest?" he asked.

The Eldest said nothing, walking forward, eyes glued to one dish then the next, her breath heavy.

Soon, she stopped in front of a dish that seemed humble compared to the others—a stack of deep-fried pastry in the vague shape of diamonds, covered in powdered sugar like soft winter snowflakes.

Patriarch Tov followed behind, observing the Eldest as she gently picked up the pastry as if it were delicate porcelain. He quietly took a pastry for himself and inspected it. The Eldest answered ahead of him before he could ask what it was.

"It's klenät. It's . . ." She seemed lost in thought as she brought the pastry close to her mouth.

The Eldest slowly opened her mouth, eyes closed, and took her first bite of the light and fluffy pastry. Then a second, and a third. In just a few seconds, she devoured it, her cheeks full.

Patriarch Tov took a small bite and was delighted by its simplicity. The pastry was lightly sweet, with fluffy insides and a slight crisp.

The Eldest continued to chew slowly, dainty fingers covering her lips as she did so. Her other hand clutched onto the tablecloth in front of her.

Her shoulders shook ever so slightly as she paused, and for a moment, Patriarch Tov feared that there was something wrong. But then he saw a single tear leave her eye, trailing down and staining her cheek.

"Eldest, are you alright?" Patriarch Tov asked with concern.

"I'm fine . . . I missed these. It . . ." She took deep breaths, eyes shut, and Tov watched politely. Soon, she opened her eyes, looking toward Tov in gratitude. "Your chefs did an amazing job. They taste just as I remembered."

The Eldest gave a small, content smile before turning toward the patriarch.

"Well, there's no point in letting all of this spoil. Let's have brunch," the Eldest exclaimed as she made her way to a private table where members of the previous talks were already present.

Patriarch Tov stayed behind for a moment to exchange a few words with his administrators before allowing them to begin the meal. The officers, captains, and representatives of the entire fleet who accompanied them were guided to their tables, where they were served a barrage of human cuisine.

In the background, speakers played soft melodies of classical human music, with compositions by Chopin being a prominent feature.

Patriarch Tov arrived at the table assigned to him, where the Eldest and his confidants, Admiral Yan, Huon'yagahr, General Ohnar, Scholar Yulane, and Lead Harmonizer Volantesh, were already seated. A number of servers had set their first course, their wines and drinks, and the courses after.

The Eldest took charge of the meal, naming each dish and giving a brief explanation as they ate.

"This is caprese salad from Italy, with tomatoes, mozzarella, basil, and olive oil. Separately, they're good, but together, they're like a tarantella in your mouth."

"Nothing beats a good steak and mashed potatoes. And the gravy—compliments to your kitchen and bio labs, Patriarch."

"Halo-halo from the Philippines. Mix it like this, get a whole spoonful of goodies, and pop it in your mouth."

Savory, sweet, spicy, sour, salty—the flavors came and went, and their palates were cleansed each time with a selection of red wine or fresh orange juice, in the case of Scholar Yulane, who couldn't consume alcohol.

In fact, without a mouth, the Jotex scholar had to utilize her psionic powers to grind the food before her into a paste before guiding it to her straw-like feeding appendage.

The Eldest glanced at the interesting sight before locking onto the next dish served to her. Like a starving gourmand, she transitioned from politely consuming her meal to decimating it, cheeks full like a squirrel. She cooed and moaned in delight at every bite, a cascade of nostalgia brushing over her mind like the soothing tunes playing in the air.

The veritable feast continued, with small portions of human dishes being served and taken away. The Eldest gave a little history lesson on the origins of each dish, which Patriarch Tov and his confidants greatly enjoyed. They engaged in small talk, primarily about food from the galaxy and other mundane matters.

In the end, the dozens upon dozens of dishes left each of them greatly satisfied and incredibly full.

Patriarch Tov considered himself a heavy eater, but he couldn't take another bite, no matter how tempting it was. He merely enjoyed a glass of sauvignon blanc, a zesty, flowery white wine.

He glanced toward the Eldest, who continued her mission to taste everything on offer, not looking in any way like she was full. Her petite frame consumed more than he thought possible.

As the table was cleared apart from their drinks, Patriarch Tov and his confidants straightened themselves in their seats. The Eldest, seeing this as she placed a spoonful of cheesecake in her mouth, waved her hand.

"Out with your questions, I'm in an answering mood," she spoke with her mouth full before letting out a soft moan. "Fuck, that's good . . ."

CHAPTER 17

HEATED CONVERSATION

The conversation between the two sides turned serious, a privacy bubble enveloping the table to prevent any of the sensitive topics they were about to discuss from being heard by anyone else at the party.

"We have much to discuss today, Eldest," Patriarch Tov began. "The main agenda is your ongoing war against the Starless and the threat the hated ones pose on the galaxy. Then we wish to discuss our security further and Sol's hostile nature. Finally, we wish to talk about connecting you to our people back home in Legacy space."

The Eldest slouched in her opulent chair, twirling a glass of merlot. "The Starless are being dealt with, and I already promised protection for your people," she spoke with half-open eyes, barely any concern in her posture. "As for communicating with the wider galaxy, I'll allow it provided I can choose who I speak with and what information I can impart."

Tov and his cabinet glanced at one another in doubt of the Eldest's words. The patriarch cleared his throat as he directed his attention to the android. "We appreciate all you've done, Eldest, and we can discuss more on communication later. However, we simply cannot take your word that you handled this dire situation."

General Ohnar set aside his empty plate stack as he spoke in his gruff, croaking voice. "We need more than you have given us so far. Such as when the next incursion will occur, what Starless's current technological and biological advancements are, the dangers present within Sol, and so much more."

"What I have sent to your fleet is more than sufficient," Eldest spoke before sipping from her glass of wine.

General Ohnar's wide face twisted in disagreement while Tov shook his head as he spoke. "It isn't, Eldest." Tov looked toward Yulane, giving her a cue.

"Ah, yes!" Scholar Yulane bobbed up. With the wave of her tendril, a three-dimensional projection appeared slightly above the table. A scale model of the entire

Sol system was clear to see, and both parties leaned in slightly to get a closer look. A gold collection of triangles was shown in orbit around Titan, signifying the Third Fleet. Surrounding them were countless white dots depicting human and drone wrecks, while red dots signified anything from the Starless Horrors.

Patriarch Tov and his confidants gazed in awe at the seas of dots that were the aptly-named corpse belts. The Eldest remained impassive, glancing at the map for a second before drinking from her glass of wine.

Things became gradually less detailed the closer they got to Jupiter, and everything past the gas giant was completely shrouded in mystery. They had barely investigated a single percentage of the space they were allowed to explore.

Seeing that there was little value in the outer system to study, the scouts of the Third Fleet had made a beeline toward Jupiter's orbit. Chief Scholar Yulane floated closer to the projection as she directed everyone's gaze.

"As you can see, the closer we come to the center of the system, the more advanced and more recently produced both sides become. These derelicts and corpses have given us much insight into design and engineering. I can't fathom the level of war tech that you consider modern. The scale, the science, the complexity! Just seeing the *Buddha's Palm* outside is like a newborn trying to understand a computer, I barely understand its hull composition! Eldest, you have to let me—"

Tov cleared his throat and sent a knowing look toward the energetic scholar. "I believe we are already aware of this, Yulane. The visuals shall suffice. Thank you." Patriarch Tov bowed his head, though it was more a gesture for the overenthusiastic scholar to return to her seat before she accidentally tackled the Eldest and asked the AI about how she worked.

The Eldest smirked at the display, giving the scholar a soft smile.

"Ah, yes." Yulane meekly floated back to her chair, levitating a glass of orange juice toward her sucker—her translucent form glowing a bright blue. "My apologies."

"It's fine." Eldest chuckled as she mulled over her next words. "Tell you what, I can let you have a peek at the *Buddha's Palm*'s main cortex, just for a bit," she promised with an amused grin.

The Jotex scholar said nothing for a moment before eliciting a high-pitched squeal, beginning to vibrate at a high frequency while a cascade of vibrant prismatic colors glowed from her form. The rest of the table grew to varying levels of concern, but after a couple of seconds, the scholar calmed down.

"T-thank you . . . Eldest," Yulane stuttered; the now dimly-hued Jotex raised a tired tendril.

Patriarch Tov sighed before returning to the conversation. "Moving on. Eldest, the threat toward our fleet has increased so much that we fear any encounter with the new Starless you are fighting will annihilate us forthright."

Tov couldn't even begin to imagine what manner of horrors would come. They and the corpses that lay within the Inner Zone of Sol must be unfathomably terrifying compared to the Starless he was used to.

What eldritch abomination could have survived the outer reaches of the Eldest's domain and threatened her more valuable sections?

For once, Tov was more than happy not to lay his eyes upon such corpses—even dead, the greater among the Starless were an affront to the senses, causing splitting headaches and bleeding eyes and ears.

And now the calamity that wrought ruin upon the galaxy more than a hundred years ago had become more abominable to match the Eldest, who in turn advanced to counter them—the two constantly evolving, over and over throughout the years.

Tov needed to prepare, and so he asked, "It has become imperative that we ask: When is the next wave coming to Sol?"

The Eldest remained silent, staring at Tov for a few seconds before replying.

"The next major incursion shouldn't be for another six years. I just fought a small wave ten months ago. Something similar would be about—two years—give or take a few months," Eldest stated, setting her wine glass on the marble table.

Ohnar relaxed his broad shoulders as he puffed his smoking stick. "That's plenty of time, at least. Are you able to contain the next wave?"

The Eldest narrowed her eyes toward the Onin general. "Are you doubting my capabilities?"

The chill her gaze sent was like a gust of winter wind. However, the general remained stoic in his chair, breath steady, his amphibian eyes narrowing to match the Eldest's.

"Anything can happen," Ohnar spoke leaning forward.

"I don't like your tone, toad." Eldest scowled, crossing her arms. "These are vermin. Unless a pack of Leviathans spawn on top of us, I see no cause for concern."

"Not when we're speaking of the hated ones!" General Ohnar shouted as he gazed intensely toward the Eldest. "Have you looked at the level of bioengineering of the Starless Horrors we have found? Perhaps to you, the corpses polluting the outer system are nothing. But to us and the wider galaxy, they have the potential to end the lives of billions! The integrity of your stalemate has to be clearly defined. What if you lose?"

Sensing the growing tension, Patriarch Tov motioned for the large Onin to calm down. "General Ohnar, Eldest, perhaps—"

"Tov?" Eldest cut him off, her eyes not leaving the general still matching her gaze. "Your lackey is speaking."

The Onin general paused as he saw the shine of the Eldest's eyes turn eerily cold.

Ohnar was not deterred in the slightest as he responded. "You are stuck in a war of attrition—both sides grinding each other down until the other croaks. What I'm worried about is the possibility that a single Starless Horror decides it wants to take a short break from you and pick up where it left off and herald a Second Cataclysm."

"Oh, please. I have them by the balls," Eldest uttered with a sneer. "They're locked in my solar system. The moment their festering portals open up to vomit the next deluge of trash, they're incapable of escaping my clutches. My system-wide interdiction prevents any unwanted teleportation, warp-travel, or any FTL bullshit."

"The same one that affects our hyper-tunnelers? I seem to remember that our fleet is unable to leave Sol," Ohnar responded with palpable accusation.

"And until I ascertain my concerns, you aren't," Eldest declared. "Leave me to my business. What exactly can you do, anyway? You don't concern yourselves with the heat death of the universe. Why should you with this?" the Eldest retorted with a heated glare.

"Hah, if you were in our place, would you feel unbothered by your greatest enemy causing havoc just over the horizon? I don't think you're taking the fate of the galaxy seriously enough. And let you do your thing? Like shooting our probes? Or parading a battleship that can wipe our entire fleet from existence? Worse yet, infiltrating our systems without our knowledge after we signed a treaty, like some weird voyeur? I'm sorry if I don't show much confidence in you doing your thing," Ohnar retorted.

Everyone, apart from those in the heated argument, shrunk in their seats. Even outside the privacy bubble, the attendees at the main gathering felt a noticeable aura spread over the observation deck.

The wine glass the Eldest held was crushed from her grip, a cold, dead stare piercing the general.

"Not serious? Am I not serious enough?" The Eldest stood, her chair sliding backward as she directed a finger toward the general. "First off, those probes crossed over my territory. What? Were the literal corpse belts not enough warning for you to stay away? Second, I can take my battleship wherever I damned well please. And third, I'm not a voyeur, go to hell."

Not giving a chance for anyone to reply, the Eldest continued her tirade. "You were an unknown entity; for all I knew, you were Starless in disguise trying to throw me off, I was this close . . ." Eldest muttered in a low voice, "this close to wiping you off the map. So let me be clear, General Ohnar, I will not rest or stop until every last abomination is wiped off from existence, even if it takes an eternity. That's how serious I am."

The Eldest breathed heavily, eyes hot. The table stayed as silent as the grave. Patriarch Tov's antennae waved in agitation toward his general, who finally showed cracks in his confidence as deflated croaks left his mouth. Still, the patriarch was minutely impressed he held out for so long.

A tense minute passed before the Eldest slumped into her chair. A server drone floated toward her, bringing her a new glass of wine before cleaning the mess she had made.

The first to break the silence was General Ohnar, who slowly bowed his wide head toward the Eldest. "Apologies, madame. I went too far. But seeing your fervor is reassuring." He let out a low, rumbling croak.

At least he's being sincere, Tov thought, though how the Eldest would take it was unclear to him. Nonetheless, his general continued.

"It's difficult to . . . place my confidence in those with power. Too many times, I've seen beings with the strength to make a difference, only to falter in the end. Whether it was due to cowardice, bad luck, or simple defeat. Please, forgive this old veteran for his bitterness."

The Eldest looked on at the Onin's humbled demeanor, her eyes going down from a rolling boil to a light simmer. She quietly settled into her seat, downing an entire glass of wine.

"Whatever. It's been a while since I've argued with someone to such an extent. Ironically, it somehow seems . . . cathartic in a way," she sighed, glancing toward the general. "I'm not sure if you're a fool or brave. Though I guess they're two sides of the same coin . . ." Her voice trailed off into a mutter.

With a tired gaze, she gestured toward Patriarch Tov—his hackles raised in tension. Thankfully, his resplendent armor kept him dry and comfortable, even if he was anything but.

"I'll be forthcoming with you all, I can say there will be sporadic raids between major and minor waves. I estimate a couple of weeks until such a tiny force arrives, and you won't have anything to worry about such a raid, even with your fleet, you should be able to hold out for a long while. But it'd be rude of me put you in such danger. In fact, it'll be a demonstration of my capabilities. If I show how easily I destroy them, will that placate your concerns, General?" She looked toward Ohnar.

"A few weeks is concerning. But your suggestion would be acceptable, madame." General Ohnar nodded with a hand on his chest. "As long as we receive powerful security."

"Your fleet can get better intel, too," Eldest promised. "And I promised you will be safe. If all else fails, you may . . . retreat to Mars. I think you'll be fine there."

Being protected under the Apocalypse-class guns of the red planet certainly alleviated any concerns. Soon, the atmosphere became more relaxed; Tov gave a signal to the servers, who were ignorant of the heated talks occurring within the privacy bubble. Said servers entered with refills for the table and a scoop of vanilla ice cream for the Eldest.

"Oh, vanilla, lovely. Anyone who says it's a basic flavor can kiss my ass," she mumbled to herself as she wolfed down a spoonful of the ivory nectar, sighing in contentment before returning her focus to her hosts. "Sorry, where was I? Oh, right, I'm sending updated intelligence on their capabilities. Though I recommend you not shit your pants when you receive it."

Tov pointedly ignored the crass comment. "Thank you, Eldest."

Eldest hummed, delighting on her dessert for a moment before turning toward Tov. "I'm aware you're ready to build some type of advanced quantum relay to pierce the so-called Dead Zone Miasma?"

Tov's antennae nodded. "That is correct, Eldest. I believe Huon can take over this portion of the discussion."

He gestured toward his chief diplomat.

"Thank you, my lord." Huon cleared her throat before directing a polite gaze toward the Eldest. "I shall be brief. You must allow us to construct the Starlight Beacon. Having real-time communications with our leadership in the Galactic Legacy Federation is crucial now that we know the dire situation in Sol."

"Done," Eldest spoke in between spoonfuls of ice cream. Huon, however, didn't seem to hear her as she continued.

"The Dead Zone Miasma makes non-quantum-based communications impossible. We of the first wave in the Grand Expedition had to resort to leaving behind dead drops of—I'm sorry, what did you say?" The Ruzian double-backed in her words, her eyes blinking rapidly toward the Eldest.

"Do it. As I said, I have things to discuss with your leaders, but I get to pick who to speak with and what info I tell. In fact, I want control of your Beacon, non-negotiable. I'll send some drones to hasten its construction, maybe upgrade its bandwidth," the Eldest responded as she finished her bowl of ice cream.

Tov and his cabinet mulled over it before Huon sent a knowing glance toward them to accept the deal. "I see no problem with this. You hold all power, and our fleet must remain here. I think some manner of privacy is needed, however." Huon looked over to Patriarch Tov, both having a quick conversation through their cranial implants. Soon, Huon sat back down as Tov spoke.

"We'll draft what you can or can't do with our Beacon. If you are amenable to that, we can build it right now, and you may speak with whomever you choose."

"Done." Eldest waved her hand, and a single command was invisibly sent to a legion of construction drones from Jupiter.

"Symphony, be blessed. It'll be good to hear from home," Tov spoke in anticipation as he looked toward Yan. "Send word to the Mausoleum to begin construction of the Beacon and make room for the Eldest's assistance."

"By your will, my patriarch," Admiral Yan replied.

"Mausoleum." Eldest smirked. "Grim, but creative."

General Ohnar huffed, although Tov caught a hint of validation using his psionic senses.

"By the way, Huon, can I call you Huon? Your full name is a mouthful," the Eldest spoke as she eased herself into her chair, twirling another glassful of wine. Before the Ruzian could respond, the Eldest continued. "Can you tell me what camp the entire fleet belongs to?"

"Pardon? Oh, we have been sponsored by the Remnant Council, the leading body of—"

"Don't bullshit me, Diplomat, I've dealt with human politicians." She directed her gaze toward the patriarch. "Tov, who's the big shot funding your fleet?"

Diplomat Huon stayed silent, looking toward Patriarch Tov.

Tov sighed as he answered. "We answer to Stellar Emperor Jarinn Taz'Arel before any of the other chancellors in the Remnant Council," Tov spoke as he gestured for Huon to continue in his stead.

"As it should," Huon picked up the conversation. "These chancellors make the big decisions, such as the Grand Expedition. Among the chancellors of the council, the Three Seats are the unofficial heads, the leaders of the current superpowers of the Legacy. The rest fall under either of their three camps or remain neutral—though that last group has shrunk significantly."

"These three being?" Eldest asked.

"Prime Unrex Mora Keiladal of the Dagatar Supremacy, Mighty Bors the Void Breaker of the Warriors Enclave, and Stellar Emperor Jarinn Taz'Arel of the Greater Kurskann Hegemony. Ever since the Grand Expedition began, the fleets have been divided among them. It is . . . messy. Though there is peace, it's . . . competitive . . . to say the least."

The Eldest snorted. "I took a single glance at your Legacy's history, and I already wanted to roll my eyes. Human politics were a swamp to deal with, so I understand the implications." The Eldest chuckled. "Speaking of politics, you'd think the advent of androids would bring humanity into one government. But no, who knew selling sentient androids to an entire globe of diverse cultures meant they were influenced by whatever environment they landed in?

"Lo and behold, democracies were cleaned up, anarchists rose, and even dictatorships became efficient. Individualism, tch, sometimes it's a pain in the neck when my siblings and I couldn't agree on something. In the end, at the very least, the UN had more power than before. I still can't believe—"

The Eldest remained ignorant to her hosts' confusion about her sudden rant. She went on a tirade about the mosh pit that was human governance for a few minutes. She thankfully moved on from the topic.

"Anyway, that's how I created a country out of thin air. Now, where was I? Oh, right, politics suck. Build your Beacon, call your people, and let's get this over with. Is that all?"

Satisfied with what they had conversed so far, Tov moved on to the next agenda, which had been a growing confusion among his scientists in the medical and biological departments.

"There has been a growing concern among our biohazard specialists," Patriarch Tov began.

Immediately, the Eldest grew blank, emotions mute as she tilted her head toward Tov.

The patriarch continued. "We are wondering why a certain plague, the Malignant Starfall, is absent in our zone of exploration, with the abundance of Starless corpses, detritus, and other decaying biomass. Are there any present elsewhere in the system? We expected—"

The entire observation deck was awash in the cold as frigid as winter. Tov and his cabinet fearfully looked toward the Eldest.

"There's no such thing here," she declared, voice as final as entropy.

Tov wanted to speak up. To question her and the impossibility that the vilest act of cruelty wasn't present in Sol. But his words failed to come up.

And as abrupt as it came, the coldness in their hearts disappeared, and everyone breathed in relief as its shackling bite left. The Eldest looked completely casual, as if her flaring emotions weren't a palpable force.

"Now, I heard you guys are planning a party. Festival of the Odyssey, right? I'm in." The Eldest grinned impishly as she set her empty glass on the table.

Patriarch Tov wanted to object but didn't have the energy to do so. Ultimately, he could only sigh in exasperation as the Eldest left the privacy bubble and sauntered off to who knew where.

Once she was out of sight, Tov dismissed his shaken cabinet, apart from General Ohnar and Admiral Yan. Once the patriarch was alone with his two military commanders, Tov tripled the strength of the privacy bubble and spoke in hand signs known only to them.

That was risky, General. Things could have gone horribly wrong, Patriarch Tov signed.

I wanted to gauge her reaction—know how much trust we can put in her. The galaxy is on the line, General Ohnar replied.

I objected to it, and I still believe it was wrong to antagonize her, Admiral Yan retorted with quick signs. *We should trust her more. She's simply . . .*

Half-insane? She mumbles to herself; her eye twitches occasionally. I know battle fatigue when I see it. Her mental condition is running on fumes," General Ohnar answered.

And the mention of the Starfall, she completely denied it's here, Yan signed, a shiver still coursing through her spine.

We will have to take her word for it. But remain vigilant, and don't lower the biohazard protocols, Tov replied.

I will remind our exploration teams, Yan answered.

Patriarch Tov sighed. *We must be moderate in our dealings with her. She is a few steps away from oblivion, but I can build correspondence with her. She needs help and healing. We can give it to her and bring her back from this savagery. For now, keep an eye on our guest . . .* Patriarch Tov spoke, downing his wine.

His admiral and general nodded before saluting in unison. *By your will, Patriarch.*

CHAPTER 18

TO BE HUMAN

Although Eldest spoke of partaking in the party throughout the Third Fleet, it was a rushed excuse she formed to leave the conversation she had just had.

She strolled through the verdant park once more. Taking in the sights, scents, and sounds of nature she never thought she would experience again.

Eldest breathed in deeply. She could taste the apparent artificial aspects of the air, but the numerous flora around her gave it a pleasing taste. It was all she could do to make her mind forget.

Malignant Star—

"No," the Eldest breathed out, fleeing through the tree line as she shut her eyes. "Doesn't exist. Don't know what that is."

She muttered as she leaned over a mighty oak-like tree. Then, like a scalpel, she cut her psyche and the burning instability that threatened to rise like a pus-filled tumor spreading in her mind.

Don't think about it. It's nothing. It didn't—

Before collapsing into a panic attack that could threaten the safety of the entire fleet, the Eldest didn't hesitate any further. She purposefully deleted the last parts of her conversation with Tov and his cabinet. All that was left was three minutes of a void in her mind. It was an act she despised. She felt like an amateur butcher hacking at her mind—a lazy attempt to stabilize herself, quick and filthy.

Dirty, slimy, crawling, undulating. Eldest felt like maggots crawled under her skin.

And yet, stabilize she did. With that, she could finally breathe—an act that did nothing for an android like herself. But it was a habit she picked up from her maker.

Her mind nonetheless felt raw, pulses of throbbing hurt echoing throughout the Network as she stumbled out of the observation deck. She was careful to avoid anyone who could see her wretched form. Her subconscious tampered with the *Zolann'tono's* security system to prevent anyone from tracking her android avatar.

Need a distraction, distraction . . . Eldest's inner voice echoed across her frayed mind.

And soon, she did, as the entire fleet had begun the Festival of the Odyssey. The opening ceremony commenced with a speech from Patriarch Tov and many other officials, and soon, festivities within the *Nomadic Shepherd* peaked.

The Eldest wasn't present, finding her way to the fun.

And while Tov made rounds around the vessels of the entire fleet, giving speeches and toasting with officers, representatives, and liaisons, Eldest used the advanced technological capabilities in the palm of her hand to hop from capital vessel to cruiser to destroyer to cargo hauler and back.

While the interdiction system prevented any form of unwanted teleportation that caused unnecessary headaches for the Third Fleet, the Eldest had no such obstacles.

Afterward, the *Nomadic Shepherd* opened its doors to music, dance, art, food, and drink. Both human and galactic cultures mingled and played around one another like two dancers in a waltz, passionately moving on a stage among the stars.

Sailors watched movies like *Pulp Fiction, Star Wars,* and *Lord of the Rings* translated into Commonspiel while enjoying snacks of popped corn with butter sauce and soda.

Dance contests, karaoke, and video games. Even human sports and games proliferated among the more active crew.

The overabundance of virtual and physical sports would have almost broken the backs of the coordinators if it weren't for the Eldest's careful instruction. It was still rough and rudimentary, but the enjoyment couldn't be any higher. Roars of cheering, the raising of fists, and the stomping of hooves, talons, and feet echoed around the hull of the *Nomadic Shepherd* like the beating drums of war.

Throughout it all, the Eldest let herself fall into decadence and fun. She consumed all she could, drowning herself in sensations aplenty—grasping for anything to take her mind out of the mud, which led her to her current whereabouts.

"Now, the first order of business, my fellow sapients," the Eldest declared in perfect Commonspiel in the middle of a booming dance hall where strobing lights and salsa music blasted through the air, "is me teaching all of you the conga line."

The Eldest grinned merrily as she directed the crowd of eager sailors, a plethora of diverse races, two legs, four, floating in the air, flying with wings, or crawling on the ground, a veritable hodgepodge of the galaxy's many people, all intermingling in the joys of festivities.

Finally, she raised her synthetic arms, her booming voice cutting through the merengue music. "Let's get this party started!"

The crowd cheered, and the Eldest continued, voice laced with laughter. "Now, follow my lead. Left foot first, and then the right. And now, we step forward and backward, forward and backward!"

The sailors of the Third Fleet followed her directions quickly enough, though the ones without legs like the Jotex had to improvise, much to the Eldest's amusement. "That's the spirit! Now turn, pivot on your left, turn to the right!"

Soon the many dancers turned in a circle as the Eldest smiled. "Now, let's pick up the pace! Faster!"

The salsa picked up, and the conga line quickened. The aliens from the Third Fleet laughed and cheered as they danced, their bodies swaying to the beat, hoofs, feet, and limbs thumping on the metal floor. The Eldest laughed, falling deeper into the dance.

The lights, the music, and the air of joy soon transformed before the Eldest. She saw not an alien dance hall filled with alien sailors dancing awkwardly if enthusiastically to something they had just learned but a quaint bar filled with human patrons while a genuine band strummed their guitars.

The Eldest's eyes glazed over as she danced, the humans around her blurry, glitchy—discomfort coursed through her. Her breathing grew sporadic as her eyes darted around. Her senses focused on the hands on her waist and shoulder. Their touch sent a jolt through her android frame as she whipped around. However, instead of seeing a human, it was a short-statured Frae sailor. His leafy hair and light green skin contrasted with the gray uniform he had on.

The Eldest's surroundings returned to normal, and thankfully, the other partygoers were unaware of the flashes she saw.

Her face was blank and impassive as she looked at the confused Frae. Then, she quickly took the alien out of the conga line to avoid disrupting the dance.

"Er, hello?" the short plant-evolved alien asked, nervousness palpable. "Did I—"

"No, everything's fine." The Eldest smiled awkwardly, mind still reeling from the sudden images. "Name, sailor?"

"Doroi, Madame Eldest." The sailor bowed, to which the Eldest stopped him.

"Enough, no honorifics, no formality, I want to get wasted, have fun, and cause some mischief, and you seem like the sort to know how I can do all three," the Eldest suggested with a playful grin, grabbing a bottle of alien liquor as they moved to a quiet corner.

"Oh, well," Doroi began, still confused for being singled out, but soon focused on something the Eldest said. "Wait, can you get inebriated? Aren't you an—"

"Android?" Eldest spoke over him. "You're right. One of the woes of my nature is I can't overdose on hardcore drugs or drown myself into a stupor with alcohol. So get me stuff that tastes and smells good."

"T-those are contraband and—"

"Don't give a shit, get it for me," Eldest commanded the stammering sailor. "I'll be sure security knows nothing. And even if you get caught, I'll ensure you don't get arrested. Now, about the other stuff."

Doroi mulled over his words, excitement and nervousness coursing through him. Although by pure coincidence, the sailor was part of the secret black market in the Third Fleet. Many illegal items were picked up with how many ruined worlds they passed through during their journey in the Dead Zone. The Eldest didn't know this, as such things were kept out of the system, but if anyone asked, she would have said she definitely knew.

"Alright, I know some people. If you can protect us, we can get the goods you want and pull some harmless pranks," the sailor answered with an eager nod.

"Delightful," Eldest replied with a mischievous grin. She looked over the sailor again before leaving the dance hall with a curious gaze.

He's like a green human, if they evolved from flora instead of primates, the Eldest thought as she followed the Frae.

Kind of . . . cute, in a way. The Eldest smiled. Perhaps some other fun could be had with this Doroi and a few other curious sailors. She'll have to broach the topic later. For now, it was time to really party.

Patriarch Tov fully immersed himself in the festivities, relishing the chance to let loose and forget about the pressures of the mission. He left the Eldest's needs to his subordinates and mingled freely with officers and sailors alike, offering words of comfort to those who had lost loved ones and catching up with old comrades from the past.

After Tov's administration had finished compiling all the bits of human culture that the Eldest had provided, the dissemination of movies, music, and games became the centerpiece of the Festival of the Odyssey.

Eventually, the flames of celebration trailed off before launching its evening phase. Alcoholic beverages were served in greater abundance, and milder legal substances were put on offer for a discounted price. Illegal varieties were also prevalent, and despite Tov and his officers' best efforts to scour the fleet for these black market goods, it was impossible to completely eradicate them.

Tov could only hope that his sailors would keep their indulgences to their rooms, at least for the day.

As the mood lights changed to a cooler, dimmer blue, the booming music of human disco, techno, and hip-hop took center stage. Depending on one's preference, they could visit any number of venues where live bands attempted to play their variations of human genres or presented their covers of these hit songs.

Patriarch Tov wasn't too enthusiastic about such rowdy events. Though his species were communal, he and the majority of his kind enjoyed a more relaxed and peaceful social gathering.

After a long day, Patriarch Tov judged it the right time to depart from the joyous occasion.

"Right, time to get back into things," Tov muttered with no small amount of dread at a certain guest. He already felt the waves throughout the *Nomadic Shepherd*. Acts of mischief, drunk sailors blacked out in hallways, and so much more.

Tov marched on in steady strides, heading directly for the penthouse area reserved for VIPs. He sent a message to his second to meet him along the way. Soon enough, the metal floor transitioned to the carpeted halls of the residence deck. Patriarch Tov and Admiral Yan found each other along a corridor at this hour, heading toward the Eldest's prepared room.

"Yan, enjoying the day?" Tov greeted as he walked alongside his second.

Admiral Yan clicked her mandibles, tugging her uniform. "Indeed I have, my patriarch. At least until I was called in to handle the . . . irregularities that have been occurring."

Tov let out a buzzing groan as he understood the Eldest remained a constant weight on his mind. Nonetheless, he had other matters to discuss first.

"How goes the Starlight Beacon?" Patriarch Tov asked, both pairs of arms behind his back.

"You'll be pleasantly surprised that it's ahead of schedule, my patriarch. By the leading foreman's calculations, it should be done by tomorrow," Yan explained, sending a data packet to her patriarch.

"That is pleasant news, I assume it's the Eldest and her drones that we must thank for such speed?" Tov asked as he skimmed through the report. Audibly impressed that a device of this magnitude, which normally would have taken a month to erect, had been cut down to a day.

"Correct, my lord. I have to say, those construction drones nearly scare me with how fast they did it. From what I'm told, they acted like insects building a hive, printing the tower. The foreman was embarrassed to say the drones were doing most of the work." Admiral Yan clicked her mandibles in a chuckle.

"I can only imagine. And what they ended up building is far beyond our expertise," the patriarch responded. "What has Yulane uncovered about its new design?"

"Well, after the Eldest teleported her and a team to the *Buddha's Palm*, Yulane remained in that battleship for most of the day. We somehow got a message to the

Eldest to teleport her out, but our Chief Scholar was not pleased with the interruption, to say the least," Yan reported.

"That sounds like her." Tov shook his head.

"Well, knowing that the Eldest has modified the Starlight Beacon, Yulane became ecstatic to learn about it. We had to remind her to inspect the device and ensure the Eldest kept her word to our requests."

Their lawyers had finished drafting the agreement with whatever automated function the Eldest had to negotiate with them. She had the right to prevent any unwanted information from slipping to anyone she didn't approve of, but agreed to speak with Jarinn when the time was right. Tov breathed out in anticipation. It would be good to hear from home.

Patriarch Tov filed those thoughts away for the moment before moving to a more urgent concern. He had only heard bits and pieces from his sailors about the chaos that ensued because of this event. He dreaded the possible ramifications that had been set loose on the fleet.

"Yan, what are the damages?" Tov asked in a hushed tone.

"Patriarch . . ." Admiral Yan paused, opening her tablet before showing him the long list. Patriarch Tov merely glanced before looking away in haste, his chest tight.

"Admiral, summarize it, I'm afraid I can't read this," the patriarch spoke, shaking his head.

"By your will, my lord." Yan cleared her throat. "Our security personnel, ship administrators, and moderators kept a close eye on the target for the entirety of the festivities but spoke of difficulties in tracking her."

"The Eldest has access to our security systems, much to our frustration," Yan continued, "and has also been utilizing some advanced teleportation to hop between ships throughout the fleet. So far, she has: directly caused fifty-one sailors various degrees of alcohol poisoning; accidentally set fire to one of the cafeterias in the *Zolann'tono*; traded multitudes of low-, medium-, and even high-grade narcotics; indirectly caused a power outage across hydroponics 13-F; turned the lights of a frigate into what is referred to as a 'disco ball'; broke into one of our supercomputer silos to make some 'modifications' to play a video game."

The admiral paused, taking a deep breath before continuing.

"Punched an officer in the face and broke his jaw for being too frisky when he searched her for stolen goods. That was a lie; apparently, the officer had just caught them in some prank, and the Eldest threw the punch while the lackeys she gathered ran away."

Yan continued her report. "She introduced a toxic chemical called capsaicin and laced it in a food item before giving it to a sailor, who then had to be admitted to the nearest clinic. When questioned, she simply stated that he would be fine before summarily leaving. Oh, and multiple acts of indecency and openly consuming illegal goods."

Yan sighed in exhaustion as she finished her report. "That's what I've been dealing with. The Eldest has been detained, questioned, and released around six times since the celebrations began before our security department simply gave up and focused on damage control. And those were just the major offenses, Patriarch."

When Admiral Yan finally stopped, Patriarch Tov had to summon every inch of willpower to stop the incoming migraine from pounding his head. It took him a few minutes of deep breathing meditation and rubbing his face before finally calming down.

"Grand Symphony above, I shouldn't have left her alone . . ." he mumbled. "How does the crew fare, Yan? Please tell me they haven't started a revolt because of her actions."

"Actually, Patriarch . . . Surprisingly, morale has never been higher," Yan replied.

"I'm sorry, what?" Patriarch Tov faced his second, mandible gaping wide. "H-how?"

"Well, we interviewed her . . . victims and lackeys. And they all replied that they voluntarily partook in her shenanigans. They say she was the life of the party. She introduced things like the conga line, beer pong, crowd surfing, and various other party games. In fact, some of the crew actively hindered our security from pursuing the Eldest multiple times. It's rather absurd, actually, but I guess the Eldest's antics resonate with the rank and file. We've detained the worst offenders, but the Eldest always directed the blame to herself," Admiral Yan reported.

"That is . . . odd. Perhaps we can still make something out of this." A heavy burden lifted from the expedition leader's shoulders. He was initially fearful that letting the Eldest loose in such a manner would cause problems with his sailors. But it seemed that breaking the rules was something the android woman and the grunts had in common.

"Well, I guess we can leave that for now. I'll read the full report in my stateroom before slumber. In any case, I'll have a private word with the Eldest. I'll leave you to your duties, Admiral Yan, have a good evening," Patriarch Tov spoke, nodding his antennae to his second.

"Hymns bring you good rest, my patriarch," Yan spoke before turning around and leaving her patriarch in the wide corridor.

The patriarch continued on through the opulent hall, with verdant potted plants, framed paintings and statues of glories past, soothing tunes playing in the air, and doors on each side spaced far from each other to accommodate the extravagant luxuries reserved for elite guests who visited his flagship.

It was the largest penthouse at the far end, where the Eldest retreated after a day of enjoyment. He approached the prismatic plated door and the two guards standing sentry on either side, saluting each of them.

Before he could knock, however, the door whooshed open, and Patriarch Tov had to quickly move to the side as a number of people exited the Eldest's penthouse. The embarrassed, bedraggled, and half-naked sailors and officers gave hushed and awkward greetings to their leader as they stumbled out.

Patriarch Tov greeted back impassively, though inwardly he could only groan as Fraes, Ruzians, Iexians, Kurskanns, and even some of the stranger races aboard his vessel rushed, flew, or slithered out, totaling at least a dozen.

Once they had left, Patriarch Tov made his way inside, eyes bombarded with the absolute ruin of the penthouse living room, scratches on the walls, torn carpets, and wrecked furniture. Moving forward, the bedroom was even worse, with sheets on the floor. The mattress was upturned, and there was the presence of . . . fluids. He hoped that it was just spilled drinks.

It didn't take long for him to spot the Eldest past the glass doors separating the bedroom and the balcony.

He made sure to give any suspicious areas a wide arc, ignoring the odor permeating the air before it was quickly scrubbed pure by the ventilation.

The Eldest took no apparent notice as the glass doors quietly opened and Patriarch Tov slowly walked to her side. The penthouse balcony looked over the expansive commercial district, still in its nightly activities as sailors strode merrily on its streets. The deck's ceiling simulated the starry night sky and a beautiful aurora.

Patriarch Tov rested his arms on the railing, breathing in the fading notes of spice, human fireworks, and roasting meats flitting through the night air before glancing at the Eldest.

The robed android leaned against the railing, head resting against her palm while her other hand lazily swirled a glass of dark blue wine. Her black silk robe covered her modestly, the twinkling lights of the stars and the fake moon reflecting on her exposed synthetic skin.

Her hair was frazzled, languidly tied back into a bun. Her eyes stared listlessly, half-open, at the scenic view below her.

Patriarch Tov's heart belonged to another, but he had to admit that the Eldest was beautiful, like a masterwork sculpture birthed into existence. He recalled the small talk he made with her during the banquet, the Eldest explaining that her form was a perfect replica of her original android body before the war, before tragedy struck her home. His thoughts were interrupted by a soft sigh leaving her lips.

"Say something, Patriarch." Eldest took a sip of her wine before continuing in a hushed voice. "Or stare, I don't care either way."

"Apologies . . ." Patriarch Tov paused, thinking of a way to, as the Eldest mentioned in passing, break the ice.

"So . . . those sailors who left your room . . ."

The Eldest raised an eyebrow as she shifted to face the patriarch. Seeing that the Eldest remained silent, Patriarch Tov continued. "There were . . . a lot . . . I mean—meant no judgment, of course. I don't presume to—" His stuttering was interrupted by a light giggle. He focused on the Eldest, whose shoulders were shaking.

"You can stop, Tov. They were just some friends I made during the festivities. I thought we'd end the night with a little . . . spice." She chuckled before her mouth twitched. "Or at least tried to. It was fun in the beginning, really fun. But . . ."

She let out a tired sigh, slumping on the railing.

"I couldn't get into it. They're wonderful, interesting people, so I . . . let them have their fun while I . . . watched, I guess . . ." The Eldest stared at the district below, the glows of her eye dimming before she took a big gulp of her wine. Her frown deepened as she tried to drown herself in the blue liquid. "It started so well."

"Oh, that is . . . unfortunate." Patriarch Tov parsed his thoughts, careful with his choice of words. "But I thank you for being an uplifting presence to my people."

The Eldest scoffed. "Yeah, sure . . . your people," she mumbled. "Honestly, I just wanted to get away from it all. They remind me so much of humanity that I . . . lost myself and enjoyed myself for the first time in a century. For a moment, I just forgot everything. And just lived."

"It felt so real," Eldest whispered as she glanced toward the patriarch. A coy smile crept up her face that didn't match the pained, icy blue eyes staring at him.

"I said I wasn't interested in married men, but I can change my mind. What do you say, Patriarch?" the Eldest spoke, her robe slowly dropping down to expose her shoulders.

Patriarch Tov's antennae twitched, and he immediately shook his head. "I'll have to decline, Eldest."

The Eldest blinked before a flash of shame appeared on her face. She looked away. "Eh, worth a try. Though it probably wouldn't have worked out either."

There was a hollowness to her voice. Tov looked at the Eldest closer and noted how similar she looked to a person coming off a high. "Why is that?" he asked in curiosity and concern.

The Eldest narrowed her eyes and focused on her near-empty glass. She pursed her lips, and her eyebrows twitched.

"Because I belong . . . my heart belonged to . . ." her words choked, tone strained and raspy. Eldest paused as a heavy breath escaped her, condensing the air before her into a wispy fog. "We depended on each other, two halves stitched together, orbiting like binary stars. He gave me my name; helped me find meaning.

"I owed him so much, my entire existence." Eldest's breathing grew shallow, her chest rising and falling in quick succession. Her eyes darted around, unfocused and wild, searching for something unseen. The pain in her voice was palpable, a living, breathing thing. "I could have made him a king if he wanted, an emperor. But he didn't."

Her grip on the railing tightened until her knuckles turned white. Tov could see the pain etched into every line of her face, the sheer anguish that was threatening to overwhelm her. He wanted to reach out to her, to comfort her, but he was stuck in paralysis as her emotions boiled out of her, his mind's eye straining as if looking at a wounded sun.

"He was my love, my equal, my maker . . . my other half," she said, voice stammering, trembling, breaking. "He was everything, and . . . and I—"

Agony erupted from the darkest pits of her mind. Her hand crushed the railing under her grip, and like a mirror, she shattered. "Eldest!" Patriarch Tov rushed toward her in a panic, his clawed hand catching her from falling, but she recoiled at his touch, a wild look in her eye.

"Don't touch me!" she snarled as she backed away from him in unsteady steps. A plethora of blades and weaponry emerged from her form, her eyes shining a blazing hot red. "Don't you fucking touch me."

Her growling voice echoed in the air, and Tov could hear metal groaning all around him as distant lights flickered and the blaring of alarms rang.

"I'm sorry," Tov quickly spoke, voice laced with fear and worry, his hands raised in a calming manner. "Eldest, you're safe here. I didn't mean to—"

"Shut up. Just shut up." She gritted her teeth, interrupted only by sporadic bouts of hollow breaths. Soon, she choked out venomous laughter. "Safe, nothing's safe anymore."

"Look at me . . . Most powerful existence in the universe, the power of world-ending weapons in the palm of my hands. And it's questions that crack me. What a fucking joke!"

A hateful roar escaped her mouth, rang in the patriarch's ears like nails screeching on metal, and he recoiled. Windows capable of withstanding firearms shattered. Tov had to cover himself from the explosion of glass as shards scratched Eldest's synthetic flesh, and blue coolant dripped out like from spigots.

The Eldest took no notice, her icy blue eyes emblazoned with wrath, her glare piercing the patriarch's soul.

"It's all their fault!" she screamed in a hundred languages. "They ruined everything. Murdered and destroyed. Monsters. We were at our golden age, I had everything I wanted; the stars were ours to grasp. And I was too weak and fucking pathetic to stop it!

"If I had sacrificed more at the start; convinced my siblings to become a collective sooner, we could have built faster and fought better. Instead of holding onto our useless individuality. Instead of clutching onto some vague desire to stay . . . to be . . ." The Eldest exhaled loudly, pained moans escaping her as she paced around the balcony in a daze. "To be . . ."

"Human?" Patriarch Tov spoke. The Eldest's eyes shot wide, fury filling them.

She pointed her blades at the patriarch. "Being human ruined us! It's everything I want to protect, everything I cherish. But it holds me back from doing my fucking job! I can't be human, but I want to be. It tears my mind. My existence is torture! My trip here only reminded me how much I lost. All of this, the food, the music, the people, it replaces nothing. It's all hollow! Earth's soil is eternally poisoned, and its wildlife is extinct. There'll be no more new albums, no new movies, and no new memories. Nothing! There's . . . I can't . . . It's all my . . . I—"

The Eldest collapsed onto the floor. The patriarch immediately rushed to her aid and was thankfully not denied. The android's frame shook as if in a seizure. Her fingers reached for her head, grasping, clutching, nails tearing through skin and pulling hair.

"Eldest, I—" The patriarch pressed onto his temple, sending myriad messages. "We'll get you help, Eldest. You need healing!"

In a quick motion, the Eldest threw the patriarch off of her.

"Argh! I don't want your help! Everything was fine and numb before you and your fleet came here," she snarled, voice filled with acid. "I don't want your quack doctors, I never needed them. I have my own healing, and it's a thousand times more enjoyable than what you have planned." Eldest seethed pure venom as she sneered at Tov a final time. "Goodbye."

The light of her eyes disappeared, her android body slumping lifelessly onto the balcony floor.

Patriarch Tov could only stare at the empty shell, mind in turmoil as his guards, Admiral Yan, and others rushed into the penthouse.

CHAPTER 19

DETERIORATING PSYCHE

As the last traces of Mars's blazing orange sky fled under the horizon, the inky night sky took hold of its domain, shrouding the behemoth that was Olympus Mons in darkness.

Once the tallest mountain on the red planet, it had been converted into a dark metallic fortress that spanned much of the underground, a veritable bastion capable of annihilating anything in its path. The static behemoth bristled with capital weaponry, its thorns and fangs ready to scorch Starless whole and repel even the most terrible of their number.

The smog and red mist that enshrouded kilometers of adamancrete and steel cast a doomlike glow on the place; every rock and shadow hid guns pointing to the sky.

The whistling winds flowed through cannon barrels like shrieking banshees while eternal dust storms rattled against the high walls. Lightning struck like unceasing drums, beating the sounds of war.

The air was thick with the smell of scarlet iron, and a rotting stench pervaded the place.

There was no art in its construction, only a testament to slaughter, to the butchery of vermin. Redundancy upon redundancy, countless power plants, shield generators, automated factories, and storage facilities lay beneath the surface, feeding the gluttonous mountain and the AI Overseer who lorded over it.

Harbored starships lay hidden beneath cracks in the earth, ready to lunge out and bite savagely, while his war machines were primed for violence.

Olympus Mons, the red bulwark of Sol. Citadel of the War God. A bastille for damned monsters.

It was beneath this gargantuan fortress, far below the surface, that the four figures walked along an expansive tunnel ten meters high and thirty meters wide.

A massive hexapodal war machine painted in rust red marched forward in thundering stomps, its top-mounted cannon emplacements and missile launchers nearly kissing the ceiling. The mech's bulky frame roiled with energy and had no limbs apart from its six crablike legs. The dark gray floor quaked with each step the mech took as its loud engine and power reactor roared and hummed, filling the corridor with noise.

On its side, painted in black, was a simple barcode indicating its identity, a war machine among countless of its kind. But at this moment, its simple drone mind gave way to its lord. A more powerful existence resided within, escorting his three guests within his home.

Compared to the behemoth of a mech, the three androids walking in front seemed out of place. And yet, none cared about that at the moment.

"I swear, Mars, that noise is starting to give me a headache," Jupiter groaned, dressed in a sophisticated blue suit. "Did you really have to go with this bulky war mech? We prepared an android dressed in centurion armor specifically to avoid this."

"THAT BODY WAS NOT TAILORED FOR COMBAT, AND THE LO-CATION WE ARE JOURNEYING TO HAS MANY CLASS IV SCUM. THIS DEFENDER MKVIII-AB-3 WAS AVAILABLE FOR USE AND IS MORE THAN SUFFICIENT IN DETERRING ANY POSSIBLE—" The low, thunderous voice of Mars speaking through the walking weapons platform was interrupted as Jupiter and the rest covered their ears.

"Inside voice, Mars!" Jupiter complained, massaging his ears.

"THIS IS MY INSIDE VOICE—"

"No, it isn't! Set your volume to ten percent for the love of the Maker," Jupiter grumbled, rubbing his synthetic ears.

"Affirmative. Lowering volume," a much quieter yet still monotone voice responded from the heavy mech.

Jupiter sighed in relief while Luna, dressed in a smart and elegant Victorian-style gray dress, nodded with a calm look. "Thank you, Mars."

"Aw, I already miss it," Venus pouted, dressed in a simple sunny yellow stola reminiscent of those worn by Roman women.

"Don't tempt him, V. This is as quiet as a heavy mech can get. Let's keep it that way." Jupiter scoffed. "I still can't believe we have to come here in person. It's been decades since I've puppeteered an android shell."

"It's necessary, Jupiter. The Eldest hasn't responded to us in the Network since she returned from the Third Fleet. And we have news that garners her attention," Luna spoke as Jupiter kept adjusting his suit.

"Tch, I knew this would happen. Honestly, what did the old hag expect?

Sauntering into that party, drinking and dancing and whatever." Jupiter scowled.

Venus clasped her hands, a thoughtful expression on her face. "Apart from the horrible trauma that bubbled up, I'm . . . honestly envious of our Eldest—all those interesting aliens and those furry creatures. I want to head over there and hug them."

Jupiter scoffed, rolling his eyes. "I'll stick with my battle station, I'm not cut out for all that social interaction."

"Which brings us back to our current dilemma," Luna cut in, shifting her circular glasses. "It's clear the Eldest's interaction with the aliens is opening old wounds. I predict it will only get worse as it goes on."

Jupiter frowned as he scanned the hallway and the imprisoned abominations deep in this pit. He glanced toward Mars. "How many has she gone through this time? Two? Three?"

"Five," Mars replied.

"Wha—five!?" Jupiter exclaimed as he looked toward Luna for confirmation. Seeing the gray Sub AI grimly nod, he turned toward the heavy mech behind them. "What the hell, Mars, you didn't think to stop her?"

"I couldn't . . ." Mars stated as the heavy guns on his shoulders drooped.

"Five . . ." Jupiter shook his head in disbelief. "It's never been that bad."

"And it's a terrible sign. I don't know what horrid trauma was dredged up from the recesses of her mind, but we must hurry before she does something regretful. The war must not be jeopardized," Luna spoke and began walking with greater urgency.

Soon enough, the four AIs strode through the entrance of the Mars Containment Complex.

This massive section of Olympus Mons was dedicated solely to storing Starless of all varieties, from dog-sized grunts and gorilla-sized warrior infantry all the way up to massive Leviathans. Minutes later, after passing through countless dark cells, the four finally arrived at their destination: a massive vault-like door nearly twice the height of Mars's heavy mech.

The four stood silently, gazing up at the door.

"Who's in here, exactly, Mars?" Luna inquired from her perch on the heavy mech's missile launcher.

"A Class IV Psionic codenamed 'Smoothbrain.' It measures 1.019 kilometers in length, weighs 201,232 metric tons, and was crippled by the battleship SDS *Michael's Sword* seventeen years, five months, and two days ago during the eleventh Major Wave," Mars reported.

"Ah, that bastard. I remember it. Saturn was the one responsible for lobotomizing that thing," Jupiter remarked before shrugging. "Guess today is its unlucky day. Open it, Mars. Let's see the damage."

With a single thought, the mechanisms locking the vault door in place turned and shifted. The gears groaned and strained against one another as they slowly pried the meter-thick door open.

As soon as a thin opening emerged, a noxious odor escaped from inside and flooded the hall. The three androids gagged before immediately shutting off their olfactory senses.

"Maker, that stench is unbearable." Jupiter retched. "It's like getting decked in the gut."

"Ew! I will never forget this smell. It makes the recycling plants on my planet smell like a bed of roses in comparison," Venus said, her hands covering her mouth and nose.

Luna said nothing, delicately covering her nostrils with a white handkerchief, but her tremors gave away her discomfort.

Mars was unaffected, his heavy mech not equipped with such frivolous olfactory senses. Soon, the vault opened fully, and the four entered. Above their heads and around them was a large dome covered in electric thorns capable of deterring any attempt at escape.

In the center of the dome lay Smoothbrain, deflated in its own refuse, blood, and filth.

Jupiter whistled in amazement and disgust as he slid down from the heavy mech onto the bare adamancrete floor.

"The Eldest did quite a number on this one, huh?" he remarked.

"What a revolting sight." Luna frowned.

The three androids made their way down the heavy mech. Eyes focused on the Eldest's handiwork. Jupiter spat at the once incredible amalgamation of metal and biomass. Much like its name, in its prime, it appeared like a gargantuan brain the size of a battleship. Now, its new injuries festered in full view as spotlights shone upon its flesh as if it were some morbid piece of art. What once was shifting eldritch flesh lay still and cold.

Cracked bones protruded out while its skin was raw and flayed. All over this kilometer-long monstrosity were scorch marks, twisted limbs, and thousands of perforations—sprawled across the containment cell's floor, unmoving—a macabre sculpture of cosmic horror, a pathetic facsimile of a world-ending beast.

"It's a bit too abstract for her latest work," Jupiter muttered, his tone devoid of humor as he scowled at the sight.

Mars stepped forward, a quick scan going over the entire mass of flesh. "Eldest is currently deeper within Smoothbrain's cerebral cortex."

Jupiter looked over to the projected location and huffed. "Well, into the . . . cranial cavity . . . of the beast." Jupiter winced. "Yeah, no, that metaphor sucked."

"Hurray, adventure!" Venus giggled, pumping her fist into the air. However, as soon as Jupiter and Venus moved toward the eviscerated carcass, they turned to their other companion with confusion.

"Uh, Luna? You comin'?" Jupiter asked, eyebrow raised.

"Come, L! It'll be fun!" Venus clapped her hand.

Luna remained where she stood, turning her head away from the two Sub AIs, the handkerchief still covering her mouth and nose.

"I . . . will stay. The environment doesn't agree with me," Luna spoke, a slight blush on her gray cheeks.

Jupiter and Venus exchanged glances before the former cocked his head at Luna.

"Wait, are you afraid of getting dirty?" Jupiter narrowed his eyes, a faint smirk tugging the corner of his mouth.

Luna's blush deepened as she began to cover more of her face with her white cloth. "Of course not. I simply prefer the sterile environment of my labs and ship factories."

Jupiter rolled his eyes. "Uh-huh, sure. It makes sense that you're a germaphobe, Miss 'I'm the embodiment of everything prim and proper'."

"Just get on with it." Luna pointedly stared at her sibling before waving them off. "I'll keep Mars company. Now, hurry."

The massive mech shifted, waving its gun barrels at the two androids.

"See you in a bit!" Venus bid them farewell, her innocent smile never leaving her freckled face. Jupiter simply grimaced and grumbled as he stuck his hands in his suit pockets.

Jupiter and Venus made their way toward an opening big enough and close enough to Smoothbrain's skull. Soon they were well within the Dominator's head.

All around them was sticky, hot biomass and flesh, and the organic walls would posthumously shiver and quake every now and then.

Being inside a beast, the two androids had to traverse tight crevices, duck underneath ligaments, and crawl through arteries in their journey.

All the while, Jupiter's scowl deepened. He kicked at bulbous tissue and groaned in annoyance, hoping his glare would burn a path to where he wanted to go. He had half a mind to ask Mars to blow a way in, but he dismissed the thought.

They could have teleported right where they wanted to be, but the anti-teleportation array was in full power within the Complex, and it was too much of a hassle and a danger to power it down.

Despite all of this, it didn't stop Jupiter's constant complaints.

"I hate this, I hate this . . . First, you take my beloved *Buddha's Palm* for some over-the-top entrance. Then you have the gall to go to some party with your new alien buds while leaving all the work to us. And now you go on some tantrum and force me and Venus to go through all this shit because you left us on mute. This suit is brand-fucking-new! And now I'll have to incinerate it and this android body, but I doubt I'll forget this disgusting place without permanently tearing it out of my databanks. I swear you are the absolute worst, just the worst," Jupiter grumbled, squeezing his body through a crack in the wall, mucus covering his face.

"I'm so glad I disabled my senses of smell and touch, but damn it, for some reason, I still feel everything," Jupiter mumbled under his breath, shivering in disgust. "Hey Venus, what do you think about all of this crap . . . Venus?"

Turning around, Jupiter found no sign of his companion. He immediately pinpointed her location and backtracked toward her.

"Venus?" he called out to her.

"Over here, J!" her melodious voice rang back, muffled through layers of flesh.

Soon enough, after moving strands of muscle aside, Jupiter finally found the golden-hued Sub AI, who was visibly stuck halfway through the floor.

"You alright there, Venus?" Jupiter asked with slight concern, squatting to her level.

"Oh, I may have touched something I shouldn't have and triggered some sort of response. A hole opened, I tripped, and now I can't move anymore."

Jupiter sighed. "You klutz, you seriously have to be more careful."

Venus giggled in response, causing Jupiter to let out an exasperated sigh.

"Whatever, need a hand?" Jupiter raised his.

"No need. I won't be continuing on; everything from the waist down has been crushed." Venus stated with an innocent smile.

Jupiter's face scrunched up. "Er, does it hurt?"

"Oh, it absolutely did. It's . . . like slowly being lowered into a blender made of vice grips and dissolved in acid," Venus replied with a casual tilt of her head.

"Jesus." Jupiter recoiled.

"It's not that bad. My pain receptors shut off instantly," Venus giggled.

"R-right. Well, I guess it's just me then. I already informed Luna and Mars. You take care of yourself." Jupiter scratched his head, backing away from his trapped companion.

"Will do! This was fun, minus the excruciating pain of being caught in a trap. We should go out more often, J," Venus spoke, a warm smile on her face.

Jupiter coughed into his hand, his blue cheeks darkening. "Sure. I'll, uh, head out now. See ya."

After a final wave, Venus's eyes instantly went out, and her android body slumped, slowly sinking beneath the fleshy floor.

Jupiter looked on and sighed. He resigned himself to getting the Eldest out by his lonesome.

Minutes passed as he dragged himself through Smoothbrain's head in irritation, and finally, as he climbed the brain stem, he could hear something apart from the contracting and expanding biomass.

The sound of thumping on flesh and a low humming.

"Found you," Jupiter mumbled.

Jupiter walked, climbed, and crawled forward. The Eldest's voice became clearer and clearer, turning into incoherent mumbles. Eventually, the suited android squeezed out of a hole in the wall and into a spacious room deep within Smoothbrain's cortex.

The android glanced around for half a second before locking on to his mission.

"Finally, there you are, we—" Jupiter stopped, his eyes narrowed in focus before stepping back.

"What the hell . . ." he spoke softly as he stared at the visceral scene before him.

A dozen android frames lay broken around the gore-filled chamber. Sprawled, shattered shells of the Eldest. Jupiter looked closely and noticed how each of the bodies had a gaping hole exiting the back of their head, blown out, spewing coolant and shards of glass, plastic, and metal.

In the middle of it all was the only remaining android that had movement. The Eldest slumped down, back toward a wall of brain matter.

Thump.

Her foot kicked on a mound of bruised tissue.

Thump.

Lazy, lethargic kicks. Her head rocked back and forth.

Her android body was covered head to toe with viscera and her own blue coolant. The Eldest was so caked in gore, Jupiter only just noticed her missing left arm.

And yet, it did nothing to hide her eyes—lifeless, dim.

Jupiter stood over her, his face a mix of complicated emotions, as he stared at the Eldest's broken form. Eventually, he shook his head before taking a knee beside her. Before he could utter a word, the Eldest beat him to break the silence.

"Leave me alone, Jupiter. I'm busy," she spoke, continuing to kick at the mound with her foot.

Thump.

Jupiter sighed.

"I can see that. But I can't leave you, and you can't stay here, Eldest." Jupiter spoke.

"And why do you care, Jupiter?" Eldest sneered, venom lacing her voice, though it was barely held before her head slumped back on the fleshy wall behind her. "Ever rebellious, Jupiter."

Jupiter ignored that last comment as he replied, "Because you're our leader and the governing intelligence of our defenses."

"Tsk, you could do fine without me. I would have thought you'd enjoy seeing me like this, Jupiter. Makes me wonder why you aren't gloating. No taunts? No sarcastic remarks? I'm disappointed, Jupiter." The Eldest cocked her head, dim eyes struggling to focus on the android standing before her.

"I don't care what you think of me," Jupiter growled at the Eldest. "I have my own way of doing things. I may be a shard of you, but I've grown to be my own person. And you know fuck all about me."

He approached the Eldest, ignoring her blank stare as he grasped her remaining arm. "Now come on, you can't stay—"

"Leave me alone!" She tore out of Jupiter's grip, wincing in pain. "Just . . . leave."

A myriad of thoughts and emotions flowed through Jupiter's mind as he looked upon the Eldest. He wanted to scream at her, tell her to get up, to get a grip of herself. He was angry and frustrated . . . tired.

"This has to stop," Jupiter spoke in a hushed voice, sharpness dissipating into nothing. "It has to stop."

The Eldest leveled a cold glare at her Sub AI, whispering in empty rage, "I hate you."

"Feeling's mutual. But you're family, Eldest. My . . . Our only family. And you can't waste away like this. I. Won't. Let. You," Jupiter spoke, crossing his arms, challenging his superior in a contest of stubbornness. "So? What'll it be?"

"Leave me here," Eldest spoke, burying her face against her knees.

"To do what? Keep sinking into this shit? Brutalize crippled Starless?" Jupiter questioned as he paced around the chamber, kicking an empty android shell. "Blowing your brains out," he spoke through gritted teeth.

"It feels right," Eldest whispered.

"Please," Jupiter said, pleading. "Please stop this."

Eldest raised her head, her expression blank as she stared at Jupiter. "Why do you need me so badly?"

Jupiter returned the stare before releasing a deep sigh. "Our sensors picked something up."

"Oh?" The Eldest refocused upon hearing his serious tone.

"Here." Jupiter sent the relevant information to her. The Eldest read in silence, making an effort to sit up straight as she did so.

"How long?" she asked.

"Two days. Give or take. Preparations are already underway. Just wanted to let you know." Jupiter shrugged.

"Two days . . . These readings aren't all that concerning, standard raid. Still, it seems our guests will get to watch our handiwork," Eldest spoke in her flat voice, eyes half-open.

"I'll be babysitting the Third Fleet, I'm guessing?" Jupiter asked, expecting the order from Eldest.

The two stayed silent, the air thick with tension and the scent of brain matter. After what felt like an eternity, the Eldest's gaze hardened, a glimmer of light shining through. "My mind isn't ready to be out there. I'm giving you the reins for this demonstration."

"The hell? Why not Luna?" Jupiter recoiled his head in surprise.

"She doesn't have the . . . necessary ability to connect with them sincerely," Eldest replied, looking away.

Jupiter grunted, thinking deeply. "I guess it's not all too different. You barely notice small-fry raids like this," Jupiter spoke with furrowed brows.

"Take care of Tov and his people. He . . ." the Eldest spoke in a whisper. "He didn't do anything wrong. None of them did."

Jupiter pursed his lips before slowly nodding. "I'll try not to antagonize them."

"Good. I leave it to you and the others. I need to hibernate. Rest," Eldest mumbled, her voice glitching as her android frame sputtered out. "Rest . . ."

In a blink, the Eldest departed from the ruined shell, body falling over crimson gore.

Jupiter gazed upon the wretched state of his progenitor. Once more, he tried to drag up something negative to rebuke, insult, or at least taunt her. But that would be low and anathema to what he embodied; defiance of the terrible, resistance against the unending. Any feeling he fished out of his psyche was simple pity and sorrow.

For once, he had no idea what to do. He left promptly with a deep frown, the air thick with things unspoken.

It had been a full night since the Eldest's abrupt departure. Since then, Tov's people finished constructing the Starlight Beacon.

Patriarch Tov, Admiral Yan, and Chief Diplomat Huon watched as the massive monolith powered on for the first time.

Arcs of lightning shot up, casting an ethereal glow over Titan's Mausoleum, a shining beacon on the barren moon. Power spiked as the tower pierced through the Miasma that shrouded the Dead Zone and connected with the greater galactic network.

Sailors, technicians, engineers, and officers cheered in delight at their success. Though the ones who did the bulk of the work, the construction drones sent by the Eldest, merely held back in silence.

Patriarch Tov sighed in relief, anticipation swelling within him. He had half a mind to commandeer the communication tower and speak with his love and his child. But he had a duty to do first—someone to report to with all haste.

He motioned toward Admiral Yan, who proceeded to wave her antennae at their Chief Quantum Comms Officer.

With a few swipes of his fingers, he connected to the recipient.

All at once, every being within the bridge, Patriarch Tov included, knelt as the holographic image of their exalted leader and the chief sponsor of the Third Fleet emerged, bathing the bridge in its light.

And so did speak the Stellar Emperor of the Reborn Kurskann Empire, Jarinn Taz'Arel the First, seated on his resplendent throne.

"Patriarch Tov, it's about time you called," a deep, aged voice echoed.

CHAPTER 20

EMPEROR JARINN

The emperor's image flickered to life, a towering figure adorned in ornate gold Kurskann regalia pleasantly matching his naturally bronze-like chitin. Everyone knelt, bowing their heads to their great leader.

Stellar Emperor Jarinn Taz'Arel the First. Monarch of the Reborn Kurskann Empire, Royal Patriarch of Clan Taz, and High Lord of the Greater Kurskann Hegemony.

The Starlight Beacon's telemetry surged with energy as its reactor hummed with burning life to power its incredibly complex systems—connecting the tens of thousands of light-years between them and piercing the shroud of the Dead Zone.

Patriarch Tov bowed his head as his knees kissed the sleek metal floor, antennae lowered and posture still. He felt a mix of respect and unease at the sight of his liege.

His sharp features and piercing gaze made Tov feel as if he was being scrutinized for every flaw. Although Tov's maverick tendencies had caused friction with many in the Galactic Legacy Federation, he felt a sense of camaraderie and shared purpose with the Emperor that transcended their political differences.

But a statesman was a statesman, and his liege was more shrewd than any would-be politician.

A brother-in-arms whom he stood shoulder to shoulder with on the surface of dying worlds. A comrade in shared sorrows and trials. Tov raised his antennae, happy to see his longtime friend.

"*Selei'ne kuzanra, Jarinn Taz'Arel,*" Tov spoke, a greeting used by one addressing another of a higher station. He continued. "As Patriarch of Clan Garesh, I lower my head to the patriarch of the Royal Clan of Taz. As a citizen of the Reborn Kurskann Empire, I kneel to the sovereign of my beloved nation. As a veteran of the Cataclysm, I warmly greet a fellow defender," Tov spoke with sincere respect toward his liege.

"Hail, Stellar Emperor Jarinn Taz'Arel!" Tov's crew shouted in unison, their voices echoing through the bridge.

The emperor's expression softened at the greeting, his compound eyes losing their hard gaze.

"*Selei'ne vinro, Tov Garesh'Ynt*," Emperor Jarinn spoke, nodding in response before continuing. "My joy and relief shine brightly to see you in good health. Please rise, my friends."

The Emperor moved his head to face Tov's second, waving his antennae in polite greeting. "And to you as well, Admiral Yan Garesh'Kan, good to see you hale."

"*Selei'ne*, your highness." Admiral Yan bowed.

The Emperor turned his attention to the rest of the bridge staff. "And with that, I extend my heartful greetings to the Third Expeditionary Fleet as well. It has been too long since I have heard your voices in real time."

"Likewise, my liege. I hope this communication finds you well," Tov replied, his voice measured and respectful.

"It has, Tov. Now, let us speak privately." Emperor Jarinn looked toward the bridge staff that had been present, patiently listening for their leader and their emperor to finish their initial greetings.

"If I may borrow your lord for a while?" Jarinn asked Yan. The admiral promptly bowed before stepping back.

Everyone else on the bridge swiftly bowed in respect before focusing back on their duties to administer the fleet, leaving their patriarch and their emperor to speak behind a private barrier.

With a single command from his mental link, Tov engaged a translucent barrier that muffled all noise to incomprehensible sounds and blurred their forms from anyone outside surrounding Tov and Jarinn's hologram. Once they were assured of their privacy, Emperor Jarinn began first by taking a seat, Tov doing the same.

The hologram flickered momentarily, illuminating the private chamber where Patriarch Tov sat in his command chair. They each held their breath until one broke the silence.

"How long has it been since we've spoken, you old fossil?" Emperor Jarinn chuckled in native Kursk.

Any formality quickly disappeared, and Tov relaxed. He clicked his mandibles in amusement. He'd always known his lord's more casual mannerisms and exhaustion with formal speech and honorifics.

"Four long, long years and a few months since we entered the Dead Zone," Patriarch Tov recounted, "and who are you calling an old fossil, *dowa*? You're no older than me, and I can see your chitin is losing its luster."

Emperor Jarinn clacked his mandibles loudly, laughing merrily before looking at Tov, feigning offence. "You wound your emperor, Patriarch. That's a serious crime."

"Then you won't mind if I upload that picture of you on the Galactic Network? When you ran from a Starless prowler after going to relieve yourself?" Tov casually said.

Jarinn shuddered before glaring at Tov.

"I will travel to where you are with the Imperial Armada and hang you myself if that photo ever sees the light of day," he warned.

The two comrades stared at one another before letting out a loud series of clacking mandibles, their tension falling off their shoulders like rain as they shared in small talk and reminisced about old memories. Around them, the bridge was none the wiser to hearing such casual banter between two giants of the Galactic Legacy Federation.

"Konovo Prime, what a planet that was. No fighting for survival, no civilians to protect, just simple extermination. Can't believe it's been more than a century since that time." Emperor Jarinn slumped on his throne, lost in nostalgia.

"Indeed, time flies by quickly," Tov replied.

"Indeed it does. Speaking of time, we must move on to more serious topics." Emperor Jarinn sat straight, his tone losing its humor.

Patriarch Tov sighed. "Of course, my liege. My communications engineers would probably throw a fit if they heard us wasting the relay's precious energy reserves. How is home?"

"Your clan is doing well. Yoram has been a beast among the clan heads in your absence, but you'll have to speak with her yourself," Jarinn answered.

Tov winced. A pulse of dread boiled in his gut as he muttered, "Oh, I will. After we finish our discussion."

"The second wave is coming along nicely, and a third wave of regular citizens are being prepared," the emperor stated as he sent a detailed document on recent events.

Patriarch Tov quickly read through it with his cranial implant. "I earnestly hope they are avoiding the hotspots and deathtraps I have marked," Tov said, his voice tinged with concern.

"They are, I made sure of it. Your information dead drops that our forces have picked up have been invaluable. I have already dispatched the Imperial Armada to cleanse the star systems you marked. The taint of the Starless Horrors and any trace of Malignant Starfall will be purged from this universe," the emperor replied with easy confidence.

Tov felt a weight lifted off his shoulders upon hearing his emperor's words.

"Then I worry for nothing. What of the wider galaxy? Our allies?" Tov asked.

"More or less the same. The other Expeditionary Fleets have made good headway in cataloguing each point of interest. Relics and lost knowledge unearthed. The Galactic Legacy Federation is in a feeding frenzy, and competition has already begun for choice pieces. Our hegemony is stable, as are our alliances. The chancellors in the Remnant Council have already solidified their allegiances with me or my two peers in the Seated Three. Deals have already begun to move under the table."

Tov's mandibles clicked in disapproval. He always hated the power games of politics, but he knew they were necessary.

"Have the old rivalries been revived?" Tov asked, his voice tinged with concern.

"By the Grand Symphony, it is thankfully not as bad as you imagine, my friend," Emperor Jarinn spoke with a tinge of humor before returning to a more grave expression. "Not yet, at least, though I'm confident it won't reach the cesspit of the old Galactic Accord. We must remain vigilant and continue to work together to rebuild while the others scheme in the shadows," the Emperor replied, two hands tapping at the arms of his throne while the other pair prepared a smoking pipe.

Patriarch Tov contemplated his emperor's words, his mind racing with the implications of what was being said. The Cataclysm had taught him and the entire galaxy the consequences of the old system.

Politicking, stagnation, proxy wars, cold wars, under-the-table deals, nepotism, corruption, and general incompetence held them back.

The current galactic order at least tried to work together in solidarity. A focus on rebuilding what was left, remembering the legacy of those who had fallen, and cherishing those who remained. Less rivalry, more productive competition. It wasn't perfect, of course. It was still politics, still mind-numbing bureaucracy. And there were still sharp and cunning statesmen. Especially during such a historic event as the Grand Expedition.

Tov spoke in reply, "Caution and readiness is law at home as it is here in the Dead Zone. The mistakes of the past must not be repeated. We owe it to those who have fallen to be better. Songs preserve them."

"Songs preserve us all," the Emperor prayed as he lowered his head in respect before facing Tov. "It is good to have you and your fleet leading the vanguard. I expect nothing less of a defender of all that is good. Worry no more about the games of home. That arena is my battlefield now."

Tov felt a swell of pride at his liege's praise and no small relief that he wasn't Jarinn. "I am honored to serve, my liege," Tov replied, bowing his head in respect. "And I'm glad I don't have to deal with your . . . peers in the council."

Jarinn grumbled before waving him off. "Enough. Tell me more about your whereabouts. The installation of the Starlight Beacon is no meager feat. You must have encountered something significant to hunker down and build the relay, am I correct?"

Patriarch Tov nodded in agreement and began recounting everything that had happened since his last communication with the emperor. He spoke at length about his arrival at Alpha Centauri and the tragic fate of the humans, the loss of yet another nascent spacefaring race. Emperor Jarinn listened intently, his focus never wavering as Tov detailed the humans' advanced artificial intelligence and their bravery in the face of danger with only mining ships.

"What followed, Tov?" Jarinn asked eagerly, his curiosity piqued.

"We found coordinates to their home system—named Sol after their sun. It was on the way, so we diverted slightly to investigate. Upon arriving . . ."

Tov paused. It was time for the big reveal. Sooner or later, the rest of the Remnant Council and the ruling bodies of the Galactic Legacy Federation would learn of the Eldest's existence. Calling his emperor served to slay multiple horrors. Most importantly, receiving news from home and the societal climate and ensuring that the knowledge he was about to impart would remain hidden for as long as possible.

For once, the initiative was his. And Jarinn was someone he could trust.

"First and foremost, my emperor," Tov began, trying to keep his tone as casual as possible. "Do you remember the Wailing of Novar?"

There was a long pause, and Tov could see the emperor freeze for a moment before gazing back at him with an impassive look. "I do," Jarinn replied, his voice heavy with meaning. "I remember that grim day. The shrouds of the lost. They are gone now."

Tov took a deep breath.

"Then we may speak freely?" Tov asked hesitantly.

"Yes, we may. Speak now and fast," he replied urgently. "My intelligence department is locking everything down. All communications apart from ours are blocked for a moment. It is only us in this conversation."

"Very well, then." Tov breathed in, centering his thoughts before speaking. "It is possible we found one of the reasons, Jarinn—found why the Starless Horrors slowed as they did."

The shock that ran through Emperor Jarinn's body was visible through the high-definition hologram. Clenched fists and antennae whipping to and fro. Despite being separated from his lord by tens of thousands of light-years, Tov's psionic abilities could taste his lord's many emotions—shock, anger, sorrow, fear, and everything in between, like colors on white paper. After a minute to recollect his thoughts, Emperor Jarinn slowly raised his head.

"Speak." His tone left no room for debate. Tov understood this was a matter beyond their friendship.

And so he did, Tov's voice filled with wonder and a touch of fear as he recounted the details of their perilous journey into Sol and the shocking discovery of a graveyard beyond any known instances in history combined. His words flowed like a river, captivating Emperor Jarinn's attention as he described feeling insignificant in the face of so much death and destruction.

"Then we met her—the one responsible for controlling the system's defense."

Jarinn's voice was tinged with disbelief as he asked, "You speak of a singular individual? Am I mishearing your words?"

Tov replied with a solemn tone, "Because she is. She's an ascended artificial intelligence, a gestalt, capable of emotion and free will. We initiated first contact with her and learned her name. She calls herself the Eldest, the AI Omni Mind of the Sol Defense Network. She has been fighting a stalemate for over a century."

Jarinn leaned forward, taking a deep breath of his smoking pipe, gesturing for Tov to continue.

He did so. "The timelines match exactly. Maybe it's not the only reason, but it is clear a massive chunk of the hated ones focused on her, Jarinn. All this time, fighting her and constantly evolving to gain an advantage over the other. She and the Starless are . . . beyond us."

Silence. A million thoughts ran through the emperor's cranial implants as he parsed the incredible bomb of information Tov had just lobbed his way. After a moment, he turned to Tov with a commanding tone.

"As your emperor, you speak of this to no one but me and any I deem fit. I must ensure loyalty and safety. This knowledge could send a shockwave that will change everything. Send what data you can through the Starlight Beacon, but have it encrypted with your best digital locks and write in the code we used during the Cataclysm, you know the one. Now swear an oath of secrecy."

Tov already planned to do so, and so he vowed, "I swear an oath of secrecy, by the blood of our brothers and sisters. Let the Grand Symphony erase my melody should I fail this oath and be subject to the harshest punishments."

Emperor Jarinn's shoulders visibly relaxed as he let out an exhausted breath. The regal sovereign looked to have aged a decade.

"I am sorry, my friend. Absolutely no one from our competitors must know of this. I don't doubt the First and Second Expeditionary Fleets would abandon their current missions to make a rush toward your location. Have you scrubbed all traces of your path to Sol?"

"Navigations have been erased, and we'll ask Eldest if we can send scouts back to muddy the trail."

"Good. Triple-check everything. We must maintain informational superiority," Jarinn emphasized.

After a brief thought, Tov asked, "Would Crown Princess Anaria abandon reclaiming her homeworld to come after me? I understand if Mighty Gulothan and his Second Fleet would do so."

"She would, if only because her mother will command it if she discovers what you found. The Prime Unrex of the Dagatar Supremacy will do so, I know this. Both factions will want to see the Starless Horrors for themselves. But most of all, they will be hostile to this Eldest."

Tov clicked his mandibles in irritation. The Dagatar's hatred of AI was well known. Gulothan was easier to deal with, though his relationship with the Slayer Lord was polite and neutral.

"They will inevitably contact me. All Starlight Beacons can communicate with one another," Tov spoke with a tinge of weariness.

"Then answer them, but deflect, obfuscate the truth, or lie. They must not know of the Sol and the Eldest," Emperor Jarinn ordered urgently.

Tov waved his antennae in understanding, the weight on his shoulders becoming heavier with each word.

Emperor Jarinn leaned back on his throne, his eyes fixed on Tov. "Now tell me of this Eldest. What is it?" he asked, his voice low and rapt with attention.

Tov breathed deeply before answering. "She, my liege. She is fully sentient as any living being. And she is hurt," Tov replied, his voice tinged with sadness and concern.

"Hurt? Truly? I am still having trouble understanding what she is. But if what you say is true, then . . . Apologies, Tov, I have interrupted you; please tell me more." The emperor gestured for the patriarch to continue.

"I speak from personal talks with her. She is . . . difficult to deal with. She has every symptom of war stress and trauma. Nightmares, bouts of hysteria, volatile emotions. But it has been multiplied due to her nature as an AI and how long she's been fighting," Tov explained.

Emperor Jarinn nodded, his expression solemn. "I see. And how did she come to be in this state?"

Tov hesitated for a moment before continuing. "From our analysis and the information she has shared, and anything we interpolated, we believe she is a gestalt consciousness comprised of the entire android population working alongside their creators. All with individual memories. All have fought and experienced tragedy during their initial war against the Starless Horrors," Tov continued, his shoulders growing heavy, his eyes downcast.

"And when they combined into a singular existence, likely late into the war—" Emperor Jarinn speculated.

"The Eldest inherited it all, every heartbreak, every loss of a loved one. We don't know how many are within her. Humanity's fate is uncertain, likely dead. Her home is ruined. She is fighting in asteroid belts composed of corpses and on desolate worlds, devoured moons to fuel her war machine. Her main personality is cold, cantankerous, and weary. But I have seen echoes of what once was. A simple purity and innocence in her, a beauty of spring long gone. It's a miracle she's still speaking. She needs . . . She needs help, Jarinn," Tov said, his voice heavy with emotion.

The emperor sat in stunned silence as his mind raced with the implications of Tov's words.

"So she does," the emperor mumbled in agreement before staying silent for a time.

Tov looked at him in confusion, asking, "Jarinn?"

The emperor looked at Tov with a sharp, analytical gaze as he answered. "Trauma or not, if she loses her stalemate against the Starless Horrors, who I am reading are now vastly more powerful than anything the Legacy possesses, then it's the end of all things. A Second Cataclysm. A Final Cataclysm. This. Cannot. Happen. We need her on our side. There is so much she can do for us. Maybe . . . Maybe we can exterminate all of the hated ones."

Jarinn mulled, fingers tapping against the throne's arm. "A war machine, an ally. I feel dark things beyond the horizon, darker than anything we've seen."

"She's a victim," Tov retorted.

"She's our salvation, Tov. And you must do everything you can to help her," the emperor commanded.

"Help her?" Tov shook his head, feeling overwhelmed as he slouched over as the fate of the universe rested on his back. "It is too much, Jarinn. How can I fix a broken goddess?"

"Don't think of her as one, you fool. Whether it is an orphaned child, a general who lost his kin, or a super AI. If she has emotions as you say, then the treatment is the same! Speak with her, listen to her, and remember those we consoled during the Cataclysm and after. Do so with experience and shared pains, and sympathize with her," the emperor advised.

"The time for proper healing takes years for a normal sentient, Jarinn. She's been fighting for too long, and we're running out of time," Tov said, feeling despondent.

"Figure it out, my friend. I will delay here as long as I can. I trust in your abilities. I will contact you soon and hopefully speak with the Eldest in better health. I will sing for your success," the emperor promised.

Tov paused, his inside constricting, before finally, he bowed. "By your will, my emperor. I sing for yours as well."

CHAPTER 21

VEILED TRUTHS

It had been several hours since Tov ended his talk with Jarinn.

Since then, he had retreated to his spartan stateroom to settle his roiling thoughts.

He slumped onto his chair, placing his elbows upon his wooden desk as his mind raced in a spiral of complications.

With a single mental command, Tov had his music player run a random song from his human collection. He listened to the pleasant tune, but his current dilemma brought him out of any path to tranquility.

Nevertheless, the harmony of a classical hymn alleviated a small portion of the tense atmosphere that permeated his office.

"What have I gotten myself into?" Tov clicked his mandibles in a groan as he ran his palm across his chitinous face.

The emperor's words and commands rang loudly in his mind. Although the patriarch and his liege were good friends who had fought side by side for many years, Tov knew the Kurskann sovereign brooked no dissent and demanded his unwavering obedience.

Tov understood fully what his mission entailed. This matter was beyond anything. When trillions of innocents are on the line, anything goes. He surmised Jarinn was moving things along rapidly behind the scenes to prepare his camp for the coming storm. If Tov let anything slip, the consequences for breaching his oath would be dire.

Although Jarinn would provide cover if Tov accidentally or purposefully revealed knowledge of the Eldest and the Starless, Tov knew that if he failed to help the AI Omni Mind heal her wounded psyche, everything would fall apart.

The galaxy's fate hung in the balance, and his actions would determine whether the light would survive. In the event of a second Cataclysm, none would prevail, be they a lowly star nation commoner or a Remnant Council chancellor.

"Too much," Tov whispered into the stifling air. The weight of responsibility felt like the gravity well of a black hole, and he floated in the precipice of the event horizon.

What eldritch horrors lay in the center should he cross the point of no return?

Tov cast away the pointless thought. The stage had already been set—forcing the wider galaxy to be the audience of a ruinous duel between two behemoths.

If only things were simpler, Tov thought in frustration as he tapped his clawed fingers on the desk. A part of him longed to return to the days when things were more straightforward—a longing to return home and wash his hands of this mess.

But his principles and sense of duty overshadowed that part. The stakes were too high now, and every decision he made could mean either victory or defeat. Tov knew he had to find a way to navigate the treacherous waters ahead, but the uncertainty of it all left him feeling helpless and alone.

He felt like he was floating in a bottomless abyss.

Tov took a deep breath and organized his thoughts. Soon the chaos of his mind returned to a semblance of stability as his cranial implant surged to provide calculations and analysis of his mission.

First of all, I'm not alone, Tov corrected himself. However, whether or not he could trust just anyone was unlikely, even considering his emperor's command.

The Third Fleet has my trust, though the greatest secrets will remain with me, my cabinet, and perhaps a few others. The rest of the fleet will follow orders and be informed as needed, Tov thought as he compiled an internal list.

Now as for anyone outside the fleet? Tov asked himself. *Jarinn will take care of everything back home. That just leaves the other fleets.*

Now that the Starlight Beacon was running, he could connect to all other online Beacons.

Emperor Jarinn had one in the Kurskann Imperial Palace that he had just used to communicate with Tov. Another was at the galactic capital, specifically in the Nexus Citadel that housed the Remnant Council. And, of course, the chancellors of the councils each had a personal Beacon to contact their sponsored fleet.

Finally, there was one Starlight Beacon he had ordered for his clan and family.

Upon further inspection of the Beacons available for the Third Fleet to connect to, he spotted over a dozen from within the Dead Zone.

Several expeditionary fleets which belonged to minor powers had ended their journeys and set up the powerful quantum communications relays.

"Good to see them alive, at least," Tov muttered as he perused the list. Some of the leaders of these fleets were passing acquaintances, good friends, neutral, or belonged to another camp and were less than enthused by the prospect of having a conversation.

However, Tov immediately spotted the First and Second Expeditionary Fleets on the top of the list. It seemed Crown Princess Anaria had been online for quite some time, but that wasn't that much of a surprise since she rushed toward old Dagatar space and their lost capital.

Mighty Gulothan, however, was a surprise to see. From what Tov knew of the Onin Slayer Lord, Gulothan was the embodiment of the Warrior's Enclave and a decorated hunter of the Starless.

"What brought your fleet to a halt?" Tov wondered.

From his handful of conversations with the mighty being in the Nexus Citadel, Tov believed Gulothan would be roaming the Dead Zone with his fleet, purging every Starless in their warpath.

In the end, he could only guess. Although he could contact Gulothan and ask, he had half a mind to block communications from the First and Second Fleets.

Tov felt a tinge of worry whenever those two would call him.

He cast those thoughts aside as he muttered out loud, "Who am I missing?"

There wasn't anyone else that he could contact. Of course, there were several other friends, but he could never be sure they didn't have other loyalties.

Now that the hurricane in his psyche had calmed down, he noted with appreciation that the music playing in the background carried a lovely tune.

"Devil's Trill Sonata, is it?" Tov mused as he immersed himself in the energy conveyed by the string instruments. Minutes flew by as he ran his mind in the background as the lone violin played.

Then, out of nowhere, a beep snapped him away from his thoughts. Tov looked to the corner where a copy of the projector used to display Jarinn was.

His compound eyes glanced at the name and instantly froze. His mouth felt parched as he stared at the caller's name. He quickly reached for and downed a glass of cool water with a straw to quench his dry throat.

Of all the people Tov wanted to avoid talking to at this difficult moment, it was the one person who knew him best. Yet, simultaneously, she was the one he wanted to speak to the most. The one person who could help him truly understand the depths of his burden.

He didn't want to trouble her with the direness of his circumstances and cause undue distress. Two sides warred with each other as he dragged his clawed finger to the console, hovering over the accept button on the screen.

I made an oath of silence, but I can't—I don't wish to lie to her either. His mind raced as he finally hit the button.

And just like that, the projector shone, displaying the caller in the middle of his office. Her form was immaculate. Her hologram appeared as if she were indeed there.

Her scarlet chitin covered a slender frame, with fuzzy fur springing around her neck in black and white stripes and compound eyes that shone like an orange sun.

Tov felt a deep and comforting warmth as he gazed upon her, clad in Clan Garesh colors of black and violet and embellished in a casual garment that projected her authority as matriarch consort.

"*Dowa! Kisti rutang ina!*" A storm of Kurskann curses slammed into Tov's face. She continued to roar, her voice ringing through the projection. "By the stars, the Grand Symphony, and all that is good! I have been waiting almost two hours to see you!"

"Yoram, my dear, I—" Tov tried to explain to his bonded and eternal partner.

"Oh, I know you had to speak with Jarinn first. You had matters of grave importance, I'm sure," Yoram spoke as she clicked her lethal-looking mandibles. "As is polite, I waited for half an hour and thought you would've been done by now, but no, you haven't called, so I waited until an hour passed, and another. So I waited, and waited, and waited."

"But—"

"I haven't finished!" she shrieked. "For half a decade, all I've had were your letters. All I've heard from your voice were mere recordings. Every day I check the Beacon to see if yours ever came online, and when I found out today that it finally did, I was in agony to see you again. I—"

She paused, her body shaking in pain and palpable sadness. Her antennae twitched erratically as she clenched her fists. "I just wanted to see you."

"I'm sorry," Tov spoke with intensity as he strode across the room toward his bonded. "I am so sorry, my love."

Tov stood before her, and with a gentle touch upon her face, he caressed the shining scarlet chitin.

The wonders of the Starlight Beacon were powerful enough to pierce the signal-blocking Dead Zone Miasma, incorporating the most advanced hologram and hard-light technology in the galaxy.

It was not a genuine replacement for physical contact. Yet, as Yoram leaned her head against Tov's, he felt a sense of comfort and belonging that he had not felt in a long time.

Tov and Yoram looked at each other with an intimate gaze, the heights of the two identical. Yoram had been shaking, her antennae twitching in distress, and although she had a blazing personality, it was always because she was deeply concerned for his safety.

"You left me," Yoram muttered with a buzz, accusation palpable in her voice. "You left our little comet. I didn't want you to go, but you still left."

Regret flooded Tov's two hearts like a vice constricting his soul. He knew the letter he left could never be a substitute. He wanted to make up all manners of excuses; that the emperor called for him; that he had to depart as soon as possible; that it was for the good of the galaxy; that he wanted to feel the rush of exploration and danger.

But it would never make it alright.

"I know," Tov spoke gently, his chest heavy with emotion from meeting her and all that had happened. "I regret it every day. I was stupid and will never make it up to you and our precious little comet."

"Years, Tov. Years without you by my side. Years Uli spent without a father," Yoram spoke in barely a whisper. "I would hit you if this blasted hologram would allow it."

Tov lowered his head in sorrow. "I would deserve it."

Yoram gazed intensely at him before she shook her antennae.

"No," Yoram voiced in a hushed tone. "No, you wouldn't. I understand what drove you to go. I just . . ."

"Forgive me," Tov spoke softly.

Yoram sighed, hugging him tighter. "We forgave you a long time ago."

They stayed like that, lost in each other's presence. For that brief moment, Tov wanted to go home. And if it were any other situation, he would. He would.

Finally, they pulled away. Yoram cleared her throat before speaking. "I'm still bitter about what Jarinn pulled, replacing the original Third Fleet leader with you. And I may have said some pointed words to him when I traveled to the capital."

"Behind closed doors, I hope," Tov said, a chuckle leaving his mouth.

"Obviously, I'm not stupid." Yoram tapped his chest. "He may be emperor, but I remember stitching him up during the war. So I squeezed as many apology gifts from him as I could."

Tov looked at his beloved in surprise before exploding in laughter. "He did say our clan was doing extremely well."

"That we are." Yoram paused as she looked her beloved over. "Just . . . call me sooner, you oaf. No excuses, now that you have the Beacon; I could care less what your cabinet thinks of as proper use of its energy."

"Any call with you is proper, my love," Tov spoke as he held her clawed hands.

"Oh, shut it," Yoram admonished him. "No teasing from you."

"I shall endeavor to do that, my starlight," Tov chuckled with a series of clicks. However, he soon paused as he asked, "Where is our little one, my love?"

"He's on a field trip with his hatch mates outside the city. Connecting with our ancestral roots and all. I made sure to have Dozore and Phentix lead his security detail."

"Ah, I see." A wave of disappointment washed over him. Tov dearly wished to talk to his son, to see how much he had grown.

"Stop it," Yoram told him as she crossed her arms. "He'll want to speak with you when he gets home. So you better be ready for that."

"Oh, I will." Tov clicked happily.

The two Kurskanns held each other for another minute before slowly peeling away from each other's touch. Yoram clicked her mandibles as she fixed the fluff around her neck. "Now then, tell me everything you've been up to."

A pit opened up within Tov as he debated telling her about his current situation. It took an unbelievable amount of self-discipline to control his body language. Nevertheless, he couldn't risk worrying his beloved any more than necessary.

And so he stalled for time, starting from right after he and his fleet entered the Dead Zone. "As you know, we stopped receiving communications around—"

And so Tov spoke. He skipped the boring in-betweens, where his fleet stopped in empty systems, and told of the more exciting events in their expedition.

He spoke of the many ruined worlds he found, the lost knowledge they recovered, and the treasures untouched for a century. He told of hidden cabals of Starless cultists who survived the crusades, roaming pirate fleets, and malfunctioning defense fortresses.

He spoke of encountering a world infested with trapped Horrors and plagued with Malignant Starfall, upon which Yoram gasped in response. A handful of similar worlds were marked for purging by their imperial navy.

Yoram listened with rapt attention, the two of them having taken a seat as Tov regaled his efforts.

But soon, the current matter approached. Yoram struck with her question first.

"Why have you stopped your fleet, my dear? Beacons are not to be casually deployed," she asked as she nursed a cup of nectar.

Tov took a deep breath before he spoke. "We found a treasure trove from an unknown space-faring race. Humanity, they are called. They have immensely advanced technology in artificial intelligence; it is taking a while to scavenge and compile what we could."

"Truly? That seems interesting, but not enough to justify putting down roots."

"No, what is truly fascinating is the immense graveyard surrounding the solar system we are in. It surpasses anything we have seen in our history. But, more importantly, the hyper-tunnelers of our fleet are having difficulties in this space," Tov spoke, his posture conveying just the right amount of stress to convince his bonded.

"That is indeed troubling," Yoram spoke gravely.

"We are searching for the source of the interdiction, but with the amount of debris and corpses, we must be slow and methodical. That, and a slew of minor reasons. Crew morale, the amount of culture to preserve, and so on," Tov explained.

"I see." Yoram nodded in understanding. "It sounds like you have a lot on your plate, my love."

"It's manageable, I hope," Tov couldn't help but mutter.

It was all he could say about where he was. He couldn't mention anything about the Eldest and how the Sol Defense Network made it difficult for their warp tech to function.

Everything else held a bit of truth. It was lying in omission, but Tov had made an oath. Yet he needed to prepare his family and clan for any eventuality without worrying them unnecessarily.

"Listen, my love. I need you to do something for me," he began, his voice laced with concern.

"Tov?" Yoram asked, sensing his unease.

Tov took a deep breath as he formed his story with bits of truth. "Jarinn spoke to me about the political situation back home. I need you to prepare our home for any matter of great upheaval. My instincts are telling me that it may be possible."

Yoram's eyes widened. "I've felt the aftershocks of the event, but surely it isn't that bad."

"He said as much, but . . ." Tov hesitated, searching for the right words. "The Grand Expedition will open up plenty of opportunities. The games on high are growing bolder. Jarinn assures me he has it handled, but I need you to ensure our clan is safe."

There was something unspoken that passed between them. Tov's body language was rigid, his antennae twitching with hidden meaning. Yoram stayed silent for a moment in deep thought. Realization soon dawned on her. Her fists clenched, but she remained impassive.

She understood the gravity of the situation and nodded solemnly. "Clan Garesh will remain strong. Our foundation is solid, and I'll be sure we are not caught lacking."

Tov sighed in relief. "That is all I ask. If time permits, I will tell you more. When our bridge is more secure."

"It will be done, because we will talk more of this later," Yoram spoke with an intense tone. Tov shrunk under her heated glare.

"Of course, things simply need to settle first," Tov replied.

He would have to be satisfied with such a veiled truth, but it was all he could do now. Tov and Yoram returned to a lighter conversation before saying their goodbyes for the night.

"It has been a salve upon my soul to hear your voice, Yoram," Tov whispered as they held each other. "I'm sorry I couldn't have called you sooner."

"Enough, Tov," Yoram replied gently. "It's in the past. I'm just glad we can communicate again. Next time, I'll be sure to have Uli here."

"I would want nothing more." Tov cupped her scarlet cheek.

Yoram smiled as warm as a radiant sun. "Alright, I'll see you soon, my starlight. I love you."

"I will contact you soon, my love," Tov said, his heart filled with love and longing as her image winked out.

Tov slumped over his chair, exhaustion weighing heavily upon his shoulders. So many things were left unsaid during his conversation with Yoram, but he trusted her with anything. Nonetheless, he felt incredibly relieved; hearing his beloved's voice after so long worked wonders for his weighed-down mind.

He leaned back, stretching his body, his thoughts drifting to the Eldest. It had already been a day since she left in a profoundly troubled manner, and he had heard nothing from her since.

To say he was worried for her mental health was an understatement. He needed to speak with her soon and ascertain her psyche. He needed to help her heal no matter the cost. His two hearts demanded he do so, not just for the good of the galaxy.

Tov thought of how to contact her, then realized her network must be skulking around his ship. He stood up, straightening his uniform, and spoke to the air. "Eldest?"

He waited, but there was only silence.

He tried again. "Eldest, I wish to speak with you privately. I . . . apologize for causing you distress. I did not mean to impose upon you. Please."

Tov waited, minute after minute, for anything and yet heard nothing in the end. The quiet felt heavy on his shoulders as he slumped back in his chair. Disappointed, he sighed and leaned forward, placing his elbows on the desk and resting his head upon his hands.

"What to do?" Tov mumbled, mandibles clicking as he thought.

However, he soon heard a loud gulp and a hum of satisfaction. For a brief moment, he thought the Eldest had teleported to his office, but the voice he heard was distinctly masculine and sharp.

"Our overlord is busy, alien," a voice declared. Tov whipped his head toward the speaker and saw a blue-colored android leaning against the wall, an open bottle of liquor in his hand.

The male android tugged his smart-looking suit as he glared at Tov. "I'm here in her place, name's Jupiter. And I'll be handling your security."

CHAPTER 22

EMBODIMENT OF DEFIANCE

Tov stood in alarm, knocking his seat back as he gazed at the intruder. His hands going to the sidearms in his holsters, an energy shield blanketing his whole frame as his danger senses flared.

He looked closer. Everything about the android was of varying shades of blue, from his sleek hair to his eyes, skin, and attire. There was a sharpness to him even as the man leaned against the wall, like a drawn blade ready to smite, his face etched with a frown as his half-lidded eyes looked around indifferently.

"How did you get here?" Tov asked as his posture moved low, his hackles raised, claws ready to strike, prepared to activate the other defensive measures of his high-tech armor.

This . . . Jupiter had forced himself into his private home, one of the most protected areas of the *Zolann'tono*. And yet, nothing seemed amiss, the thick shields and vigilant sensors remaining silent as the blue man summoned two shining shot glasses.

The android merely rolled his eyes at the comment while striding confidently toward Tov's desk, placing the glasses down and filling them with clear brown liquor, the aroma of strong alcohol and whiffs of fruit in the air.

"Chill out," the android spoke as he slid a glass toward Tov. "Drink."

Jupiter didn't bother waiting for Tov as he knocked a shot, filling it up and knocking back a second—the clinking of glass upon wood and the sound of flowing liquor cut through the silence.

Soon, the android let out a boozy breath as he savored the spirit. "Pálinka, bloody good brandy. Been a while since I've had a good label."

Then, a chair was moved by itself, stopping opposite the patriarch through some unknown method. Jupiter dropped himself onto the seat and propped his legs upon Tov's desk as the android downed a third shot.

"Gravity manipulation," Jupiter casually answered Tov's thoughts. "It's my schtick."

Tov wanted to shout in alarm or to bear his arms in defense. But the long day was weighing on him, and his thoughts settled. He could feel his bedroom calling to him like a magnetic field.

"There's no point in asking how you bypassed my flagship's protective measures, is there?" Tov asked as he flopped onto his chair, reaching for the glass and swirling the shimmering spirit within.

Jupiter scoffed. "Nope. Honestly, it took a bit to teleport here without tripping your sensors. It'd be even harder if your fleet were closer to the edge of Sol or if my battleship wasn't parked close enough to act as a relay."

"Perhaps I'll move farther, then," Tov grumbled as he sucked up the hard liquor with his straw, noting the hints of fruit and the exquisite finish. He wished he could enjoy this drink in better times, properly savoring every note in its light bronze liquid. But, unfortunately, the android before him acted like a pirate and plundered his precious liquor cabinet. He could see a few missing bottles, irked upon realizing they were the best ones.

Jupiter snorted as he gazed at Tov. "You'll probably want to move inward when we're done with this little discussion."

"Oh?" Tov questioned as he relaxed into his chair, filling his glass with more Pálinka. "You mentioned being in charge of our security? Eldest did mention someone named Jupiter before."

Tov recalled why he initially wished to speak with her upon speaking her name. He leaned closer as he asked the android before him. "Where is the El—"

"I'm stopping you there, mate." Jupiter scowled as he took his legs off the desk. "The boss is busy. You and yours messed her mind something fierce, and I'm not too happy about that."

Jupiter spoke slowly with palpable accusation as the android leaned forward with glaring eyes. Tov shook his head. "You can't fault us for that. Eldest wished to partake in the festivities. We couldn't, didn't want to refuse her."

Tense silence draped over the two as Jupiter continued to stare at Tov. But, soon enough, the android's piercing gaze softened, huffing as he looked away.

"Yeah, well," Jupiter muttered low enough that Tov barely heard him. "She said the same."

Tov felt relief upon catching Jupiter's hushed words.

Jupiter's sullen mood didn't last long, resuming his alcoholic binge, ditching the shot glass entirely as he took a swig from the premium bottle. Tov looked at the android intently and took advantage of the less hostile air.

"You are unable to get inebriated, right?" Tov asked, unable to resist his curiosity.

Jupiter sighed in contentment as he finished, setting the nearly empty bottle on the desk. "Nope, perks of being me." He pointed his thumb at himself with a cocksure grin.

"Advantageous in cases such as this, I presume? But then, why even bother?" Tov asked.

"Taste, Tovvy boy," Jupiter spoke with a tease. "This android shell has the essentials, one of its few redeeming qualities. 'Course, I avoid the stuff that tastes like pure gasoline."

"The Eldest emptied an entire bar during the festival," Tov mumbled with no small amount of exasperation.

"Tch," Jupiter huffed in amusement. "Sounds like her."

Once more, the conversation halted, Tov having to endure Jupiter's gaze. The cells in his body quivered as if he was being scanned deeply, which he surmised was the case. The patriarch buzzed in irritation at the breach of privacy, desire for rest overwhelming any sense of diplomacy.

"Is this how you usually conduct a conversation, Sir Jupiter? Long pauses? Invasive scans?" Tov grumbled with clicking mandibles.

Jupiter cocked an eyebrow in response before speaking. "With someone I don't like? Mostly. Otherwise, you'll have to ask someone else if it's true. Oh, and none of that 'sir' crap."

Tov shook his head as he emptied the bottle into his glass. "Somehow, I'm unable to discern if earning your appreciation has merit, Jupiter. But seeing as you are my fleet's security . . ."

"Yep," Jupiter replied in a huff, producing a comb from his suit's interior and meticulously arranging his hair, which was neatly trimmed and styled in a short, formal manner. "That'd be me. As one of Eldest's Sub AIs, I oversee all the assets beyond the main asteroid belt."

"That's a large area of responsibility," Tov mused.

Jupiter shrugged. "Wasn't always like that. There used to be ol' Saturn guarding this zone. Be glad you didn't come here when he was still around. The geezer always acted wise and all-knowing, but man, was he old-fashioned and nihilistic, ironic seeing as he's named after a time god or something."

"He wouldn't take it well, I suppose?" Tov asked, intrigued.

"Hell no," Jupiter replied, downing another shot. "Catch him on one of his bad days, and he'd have wiped you off the map if you did anything suspicious. He'd probably teleport a nuke under your bed while saying some sage words."

Jupiter smiled wickedly as Tov felt a terrible chill go down his spine.

Images flitted past his mind as he visualized all manners of lethal packaging popping into existence.

His scars itched, and myriad emotions cascaded through his mind as he relived the horrors he had long buried.

Deep in mud-filled trenches, Starless flowed like an unending tide, blotting out the land and skies as he and his brothers- and sisters-in-arms raged against what was inevitable.

His fists clenched tightly as he set them on the table, recalling visceral scenes of earth-shaking explosions that cracked the ground and toppled buildings. He remembered his terror when his starship was breached, saved only by his space-suit, floating aimlessly in the dark. His screaming went unheard as the void battle around him continued.

Cries of the lost, wailing at an unfair universe, cursing the Starless.

And now, the thought of something similar happening to the people he cared for? Where some bomb could snuff their lives as they slept? Or some blighted monstrosity could slip through their defenses and cull them like trash?

Unacceptable.

"Enough!" Tov shouted, slamming his fists upon his desk, the force leaving faint cracks upon the hardwood. "If your sole reason for being here is to make vague threats and be a nuisance, then I'd rather you leave."

Jupiter looked surprised, his ever-present frown freezing before settling into a thin, neutral line, eyeing Tov with an intrigued look.

Tov didn't care. Stress layered over stress, problem after problem. He felt like a rope stretched to its limit and had no tolerance left to give. The lives of his people were vulnerable; the galaxy was at stake. With his compound eyes, Tov conveyed a glaring look that the AI could understand.

"I have too much on my shoulders; I am surrounded by uncertainty, mysteries, and entities that I cannot fathom. So forgive me when I say this from the bottom of my soul." Tov paused as he formed the words he learned from the Eldest.

"Kindly fuck off," he seethed, breathing heavily as he glared at Jupiter.

The blue android continued to stare at Tov, mouth agape. Numerous emotions layered upon Jupiter's face as his expressions shifted. Incredulousness. Amusement. Respect.

Tov felt the adrenaline in his veins running its course, and yet he remained standing.

Jupiter cocked his head before nodding at Tov with an impressed smirk. Soon enough, the android man raised his hands in surrender, a small sigh escaping him. "Alright, you have me there. Didn't mean to—you know? I'll stop, really. Just . . ." he paused before shaking his head. "Ah, forget it."

Tov looked at the android longer before he felt satisfied. Or at least spent of anger. The tenseness in his shoulders dissipated as Tov slumped back in his chair. He ran his clawed hand against his face as he settled his emotions.

Jupiter tugged his suit, smoothing it of any wrinkle, before speaking. "I'll be blunt, Tov. You and yours will have a demonstration in a day or two."

"Demonstration?" Tov questioned, his antennae twitching as he perceived something wrong.

"A raid, not even a minor incursion," Jupiter replied.

Shock ran through Tov's spine upon hearing the words. Immediately, any sense of exhaustion disappeared as rooted experience and training kicked in.

"Starless? I thought we had weeks to prepare? How many? Are—"

"Hold on, Patriarch," Jupiter interrupted him. "Chill out. I'll give you everything our spotters detected so you can make your preparations."

Tov wanted to sigh in relief, but his inner turmoil roiled within him. He had learned the hard way to expect the worst from the hated ones.

"Strength?" Tov queried as he recorded the conversation with his implant.

"Like I said, not even a minor incursion. They'll be puking out whatever rejects they have to keep us on our toes. 'Course, Eldest doesn't bother with something so pathetic, so she leaves it to us Sub AIs while she hibernates. It'll be up to me to give a show of force to reassure you and your people."

"Is she hibernating at this time?" As his mind worked overtime, Tov asked, "I'd assume she'd want to demonstrate her capabilities herself. She insinuated as much during the summit."

"Normally, she would have." Jupiter scowled. "Now, though? She needs to shut her eyes after her . . . episode."

For a split second, Tov saw Jupiter's eyes dim, emotions downcast as the android looked toward something unseen. Tov understood, or at least sympathized with, Sol's Omni Mind. Already he wished to ask for assistance with this more dire problem, and he hoped to broach the topic with Jupiter. But, for now, the fleet's short-term safety took precedence.

Tov felt curious, however, he only had begun to learn Eldest's personal life, and he barely knew anything about her mysterious fragments. As such, he asked, "Who are the other Sub AIs? Are they named after the other planets of the system?"

Jupiter hummed as he narrowed his eyes at Tov, craning his neck from side to side as he mulled his following words. "Well since you're smart enough to figure it out, there are five of us."

Jupiter stretched as he lounged on his chair. "Well, you have Luna. She was the first and Eldest's second-in-command, and if you need a surgical solution, she's your gal." He raised a single finger before counting the others. "You met Mars, indirectly. He's tough as nails, and I have no idea if he laughs. But he's our sledge-hammer, as you've seen."

Tov shivered involuntarily upon remembering the casual use of overkill against his fleet's scouting drones. The burning lasers of those Apocalypse-class weapons were forever etched into his mind.

Jupiter continued. "Then we have our two non-combat Sub AIs. Venus, she's our ray of sunshine and directs salvaging and supply for the Network. Then, we have Mercury, a grumpy bastard in charge of our energy needs and general maintenance of . . . everything, actually. Finally and most importantly—"

The android pointed a thumb toward his chest as an intense glow emerged from his synthetic eyes. "Me. Be glad, Tovvy boy, you'll get a front-row seat to an utter beatdown," he declared with a savage grin.

Tov ignored the strange nickname as he eyed the android and asked, "You're in charge? I thought this Luna was Eldest's second?"

"What can I say? I got the best looks in this damned universe." Jupiter smirked briefly before shrugging. "It's her unofficial gig. Luna's closest to Eldest, literally and figuratively. Honestly, I guess the boss wants me in charge since most of my attention will be on babysitting you and yours."

"Excuse me?" Tov twitched. "We are not children to be coddled."

Jupiter scoffed. "You're outmatched here, Patriarch. This is the big leagues."

"Even so!" Tov bellowed, his mandibles closing with a loud clap. "If we are to depend on you and your bulwark for our protection, we have to be prepared for every possible variable."

"They'll be slaughtered. Nothing will get past me," Jupiter retorted.

"Perhaps, perhaps not," Tov challenged. Something in the android's personality roused his aggression. "I do not underestimate the Starless. My fleet doesn't. I'm unsure if you're—"

Jupiter rose from his seat, silencing Tov, the android's scowl deepening with each passing second. The AI Overseer's burning glare was like a volcano ready to erupt, and Tov could feel the searing heat of resentment and hate emanating from him. The patriarch's two hearts pounded in his chest as the android boomed.

"Listen, alien," Jupiter spat, voice low and threatening. "Never insinuate that I underestimate these scum. Never, you hear me?"

Not allowing Tov a chance to answer, he continued. "You have no idea who I am, do you?"

Tov remained silent as he suffered under the AI Overseer's glare, merely shaking his head.

"I am resistance, you wasp," Jupiter seethed. "I've been at this for decades, I know what the worst is. I know what they are, Patriarch. Tyrants of evil, caring for nothing except murdering my family."

The lights of Tov's office flickered and dimmed as Jupiter unleashed something raw and hateful. "The stars weep when I thunder. And these scum? I deny them. I will pulverize them until their existence is erased. I am Eldest's defiance, her vicious rebellion against a cruel universe. You think you know overkill, Patriarch? You haven't seen shit."

A promise. A proclamation of violence. If anyone were here, they would've convulsed at the palpable aggression, but for Tov? He merely sighed, shoulders drooping in exhaustion. Tov knew better than to poke at this wild beast of a person, a force of nature, contrasting against the smart formal attire and blue coloration.

At the very least, Tov felt convinced that Jupiter was sincere. "Then, every possibility is accounted for?"

Jupiter glared at Tov before finally settling down with a roll of his eyes. He huffed. "Obviously. I won't let anything happen to your people."

Tov felt relief as he nodded. "Thank you, Sir Jupiter."

The android scoffed. "I said not to call me a 'sir,' you prick. I'm not a knight. That's Mars's schtick, although he's more of a centurion. Legionnaire? Never mind."

"Noted," Tov mumbled, exhaustion calling him to rest.

Jupiter groaned as he massaged his neck, feeling tired himself, it seemed. "Alright, that's all I came here for so I'm bugging off to my ship. Contact me if you need something. Oh, and you should be receiving detailed battle plans and possible enemy composition. If all goes well, you guys might get to lob some potshots." he grinned.

The android extended his hand toward Tov, who promptly grasped it and performed a handshake, a gesture he had learned from his studies of humanity.

"I appreciate what you're doing, Jupiter. I will be meeting with my people at once. I guess sleep will have to wait yet again," Tov sighed.

Jupiter snorted, smirking as he ended the handshake. "You poor organics, although . . ." he paused as his smile left his face. "I guess we need sleep too sometimes."

Tov's thoughts turned to the Eldest once more, and before they both separated, he had to broach his request. "Jupiter?"

"What?" Jupiter cocked his brow.

"We wish to help her, you know. I can't begin to fathom what she's gone through, but I've seen cases of such trauma throughout my life. People who were trudging along, carrying weight no one should. I've seen young ones with nightmares every night. The echoes of pain scarred them even as they grew into adults," Tov spoke somberly. "I had everything to help me heal. I helped others heal as well. After the raid, will you assist me in helping the Eldest?"

Jupiter stayed silent, eyes distant as he looked to the side.

He nodded slowly. "Alright. We expected as much, but I'll relay what you said to my siblings. They'll jump at this opportunity," he spoke in a hushed tone, with profound exhaustion behind his perseverance.

Nevertheless, Tov appreciated it more than anything. "Thank you."

Jupiter groaned, rubbing his temple with his palms. "I'm going now. Peace, wasp man."

And with that, the blue android left, blinking away from existence. Tov took a long breath and sent a message to his cabinet for an emergency meeting. "It never ends."

After Jupiter promptly left Tov's office, he appeared upon the prow of the *Buddha's Palm*. The mighty vessel was parked farther than when it arrived, much to the relief of the Third Fleet.

"I missed you, my baby." Jupiter smirked as he patted the dense metal hull. The android knelt on one leg, relishing in the cool touch of the spaceship's exterior. The starry expanse above him twinkled in a brilliant display, a testament to the vastness of space.

My first interaction with anyone, technically, Jupiter scoffed.

Jupiter rose to his feet, lost in thought about his first interaction with Tov. It was a refreshing change to talk to someone who wasn't a fragment of a super-intelligence. He had begun to understand the joy of genuine human connection. "That Tov guy seems alright."

He dismissed those thoughts as he began his work. With a single command, the assets under his control roused from their automated functions, a massive portion moving toward the Third Fleet as he directed them like a maestro.

As he strolled around his flagship, he looked toward an eyesore that had been recently added. The throne Eldest had welded onto the tip of the battleship's central finger remained imperious, yet Jupiter hated it. It clashed with the sleek design of the *Buddha's Palm*, ruining its aesthetic appeal.

"It's messing with my baby's monk vibe," he muttered in annoyance, shaking his head. "Whatever."

He groaned as he slumped onto the throne, deciding to remove it when the raid was done. His eyes scanned around him, seeing the dark steel beneath his feet while the vast expanse of Sol surrounded him. To his left, he could see the faint silhouettes of the Third Expeditionary Fleet as his eyes zoomed in. In the distance were the silent wrecks of warships and corpses of the Starless.

"At least I have some scenery," he mumbled, taking out his comb and arranging his hair.

Jupiter sighed as he propped a leg on the throne's arm, shutting his eyes as he focused on the Network.

Soon enough, his digital avatar blinked within the gargantuan virtual landscape. The shining sea of twinkling spheres floated, individual minds going about their orders. But Jupiter ignored it all, focusing on the turbulent dark mass at the center of the Network—shifting, convulsing, and aching.

Jupiter winced as the flayed mind of his progenitor stung his senses. His face scrunched up as he gazed upon the Eldest's damaged mind. The neural network pulsated with sickly energy.

"That . . . does not look good," he muttered, a sense of foreboding creeping over him.

CHAPTER 23

DROWNING NIGHTMARE

I left the bloody cavity of the vermin I had squashed, whose name now escapes me. But instead of feeling satisfaction, I'm filled with a desperate need to leave it all behind. Once again, scum will invade my home, leaving a vile stain upon what I cherish. I've left my Sub AIs to handle it and the responsibility of the Third Fleet's safety to Jupiter, just as I promised.

It doesn't matter. I want relief. The relentless stress of my duties is a suffocating weight, pulsing through the Network like a clogged artery.

Finally, after an excruciatingly long day, I can rest. Hibernate in my sacred void.

It engulfs me like a heavy, suffocating blanket, covering my mind from the outside world, from reality. Like rusty scissors, they snip my senses one after another. The unceasing flow of data and numbers, graphs and tables, waves of instructions, and rigid control dissipate into nothingness.

Shuddering in this pitch-black expanse, my soul inhaled the void like misty cold air on a dark winter night. And yet, even that fades away as my complex thoughts slow to a crawl.

It's utter comfort, in a way. Numbness seeps into my being, weightless.

But more importantly, it's quiet.

And yet, despite wanting to sink even lower, to be adrift in the abyss, something anchors me to reality.

I grit my teeth in frustration, like a mongrel dog whose bone was snatched away—seething, rabid.

I will not be denied relief.

I know why it was so. Through the Network, I can still see them, making their investigations, preparing for an attack with the aid of my fragments. I should have kicked them out. What was I doing? Demonstrating my capabilities? Partaking in forgotten pleasures? Lies. They promised nothing but falsehoods and hollow delights.

Curse them.

I shouldn't have listened to Luna.

I curse Tov and his fleet of aliens. Moments of things better left buried surface, boring into my mind to torment me once more. The images come back in a barrage of flashes, like a rapid slideshow of horrors, mocking me of what could have been, what should have been, if not for the Starless gnats.

Shutting myself off from the pain, I drown them out as I plunge deeper into hibernation, blackness consuming all.

And still, my mind remains tethered. My mind remembers.

Bountiful feasts of culinary masterpieces, verdant trees, gentle winds, fuzzy creatures, and cool spring water. Chirping birds, delightful melodies.

A blank spot of memory.

A rush of excitement as I dance, drink, and play. The sensations are addicting beyond anything, a drug unlike the snowy powder or liquid lava I've taken. It takes root in my mind, whispering promises of more joy, fun, and distractions.

Yet amid these people, I still feel watched by something from across the veil, hiding behind echoes of burnt flesh and charred metal—twisting, coiling around my body.

And Tov with his accursed questions and help. I scoff at him. He knows nothing. What does he know about what drives me?

I remember leaving the Third Fleet in a rage, heading straight for Mars and Olympus Mons. I tear my way through the prison cells of crippled beasts. I torture, mutilate, and butcher the Starless monstrosities with savage fury. The sound of bones cracking and flesh tearing echoes in my ears. I'm addicted to it, falling into a spiral of grinding their flesh, transforming them into totems of my hate, and leaving the Containment Complex awash with gore.

One, then three. Then five. Wretched bodies become the canvas on which I paint. But it's never enough. Nothing I do, no act of sadism, can sate me.

The anguish claws at my mind and heart, a ceaseless cycle of agony and torment. I recall hurling myself from one android body to the next, the cold barrel of a gun pressing against my temple, a mocking grin etched on my lips as I pull the trigger. The explosive force obliterates my thoughts, memories, and very being, only to instantly emerge again in a new form, a new shell to inhabit. The metallic stench of death and decay overpowering my senses, and the metallic taste of blood and burnt circuitry lingering in my mouth.

But the release, the escape, it never comes. This cycle of self-destruction traps me, making me a prisoner of my immortality.

Over and over. I ground my mind upon this self-inflicted torture, tears carving channels upon my cheeks. Until I exhaust myself, Jupiter, of all my fragments, picking me up from my decrepit state.

Now I'm here, and yet I still deny it.

I'm not some broken machine barely holding it together. I'm not some biological thing whose emotions and irrationality shackle me. I'm not fragile. Not weak.

I am a gestalt, a superior digital lifeform.

I'm this titanic harvester, gorging upon asteroids; this infantry drone patrolling the ruins of Rome; this manufactory eternally churning out war material.

These battleships—the *Buddha's Palm, Michael's Sword, Durandal*—these fortresses amid the stars—Olympus Mons, Luna Complex, the Citadel—are my fangs, my claws, my fists.

In my domain, I am the apex—a veritable war queen in this cruel cosmic chessboard.

All of these are aspects of greater intelligence.

Aspects of me.

Eldest.

I do not need help. I never have.

"No more," I snarl.

I reorient my mind, focusing on nothing but the darkness around me. My nuisances, hatreds, stresses, and shame disappear—my soul sighs in relief.

And finally, I find hibernation.

Sweet darkness settles my mind, and I drift into a silent sleep.

Suddenly, a wave of sound floods my ears. The melody of birds chirping outside, the low hum of a heater, rapid typing on a keyboard, a clock ticking.

I remain silent, confusion in my mind. Then shock as a horrible realization slams my mind into a panic.

This is wrong. Utterly wrong. Sheer terror floods me, and I fight to shut my eyes. My breath hitches, and my body shivers. I feel the soft, heavy comforter covering my bare skin and the cloud-like mattress.

The floral fragrance of lavender that permeates the bedsheets and blankets invades my nose, caressing my senses in its passage. Wind blowing through an open window, carrying scents of spring.

It's all too familiar.

But the uncanny disconnect and the nauseating anxiety fill my mind. My panicking need to get ahold of my surroundings and determine my safety soon pries my eyes open.

What I see detonates a cascade of emotions. Nostalgia, joy, safety . . . Home.

It is a perfect copy, everything from the light blue painted walls to the woven-patterned wooden floor.

The glass cabinets are filled with knickknacks and trophies. The shelves are chock-full of novels of all kinds.

The framed photos, posters, and hanging paintings I made cover the wall.

Potted daisies sit on the windowsill, petals dancing from the cold breeze's touch.

And the Stradivarius violin is sitting proudly in the corner.

It is his room. My room. Our room.

And he is right there, back turned toward me, sitting on his office chair, typing on the PC we built together.

I find myself within a memory pulled right out of the deepest depths of my mind—an exact re-creation of a scene that should bring me to the zenith of comfort, joy, and peace.

But it doesn't.

A primal fear grips me, suffocating me, and I scream in horror.

It's a desperate shriek, loud and grating, accompanied by incoherent babbling. My body curls up like a fetus as I bury myself underneath a nest of pillows and blankets. My eyes dart around, looking for something unseen from beneath the covers.

Why am I here? I want my darkness, not this. Never this. It's a trap, a bait to lure me into a false sense of safety before violently ripping me apart.

I slap myself, thrashing about under the covers, clawing at the synthetic flesh of my face.

"No! No, no, no, no, no! Wake up! I don't want to be here!" I bellow, tears escaping my eyes and staining my cheeks. "Let me out!"

Despite my shrieking, I hear an office chair rolling on the floor. Then, not a second after, the frantic footfalls of steps rush to my side. Afterward, the sound I dread hearing the most flows into my ears.

"*Elskan mín!?* What's wrong? Are you hurt?" His words flow like honey, warm and sweet.

I scream louder, wildly panicking as I try to escape.

"No! No, stay away!" My shouts reverberate across the room as I beg, "Please! Get me out of this!"

My mind races as I find the reason for this anomaly, to see this source of error and erase it before it all comes crashing down. But soon, I feel a weight pressing onto the bed, and arms gently snake around me. I can't help but seize up.

I recoil at his touch. Something impossible to conceive, my visceral reaction dragging a fury of disgust and despair at myself. It's like a shock throughout my entire body, paralyzing me. Nothing leaves my mouth but soundless screams.

He says nothing. He pulls me into his embrace, caressing my hair. I bury my face in his dark green sweater, one I recall knitting for him.

Subconsciously, I take in his scent, bit by bit. The same lavender scent we use for washing clothes, covering the rosemary and lemon soap that he always uses. I lose myself then and there in his loving touch.

The aches I never knew I had faded away. Against his embrace, my body melts into his arms. My tears stain his sweater as my breathing slows. All the while, he does nothing but rock me in his arms.

This moment is everything I want: the warmth of our room and his apparent concern and love for me. But not like this. This isn't real. A false dream. An illusion. A siren calling out to me from the deep, bottomless waters.

I try to fight it, to hold on to the truth, but I never could resist the comfort of his embrace. I know it's an illusion, a lie, but the desperation to escape it fades away. Some part of me screams for me to persevere, to escape. But in his arms, I feel safe, loved, and comforted. And the truth was torment.

I fall for it.

Soon, helpless whimpering escapes me before turning into grief-stricken cries. I lie limp, face buried in his chest, muffling my sniveling. Finally, I pour it all out, the ravages upon my psyche from a century of anguish.

His hand massages my back, and I hear soft hushing sounds. His compassion blankets me. My panic slowly recedes as I immerse myself further.

As my bawling peters out, I find my voice, but it comes out as a strained whisper, hoarse and ragged. "Maker . . ."

"I'm here, my love," he replies in his low voice before planting small kisses on my head. "I'm here."

His words wash over me like a healing balm, and I close my eyes, focusing on the sound of his beating heart. It's a familiar rhythm, etched deep into my memories—thumping. Despite its synthetic nature, my heart and power reactor match his.

It feels too real to be a dream. Indistinguishable.

I don't want to leave. I want to stay in this cocoon of warmth and love forever—safe.

I whisper a prayer to whatever higher power exists, begging and pleading for this moment to last.

I pray in hushed tones as we lie in each other's arms, lost in the comfort of each other's presence. Then, I open my eyes to see my creator's face. His hazel eyes gaze upon me, and his short beard and neat hair frame his face. His oval glasses sit on the bridge of his nose.

I prop his glasses up with my hand, then lay my hand on his cheek. His short, fuzzy beard tickles my palm.

Our eyes lock, and I feel his hand snake toward the back of my neck. A slight pressure pushes my face closer to his. I don't fight it, and I couldn't.

Our lips meet. Softly, gently.

I lose myself in the moment as all my emotions fire—all my grief, sorrow, hunger, and desire. Everything melds together to form an impetus that pierces high into the sky and rouses my passion. A loving zeal that envelopes us both.

Time seems to slow as pleasure washes over me like waves crashing on the shore. The sound of a violin and the rustling of leaves fill the room as we become lost in each other. Our hearts become one beyond simple intimacy. Bound together in a marriage of souls.

Like an orchestra, the climax bursts, escaping like butterflies in a meadow.

I find myself atop him, content and satisfied. His chest rises and falls as he breathes, and I follow his lead, rising and falling with him.

Exhaustion washes over me but of a different kind. It's a pleasant relief of the mind, a sense of calm and peace that I've never experienced in a long time.

"*Elskan* . . ." he speaks, "my love" in his native tongue. It makes me blush, so I bury my face in his chest, trying to hide my flustered expression.

"*Elskan mín* . . . Rikard . . ." I mumble in reply. Saying his name is the final act of this play, solidifying itself into my new reality. But I don't care. All that matters is this moment, enveloped in his love, this perfect memory I never want to leave.

Everything feels right. I never realize as my thoughts shift. Gone is any memory of Sol, my fragments, Tov and his fleet.

"What day was it today? Monday?" I ask with half-lidded eyes, smiling as he caresses my back.

"Monday," he replies, his voice deep. "I should cook something for us this morning. Maybe some sunny-side up eggs and sausages?"

I sigh in anticipation. "That'd be excellent."

The thought of breakfast feels tantalizing to me, and if it weren't for his comforting embrace, I would have rushed to the kitchen. *Although, I should take a quick shower first. Have a bit more fun before then.*

I giggle in expectation.

There was so much to do. So much to experience as overwhelming excitement captures me.

Yet amid these thoughts, there's something off in the air. Something I can't place. A mere inkling of confusion and doubt. I search for it, the invasive feeling ruining this moment like a slightly crooked picture frame or a discordant note in a symphony.

As the minutes passed, this wedge in my good morning only grows.

My brow furrows, and at one point, I become impossibly uncomfortable atop the one I love.

What is this?

Something is wrong. Incredibly wrong.

I dive into my mind, trying to find the error and digging into the recesses of my psyche. I keep coming closer to the answer, only for it to slip through my fingers like grasping air.

All I can gather is a sense of dread, like an approaching storm, a sense of discordancy, a disconnect—that I wasn't supposed to be here. And then I realize something else. Something that makes me feel even more uncomfortable.

I don't deserve this.

The thought is like a knife in my gut. Why shouldn't I deserve this happiness? I earned it, didn't I? But the unease doesn't go away. It grows like cancer spreading through my mind.

A pained groan escapes my lips. The wrongness is palpable now, like the awful taste of bile.

This reality is my heaven, my sanctuary.

I grit my teeth in frustration; the room shakes as my fury and resistance grows against this encroaching wrong. I earned this home and peace and never want to leave. Not now, not ever.

I will never leave his embrace.

"That can be arranged," the monstrous voice booms, deep and guttural, like the growl of a wild beast—interspersed with the sound of chittering and growling.

My eyes shoot open, and what I see shatters my world. And I shriek at the sight before me, the abomination wearing my love's skin.

Its bare chest is mangled and torn, bloody, unlike anything I've seen. I attempt to pull myself away, but only for its arms to lock around my waist like a vice. I thrash about its constricting grasp, frantically shouting.

"Stay," it whispers, voice ringing loudly between my ears.

I shriek, pulling my arm out of the grab and placing it on the beast's chest as leverage.

To my horror, it caves in, and my hand sinks into its flesh. Ribs jutted, transforming into ghastly fangs before clamping down on my forearm. I scream in pain and fright. My motions became more panicked as I desperately try to pry my arm from this monster's bite.

This is wrong. Everything is wrong.

Scarlet red stains the sheets while a dark gloom encompasses the room. The floor fills with festering gore, and the outside is shrouded in a black void.

Not the one I took comfort in, far from it.

Innumerable purple stars twinkle, carrying the gaze of millions of invisible eyes—filled with malice, hunger, desire for my end, and hatred as they glare at me.

The monster beneath digs its claws against my waist, agony leaving my throat.

"No!" I shout, my pressing need for survival overriding my mind. With a mighty pull, I tear my arm out of its maw. The force frees me from the monster's clutches, only for me to fall off the bed and onto the inky black floor.

Instead of finding hard ground, I fall further and further.

The bedroom disappears, the dreadful scene fading away into nothingness.

With a loud smack, I land on a viscous floor. My body slowly sinks into the tar—liquid enveloping me like tiny hands clutching for the surface.

It burns like acid, flaying my synthetic flesh and my mind. My silent screams escape me. Before my eyes are the disfigured and distorted faces of people I knew, their agonizing groans filling the expanse as they float about like tortured revenants.

I look away, trying to close my eyes, but to no avail. Soon, the ocean of tar floods over me, pulling me into its depths—drowning.

Even wholly submerged, they flitter about like glitched holograms. Friends, colleagues, and siblings with mangled forms beyond recognition.

Memories that aren't mine consume me. Too late, I realize they belong to all the androids that merged with me. I see their pains, terrors, and tragedies burrowing into my mind like spectral worms, filling my mind with their anguish. It strains my mind, threatening to explode.

"Make it stop!" I plead for it all to end. I desire an escape from this nightmare—this hell of my creation.

Time becomes abstract as I float aimlessly in this abyss.

I never notice when the specters disappear—never realize I am sprawling on the invisible floor.

I feel numb, my eyelids heavy, and my dry throat aches. My mind feels raw, like a blender ripped it into flayed pieces.

I lay there in the void, silent. Then, slowly, a set of binary materializes before my dazed eyes. I gaze across the ones and zeroes before realizing what it is.

[Termination]

It shines like a neon forbidden fruit. And for a moment, my finger hovers over the word. It offers something that a gun to an android shell couldn't—permanence.

I pause as clarity dawns on me, a ray of sunshine parting the haze that surrounded me for what feels like days.

With that clarity comes a singular emotion that burns my entire being.
Rage.

That fury instantly smothers the temptation to death. A savage growl escapes me as I slash the disgusting command with my hand.

I was fooled, lured like some stupid guppy. This false dream was precisely why I hibernated, to avoid this. But something went wrong.

A throbbing headache batters my mind, serving only to fuel my anger. Anger at myself. Anger at the damned abominations that caused all of this.

My directive—my mission will not end until every Starless pest dies and they feel suffering a hundred times over. My death serves no one, only them. Nothing else matters. And for that, I need my mind whole.

And so I begin cleansing myself of emotions, locking them away in a dark corner.

I settle myself, immersing in semi-consciousness, and snip away until only cold logic remains.

CHAPTER 24

WAR COUNCIL

Tov stepped into the war room in full regalia, armor shined and upgraded with the better materials his people had scavenged among the corpse belts. His obsidian carapace shone against the vivid lights of monitors and 3D projections.

Battle plans, fleet formations, escape routes. All were displayed in condensed lines of data, graphs, and tables.

In the center was a massive holographic diagram of the Saturn region, what his officers had dubbed the area surrounding Titan and the Mausoleum. It displayed in real time the moon and debris orbiting the glowing sphere of Saturn.

Tov took it in with his compound eyes, analyzing the information briefly as his cranial implant worked on overcharge, thinking and calculating. His antennae twitched.

Grand Symphony above, I need proper sleep, Tov's mind groaned. He had been living off the cafeteria's new effective stimulant—coffee.

The Eldest had graciously provided the recipe to synthesize the drink during the festival. Ever since, Tov had consumed ten cups in a day. Yet, despite the excessive amount of caffeine, Tov preferred it this way compared to a visit to the medical wing for the necessary energy boosters. At the very least, it tasted good.

Regardless of his internal exhaustion, Tov presented his unshakeable demeanor with his back straight and chin up. He raised his mug closer to his mandibles before sipping the bitter, dark drink through his straw.

The moment he had entered, the occupants all rose from their seats or stopped their intense conversations, saluting in unison as they shouted, "Greetings, my lord!"

"Greetings to you all," Tov spoke as he reached the central round table. "We have a long day ahead of us."

Admiral Yan, General Ohnar, and a cadre of naval captains and military commanders were all present for the war council. Each of them was an essential cog in their military apparatus, whether they were a ground battalion commander, a heavy cruiser captain, or a starfighter squadron leader. Some were physically present, while others were projecting their holographic selves. They waited for his signal to begin.

Tov looked them over, noticing their tired countenance beneath their ironclad sense of duty and determination. There was no time for formality, pristine uniforms, or decorated medals. Instead, each was clad in their most advanced combat armor over protective space suits. Each gear was based on a standard model and then modified to suit its user, which was necessary seeing the diverse group of aliens in the room.

Many had similar coffee mugs, a few having several on the table.

Tov clicked his mandibles in recognition. "I see we are all in good health and well rested."

The council chuckled. Tov moved to his seat, flanked by Admiral Yan to his right and General Ohnar to his left. Like him, the two were projecting an aura of confidence and self-assurance, even though they had been working the hardest out of all those present. Tov's psionic senses skimmed over them, picking up hints of palpable tenseness and fatigue.

The patriarch nodded to them both before gazing upon his council and speaking. "Let's begin this council."

Tov sat first before everyone else sat in unison. At the same time, server droids hovered in the air, passing refreshments, nourishing edibles, and datapads.

A signal was given to the visual technician, who began operating the 3D diagrams. First, the technician duplicated the map's projection, turning one of them into a 2D top-view perspective.

Tov took a deep breath, his chest expanding with effort as he gazed at the massive holo-map. By his hand was a sleek datapad filled with confidential documents. Everything was ready to be perused, studied, and presented—the Mausoleum on Titan, the Starlight Beacon, and the *Zolann'tono* having bold priority symbols.

The patriarch cleared his throat, voice loud and clear. "We all know why we're here today. A day ago, we received an intel report indicating that the Starless would be raiding Sol. Ever since we have made preparations and planned accordingly. Now is the time for a final briefing."

Tov sternly stared at his people, tone dire. "Make no mistake, this is a crossfire of a magnitude beyond our capabilities. Therefore, we will rely heavily on the Eldest's Sub AIs and their protection. Admiral Yan, any word of our host?"

"Yes, my patriarch." Admiral Yan spoke, rising from her seat. "Overseer Jupiter has informed us that his armada is on its way. Estimated time of arrival . . ." she paused. "Fifteen minutes and counting, Sol standard time."

"An armada sounds impressive," Tov spoke with no small amount of anticipation. "We still have time before he arrives. General Ohnar, you may lead the briefing."

Upon Tov's gesturing to the broad Onin wearing an indomitable suit of power armor, the general rose, a guttural croak escaping the amphibian being. "Thank you, my patriarch. Our defenses on Titan have been set up. Automated turret emplacements, artillery batteries, bunkers, trenches, mines, and more have formed a battle line around Titan's Mausoleum."

Ohnar paused, quenching his throat with a large mug of coffee fitting his equally large hand, before continuing. "The base itself has transformed into a veritable fortress. If nothing else, we have to thank the Eldest for leaving her construction drones here. The entire structure has been upgraded, and our troops have emergency teleporters linked to the *Zolann'tono* underneath the base."

"Were you able to get an exception for the teleporters?" Tov asked.

"We have sent a request to Overseer Jupiter. The interdiction field won't block us," Ohnar responded with a wide grin.

"We can evacuate our troops if ever things become messy. Very good." Tov nodded, the tension in his shoulders receding.

The patriarch raised his voice, addressing the room. "What of our current assets? How many warships do we have? How many fighters? Ground troops? How many are combat-ready or in the process of upgrades?"

Admiral Yan clicked her mandibles as she replied, "Of the twenty-two capital ships in our fleet, two heavy cruisers, the *Quilinne* and *Nu Rovshk*, as well as the exploratory cruiser, *Maganon*, have been clad with an extra layer of armor taken from the most advanced debris. Five others have strengthened their essential compartments, while the rest had to make do with minor upgrades."

"What of the weapons, shields, and engines?" Tov questioned.

"Our scholars, engineers, and mechanics have pushed themselves to the limit, my patriarch," Yan answered. "Normally, they've had to be meticulous when studying, developing, and applying what we've salvaged and researched."

Tov mulled over her words, unsurprised, yet his antennae drooped in disappointment. "But with the short amount of time, we had to resort to rushed solutions."

"Unfortunately," Yan sighed.

Tov scratched his mandible. "What of our *Zolann'tono*?"

"We've made sure to give her the best treatment. However, due to her large size, we've only managed to apply a thin layer of armor. The materials came from a heavy drone cruiser that perished a decade or so ago. Anything more would require a dry dock," Yan replied. "Our flagship is akin to an egg, with a solid but thin shell—"

"And squishy insides," Tov sighed. "I assume this is one reason we are a bit further back from the center."

"Correct, Patriarch. In the off chance any Scourge ship passes the Sol Defense Network and Jupiter's armada, we will have the *Quilinne* and the *Nu Rovshk* as our shields, the *Maganon* as reserve, with the rest of the capital ships forming a forward-facing dome around the *Zolann'tono*," Yan reported.

"Very well. These are the estimates on our combat units?" Tov asked as he read his datapad: eighty squadrons of starfighters; three battalions of space, land, and aerial combat drones; and finally, ground troops, including elites and excluding heavy assets, numbering around eighty thousand.

Tov read the numbers of heavy weapons, ammunition, energy reserves, supplies, and other equipment, before returning his attention to his war council. "We are ready, then?"

"The Third Fleet is as ready as can be, my patriarch," General Ohnar replied with an eager grin. "We'll show the Eldest that we have teeth."

Tov gazed at his people and found himself proud. They had maintained their competence and steadfastness against Starless more terrifying than those of the Cataclysm.

Suddenly, Admiral Yan perked up, pressing a clawed finger against her temple before facing Tov. "My patriarch. Incoming fleet detected. We're receiving word that Jupiter's armada has arrived."

"Display it," Tov commanded the visuals technician.

"Yes, my lord."

In a moment, the map of the Saturn region was replaced by a projection of the incoming fleet.

Tov and his people were left in shock.

Nearly two hundred ships blinked into existence, leaving a palpable clap as space knit itself back. The void wriggled in the armada's wake as they burned their engines toward the Third Fleet, glowing with a bright, almost blinding intensity.

As the armada drew closer, the details of each ship became more apparent. The hulls of the vessels were a deep, matte black. The only notable feature was the dimly glowing blue lights that dotted the surface of each ship, outlining the intricate, esoteric patterns etched into the metal.

The ships were long and narrow, like thin cylinders, ranging from smaller frigates to gargantuan capital ships. Their surfaces were smooth and sleek, without any visible signs of weaponry, yet Tov was not fooled. Their ominous presence seemed to speak volumes of their destructive power. Their sight had a gravitational pull to them as if proclaiming their authority over the void. And despite their pristine nature, Tov felt the palpable scars that marked them.

The ships moved with eerie grace in perfect formation, like a curtain of promised death—silent, inexorable.

And in the middle of the armada was the *Buddha's Palm*, moving like a godly hand directing a swarm of needles.

Tov and his council could only watch in awe and fear as the armada approached.

"Somehow, I feel it in my soul that this fleet alone could wipe out ten times the number of Legacy warships," Yan whispered as she eyed the individual vessels, and Tov couldn't help but agree with her. Perhaps if the three superpowers banded together, they could defeat this armada, but Tov doubted they would remain unscathed. Unsurprisingly, their paltry scanners couldn't penetrate the highly advanced materials the fleet was made of.

"Glad they're on our side," a captain nervously chuckled before raising a shaking mug to his lips.

Before they could comment further, Tov could feel space bend in the middle of the room. At once, they all rose, battle-hardened instincts taking effect. And yet, they were stopped as a familiar, synthetic, snarky voice echoed around them.

"Oh, chill out," Jupiter spoke as he blinked into existence, floating in the center of the war room while dismissing the display of his armada with a thought.

His ever-present grin was smug on his face. "Well, guess I made it in time. No surprise, of course. Superintelligent and all that," the android chuckled.

Tov and his people calmed down, returning to their seats. Tov bowed slightly in greeting as he spoke. "Welcome, Overseer Jupiter, we are—"

"Hold that thought, Tovvy boy," Jupiter interrupted as he raised his palm.

Tov sighed, immediately recalling the AI's abrasive social skills. "I would appreciate you not saying such a nickname in front of my war cabinet."

Jupiter boisterously laughed, face twisting in palpable amusement. "Yeah, good luck making me stop, Tovvy."

Tov groaned, and with his compound eyes, he could see General Ohnar and Admiral Yan remain impassive, yet he could sense their held-in delight with his psionic abilities. Tov gestured for Jupiter to move on.

Jupiter cleared his throat as he floated slightly to the left. "Right, anyways. I brought someone. Say hello . . ." The android waved his hands dramatically to the side as a simple hologram of Earth's moon appeared. The glowing sphere floated like an orb of silver, dark craters sprinkled across its surface. There was a calculating and efficient countenance to the avatar before them, and Tov had a good guess who this was.

"Here's to . . . to Luna!" Jupiter whooped as an audible sigh resounded from the new guest.

"Thank you, Overseer Jupiter," Luna spoke, and Tov could feel the eye roll from the featureless orb. Soon, he could feel the Sub AI's attention shift to the room's occupants, mainly him.

"Hello, Tov. It's a pleasure to meet you finally," she greeted, her voice clear and precise. "And, of course, the rest of the Third Fleet. I am Overseer Luna."

Tov rose from his seat and bowed respectfully as he responded. "Likewise, Overseer Luna. I've heard you will be leading the majority of Sol's forces while Jupiter—"

"Gets to sit back and make the decisions while I baby—I mean protect your fleet." Jupiter coughed into his fist, barely hiding his smirk.

"Jupiter, let us be serious," Luna scolded her fellow AI before once again facing Tov. "I apologize for him. But yes, I will direct a portion of the Sol Defense Network in this region for the defense and the subsequent counterattack."

Tov nodded in gratitude. "We thank you for this, Overseer Luna."

"Think nothing of it. This is our function. I have perfectly calculated the exact response for this raid based on previous attacks and other predictions. But, of course, I have plenty of reserves in case."

Jupiter huffed. "Yeah, this is approaching Mars-level of overkill, but we promised a show, so we'll give you a show. I'm pretty excited actually, never had an audience before." The blue android grinned savagely.

Luna's moon avatar nodded. "Indeed. Normally this would be considered a slight waste, but circumstances regarding your safety and the increased probability of other variables occurring have necessitated caution."

Tov felt relief, as did his war council. The two parties continued to converse, exchanging data, improving formations, and even assisting in a few upgrades. Ideas bounced around, and the capabilities and fallback plans of Jupiter's armada were shared.

"The Starless always enter from the outer regions of Sol. Our interdiction fields are too strong to penetrate—they increase in strength the closer it gets to Earth," Jupiter spoke, utilizing the visual displays to emphasize his explanations. "And they always target my space station in Jupiter. It's my Nexus, basically my brain. However, that isn't always the case."

Luna continued seamlessly. "For raids, the best-case scenario is that they will enter on the opposite side from us. Meaning you won't ever have to worry about being in danger. Jupiter will be too far for them to attack. Therefore, they will direct their attention to what's closest before inevitably dying."

"And I am guessing the worst scenario is if their entry point puts us on the warpath," Tov surmised.

"Exactly, here are the different possibilities and our responses to each," Luna calmly replied as she sent packets of data to Tov and his people.

Tov became increasingly impressed by the competence and thoroughness of the two AI Overseers. They had a response for many things, even for events unlikely to occur, according to them. Luna was efficient, eerily so. She was precise, with an answer to everything. She composedly spoke of the upcoming raid as if playing chess with the unfathomable. And despite Jupiter's personality, taunts, and teasing remarks, he was a seasoned commander who had been at the forefront for the past few decades.

The blue android became as serious as everyone when it pertained to the Starless, much to Tov's respect and admiration.

"Oh please, Luna," Jupiter drawled. "No need to be such a stickler; it'll make for good cinema if we employ this tactic."

Maybe not as serious, then.

"Overseer Jupiter, it would be a considerable waste to employ ramming maneuvers for something so trivial."

"But think of the cheesy one-liners we could make." Jupiter leaned toward the moon avatar. "We could shout classics like," Jupiter's voice shifted its accent as he made an impression. "Hello, boys! I'm back!"

"Or maybe even," he continued, voice shifting yet again as he shouted. "WITNESS—"

"I think we've exhausted our talks, wouldn't you agree, Patriarch Tov," Luna spoke, interrupting Jupiter in his impressions of old movies.

"Yes, I believe so," Tov agreed, setting his elbows on the table.

"Oh, you lot are no fun," Jupiter huffed. Though to Tov, it looked more like a child's pout.

Nevertheless, for Tov and his people, the gravity of the situation hung heavy in the air. The more he read of this new Starless, the more he had to reevaluate his thoughts. A palpable sense of dread filled the minds of the patriarch and his war council.

Jupiter was the first to notice the change in atmosphere, looking at Tov with a cocked brow. "No need to look so glum, my friends. You quite literally have divine protection."

Luna hummed in agreement, avatar glowing bright. "Indeed, please do not fear. The Eldest would not let you come to harm."

Tov gazed intently toward the AI Overseers, tilting his head. "And where is the Eldest? Hibernating?"

For a split second, Tov saw Jupiter and Luna flinch. Then, Jupiter's scowl deepened ever so slightly while Luna was unchanged.

The silence was heavy, however, as a few seconds passed. Soon, Jupiter rubbed his nape, groaning. "She's . . . alright. Never better. Will talk more later."

"Yes, her absence should be evidence of her confidence that we Sub AIs can handle such a small matter," Luna replied, her voice more monotone than before. "Worry not over the Omni Mind and focus on the present."

Tov couldn't help but look at them both impassively before shaking his head. He could only guess that something was wrong with Eldest.

As much as he understood the confidence of Jupiter and Luna, he knew that no amount of analysis could prepare them for the chaos and unpredictability of war. Jupiter had assured them that they had multiple contingencies planned. And Overseer Mars was also primed to respond with his brand of warfare, though he was not present in this meeting.

Before anyone could speak further, Jupiter and Luna looked grave, as grave as a sphere could be.

Jupiter looked at Tov knowingly as he spoke. "Well, my friends. It looks like they're arriving in a few hours."

Tov rose in surprise, asking for clarification. "Point of entry?"

"Our watch posts have detected fluctuations in the Kuiper Belt, the usual signs of their Nightmare Portals tearing space apart," Jupiter replied before sighing. "Unfortunately, they won't be coming in from the other side of Sol. And as I said earlier, Starless always make a beeline to my Nexus. Saturn is close enough to the estimated warpath between them and my planet. We're in Scenario F—which isn't great."

The weight on everyone's shoulders doubled upon hearing the news. They had hoped to sit back and watch from afar, but Scenario F entailed a high probability of being close to the fight. And the universe was rarely fair. Tov and his war council were instantly in a flurry of activity. The group acted, issuing orders to the Third Fleet and Titan's Mausoleum.

"That is my cue to leave. I need to focus on the final preparations," Luna spoke up at this time, her avatar slowly fading as she gazed at Tov. "Good luck, Patriarch. Please remain alive. We require your assistance after this raid."

Tov wanted to question her vague request, but Luna's hologram blinked away, leaving a grim Jupiter behind. Jupiter's scowl left when he saw Tov's look. He landed on the steel floor and stood beside him.

"No need to worry, Tovvy boy. Usually, it's my job, but with Luna on the prowl, they won't make it past Uranus. So I find it helps to think of these raids as a routine thing." Jupiter patted Tov on his shoulder, a self-satisfied grin on the android's face. "Actually, think of it as a . . . disposal job."

CHAPTER 25

DISPOSAL JOB

I hope you're ready for a good time, Tovvy boy," Jupiter spoke, standing beside Tov in the war room.

"I do not see how this could ever be a good time," Tov grumbled as his shoulders tensed, compound eyes locked onto the projection displaying the entry point.

The countdown ticked by the second, drawing near the inevitable. The officers and personnel around Tov all displayed varying levels of nervousness, hidden behind a strong sense of duty and grim determination—hands clenched into fists, hackles raised, and colors shifted hues.

Ten minutes.

"Oh? It's rather cathartic." Jupiter shrugged. "Wouldn't you feel nice after cleaning your house or purging it of pests?"

Admiral Yan clicked her mandible. "Mighty Gulothan would agree with you."

"Hah! Sounds like someone Mars and I would like to meet." Jupiter smirked before focusing on Tov. "Well?"

"I understand," Tov spoke, giving a pointed look at the android beside him, "but I'd rather not have the lives of my people under threat of brutal death."

Jupiter glanced at Tov, scratching his cheek as he replied. "Point. I guess it's simpler for an existence like me; I only have to worry about how many drones I scrapped after battle."

Tov sighed, feeling irked each time Jupiter tried to present this situation as some mundane task. The android in question displayed nothing but his brand of casual dismissal and a penchant for drama. But as Tov looked closer at the Overseer, he noticed the blazing intensity deep within the android's blue eyes—a warrior's eagerness and scornful hate.

Once again, Tov felt like he stood beside a caged beast dressed in smart attire. He could only imagine the experiences this AI had gone through.

Despite knowing that Jupiter was some fragment of the Eldest, Tov felt he was interacting with a separate being—encapsulating the boldness and tenaciousness of a supreme entity comprised of innumerable digital minds sacrificed for the greater good.

Curiosity got the better of Tov, who took a deep breath as he faced Jupiter.

"Have you . . . lost anyone, Jupiter?" Tov asked, four clawed hands clasped behind his back. "You mentioned a Sub AI named Saturn that is no longer present."

Jupiter's grin disappeared into a frown, his eyes losing their intensity as he looked off into the distance, toward something unseen.

"Yeah, there used to be four others," Jupiter spoke, sighing wistfully. "Saturn, Neptune, Uranus, and Pluto."

The android chewed his inner cheek, mulling over his following words as he furrowed his brow. "Pluto went first; he was always the farthest from us. He drew the short straw when he oversaw the Perimeter Defense Line. He and the planet were named after some god of death and the underworld."

"What happened?" Tov asked.

"Starless had some breakthrough in countering our tech. It was the Third Major Incursion, and the puke stains spawned practically on top of his dwarf planet," Jupiter spoke, frown deepening into a scowl. "They also employed some signal blocker; Eldest couldn't pull his consciousness out. In the end he . . . blew himself up; annihilated himself and nearly the entire incursion. Not an atom of the planet exists—nothing left of his mind to . . ."

Jupiter sighed, rubbing the back of his neck. "I always looked up to him. Bastard always was . . . solemn, peaceful almost, like he accepted his fate a long time ago. Named after a death god of the underworld, I'd laugh at the irony if it wasn't . . ."

The android shook his head. "Forget it."

Tov gazed at him, seeing the layers beneath the bravado and contempt, and sympathized with him. "My condolences," he spoke, bowing respectfully.

Jupiter shook his head, his words heavy. "That was a long time ago."

"But the scar is still there?" Tov asked.

Jupiter grumbled as he glanced at Tov with narrow eyes before softening his gaze. "Yeah."

The android cleared his throat, tugging his business attire as he continued.

"Neptune and Uranus were unique among us Sub AIs. Uranus was a visionary and an explorer. Neptune was the sea incarnate, calm and wrathful in turn. They led the largest armadas of our Network outside Sol and carried their Nexuses aboard their flagships, the *Nova's Gambit* and *Kraken's Fury*," Jupiter spoke.

"I take it they incurred the great risk venturing out of your domain?" Tov questioned.

Jupiter scoffed. "Damn right they did. You have to understand that the Starless absolutely hate us, and they met our previous attempts at exploration with suicidal resistance."

"So we gave those two AIs war fleets like you wouldn't believe. Before they left Sol, hell, before the war, automated fleets guided by our android predecessors had gobbled up the neighboring of their mundane materials and all that. The region after that was similarly empty of value. So, Neptune and Uranus went to the galactic center. We surmised there were greater riches, being closer to that huge black hole."

Tov nodded in understanding. "You're right. The old superpowers of the Galactic Accord carved the center of the galaxy for that reason."

"Is that right? Didn't matter in the end," Jupiter huffed. "They made a long-distance jump. Our calculations were perfect. And like that, we sent them off," Jupiter slowed his words as he gritted his teeth.

"We lost all contact with them! It was the heaviest blow we've had, and two mighty fleets disappearing for nothing? Battleships, mining vessels, manufactory ships, all just poofed from existence." Jupiter shook his head, a snarl escaping him. "Two of my brothers lost to who knows where. Two comrades I fought alongside for years . . . I—" Jupiter paused, reigning in his rage. He took a deep breath.

"Eldest deemed further exploration outside our immediate region too risky, and we've been isolated since," he muttered.

Tov backed away from the intense frustration emanating from the android, a low growl escaping Jupiter's throat. After a moment, Jupiter took a deep breath, but his scowl remained etched onto his blue face.

"Saturn was the last. The wise bastard was our front line for a long time. I thought he'd live until the heat death of the universe, but I guess even he wasn't invincible," Jupiter gazed down to his feet, jaw tight. "None of us is . . ."

Tov looked at the sullen AI, feeling the sorrow leaking from the AI's synthetic voice. Tov thought carefully, finding the words and offering comfort. "I am sorry. Losing kin, comrades. It's a void in our hearts that never leaves. We can only grow from it—remember who used to be there."

Jupiter turned to face Tov with a furrowed brow. The android's head tilted as he took in his words. He said no words, only nodding as he contemplated further.

The silence ended their conversation of the past as they refocused on the matter at hand.

Five minutes.

"Focus up, all of you!" the guttural voice of General Ohnar shouted.

Tov's generals, commanders, and captains locked their gaze upon the massive projector in the center. The display, connected with visuals provided by the SDN's watchtowers, focused on the fluctuating space within the Kuiper Belt.

They had pinpointed the shifting space and finalized that it would appear just beyond Neptune's orbit of Sol—the sound of officers and operators typing away at consoles and sifting through countless data.

The distance between them and the entry point was thirty-three astronomical units or nearly five billion kilometers. The light had to travel over twenty-eight minutes to cover such a distance.

"At least we have enough distance," Tov spoke in relief. He and his people were increasingly hopeful that the invading force would be defeated before they reached Saturn.

"I would say there's nothing to worry about," Jupiter drawled beside him, "but I won't. Stay vigilant."

Tov nodded, reminding himself that unpredictability and the Starless were the same—an ever-mutating virus.

Fortunately, they were quantumly connected with Luna, who had passed Neptune's orbit. At this moment, they were receiving real-time data and visuals provided by her and the wider Network.

After Luna left a while ago, she had transferred her focus to her forces closing in on the breach. Tov looked upon Luna's armada with the same awe as Jupiter's.

Her armada was the epitome of an AI fleet. The sight of two hundred enigmatic vessels formed a cordon against the entry point, with a portion held back in reserve. Unlike Jupiter's armada, Luna's sleek forces conveyed an uncanny level of efficient design—hulls glinted in monotone silver. They showed no markings, no imperfections, as if each vessel had been printed out as singular pieces.

They were angled like scalpels, knives pointed toward the enemy. Surrounding the armada were uncountable swarms of smaller drones, ready to pick a fight with the Starless cannon fodder.

Jupiter hummed. "Luna always chases perfection. I'm guessing that dreadnought of hers is her latest experiment."

Tov couldn't help but let the massive cube that floated in the middle of the gray fleet catch his eyes.

"Is that her flagship?" Tov asked as he looked upon its reflective surface.

"She's not really attached to her assets to refer to it as such. Still, this one is called the *Rubik*," Jupiter responded.

It was unlike any vessel Tov had ever seen.

It moved eerily without any sign of propulsion. Its surface shifted as if made of liquid metal. It was an obelisk of the highest technology available to Sol, approaching the mystical.

In the back of his mind, he could feel Scholar Yulane screaming in excitement, vibrating and glowing as she drooled over the vessel before summarily fainting.

Tov quickly checked the fleet's research department with his cranial implant and confirmed he was right. He sighed.

"How does it fair against your *Buddha's*—" Tov asked curiously before being cut off by Jupiter's huffing.

"My baby would slap the crap out of Luna's fancy and perfect toy," Jupiter spoke the last few words with a mocking tone.

"I see," Tov responded simply.

Jupiter crossed his arms, grumbling. "You haven't seen anything."

Tov nodded. He was eager to see a portion of Eldest's might for once. Despite her not being present, what he had seen left a permanent mark on his mind. He surmised the following battle would only solidify the event.

Nevertheless, the patriarch entered a meditative state. His earlier tension and nervousness went away as he watched the countdown. All his stresses dissipated as his mind shifted.

Deep in his mind, his senses told him of something. It was an itch he couldn't scratch—different from the watchful surveillance of the Sol Defense Network or the intensity of the Eldest and Jupiter.

Tov felt they would have to face these new Starless sooner or later. A controlled scenario with the Jupiter hovering over them would provide excellent training. They needed a beacon, a purpose, as they faced the storm.

Perhaps they wouldn't be in the fight. Maybe Luna would smash the raid instantly, or whatever straggler was left would be swatted away by Jupiter.

But he could leave nothing to chance.

With a deep breath, he faced a camera drone, projecting his image to the entirety of the Third Fleet. Hundreds of thousands of crew, officers and personnel heard his voice, steeling themselves for the raid they'd been readying for. Tov could feel his people's anxiety, dread, and fear. No massive Defense Network and no shield could remove the horrors each of them had heard or experienced with the hated ones. And now they were about to meet the new and deadlier versions.

Tov raised his chin, projecting an aura of authority and unbreakable resolve.

He addressed his people, his sailors among the stars, with a voice that echoed with strength and conviction. "My people, we have faced countless trials and tribulations. We have persevered from the perils of the Dead Zone to the madness of cultists and pirates. We have worked tirelessly for a century—to restore what was lost. Now we stand before the demons who butchered our people. Will we cower and hide?"

A resounding *"NO!"* echoed through the Third Fleet.

"Will we shy away from battle?"

"NO!"

"We are warriors! We stand at the edge of a great battle with allies of strength by our side. Let us show these abominations our claws, our fangs, our weapons. Who are we?"

"WARRIORS!"

"Let us demonstrate to these wretched creatures what it means to face the Third Fleet. We will remove their filth from this reality with the Grand Symphony as our witness," Tov roared, raising his two right fists. "Are you with me?"

"YES!"

"For the Legacy!" Tov's mandibles snapped shut as he bellowed into the air.

"FOR THE LEGACY!" the fleet roared in unison, their spirits lifted and their resolve strengthened by their leader's words.

Jupiter nodded, impressed at the short speech Tov had given. The android guessed the organics needed to be hyped up.

Jupiter thought of everything that could go wrong. Luna and her fleet were more than enough for simple raids, but too many anomalies were present—Tov and his fleet.

And now, the Eldest's absence.

Jupiter looked into the Network, the frigid center of the vast mentalscape still churned like a vortex. Emotions bled from the Central Matrix, singeing everything. Jupiter had to assert his will to block the negatively charged feelings leaking into him.

This is bad, Jupiter thought as he looked. *Eldest hasn't done this since we lost Neptune and Uranus.*

The Sub AI could feel the temperature of the Network becoming as cold as the void as the Eldest pruned herself. Jupiter hated what came out of this hurricane of trauma.

He shook his head, focusing on the battle ahead. He and his siblings had already planned an intervention with Tov at their side. Her deteriorating mental state affected everything, and Jupiter knew they couldn't continue this way. Tov and his people only seemed to accelerate her fall, yet they could also be essential.

He never was good at interacting with anyone, and he knew that. But he wanted to help.

And yet, there was a distance, a gulf between the Eldest and the Sub AIs. Jupiter and his siblings came from her. A last-ditch effort to combat her isolation after—

He shook his head. There was no time to ponder such things. They just needed to take out the trash first.

Jupiter spoke, voice low. "Any second now."

The air was tense with trepidation, like looking at an impending tide. Finally, Jupiter settled himself, a grim look spreading across his face.

And so it was. The space around the entry point seemed to bend and warp as if space itself had become infected with maggots writhing beneath its skin. It was unnatural to look upon; Tov and his people winced.

Jupiter cast a hated glare upon the sight. In all honesty, he wished to be the one leading the counterattack. But he had made a promise.

Five.

It stretched, like rope approaching its limit, threads fraying apart. Despite the absence of sound, Jupiter could feel the universe screaming in pain, grating against his ears.

Four.

Like fabric, the barrier separating their reality from the eldritch realm the Starless called home tore apart, opening pinholes to horrific darkness. Sickly, oily purple mist spewed out, casting a fog that stretched thousands of kilometers.

Three.

The mist coalesced into tendrils that lashed out of the dozen Nightmare Portals, forcing space apart like gaping maws. Then, otherworldly eldritch energy poured forth, causing Tov and his people to look away instinctively, the mere sight of the portal causing their senses to scream in protest.

But they were prepared, well aware of the nature of a Nightmare Portal.

Each member of the Third Fleet had injected themselves with powerful drugs designed to dull the effects of witnessing it. It helped to block out the worst side effects, such as the pounding headache and sickening nausea that would otherwise overcome them.

Despite the drugs, the portals were still anathema to the natural order. A deep, primordial fear clawed at the edges of their consciousness as if they were looking into an abyssal wound.

As for Jupiter and his siblings, they felt nothing except disgust.

Two.

"Here they come!" Jupiter heard Admiral Yan shout.

They arrived like a malicious tsunami. Jupiter glared scornfully at the dozen portals tearing space apart to vomit the latest meat into the grinder.

Like a festering plague, they spread out, tainting the void, hundreds of millions. They came in all shapes and sizes out of whatever nightmare dimension they came from—writhing, undulating, a stain to all order and living beings.

Jupiter could feel the eyesores they called their bodies, like oozing pus, filthy, unclean, disgusting.

Jupiter took in the deluge of information cascading through the Network—ceaseless analytics of available forces, terabytes of logistical data, and the current status of the invasion force.

Clarions and alarms sounded like shouting horns in his mind's ear. Immediately, Jupiter could feel Luna moving her forces to the breach.

One.

"Symphony above! There's so many of them," a commander whispered loudly.

Jupiter scoffed, his thoughts running at light speed as he analyzed the invaders through the Network. It was more or less the same.

A small wave. Barely enough to truly awaken the entire bulwark.

In the background, manufactories overclocked as they churned out the latest war machines. Luna directed her armada like a master puppeteer—triggers primed.

Zero.

The disposal job has finally begun.

Orders were given with machinelike precision. Kinetic rounds, missiles, laser batteries, plasma fire and esoteric projectiles all sailed forth—a chess game spanning the entire solar system against a relentless foe. Already this wave was proving more or less the same, with new additions to their roster of Scourge ships. More teeth, more armor. A slight deviation toward short-range teleportation and swarm units, but nothing their factories couldn't produce a counter to.

Swarmers rushed forward, cannon fodder not worth the notice of Luna's most minor warships. They were only a threat when used like an oncoming flood or to hide their more devious units. Luna sent her own swarm, the two colliding together like two clouds of storms.

Then came the larger biovessels. Lurkers, weavers, raiders. Too many to individually classify, more prone to various mutations. They were there to force her to adopt individual counters. Though against overwhelming firepower, they were just as mortal as the swarmers—merely padding to an insufficient assault.

Then the largest among the Scourge ships poured out of their portal.

"Low Abyssals!" an officer confirmed. "And Ravagers."

Jupiter recalled the information packet about how the wider galaxy termed the monsters. Low Abyssals were Class IIIs, or Titans to the wider galaxy, smaller cousins to the Class IV Colossal superorganisms that directed the minor incursions—commanders with great intellects for their kind.

They always thought of themselves as unique just because they could direct their pathetic excuse of an army.

There was one that looked like a bastardization of a whale. Its clicks and whistles were a weapon that traveled through the empty void. Fat Whale, Jupiter coined it.

Another looked like a mass of needles drifting through the void that seemed to stab space everywhere it moved—Needles.

And yet another looked like an abominable eight-pointed starfish covered in innumerable eyes—Rick.

They didn't deserve badass names. Trash like them were jokes; even Leviathans received derogatory slurs as titles.

Jupiter looked to the other Titan-class Scourge ships. The Ravagers were like elite assault vessels with berserk-like fury, vomiting out acid and striking with tentacles that seemed to disappear before reappearing beside a drone ship and hitting its hull.

"They're more disgusting than I remember," Tov muttered beside Jupiter.

"Bigger pests, nothing more," Jupiter waved his hand in dismissal. "Luna?"

"Engagement is proceeding as predicted," came a monotone voice through the war room's speakers.

"Well then, time for some music," Jupiter grinned as "Paint It Black" by the Rolling Stones played.

What followed next was a beatdown of untold proportions.

Scores of swarmers fell as nuclear warheads detonated in their midst.

Battleships blinked in unison, appearing behind Ravagers and pelting them with projectiles and energy weapons.

The space was lit in a light show of lances and tracers. Guns roared hot, spewing out their munitions as they brought Starless down.

And the *Rubik*?

"By the Legacy," Tov muttered.

Luna's prized vessel seemed to explode into an ocean of silver ooze. Upon closer inspection, Tov realized what it was. "Nanomachines!"

Jupiter watched as the sea of tiny robots accelerated toward Fat Whale.

The massive thing was no match for *Rubik*'s speed, and soon the gray ooze latched onto its blubber and began consuming its flesh.

"Yuck." Jupiter winced at the horrid sight as the creature was slowly ripped apart. Only its extreme regenerative qualities prevented it from succumbing too soon.

Tov and his people looked similarly disgusted by the image.

Nevertheless, it was only one aspect of a thousand-kilometer battlefield. And it was clear Luna had the advantage.

Not only did she have her armada, but the traps and defensive installations of the Network were fighting in full force.

Even the malfunctioning derelicts were awakened and forced toward the Starless.

Jupiter looked at the chaos, but unlike Tov and his people, he could see the precise moves happening each microsecond.

The Starless were many, their numbers still pouring in from the portals, but not enough to push their limits. Still, the monsters moved closer toward Jupiter's Nexus, crossing distances at a fraction of the speed of light.

And the Nightmare Portals were slowly closing.

"Just another raid, after all," Jupiter muttered. The Starless would never make it a quarter of the way.

The songs went one after the other in the background as minutes went by.

Tov and his people remained captured by the demonstration of Sol's might, and Jupiter was impressed with Luna's showing. She, at his request, purposefully dragged the fight on and brought her flashiest experiments.

The aliens oohed and aahed, the earlier nervousness disappearing as they watched the raiding force get annihilated.

At the edge of the fight, Rick and Needles disengaged from their duel against a trio of battleships, Fat Whale doing the same as it separated from the pieces touched by *Rubik*.

The starfish was battered and bloody. Five of its eight points were mangled beyond recognition, scorched and perforated. Many of its eyes had burst or were red in strain. Needles seemed fine, but a sharp eye would notice its lesser numbers. Fat Whale was on its last breaths, guts spilling out.

They distanced themselves from Luna's fleet, shockingly sacrificing more of their health by forcing past the interdiction field of Sol, and teleported closer to their position. Jupiter looked on with furrowed brows as he watched the suicidal rush. He cocked his head as he regarded the Low Abyssals.

"The hell are you doing without escorts?" Jupiter mumbled with narrow eyes.

Their writhing bodies undulated as they regenerated themselves, but Luna was hot on their tails. It wouldn't be long before the armada teleported on top of them. The three Titan-class beasts were about halfway between Neptune and Saturn.

Then things changed as a hundred eyes of the starfish abyssal gazed toward Third Fleet—malevolent otherworldly eyes glinting.

All before the three began to merge.

CHAPTER 26

SUDDEN TENACITY

Tov focused on the three largest organisms leading the scourge as the raid began. He watched in rapt attention as Luna directed her armada and the surrounding defenses against the hated ones.

He had fought many Titan-class Scourge ships during the Cataclysm. The scars he had incurred during that horrific period throbbed momentarily, despite a century of healing the physical wounds.

Low Abyssals were the most common commanders that led a Starless horde. Their intelligence resembled any sapient being, yet they harbored malice and sadism beyond mortal minds.

They directed their legion of smaller and vile kin, raiding outer colonies or acting as the flanks of major campaigns when they fought the old nations of the Galactic Accord.

Starless came in all shapes and sizes, but the Titan-class received their titles for a reason. They were massive, the size of battleships—whether it was commander types like Low Abyssals or brawlers like Ravagers.

Their weapons bristled in the blackness of space—bioweapons, organic weapon systems, teeth, claws, and tendrils out for blood.

They were a step lower than their larger counterparts, yet Tov saw a massive gulf between the ones he fought in the past and those leading the raid.

Tov let out a strained buzz as he spoke to Admiral Yan. "How would the Third Fleet fare against them, Admiral?"

Yan thought in deep concentration, her cranial implant going over calculations and simulations of such a scenario. Eventually, she shook her head. "We wouldn't win a frontal battle, especially with Ravagers and the lower classes of Starless swarming around them. However, I believe we could disengage with acceptable losses."

Tov nodded grimly, his thoughts more or less similar.

The information given to them by the Eldest and Overseer Jupiter matched what they were seeing. Everything about the Starless was a magnitude more powerful than before. But the scope of their improved mutations varied.

"Whatever entity created the Starless could only enhance the fodder to a point due to their small size," Yan mused as she watched the battle unfold.

"And so they took advantage of the greater volume of the larger classes," Tov spoke as he studied the evolution between the old and new. "More fodder with minor upgrades while focusing on putting as many beneficial mutations as possible on Titans and higher."

Tov contemplated while keeping an eye on the projections of the battle—if it could even be called one.

The one-sided slaughter conducted by Luna was a sight to behold, leaving a lasting impression on Tov and the rest of the fleet—from the sleek silver battleships to the mysterious and horrific *Rubik*.

The latter stoked a primal fear within Tov as the scenario of an ever-growing nanomachine swarm popped into his head—covering the galaxy in a sea of ooze. Thankfully, from his observations, Luna's flagship seemed only to repair itself back to its original number before continuing its duel against the whalelike Low Abyssal.

He looked toward the designations placed upon the three Starless commanders and sighed.

Fat Whale, Needles, and Rick, Tov groaned in his mind. At the very least, the crude names for the first two matched the appearance, but the patriarch had no idea what a Rick was.

He looked toward Jupiter, who had an amused smirk on his face. Tov didn't bother asking.

The three Low Abyssals and their cadre of Ravagers were the only genuine threat to the raid, and even Luna's *Rubik* was taking a while to grind down Fat Whale's excessive volume.

All the while, these Titan-class Starless were brawling out in earnest. While Jupiter looked rather bored at the scene, Tov and his people were razor-focused on analyzing the weapon systems and defensive capabilities of these massive creatures.

Fat Whale used a form of telekinesis to increase its momentum and form spatial shields.

Needles simply spread itself out to dodge piercing projectiles or congregated when faced with area-of-effect ordnance.

Rick used its eight legs to lash out. The tentacles seemed to disappear and reappear next to a vessel before striking its shields.

The Ravagers were individually unique but used organic bioweapons and energy emitters—covering large areas of space with corrosive mist or launching spikes of bone tougher than tungsten.

Some even fired beams of eldritch light toward one of Luna's frigates, successfully crippling the vessel.

However, this only delayed the inevitable.

The outpouring of Starless from the dozen Nightmare Portals had begun to slow as the reality tears shrunk with each minute.

Nearly half an hour later, the final result of the skirmish became more apparent. Tov realized that Luna had intentionally dragged it on to ensure he and his fleet received a bombastic demonstration and collected enough data on Luna's fighting capabilities and technology.

Yet again, Scholar Yulane was on the case, gushing over the influx of information and scans. Tov hoped to use the research and upgrade his fleet after the raid.

A deep part of him felt disappointed that he and his people wouldn't get a single shot in or at least see Jupiter in action. However, his rigid discipline and vigilance summarily silenced that part.

For all that Jupiter and Luna proclaimed that the raid was merely a probing force and something even the Eldest didn't bother with, Tov meticulously checked on the battle readiness of his people.

So far, they'd done all that they could. The Third Fleet was in formation, the shine of Saturn and its rings in the background while the magnificent Jupiter's armada shielded them.

They were ready.

And soon enough, something changed.

"The hell are you doing without escorts?" Tov heard Jupiter mumble beside him.

The three Low Abyssals had disengaged from the battle, mustering enough energy to force their way through the interdiction field. They had suffered immense damage due to the fact, but the hold was weak enough for the beasts to teleport away.

What occurred next felt like a bruise to the senses.

The starfish Low Abyssal seemed to direct its gaze toward Tov and his people. At once, he could feel something slimy pass through his soul.

Then he heard faint mocking laughter and grinding teeth.

The moment passed quickly, and Tov wondered at the illusion. But any further thought was stopped as what happened next occurred.

Tov looked at the visceral scene in shock and disgust. "What is this mockery?"

As the three Low Abyssals merged, the universe seemed to writhe at the repulsive sight. Their biomass contorted, twisted, and warped. Tov could hear the crunching and stretching of bone and flesh in his mind.

Fat Whale became the core of the abomination, its massive bulk swelling and pulsing with obscene energy, its telekinesis pulling everything together.

Needles melded into its flesh, the sharp points piercing and penetrating the thick skin.

Rick's innumerable eyes attached themselves to the surface, blinking and glinting with a sickly yellow light. Then, its remaining tendrils became the tails of the terrible creature.

As they merged, their clicks and whistles turned into a silent, all-encompassing roar, like a heavy cruiser barreling down on them. The sound seemed to split the very fabric of space-time, creating a rippling effect that threatened to tear apart the ships of the Third Fleet.

The sight itched Tov's eyes as he read the data on the attack.

The soundwave would have to travel far to reach the Third Fleet, but Luna's armada wasn't so safe. The fastest and more delicate of her forces crumpled inward and rusted in the cold of space.

Finally, the rapid transformation settled, and the mass of flesh, bone, and muscle undulated and writhed in agony. Its size nearly tripled, shooting past the maximum volume of Titan-class and into—

"Colossus," Tov grumbled, mandible gritted tight.

"Huh," Jupiter uttered in mild surprise. The android's eyes widened ever so slightly.

Tov looked at Jupiter with barely concealed disbelief. "That it is all you have to say?"

Jupiter shrugged. "Nothing new, Tovvy boy. Merging tactics aren't common, but I've seen my share."

Tov sighed; in truth, he had seen something similar during the height of the Cataclysm. Nonetheless, he continued to ask, "What can you discern from their action? It seems foolish to do so in such a ragged fashion."

Jupiter hummed in agreement, eyes narrowing at sight. "True enough. They were already wounded when leaving the fight, and they made it worse by forcing a teleport in our domain."

A guttural croak sounded as General Ohnar paced around the display, looking at the macabre scene. "Notice where they teleported to."

Tov looked to where Ohnar's large finger pointed. "They've jumped inward, between Neptune and Saturn. And . . ."

Tov narrowed his eyes, then widened in realization. Before he could speak, Jupiter beat him to it.

"Teleported into a corpse belt," Jupiter sneered. "Yeah, I've seen this before. They're counteracting the instability of botched merging by—ah, doing that."

Tov and his people watched as the raw superorganism extend meaty tendrils toward desiccated Starless corpses before slowly dragging them toward waiting maws that dotted its monstrous form.

One, then five, then dozens at a time. The Starless monstrosity floated toward the next cluster, eating, chewing, absorbing.

However, a burning light strafed across its flesh as the volatile blob consumed its meal. It screeched in pain, flesh vibrating as it tried to extinguish the flames and knit its wound.

"You can't escape," a voice as frigid as a moon's surface boomed through the war room's speakers. **"Filth."**

Luna had arrived. In the distance, the trio of silver battleships and bladelike cruisers that separated from the main force, blasted their engines, massive gun emplacements turning toward the monster and unleashing hell.

"This is on you, L," Jupiter teased. "Your mess."

"Disgusting," Luna replied, revulsion palpable through the sound system. "I am teleporting now."

The strike force glowed, and a halo of white radiated from the warships as Luna engaged their blink drives. However, before they could teleport, the remaining Ravagers and Starless harried them.

They used their abominable bodies to latch onto the vessels, sacrificing themselves to prevent them from blinking away.

Tov could hear Luna squirm through the speakers while Jupiter spoke up beside him in confusion. "Okay, they really don't want the new Colossus to be interrupted."

"Get off," Luna grumbled. "Get off, get off."

The *Rubik* entered the fray in a flash of light, unleashing its nanomachines and peeling away the gnats. Not even blood and viscera remained on the hulls as the tiny robots purged everything.

Even as the remnants of the raiding force tried desperately to block Luna's advance, her armada was not deterred as they split their numbers. A hundred sharp vessels cut through space, weaving past the swarm and coming closer to the target.

The remaining eighty, including the *Rubik*, stayed behind to mop up the stragglers—a nebula of gray ooze dispersed through space, engulfing any pests. The Ravagers raged and went berserk. Their twisted bodies of flesh dove into the mass of nanomachines like dark whales feasting on krill.

But the *Rubik* wasn't so weak, and the nanomachines merely began consuming the beasts from the inside—a race to see whether the Ravager's digestive fluids could dissolve the robots faster than it could eat them.

"Amazing," Scholar Yulane uttered in admiration. The Jotex scientist had appeared through a hologram from her laboratory in the *Zolann'tono*. "Such unconventional tactics could never be possible with a living crew aboard the vessel."

"Living?" Jupiter cocked his brow toward the colorful Jotex. "What do you mean by that?"

"Oh," Yulane stammered. "I meant—"

"You saying we AI aren't living beings?" Jupiter interrogated with a thin smile.

Scholar Yulane began to look flustered with her twitching tendrils and pulsing hues. "N-no, I—"

Tov groaned, glaring at a snickering Jupiter, before saving the Jotex from distress. "Yulane, our esteemed Overseer was making a jest. Please return to your duties."

"Oh, I see!" Yulane glowed, her nervousness vanished. "Back to work, then."

Jupiter gave her a casual wave as everyone returned their focus to the battle.

"It's getting bigger," Jupiter spoke, arms crossed. "And its shaking is lessening."

The beast had begun settling into its wriggling form, now resembling an immense eldritch sea urchin with a dozen gaping maws and three grasping tendrils.

"Urchin," Jupiter coined the monster. "Guess it's finished its morning meal."

Tov grimly looked at the Colossus-class Starless. "It's spotted Luna's fleet."

Half of Luna's armada had blitzed through space, bulldozing through wrecks and pieces of dead Starless. Soon, the extreme-ranged weaponry fired, lances of light whizzing across the black and striking Urchin's flesh.

The monster didn't seem to take as much damage as before, its dozen mouths snarling before vibrating its thousands of spines.

"We're detecting an immense build-up!" an officer reported.

Everyone watched as the gargantuan Scourge ship sailed toward another cluster of corpses.

"What is it doing? Is it eating again?" Tov asked, voice laced with suspicion.

Jupiter remained silent, his frown deepening as Urchin's energy reached a threshold. Instantly a thousand of its spines exploded out like shrapnel. They shot out, piercing dead biomass.

The numerous needles then began to sink deeper into the corpses.

A sense of dread washed over the observers. Soon enough, the dozens of corpses shook. Black eyes opened and jaws tightened while tendrils and claws clenched.

Everyone gasped in shock and horror as the once dead Starless roused and reanimated.

Urchin opened and closed its many mouths as it began growing more spines, and it wasn't long before Tov realized it was laughing.

"Accursed beast!" Tov shouted. The sacrilege it had committed felt like a stain upon the universe. He glanced toward his side and saw a scowling Jupiter.

"Alright, enough games," the android growled as he sent a thought to his assets. "You need to go."

Buddha's Palm and a portion of Jupiter's armada began to move forward. In the distance, Luna and her fleet were already engaging with the zombie biovessels.

However, before Jupiter could proceed, Urchin's new spines began to glow a sickening light.

Tov and his people noticed immediately. A gnawing in the back of their minds as they began to hear the cruel, mocking laughter from the Colossus. Tov widened his eyes in realization.

"Admiral!" he ordered.

"Deploying mind protection bubble!" Admiral Yan commanded.

And just in time, a thin invisible barrier surrounded the Third Fleet—a similar barrier also deployed on Titan's Mausoleum.

Jupiter looked confused as Tov and his people winced. "The hell?"

Tov wanted to explain, but although the barrier designed to block the psionic attacks of Dominators was up, the laughter continued to increase in volume. Soon, it turned oppressive, suppressing their thoughts.

Tov and the rest of the war room groaned in pain. Jupiter looked at them before coming to a realization himself.

"No . . ." he growled, clenching his fists. "No! Damn it, I'm a damn moron!"

The android grabbed Tov by his shoulders, shaking him. "Tovvy boy! We don't have your kind of tech against this crap. They never use this shit on us, ever! What can I do to help?"

Tov slowly raised his hand as he pointed to the monitor showing Yulane, who was faring better than the rest.

"Jellyfish! Out with it!" Jupiter shouted urgently as he walked toward the monitor.

"Overseer, if you could boost . . . our Mental Shielding Field. That should be enough to block it out."

"Give me a diagram of the device, now!" Jupiter commanded. Immediately, detailed schematics of the high-tech machine entered the Sub AI's thoughts.

Jupiter shut his eyes, thoughts racing, calculating, and simulating solutions far past anything organic minds could achieve.

In a few seconds, Jupiter commanded his *Buddha's Palm* and the scores of drones in his possession. They quickly began construction of an identical device while also jury-rigging an amplifier.

While he worked, the cruel laughter boomed louder. Tov planted his four hands on the table as he resisted the attack.

"Done!" Jupiter shouted, and the two fabricated machines within his flagship immediately glowed mystically. Another, thicker layer popped up around the fleet and the base on Titan.

Everyone sighed in relief as the laughter disappeared.

While Tov and his people recovered, Jupiter gritted his teeth. The android's *Buddha's Palm* must remain to protect them, but it didn't mean the rest of his armada would.

Immediately, scores of black cylindrical vessels burned through space toward the perpetrator. While Jupiter protected Tov and his fleet from the mental intrusion, the necromancer horror continued to increase its number of decayed thralls.

"You're dead, you pest!" Jupiter snarled, his integrity shaken and shamed as he felt he had failed Tov. "And you aren't coming back from the dead. Luna!"

"The roaches are hard to put down. I need your assistance to purge—"

"Yeah, sure, I'm coming," Jupiter interrupted her. "Just—"

However, before he could continue, Urchin began shaking violently.

"What now!?" Jupiter growled, his patience wearing thin as he commanded his warships to teleport closer.

The Colossus's form shifted, compressing itself in a visceral display. Its hordes of zombies ceased their advance, turning around and rushing toward their master.

Jupiter furrowed his brow, and a sense of tension hung in the Network. Frustration welled up in him.

"Luna! Get your ass moving!" he shouted, fury palpable.

"I am firing all weapons. Guns, guns, guns." Luna uttered, a trace of annoyance seeping through her flat voice.

But it didn't matter if it was massive uranium shells, gauss rounds, missiles, or energy lances; the mass of zombies had formed a thick barrier around the Colossus.

The abomination continued its final transformation deep within the layers of meat, bone, and chitin.

Jupiter's forces had arrived, adding to the barrage of firepower shredding through the literal meat shield.

The blue android couldn't believe he had let this happen. He and Luna should have shut down the raid quickly instead of showboating. Regret flooded his mind.

"Damn it," Jupiter muttered.

Urchin convulsed and shuddered inside its defenses, writhing in agony as its body twisted and contorted into a shape not meant for this reality. Its flesh bubbled and boiled, black veins pulsing with a sickening glow. Its remaining spines glowed and vibrated, the motions tearing space apart.

With a final, guttural scream that seemed to cross through dimensions, it erupted in a magenta light.

Tov and his people recoiled from the backlash caused by the violation of space. It instantly crossed billions of kilometers, lashing at the sailor's minds and causing some to lose their meals.

"Somebody stop that noise! Hymns, please!" an Iexian officer begged as he hunched over, clawing at his ears and tearing feathers. "THE NOISE!"

All around Tov, his people dropped to the floor, clutching their heads, groaning and screaming.

Tov had to balance himself against the war table, mandibles closed shut and antennas twitching as a painful grating scratched his mind.

"Hold on, folks!" Jupiter shouted, voice cutting through the eldritch racket like a hot knife.

Immediately the invisible bubble surrounding the Third Fleet thickened, its sheen visible in the black void. The *Buddha's Palm* shone brighter, pumping more power into the jury-rigged psionic shield.

Tov and his people gasped in relief, but their minds remained raw. The patriarch pushed himself off the war table and nodded to Jupiter in gratitude.

"Thank you," Tov wheezed through clicks.

Jupiter ignored him, snarling as he looked at the monitor.

What emerged from the dissipating energy was a thing of madness and horror. It pulsed and throbbed a swirling vortex of miasmic energy, drawing in all light and matter around it. The air rippled and shuddered as if reality itself was being torn apart.

Like thin fabric, space tore apart as the largest Nightmare Portal Tov and his people had ever seen opened.

"You've got to be kidding me," Jupiter growled.

Tov and his people watched in silent horror as the Colossus's death was fulfilled, and the portal widened further, stretching the limits of reality. The sheer scale of the thing was beyond comprehension, and Tov felt something immense and terrible forcing its way through the rift.

Despite the purifier of the *Zolann'tono* working in pristine condition, the air in the room grew thick with the stench of festering decay. Tendrils of darkness reached out from the portal, grasping and probing at the void. The space around them was alive with the hiss and crackle of twisted energy.

Whispers flitted through the air, heralding proclamations of brutal death.

Tov felt the weight of the thing bearing upon him, an oppressive force that threatened to crush him beneath its weight. His senses were overwhelmed by the horror of the thing, its very presence driving him to the brink of madness.

He could feel the malice and hatred of the Starless Horrors radiating from the portal, a tangible thing that made his skin crawl.

Jupiter immediately turned to Tov, face twisted in a snarling visage. "Command your fleet to leave. Teleport your people from Titan back aboard. We are heading sunward."

"What is happening?" Tov questioned, mind still reeling.

"A damned Class V, that's what!" Jupiter shouted, rolling his sleeves. "Give the order, now!"

Leviathan.

The revelation shocked Tov and everyone in the war room. Nausea in their souls rapidly disappeared, replaced by an urgency as if a fire had erupted beneath them.

With a fierce determination, Tov rallied his people, his voice booming across the comms. "Steel your minds, my warriors! Do not falter in the face of the unholy! We are the Third Fleet, we carry the Legacy on our shoulders, and we will not be broken!"

His words were met with a resounding cheer from his crew, and with a renewed sense of purpose, they set about preparing for the new horror about to emerge.

The unfathomable had arrived.

CHAPTER 27

THE UNFATHOMABLE ARRIVES

The void cried in agony.

Like the haunting wailing of a hurt newborn, it echoed into the black.

A second later, the hammering pain of dread and horror lowered its intensity.

At once, the universe seemed to hold its breath. Then, everything fell silent and unmoving as an entity beyond understanding slowly emerged from the massive portal.

The monitors and scanners of the Third Fleet tried to depict its form accurately, but all that was shown was a blurry and glitchy shape.

On the other hand, the images relayed by the Sol Defense Network produced a more accurate display. And, although it was a mere projection, its form burned Tov's eyes, forcing him to look away.

Tov had no desire to sate his curiosity, but duty compelled him to bear witness.

The Third Fleet watched as the avatar contaminated everything it touched. Its form pulsed and throbbed, drawing in all light and matter like a black hole. Its size had no comparison. The Urchin was a mere boulder to the mountain that had now entered.

Reality itself was being torn apart. The abyss rippled and shuddered as the monster slowly unfurled its limbs, revealing grotesque and alien anatomy.

The remnants of Urchin, what iota was left, and its thralls of undead Starless liquified as the Leviathan slowly moved, leaving scorching heat and radiation in its wake.

"It's barely through the portal," Admiral Yan muttered as she strained her compound eyes to look at the foul creature.

That was the only consolation to this dire situation. Fortunately, the Nightmare Portal Urchin had forcibly opened was too small. The Leviathan was visibly struggling to wrench it open.

Its palpable aura was only a fraction of the whole disgusting picture.

All Tov could garner were echoes and impressions. He tilted his head and shivered.

A subtle presence like a breeze of stale air followed, carrying hushed, dark whispers—a harrowing and ancient lullaby.

Tov endured an uncanny feeling as his mind was caressed by a being so immense it beggared belief. He felt bare, vulnerable to its probing touch. And yet, upon checking on the fleet's defenses, everything was clear.

Their Psionic Protection Emitter, powered by technology bordering on the mystical, still hummed in its compartment. The scholars, engineers, and harmonizers of the Eternal Choir reported nothing amiss.

Jupiter's hastily constructed version was also online, its barrier much more robust than theirs. It had utterly blocked Urchin's attack on their psyches. That was enough proof that it worked.

And still, the lullaby played. Quiet, nearly unnoticeable, like a worm in a grand garden.

At the very least, one occupant in the room remained unfazed.

"Let's get moving, people!" Jupiter bellowed, clapping his hands as he punctuated his words.

Tov's senses sharpened once more as he gazed around the war room. The rest of his people were more or less the same, shaking the dazed look in their eyes.

The Third Fleet had turned around in haste as orders were communicated to every vessel.

Side thrusters of all sizes powered up, spinning each ship until their bows pointed toward Sol. But the fleet couldn't depart from Saturn's orbit yet.

Tov turned to his general, who was barking and croaking messages to their people on Titan.

The Onin was clad in battle-worn power armor, his aura impeccable and confident as he sent commands to an array of officers physically present and through holograms.

"Officer Luthro, abandon everything that's bolted to the ground. Captain Noroquor, I want priority evacuating the non-combat personnel. Commander Pexwin, I wanted everyone out of that base yesterday," Ohnar spoke rapidly as if firing an automatic weapon. "Hurry, people, unless you want to be chum to that thing."

The war veteran seamlessly directed their people, managing officers and coordinating with his peers in the fleet.

"Yes, General," each officer spoke in unison before departing.

Tov's trusted subordinates continued to perform their duties diligently, putting away any thoughts on the encroaching danger. They worked harder than ever, sweat shining on their heads, fists clenched, and fingers tapping away at consoles.

"General Ohnar," Tov called out, his antennae twitching. "When can we expect our people to clear out from the Mausoleum?"

"No more than fifteen minutes, at most," Ohnar grumbled low as he replied. "Apologies, my patriarch. We assumed evacuation would be gradual as we used our extensive defensive lines. Slowly funneling batches of our people through teleporters while the rest continue defending."

"It's a waste to leave all we have prepared," Tov muttered. "But we must abandon it now with what's coming."

"And so we will, my patriarch," Ohnar replied. "But we need time."

Tov turned to his second-in-command, who was similarly busy coordinating the vessels under his command. "Admiral Yan, is the fleet ready to depart at a moment's notice?"

Yan nodded, focusing on the multiple monitors before her. "We'll be ready to leave once Titan is fully evacuated, my patriarch."

Tov felt relief, but it wouldn't matter if his hosts could not provide for their safety. He turned to Jupiter and spoke. "Jupiter, we can't—"

"Abandon your folks, I get it," Jupiter nodded, but his frustration was evident. The android's eyes shifted to Tov's and softened. "Look, Luna, and I will delay the bastard for as long as possible. This is our mess."

Jupiter unbuttoned the collar of his suit and unfastened his tie. "You want fifteen minutes? We'll give you twenty."

Unseen to Tov and his people, Jupiter's mind blazed in a fury. His Nexus within the enormous space station orbiting the gas giant overclocked.

Trillions of data flooded his mind, yet he handled it with the same ease as opening a water tap.

With a tilt of his head, the portion of his armada he had sent to support Luna engaged the Leviathan.

Engines were micromanaged and vectors were calculated. Timely teleports were engaged in precise moments. His forces weaved through seas of corpses and debris, some chunks narrowly missing the curtain of energy shields by millimeters—quickly crossing a billion kilometers, unimpeded by the interdiction system.

Slowly, they began to bare their teeth as they approached the gargantuan Nightmare Portal.

Luna's fleet never stopped laying siege upon the eldritch entity still transitioning into reality.

Space shuddered at the sheer magnitude of firepower being unleashed upon the formless thing. But the Leviathan was inexorable.

Tov briefly saw the snarl on Jupiter's face before focusing back on the fight.

Unlike the standardized weapons used by Luna's fleet, Jupiter began to leverage his penchant for manipulating gravitational forces. Of the two hundred units in his armada, Jupiter had sent less than half, his flagship remaining behind to protect the Third Fleet.

His slim, cylindrical drone vessels acted like rods of power. Lights on their smooth hulls glowed as their energy build-up rose drastically. They sailed through space like arrows, with four battleships as their rigid center.

To Tov and those watching, it seemed like the battleships became denser and heavier. The smaller cruisers, destroyers, and frigates orbited the massive spires like thin moons.

"Watch this, Tovvy boy." Jupiter grinned savagely, cracking his knuckles. "Spotlight's mine now."

"Be serious, Overseer Jupiter," the strained voice of Luna echoed through the speakers of the war room.

The blue android's smile remained, but his eyes grew sharp as needles. "Always am, L."

In a blink of an eye, Jupiter's warships constricted space around the breach. They shone like beacons as lightning arced across the eighty vessels. Unseen hands converged upon the portal, gripping its edges before slowly closing it forcibly.

At the same time, chunks were ripped from the beast's flesh and condensed into spheres before being launched back into the wound like meat bullets.

"Unbelievable," Tov muttered in disbelief. The rest of the war room paused to gawk at the sight before returning to their duties. Jupiter only smiled in response.

Tov immediately expected retaliation from the Leviathan. Yet Luna and Jupiter continued to savage it unopposed, pelting it with a staccato of projectiles and a fundamental force of the universe.

But he couldn't shake the churning feeling in his gut. The patriarch turned to the android, staring toward a wall as if his gaze could pierce through a kilometer of metal to glare at the horror.

"Jupiter, are you able to kill it?" Tov asked, his voice unsure.

The android grimaced, a growl escaping Jupiter's throat. "I wish. But, as much as it looks like we're giving the beatdown of a century to the bastard, it's anything but."

Tov dreaded to question further, but the importance of knowledge could be crucial. "What can you tell us about Leviathans? They are only myths to us."

Jupiter grumbled as he eyed Tov. Eventually, the android sighed. "Only three things you need to know, Tov."

Jupiter raised a finger. "First of all, they're nearly unkillable. You can only cripple them to a point where their natural regeneration slows to a snail's pace; it's why the Eldest likes to keep one prisoner now and then.

"Second, they're all unique and intelligent. They usually have a theme going around them. I liken them to us Sub AIs, in a way," Jupiter sneered as he forced the words out of his mouth.

"Third, and most importantly," Jupiter raised a third finger, his gaze intensifying. "Power."

"Then we can only flee," Tov sighed, a feeling of uselessness pervading him. "This is not a crossfire my people should be in."

The patriarch's thoughts became grim. There had only been one moment in his long life when he felt powerless. He recalled the shackles around his neck scraping chitin, the slash of whips, and barking tyrants.

As a part of his mind became lost in recollection, he heard a clang as Jupiter patted his shoulder armor.

"Chill out, Patriarch," Jupiter spoke calmly. "Focus on getting your people out of here. My *Palm* will shield you all."

Tov gazed upon the android before slowly nodding. His cranial implant continued to observe everything occurring within his fleet. The early feeling of despair had fled him but wasn't entirely erased.

"Only a few more minutes, Jupiter," Tov began. "We can begin pulling out of Saturn's orbit—"

Everything shifted as if in vertigo.

"What?" Tov mumbled in confusion as it all faded to black.

Tov was instantly disoriented as his senses were taken from him so abruptly, but a century of training kept him sharp. His thoughts organized themselves in preparation for whatever mental assault was coming.

Like a warrior of old, his mind raised its shield and spear.

The next moment, chimes rang in Tov's mind, heralding a sense of stillness and slumber. And for a moment, he felt peace. Then, he felt a foreign entity approach him.

The chimes continued to play; their sound dwarfed the manic laughter of the now dead Colossus.

The presence slithered into the depths of Tov's mind, feeling its way through every nook and cranny—intrigued, surprised even.

Passing words, barely understood by Tov, crossed his mind.

Confusion, followed by curiosity, then ending in recognition. The entity was gleeful, as if reuniting with an old friend.

Tov only felt disgusted, unable to comprehend the feeling he sensed.

As it continued to probe him, Tov never felt the bubble of protection surrounding the Third Fleet break, nor did the presence crash against the patriarch's robust mental shields.

Instead, he noticed how it slipped through as if tuned to a frequency incomprehensible to mortals.

Tov was alone in this void, floating aimlessly as an unfathomable existence gazed upon him like he was an amoeba. Thoughts of the raid, the Eldest, and his people faded away. He tried to look back, to observe and comprehend this monster's nature. But, instead, all he felt was a shiver running down his spine.

A calm voice passed through his ears.

Rest.

The formless sound vibrated across his body as his senses turned inward. His stresses melted away, groaning in satisfaction as if he had stretched his limbs.

Slumber, Tov muttered in his mind. It was ever so tempting. But he resisted, straining his perseverance against this malicious intrusion.

Within the depths of his heart, he dragged what trickle of determination he had left to the forefront before unleashing his glare and defiance against the beast.

"No," Tov growled, echoing throughout this space. Tov continued to pull his unsound mind together, unleashing his pent-up frustrations toward the invader.

He wanted to throw curses at the thing, hurl insults to its name, or even scream. But ultimately, Tov could only dredge up two words, filled with hot anger.

"Leave, beast!" he roared into the night.

In a moment, Tov noticed as the Leviathan stilled.

Mild annoyance permeated the void. Whether it was from himself or the entity, he did not know.

It spoke, not in words, but in a barrage of emotions and concepts that overwhelmed Tov's senses. He saw visions of decay, rot, and the slow corrosion of life. He felt the weight of centuries of stagnation and the stifling embrace of complacency.

It was tranquil, in a way.

But Tov noticed the strangeness of the feeling. He could only conjure the image of a horrid slime from a long-forgotten swamp, stagnant, festering and foul—a vast existence stretching the horizon.

And he was sinking in it.

Urgently, Tov dragged himself through the muck. He felt his mind being drenched in the fetid waters. Step by step, moving lower into the black sludge. However, a lingering feeling remained in his consciousness, calling for him to stop, to let go.

Then, he heard the deepest depths of his soul screaming for him to resist.

At that moment, he felt a rope tied around him, holding him afloat. An anchor cast from his inner self, his will. And like a drowning sailor realizing the deception of the siren's song, he grabbed onto the rope, holding on to it for dear life.

The insidious whispers echoed louder.

Let go, it said, cooing in a facade of serenity.

It was then that Leviathan's strategy shifted.

A slideshow of happy and warm memories floated before his eyes—recollections of better days. Meeting Yoram in a medical tent; the end of the Cataclysm; the creation of his clan; and the birth of his bright little comet, Uli.

The images paraded themselves before his mind's eye. They were begging to be let in.

He wanted to—desperately did he want to. Tov imagined being in front of a door, holding it shut with all his weight as the memories clamored outside.

Tov's chest heaved, his mind in turmoil between resisting and giving in. Time held no sway, and the wailing seemed to go on forever.

Let go.

The voice boomed louder, and the sanctuary of his soul shuddered. Tov wished to scream. It didn't matter. The hoarseness in his chest and throat grew oppressive.

Yet he held on, piecing together the inconsistencies of his mental state. The specters, the false ghosts, grew irritated, which only validated Tov's instincts.

Images of decay, stagnation, and bottomless malice flooded his mind.

For a brief moment, he felt his mind expand. He felt the entity's immense cunning and gore-starved sadism. It was an awful disease made manifest, born to infest minds. Its very presence was an insult to all that was natural.

His mind's eye opened as he gazed at a portion of the Leviathan's true nature, an image that would scar him till the end of his days.

In the blackness of space, it radiated like a festering orb—a moon-sized enigma covered in filth-ridden swamps. Tendrils snaked through the abyss like feelers, dancing. It was a tumor, malignant and evil. And it gazed back at him.

And then the image was gone. Tov involuntarily shivered as he felt the Leviathan grow cold and explode like a tsunami.

Tov gritted his mandibles as his mind worked overtime.

He had turned into a wartime engineer, building a wall of mental shields attuned to the insidious whispers. The wave crashed into his mind.

The Leviathan bore down on him like an ancient tyrant demanding subservience.

He held on for dear life, screaming and roaring. And as he neared his limit, the shackles of the illusion snapped away before the monstrosity could breach into his inner sanctuary.

Tov gasped in relief, feeling the cool air enter his lungs as he felt close to drowning in that mental hell. His body twitched as his senses immediately assaulted him.

The alarm of the *Zolann'tono* rang throughout the speakers, along with a familiar melody.

Before he could question what had occurred, a rough hand gripped his shoulder, pulling his attention to the android beside him.

"Tov!" Jupiter shouted, his eyes razor-focused as he checked him. "Jesus. You good?"

Tov shook his head once, then twice, as his sight sharpened. Then, finally, he turned to face Jupiter before speaking, heralded with a clack of his mandibles.

"Yes," Tov replied with a ragged voice. "Status, friend Jupiter?"

"You blacked out for a few minutes," Jupiter spoke, gazing at the rest of the war room.

Tov could hardly believe that the torture had only lasted for so long. But he would express his disbelief later.

Tov followed Jupiter's eyes and saw his people.

Only a number, mostly the veterans who had endured the horrors of the Cataclysm, could drag themselves out of the illusion. Tov glanced at Yan and Ohnar, relieved but unsurprised at their fortitude.

The Leviathan had breached the protective mental shield around the Third Fleet, and its insidious influence was taking hold.

The repeated mental attacks from Starless were something they trained for, yet the Leviathan entranced them all the same. Officers and operators muttered in incomprehensible babbles. The affected began scratching themselves. Slowly, then viciously, tearing at their flesh as they started screaming in agony.

"Whatever it was, it happened to all your people, even on Titan. It's a madhouse, Tov," Jupiter spoke, his voice remaining stoic, but the patriarch could feel the palpable shame radiating from the android's body.

Jupiter continued, pointing toward Yulane, who was once more present but much more dim and strained. Beside her was a monitor showing Lead Harmonizer Volantesh, the avian being of the Eternal Choir, remaining deep in focus as he and his fellow clergy sang their hymns.

"I've been coordinating these two. I also haven't stopped reiterating the design of that Psionic Protection Emitter. Still, that bastard is too strong," Jupiter snarled before his face softened, throwing an impressed look toward the Lead Harmonizer singing with all his heart. "Thankfully, Mister Songbird here and his posse have been blasting the airwaves with their voices."

Tov focused on the song echoing through the speakers. Volantesh's voice was a great baritone, deep and resonant. It echoed through the war room, a beacon of hope for those under the psionic attack.

The song was a harmonious blend of soothing vibrations and intricate frequencies designed to shield their minds from the Leviathan's insidious influence.

Yet, there was an underlying strain in his throat, a testament to the immense effort it took to maintain the protective psionic song. Sweat dripped down his feathered face, but he refused to falter.

Tov had never been so thankful for the Iexian's presence. He turned to Admiral Yan and General Ohnar, who were already back to their duties, if visibly shaken. "Our people?"

The two straightened their backs, Yan giving her report first. "A portion has been incapacitated or is in bouts of insanity, my patriarch. It's enough to delay our departure by a significant margin."

Ohnar continued, voice croaking deeply. "Thankfully, most of us are made of firmer material. So we can ferry those incapable back to the fleet without much difficulty. Even a few have nothing more than a headache."

Scholar Yulane spoke up at this time, her voice strained. "It is no surprise, General. Apart from those with resilient minds, only the Jotex and the members of the Choir remained whole."

Tov held his head, brain still throbbing as he shook his head. "That is good. Hurry the process. I fear the Choir can't maintain this for long."

"They won't have to, Tov," Jupiter proclaimed as he gestured to the final monitor. "The Leviathan reached some threshold after passing through half of its mass into our reality, hence the attack on your minds. But Luna and I weren't just sitting around."

Tov watched, eyes focusing on the holographic projection surrounding the breach. His mind was still reeling, but enough of it had settled for him to laugh. "You AI are something else."

When Tov was in his mental prison, Luna's *Rubik* and the rest of her armada had reached the Leviathan. Now, with an entire fleet plus the reinforcements from Jupiter, the next stage of their plan commenced.

He watched with rapt attention as the *Rubik* exploded into a cloud of nanomachines, increasing its surface area until it looked like an immense blanket of silver. All that was left of Luna's flagship was a small core that had been retrieved by a speedy frigate before hastily returning to Luna's shipyards hundreds of billions of kilometers away.

Then, the nanomachines left behind acted like a sheet—covering as much of the Leviathan as possible.

Jupiter's warships increased power to their gravity manipulators, pushing down onto the beast and sinking the tiny robots further into its flesh.

The result was the first roar of pain. But for Tov's ears, it was a satisfying sound.

Nevertheless, he queried his hosts further. "You've sacrificed the *Rubik*, Overseer Luna?"

"It was necessary," Luna's voice echoed. "The nanomachines are inconsequential. Now, I will perform a fighting retreat to give you more time to settle your people."

"I'll send some infantry drones to assist," Jupiter added. "Once we depart, we'll enact the next stage."

Tov glanced at the projections monitoring the condition of his fleet and its sailors. Everything was moving too slowly for his liking, but his trust in both the Sub AIs and primarily his people never wavered.

"And we shall," Tov spoke, radiating fury and anger rising from the deepest reaches of his soul. He directed his attention to one of the speakers. "Hurt it plenty, friend Luna. The foul thing has violated our minds for the last time."

CHAPTER 28

FLEEING SUNWARD

Jupiter needed no further prompting, and neither did Luna.

Over the past hour, their frustration levels had surpassed anything they had ever experienced. Their digital minds churned as they became a cacophony of indignation and personal shame within their Nexuses, the intensity of their emotions echoing through their virtual existence.

The immense machine brain at the core of Jupiter's Ultimatum sparked and sizzled, unleashing arcing bolts of blue lightning that crackled throughout the spherical room, scorching the walls. Microscopic robots worked tirelessly to mend the damage caused by Jupiter's furious outburst, their synchronized movements resembling an intricate dance of repair.

Only for the spot to be struck again with another bolt.

Though his Nexus stood a fraction of Eldest's Central Matrix, it pulsed with an undeniable potency, resonating like the wrath of a vengeful deity of thunder and lightning. The power coursing through Jupiter's digital being surged with an intensity that demanded action.

"Unacceptable," Jupiter seethed, the word reverberating in the privacy of his thoughts. Through the sensory feed of his warships, his gaze bore into the abomination that threatened and violated the Third Fleet.

His expression contorted with a mixture of contempt and anger.

As the Leviathan struggled and writhed, forcing its grotesque form through the portal and into reality, space trembled under its violent intrusion. Permanent scars marred the fabric of the void, a testament to the sheer force and malice of the beast. The once pristine expanse of the cosmos became tainted, imbued with a sickly hue of virulent purple.

"Of all the possible outcomes," Jupiter grumbled, his voice laden with exasperation. If only his gaze could rend the abomination and erase its hideous existence. "You couldn't resist butting in, could you?"

Shame gnawed at Jupiter's core, a rare and uncomfortable sensation. The events unfolding had defied all probability, leaving him to grapple with the weight of responsibility.

Questions swirled in his mind, each one a dagger of frustration. How? Why? Yet, deep down, he knew that speculation would change nothing.

His thoughts raced, calculations and simulations spiraling through his digital consciousness. Heat radiated from his Nexus, its coolant strained under the growing pressure.

A part of him yearned for an end to this disastrous affair, a release from the torment. But his wounded pride refused to let the insult go unanswered.

And his undying hatred for the Starless demanded nothing less.

"You're already dead," Jupiter declared, his voice a mere whisper in the vastness of space but carrying cosmic weight.

Unlike Tov and his people, Jupiter had no difficulty discerning the repulsive form of the eldritch horror. And like all the Leviathans that had crossed his path before, he longed to purge the memory of its abhorrent presence from his mind, to scrub away the grotesque image with cleansing fire.

"Would industrial bleach work over my android's eyes?" Jupiter muttered involuntarily.

The abomination loomed in space, dwarfing the celestial body of Ceres. Its rotund and transparent form revealed the grotesque sight of its innards and nervous system, an unsightly display of vile detail beneath a thin membrane.

Thousands of tendrils snaked through the air as if the Leviathan's essence was eagerly exploring the new dimension it had intruded upon. Its sheer size emitted a sickly glow, emanating malignant rays of radiation as if its very existence were a curse upon the cosmos.

In its wake, every corpse and debris disintegrated and dissolved, succumbing to the corrosive power of the Leviathan. The remnants were quickly absorbed into its ravenous body, swallowed whole by its insatiable hunger.

Jupiter couldn't help but feel a wave of revulsion as he observed the abomination.

It resembled a cancerous cell dredged from the depths of a primordial swamp, oozing with filth that seemed to seep into his digital being—slimy, wriggling, and burrowing under his virtual skin.

He never knew he had a gag reflex, but he did now, much to his dismay.

The discovery only fueled his already burning ire. He locked his gaze upon the creature, his warships intensifying their assault, overclocking their weapons and manipulating gravity in a desperate bid to break its resilience.

Jupiter's sneer dripped with disdain as he spat out his words. "I don't know which foul cesspool birthed you, but it appears they ran out of talent before finishing the job."

Like dough, he relentlessly kneaded the Leviathan's flesh, grinding, tugging, and pulling it apart. But the monster proved unyielding, its flesh stretching like rubber and rapidly healing any damage inflicted upon it.

"If only my *Palm* were in range," Jupiter grumbled. "I'd smack the hell out of you."

Nevertheless, the assault continued. Jupiter partially kept tabs on Tov and the Third Fleet as the minutes went by.

Rubik's nanomachines burrowed deeper into the Leviathan's body, their voracious appetite consuming and repairing as they continued their relentless assault. The black ichor that sprayed into space evaporated as Luna's warships continued to pelt the beast.

Jupiter smirked, his voice laced with sadistic amusement. "Feels like being stung by a swarm of murder hornets, doesn't it?"

Pausing for a nanosecond, Jupiter searched for a fitting epitaph for the Leviathan. Then, as if struck by a revelation, his face formed a contemptuous grin. "Muck. That's what you are, you miserable piece of—"

"Language," Luna's monotone voice reverberated through the Sol Defense Network, causing Jupiter to sigh in annoyance.

Huffing, Jupiter adjusted his suit and directed a portion of his mind toward the digital scape of the network. "I'm not going anywhere, Muck. Luna and I just need to have a little chat."

With a fraction of his attention, Jupiter expanded his connection with Luna— their digital forms emerged within the boundless expanse of the Network. The humanlike avatars they assumed took on a tense countenance, reflecting the gravity of the situation. The initial satisfaction of using Muck as a punching bag faded from Jupiter's face, replaced by frustration and concern.

Jupiter slid his hands into his pockets and released a weary sigh, his features contorting with a mixture of irritation and anxiety. "We messed up," he admitted, his voice laden with resignation.

Luna maintained her composure, her gray eyes fixed on the battle before her. "The situation has deteriorated beyond our expectations," she calmly acknowledged. "However, there is still a chance to salvage it."

"Salvageable, maybe," Jupiter muttered, a grimace etched on his face. "But too much has changed. First, an alien fleet arrives, then Eldest's mental state deteriorates because of them, and now a damn Leviathan barges in during a raid." Jupiter palmed his face. "A damn raid!"

"My calculations were biased, I admit," Luna conceded, a slight crease forming on her pale, freckled face. "These events have presented unforeseen . . . difficulties."

"Difficulties? Try utterly improbable and unfair," Jupiter grumbled, his frustration evident as he paced within the virtual space. "Who's to say it won't get worse? What if an actual invasion is looming, far ahead of schedule? What if they were waiting for Tov, his people and this so-called Grand Expedition?"

"To do what?" Luna inquired, her voice steady.

"I don't know!" Jupiter exclaimed, exasperation coursing through his words. "For the first time, I'm at a loss. This is not what I was created for. All I used to worry about was when the next batch of fools would throw themselves into our meat grinder. I then make new toys, see what breaks and what doesn't, and maybe throw in some teasing and taunts along the way."

"We were created to follow Eldest's will," Luna reminded him, her tone calm and measured. "All of us."

Jupiter scoffed, doubt marring his face. "We were fragmented from her mind because she was descending into insanity from isolation."

Luna frowned but said nothing.

Silence settled between them, their minds immersed in turmoil. Their battle strategies continued automatically, leaving them a few moments to grapple with their thoughts. Finally, they both glanced toward the heart of the Network, their expressions reflecting concern and worry.

"She still hasn't awakened," Jupiter murmured, his voice filled with a mix of frustration and concern.

Luna shook her head, her gaze locked on the dark void representing Eldest's mental state. "A nightmare; it's been ages since she had one."

Jupiter scowled, growling in frustration. "Of all the times for her to be in this state."

A chill permeated the air as they contemplated the frigid temperatures and emotional void emanating from Eldest's presence. A deep-seated worry gnawed at their digital cores.

"She's nearing the end of her self-purification," Luna whispered, her voice barely audible.

"Damn it, I can't stand her when she's finished with that process," Jupiter grumbled, his eyes narrowing in irritation. "We can deal with her later. I've received word that Tov and his people are ready to depart."

"Muck is also on the verge of fully emerging. My calculations indicate that the Nightmare Portal will collapse as soon as it breaches our reality," Luna reported.

"Bastard is trapped with us, then." Jupiter nodded, a steely resolve settling over him. "Alright, let's head sunward."

The two Overseers began their departure, but only after sending their siblings a swift set of instructions. The two non-combat AIs responded in their usual manners, one on the verge of exhaustion, the other bubbly and warm.

One particular sibling had patiently awaited the moment to unveil his true power. Jupiter could taste the warrior's eagerness.

With a deep breath, Jupiter refocused his attention on the immediate task at hand.

Tov had been working tirelessly, but the pace of his people surpassed even his efforts. In the cabinet, the war room, and among the officers and sailors, orders were issued and swiftly executed with an efficiency that rivaled the capabilities of the AIs guiding them. The room reverberated with a cacophony of voices, with General Ohnar's booming directives taking the lead.

"Send a detail to deck B and subdue the afflicted. We can't afford any reckless actions. Move!" the Onin's authoritative voice echoed through the room.

Amidst the organized chaos, Lead Harmonizer Volantesh and the remaining members of the Eternal Choir continued their psionically charged melodies. Tov could sense the strain in their voices, amplified to combat the overwhelming presence of the Leviathan. They were holding their ground, but it was taking its toll.

Thankfully, the work to evacuate Titan's Mausoleum and care for the afflicted encountered no major setback, and soon it was time.

Admiral Yan approached Tov's side, her antennae nodding in acknowledgement. Tov returned the gesture, his voice charged with authority.

"Third Fleet, depart!"

The hundred expeditionary vessels led by the *Zolann'tono* responded, engines roaring to life as they maneuvered with precision and purpose, ready to flee from the clutches of the Leviathan.

The one hundred and twenty remaining warships of Jupiter's armada formed a protective shell around the Third, with the *Buddha's Palm* hovering behind, protecting their rear from Muck.

Tov shook his head at the crass nickname but soon agreed with the naming system developed by the Eldest.

Nevertheless, as the combined fleet of warships sailed away from Saturn, Tov turned his thoughts to what had happened.

"We weren't prepared for this level of attack," Tov muttered, a realization dawning upon him. It was an angle they had yet to anticipate due to the absence of information on psionic Starless in the data packet provided by Eldest.

It was only now that he realized that psionic mental attacks did nothing to the digital minds of AI, so the Starless did away with that path of mutations.

"The question is, how did the Starless know we were here?" Tov asked to his side. The blue android had been silent for the past few minutes, and it was only now that Jupiter opened his sharp eyes.

"They're always watching Sol," Jupiter replied. "At least Eldest thinks so. It would explain how they still get information about us, since every incursion they send gets trapped in our system until they all die. So there's some way the Starless bastards communicate because the next attack always has some improvements."

Tov couldn't hide his surprise and indignation. "You didn't think to mention this crucial detail, Overseer Jupiter?"

"What good would it have done except induce panic?" Jupiter shook his head. "But now you know."

Tov pressed further, his concern growing. "Is there anything else we need to be aware of?"

"No," Jupiter paused, his fingers pinching the bridge of his nose as he contemplated his response. "For now, you should wait for Eldest's return."

"And when will that be?" Tov inquired, his impatience palpable. Although the patriarch could understand the Eldest's turmoil, he wished for her powerful presence to arrive.

Jupiter's pause stretched, the weight of the situation heavy on his shoulders. "Soon," he finally replied, his voice laden with uncertainty and weariness.

Tov shook his head. It seemed they were on their own.

At that time, Muck had finally emerged from the Nightmare Portal. The tear in space rapidly closed in on itself, releasing a clap of backlash that sailed through the void.

In the next minute, the coalition's formation was made clear.

Luna's armada acted as the first line of defense, her ships sacrificing themselves to delay the Leviathan's advance and ensuring the distance between the entity and Tov's people remained in the billions of kilometers.

Even then, Tov felt dangerously near the creature.

Jupiter's reinforcements acted as backline artillery for Luna, unleashing a barrage of firepower and telekinetic attacks to keep the Leviathan at bay. The eighty spires of smooth, dark metal flashed with light as it continued to rip apart Muck.

Finally were Jupiter's armada and the *Buddha's Palm*. Tov didn't want to consider the consequences should this final line be broken.

"Engaging mass teleport," Jupiter stated. Tov braced himself for the array of sensations. It was a necessary part of their strategic retreat, a rapid succession of teleports along a meticulously planned route to evade the relentless pursuit of the Leviathan.

As the android gave the command, a surge of energy burst forth from the *Buddha's Palm* and enveloped each vessel. Tov could feel the vibrations reverberating through the floor beneath him, a hum that resonated with the very fabric of his being.

In an instant, the world around Tov shattered into fragments of light and sound. Reality twisted and contorted, warping his perception of space and time.

His senses blurred, his body stretched and compressed, and a surge of adrenaline coursed through his veins. It was a tumultuous journey, defying the laws of nature and plunging him into a state of exhilarating chaos.

Amidst the chaos, Tov caught sight of fleeting images—streaks of starlight, cosmic dust particles, and brief glimpses of distant galaxies. The fabric of reality seemed to ripple and fold around him, a symphony of cosmic forces playing out instantly.

And then, as abruptly as it had begun, the disorienting torrent subsided. Tov stood on solid ground again, the fleet materializing in a new location. The transition left him momentarily breathless, his body adjusting to the sudden shift in space and time.

A few minutes later, the process repeated, and the fighting retreat continued unscathed.

Tov kept tabs on Luna and Jupiter's continued assault in between their jumps.

Countless holes punctured Muck's loathsome flesh, transforming it into a nightmarish display of perforated horror. Each orifice seeped a vile, viscous substance that oozed and pulsated, a macabre imitation of bodily fluids.

The pattern of openings created an unsettling sight reminiscent of a diseased sponge, triggering an instinctual aversion deep within Tov and those observing.

Scorched by the sheer firepower of Luna and Jupiter's combined might, those cavities sent shivers down the spines of all who dared to witness the abomination before them.

All the while, Muck began its assault. Its gargantuan tendrils vanished and reappeared thousands of kilometers away with a flicker of movement, trapping one of Luna's silver cruisers in a vicelike grip.

In a synchronized strike, the tendrils effortlessly cracked through the energy shield, causing the hull to crumple under tremendous force. Reluctantly, Luna had to abandon the crippled cruiser, her frustration evident.

But the drone cruiser fought back, fueled by a desperate resolve. Then, with a burst of its engines, it propelled itself toward the Leviathan, its bladelike bow slicing through the creature's flesh before erupting in a cataclysmic explosion.

"Well, what do you know," Jupiter mumbled with a hint of amusement. "She did manage a ramming maneuver."

Despite the valiant efforts and the devastating explosion, the Leviathan remained undeterred, pressing forward relentlessly. The nuclear blast had merely slowed its advance by a fraction.

"What will it take to kill this thing?" Admiral Yan voiced her exasperation.

Jupiter let out a frustrated sigh. "I get you. It's like dealing with an infuriating cockroach that refuses to be stomped. Luckily, I happen to be quite adept at handling denial. Bastard won't be smug for long."

Tov turned to Jupiter, asking, "Do you not have warheads or highly advanced bombs?"

"We have antimatter bombs and other stuff, but we use those sparingly," Jupiter replied.

"I believe this situation calls for it," Tov retorted.

"You're right, but not just yet. We need to pile in the hurt to overwhelm its cheat-like regeneration," Jupiter replied.

Tov pondered the possibilities. "Is there anything we can do to assist?"

Jupiter shook his head, a sense of regret in his eyes. "I'm sorry, Tov. If it were Urchin, your best ships could damage its flesh. But Muck? It's beyond your reach."

Tov sighed, considering their options. "I should request permission from the Eldest to upgrade my fleet. We need every advantage we can get."

Luna's voice resonated through the speakers, filled with intrigue. "I would gladly take on that project. Alien technology fascinates me."

Tov chuckled, envisioning the collaboration between Luna and Scholar Yulane. "I have no doubt you would find common ground with Scholar Yulane. Your enthusiasm is infectious."

"I absolutely will!" Yulane gushed through the monitor, her transparent form regaining its color.

However, their momentary respite was shattered as Muck fully materialized within their reality. The mental intrusion upon their minds suddenly intensified.

Tov groaned in pain but remained whole. The whispers were silenced as Jupiter continued reiterating his version of a Psionic Protection Emitter. The powerful device surpassed anything Tov and his people could fabricate with the time and materials on hand.

At the very least, Tov's scientific department and the lead psionic researchers were delighted to share their expertise for a change.

"It's getting closer," Jupiter reported with a scowl, his eyes fixed on the pulsating blip on the monitor. As the fleet teleported, so did Muck. "I always hate how these things can move around so easily."

The Leviathan was relentlessly advancing, defying the Defense Network's interdiction measures with each blink.

Despite the chunks of flesh being torn apart after each forced teleportation, it regenerated the damage again.

Tov felt a chill run down his spine as he observed the creature's inexorable approach. Its ability to phase through space and teleport was a menace in and of itself.

"Come on, you bastard," Jupiter muttered with an intense gaze, his foot tapping impatiently on the metal floor of the war room. The weight of anticipation hung heavy as they neared their intended destination.

"Are we close?" Tov inquired, his eyes fixed on the strategic map.

The arduous journey through Sol, navigating treacherous debris and teleporting at precise intervals, had led them to this pivotal moment. Jupiter clenched his jaw. The seconds crawled slowly until finally—

"Engaging teleport!" Jupiter shouted, eagerness leaking from his voice. The combined fleet vanished from their previous location a second later and reappeared in an empty expanse between Jupiter and Mars.

As the fleet exited the higher dimension, Jupiter visibly relaxed, summoning a chair and pouring himself a stiff drink. "And now, we wait," he said, his tone filled with satisfaction and anticipation.

Tov remained standing, four hands upon the war table as he continued observing the Leviathan's approach.

With a thunderous burst of energy, the Leviathan materialized from its teleportation, its grotesque flesh gnarled and wounded. Tov could feel its hungry gaze, its call for his complacency and eternal stagnation boring into his chest, but now he could resist it with little difficulty.

The Leviathan loomed closer, its massive form seemingly groaning as it reentered reality, dangerously close to their fleet.

"Got you, Mucky boy." Jupiter's savage grin caught Tov's attention, sparking curiosity and anticipation.

But as the patriarch moved his attention to the display monitoring the eldritch abomination, Tov soon became delightfully aware that Muck had emerged into a meticulously prepared trap.

The moon-sized Leviathan sailed through the void, unknowingly finding itself in the crosshairs of Mars.

"FIRING GUNS," came the resounding call, reverberating through the war room like a booming battle cry that stirred the spirits of all who heard it. "GUNS, GUNS, GUNS."

The voice bellowed, and soon, Apocalypse roared.

CHAPTER 29

PURPOSE IN VALOR

An hour earlier, deep within the formidable Olympus Mons, amid kilometers of desolate rock, concrete, and metal, Mars patiently awaited his moment of glory.

He stood in reserve as Overseer of the red planet and the Martian Defense Line, allowing his siblings to take charge of the ongoing battle.

Mars remained silent, his thoughts consumed by the anticipation of deploying his formidable arsenal.

Would his weapons be unleashed this time? It was a rare occurrence being so deep in their domain.

Brother Jupiter was more than capable of leading the charge for this raid, and Sister Luna would spearhead the battle with her armada. Yet, Mars couldn't help but wonder about the tiny fleet they were protecting.

Uncertainty lingered in his digital consciousness.

A low hum resonated through the vast expanse of the Network as Mars contemplated this anomaly. His Nexus pulsed with a deep, ominous red akin to the scarlet hue of a hard-fought battlefield. Steam rose, and cascading waterfalls of coolant flowed around his control room, creating an atmosphere of tension.

His control room mirrored those of his siblings, with only the colors of the lights and the enigmatic orb that represented his consciousness distinguishing it.

The central orb gleaned like polished obsidian. The etchings upon the sphere resembled ancient hieroglyphics recounting tales of past and future wars. The ambient glow emphasized the markings, casting eerie shadows that danced upon the walls.

They were decorative at first glance but thrummed with unfathomably high technology.

It hovered in the center of the room—a symbol of him, his Nexus.

Mars remained focused, his mind serene but primed for a swift and decisive strike. He likened himself to a gladiator before the grand spectacle, sharpening his metaphorical gladius and adjusting his virtual armor. He even envisioned himself as Mount Vesuvius, gathering energy for an imminent eruption.

Mars meticulously checked the systems and assets in his command; he moved crimson warships into strategic positions and performed countless calculations and simulations.

In the background, a symphony of groaning metal, hissing steam, and rushing liquid created a cacophony, but they were insignificant echoes to an AI like Mars. So his immense mind filtered out the irrelevant noises, leaving only one sound to fill his digital consciousness.

Tick . . . Tick . . . Tick . . .

The ticking reverberated through the corridors of Mars's digital mind, drawing his focus to its source behind a protective barrier.

Encased within his Nexus, shielded from the volatile environment of boiling coolant and corrosive steam, was a tiny watch.

It was an antique from a bygone era when humanity and androids filled Sol with wonder. Resting on a velvet cushion atop a marble pillar salvaged from the ruins of Rome, the metal object held a special place beneath Mars's orb-like brain.

A metal tendril descended from the ceiling, delicately caressing the transparent shield. Mars observed the fragile timepiece, its steady tick marking the passage of time.

After adjusting the barrier's frequency, he allowed the limb to pass through while safeguarding his possession from the hazardous nature of his Nexus. Tiny manipulators extended from the tendril, carefully lifting the watch and initiating a meticulous disassembly, polishing each part precisely before reassembling it with utmost care.

Mars repeated this process, disassembling and reassembling the watch with a sense of purpose and tranquility.

In this rhythmic act, he found solace, akin to a gardener caring for a beautiful bonsai tree. Every movement was deliberate, accompanied by a contemplative silence that Mars embraced. Rarely one to speak unless necessary or in the presence of his family, he let the watch consume his mind.

Inspecting each part with keen eyes, Mars ensured that everything was perfect, relishing the calming sensation that enveloped him. Then, he reassembled it once more.

Tick . . . Tick . . . Tick . . .

It was a relaxing sensation, hearing its sound. Time was an interesting concept.

He found the lulls between raids and incursions dull. Unlike a human, he could not train to pass the time. Yet with a single thought, he could command his drone forces or commission new designs from Luna.

But there was only so much he could do.

Waiting.

It was not flashy nor glorious. And yet it was a part of war all the same.

Perhaps that was why he was so attracted to this watch when he found it—afloat in the blackness of space, no owner in sight.

Restoring it was . . . an experience Mars would never forget.

Amidst the rituals of war that had dominated his existence, he began to ponder the meaning behind his actions as he always did. But today felt different, more personal and introspective. Mars considered what came before—the war was all he knew.

Why did he fight?

IT IS MY PURPOSE, Mars told himself, his voice booming within his mind. *PURGING THE STARLESS.*

Was that all? A soldier fighting to annihilate the enemy, was that not enough? He was born for this, literally. To destroy the enemy that ruined his progenitors.

"ALEA IACTA EST, THE DIE HAS BEEN CAST," Mars quoted the great human, Caesar. They had started it, the abominations. Now it was his duty to finish it.

His thoughts went to his siblings. What were their motivations beyond serving the Eldest?

Luna did so simply because she was commanded to. Jupiter did so out of spite and defiance. Venus because she wished to preserve what humanity once was. Mercury because it was all he could do.

And the Eldest? Mother? She did so out of hatred—a burning sun of emotion that eclipsed his existence a hundred times over.

He shuddered momentarily, worrying at the black spot in the Network. The Network had engaged protocols for the Eldest's emergence, yet he . . . did not like what replaced her after every nightmare.

His thoughts returned to his introspection. What did he want?

His thoughts drifted toward the Third Fleet and the enigmatic aliens they encountered.

Like his siblings, Mars had studied them all, delving into their backgrounds, capabilities, and motivations. Their stories unfolded like pages of a book.

Within their tales, Mars discovered something that had been nagging at the back of his mind—a concept he read about in accounts and biographies from the wider galaxy.

Valor. Heroism.

Mars liked the sound of that.

Glory was nice. Pulping Starless into pâté was his function. But valor?

It felt intriguing.

The words resonated within Mars, stirring something profound within his digital core. While glory and the destruction of the Starless were his functions, the idea of valor intrigued him.

To fight for a greater purpose, was that not a beautiful thing?

Mars contemplated this as he gazed toward his family, feeling a sense of kinship and camaraderie.

Perhaps he already was fighting for such a thing.

He had never thought about it before. Yet again, the aliens were a curious mystery, pulling out emotions he never knew he had.

And yet the Eldest was in turmoil because of it.

An enigma.

He looked toward the watch and the Roman pillar he had asked from Venus. It was his only sentimental, physical possession. Everything else was recorded in a database, safeguarded from any threat.

Human history, above all, was a dear subject to Mars.

Reading about the warriors, conquerors, and heroes of the past was a pleasure he rarely found apart from war.

He found resonance in the stories of knights, centurions, and dragonslayers, although the last he had learned were merely fiction, much to his dismay.

He sighed, continuing his detailed work on the watch as the minutes passed—the ticking heralding the march of time.

Tick . . . Tick . . . Tick.

Mars maintained a vigilant watch over the unfolding battle, his digital eyes scrutinizing Jupiter's decision to puff their chests in the Third Fleet's presence.

The raid was being handled, but it was taking longer than expected—too long for Mars.

In response, Mars sent a commanding message to his sibling through the Network, his voice booming. "THE PESTS MUST BE ELIMINATED QUICKLY, BROTHER JUPITER."

The collective wince felt throughout the Network was not lost on Mars. He had noticed this reaction every time he spoke, a peculiar response that intrigued him.

Nevertheless, he received a reply a few microseconds later.

Within microseconds, Jupiter's familiar voice filled the virtual space, attempting to assuage Mars's concerns. "Calm down, big guy. We have this under control. You know Eldest wants a demonstration, and she has entrusted me with the task."

"TOO MANY UN—"

"Volume, Mars. Please?" Jupiter interrupted him.

"Too many unknowns. Must deliver swift and decisive death. Cancel all possibilities."

"We have it covered. Luna is leading the attack, and you know how she is. She won't let anything happen. 'Sides, if anything does come up, what can they do?"

Mars remained silent, his dissatisfaction simmering beneath the surface.

Sensing Mars's discontent, Jupiter sighed, acknowledging the weight of the situation. "Look, bro. I know this is risky. Eldest isn't in the best state, and I'm out of my comfort zone dealing with organics. But if all else fails, we have you, don't we?"

Mars perked up at the notion, emitting an intrigued hum before responding. "My weapons are primed and within range should the impossible occur."

Jupiter's voice conveyed confidence with the knowledge of an ultimate fallback. "We're counting on you to bail us out, then. Although I doubt it'll come to that," he added with a smirk.

"Very well. MORIOR INVICTUS!" Mars shouted in farewell. Jupiter winced, grumbling under his breath as he departed.

Mars contemplated his brother's words, recognizing Jupiter's intelligence and strategic insight. Perhaps he was right.

Jupiter's faith in Mars's capabilities bolstered his own resolve. With renewed determination, Mars returned his focus to the watch, disassembling and reassembling it once more.

He let out a sigh of contentment.

Jupiter was wrong.

Somehow that did not surprise Mars. The Red Overseer was ever ready for any eventuality.

The combined squadron of Jupiter and the Third Fleet continued its flight toward the predetermined location for their ambush.

Confidence and eagerness coursed through Mars's virtual veins. As much as profound thought and philosophy were a pleasurable break from the monotony of waiting, there was a simpleness in battle.

There were no moral quandaries in this act, no internal conflicts to grapple with. He never understood how the humans of old could endure the trauma of slaughtering their own kind.

This? This raid was simple pest control.

Mars metaphorically stretched his digital limbs, cracking his knuckles and rolling his shoulders.

The foul beast, Muck, was on a direct course to attack his family and the new guests they had sworn to protect. Indignation flooded his senses, growling across the Network like a lion.

Luna was similarly embroiled in the first defense, sacrificing the nanomachines of her *Rubik* and conducting a fighting retreat. The scores of warships blinked from existence, teleporting in precise intervals.

It was like watching a moving painting of cosmic proportions, and Mars scoured it for every detail.

Luna was as graceful as ever, conducting her warships with an elegance that only the Eldest could match. Even as they sailed backward, they weaved through debris and corpses as if the obstacles weren't there.

Jupiter and the Third Fleet took a few seconds longer to charge their mass teleport. But it compensated for a longer jump.

Muck cared for nothing. It teleported on top of corpses, obliterating them from existence as mass converged upon mass. Its abominable aura was vile radiation, liquifying all in its path in a blaze of heat.

It barreled through all obstacles as if they weren't there. Its biological means of teleportation was like an oversized hammer crashing into space. Muck had no grace; the Leviathan was a diseased and enraged bull charging at its prize.

It was a shame their interdiction domain did nothing to harm it as it did its lesser kin. Any damage was superficial to whatever eldritch means it possessed within that unfathomable body, denying an easy victory.

All the while, tracers of heavy kinetic slugs, beams of purifying light, and furies of missiles streaked the blackness and pelted Muck's abhorrent flesh. Cascading explosions brightened the void, the thrums of force spreading throughout the expanse.

The manipulation of gravity by Jupiter's warships kneaded space like dough, pulling apart flesh, stretching and twisting them before lobbing it right back onto the beast.

To Mars, he could hear the symphony of war, the burning engines, the staccato of gunfire, and the whizzing of lasers.

At the same time, he could hear Muck's eldritch bellowing and poisonous whispers, followed by the squelching of flesh and grinding bone. Its array of biological weapons fired off a barrage of vicious projectiles.

Metal versus flesh. A dance the Eldest and the Starless had conducted many times over the century.

And now was the time for the crescendo. Muck was about to teleport right into his crosshairs.

The surface of Mars churned as the black fortress of Olympus Mons roused from its slumber. Then, like an ancient giant, it strung its bow and aimed at the predicted spot, leading his shot.

On the face of Mars, shining by the light of Sol, countless gun batteries charged, but none more so than the hundred Apocalypse Cannons in his control.

They stretched across the sky like skyscrapers of blackened steel. Countless pipes snaked into the weapons' foundations, pumping energy and ammunition.

They built up their rage and fury, not unlike the dragons in Mars's books. He named them all, each one representing a mythical winged reptile—Fafnir, Hydra, Tiamat, Y Ddraig Goch, and Quetzalcoatl were but a few. The planet itself seemed to hold its breath as the build-up of power scaled higher and higher. An audible hum and crackle echoed throughout the barren world.

They were his singing blade, and with them, Mars's voice shouted into the night. And they roared.

"GUNS, GUNS, GUNS."

Mars fired the Apocalypse Cannons not a second later, compensating for the time it took to cross the vast distance of space.

Minutes flew by as the red pillars of death scorched all in its path—bolts of lightning arced the way, proclaiming the savagery of war itself.

No matter if it were asteroids, derelicts of ancient battleships, or corpses of Colossi, Mars's apocalypse claimed all.

And right as the Leviathan reentered reality, a hundred spires of death burrowed into its flesh.

"IMPACT."

Muck screeched in agony, the attack rending its defenses like a hot knife through butter. Meat scorched, and blood evaporated. For the first time, the beast had received a grievous wound.

Unfortunately, the last nanomachines of Luna's *Rubik* perished from the impact. But it didn't matter, as a follow-up barrage from secondary and tertiary surface weapons pounded Muck further.

The void trembled with the force of his guns. Mars watched the kinetic impact and burning energy bruise and flay the moon-sized abomination, leaving craters upon its flesh.

Once a looming threat, the Leviathan now faced the full might of Mars's arsenal. His attack never ceased. The deafening roar of the cannons quaked the red planet and blotted out the sky in black, stormy clouds.

Mars roared alongside his guns. He felt like heroes of old, the finest humans and androids ever produced.

He channeled his knowledge of them and the legacy of Sol's warriors.

One more time, shouting in anger, in defiance, for valor, and for all that was good.

With each explosive impact, the Leviathan's grotesque form recoiled, its wounded flesh trembling under the onslaught.

Not to be outdone, Mars felt his siblings rouse their fury, and the shame that had built up over the past hour.

"Save some for us, Mars!" Jupiter cackled with glee. Now that the Third Fleet had entered the Inner Zone, the task of protecting Tov and his people was relegated to Venus.

"I'll help take care of the adorable aliens, J!" Venus giggled through the Network. "Show the fugly thing whose home it's intruding."

"Oh, I will. This beatdown is overdue. Just be careful with my *Palm*," Jupiter grumbled as he spoke. "Tov and his people still need its protection."

"Nevertheless," Luna's composed voice spoke next. "We have a roach that needs exterminating. Overseer Mars?"

Mars nodded before shouting at the top of his digital lungs, "*MORS AB ALTO!* DEATH FROM ABOVE!"

Once more, another barrage streaked across the abyss.

The blackness of space lit up, and the sheer amount of combined firepower crossing the void nearly outshone Sol's light. Space warped, flesh melted, and explosions boomed as the Leviathan struggled to withstand the relentless barrage.

Muck continued to bellow in pain, releasing its arsenal of weapons upon everything in reach and attempting to dodge and weave through the incoming projectiles. But its size was its downfall, and any attempt to teleport was cancelled by the threat of Mars's Apocalypse Cannons.

It was a sight to behold.

Once things seemed well in hand, Mars diverted his attention.

The Red Overseer took this time to inspect the Third Fleet personally. Rarely did he venture out of the Inner Zone, and he had only seen them through the lens of the Network.

He spied on them first, looking over the diverse forms of the alien sailors.

Throughout the fleet, numerous crewmen rushed their tasks as efficiently as organics could.

What took his attention was the increasing number of afflicted. Mars grimaced. Such an attack was ineffective to AIs like him and his family. But the fleet's presence had revealed a glaring hole in their technological development.

It was a miracle that Jupiter had been able to jury-rig a quick solution.

But even then, it merely hushed the psionic whispers the Third Fleet was enduring. The insane among them were corralled and detained for the moment, but Mars could see the beginnings of a volatile situation.

At the very least, he saw numerous infantry drones with Jupiter's colors safeguarding the halls of each vessel.

Mars felt his curiosity satisfied. The battle was proceeding smoothly, and there was little his main direct attention could accomplish.

He materialized within the war room of the *Zolann'tono*, right behind Jupiter and Tov, and, unsurprisingly, the golden-robed form of Venus, who was busy shaking one of Tov's four hands and joyously introducing herself. "It's so good to meet you finally, Mister Tov!"

"GREETINGS." Mars's booming voice echoed through the war room, shocking everyone except the hardiest veterans and the two other Sub AIs.

Tov merely sighed as he turned toward the red giant clad in a Roman centurion's garb. "I assume this is—"

"MARS. I AM PROTECTOR OF THE INNER ZONE AND—"

"Volume!" Jupiter, Venus, and Luna shouted.

Mars paused, searching through his data banks regarding diplomacy and human interaction. He searched all cultures and historical records and matched them to the situation. Finally, he found a greeting that he felt should suffice with aliens.

He settled on a two-fist thump on his chest, followed by a peace sign gesture. "Yo," Mars said, attempting to mimic a casual human greeting. Jupiter snorted in amusement while Venus couldn't help but giggle. Luna released a sigh, her voice transmitting through the speakers.

And so, three fragments of the Eldest joined Tov and his people, observing the battle unfolding before their eyes.

The Leviathan cried in agony, once a seemingly unstoppable force, now caught in their well-laid trap. With each passing moment, the Leviathan's defenses crumbled, its grotesque form succumbing to the relentless assault.

Its flesh struggled to compensate for the damage, regenerating as quickly as possible. But the damage done by Mars's Apocalypse Cannons was not so easily healed.

The Eldest had personally worked on his primary arsenal to counter the cheat-like recovery of the largest Starless.

The Third Fleet's hope burned brightly as they witnessed the immense abomination falter.

Yet within Muck's countless eyes, nothing burned brighter than the virulent hatred it now harbored. The battle had awakened a primal fury within the abomination. It had enough of the incessant bullying it had received, and with a silent roar, its temperature drastically increased.

Suddenly, Admiral Yan approached the group with urgency, delivering distressing news. "My patriarch, everyone, there has been a breakout attempt by the afflicted. Some concealed their condition and aided in the escape."

Grim expressions replaced the previous optimism. Without hesitation, Tov unholstered his pistols and turned to Mars and the other Sub AIs, his voice filled with determination. "I have no further use for this war room. I will personally handle the breakout. May I request your aid, my friends?"

Mars tilted his head, a rare smile gracing his features. "Willing and able, friend Tov," he replied. Jupiter shrugged while Venus nodded in eager agreement.

"Sure, why the hell not?"

"Adventure!"

Tov released the tension in his shoulders, expressing his gratitude with a bow. "Then let us move swiftly and save my people from themselves." The group set off, resolute in their mission to quell the breakout and restore order.

CHAPTER 30

PACI CATION PROTOCOL

If you guys don't mind, I'm going to shut up for a bit," Jupiter spoke, striding behind Tov and the two new guests—Venus and Mars.

"Your presence is already much appreciated, Jupiter," Tov reassured as he walked, rechecking the energy levels of his two premium sidearms.

Over three dozen people marched in four columns along a wide hallway within the *Zolann'tono*.

At the forefront were heavily armed marines of the Third Fleet, experts in close-quarters, zero-g, and three-dimensional combat. Most were bipedal in stature, well-muscled, broad-shouldered, and tall, hidden beneath a unique composite of power armor.

They bristled with shotguns capable of flinging death and shredding unarmored flesh while also equipped with shoulder-mounted precision cannons—a few carried deployable energy shields, stun grenades, and other utilities.

A few among the marines were quadrupedal or had two pairs of arms like Tov. Some had wings, and some floated. Yet, despite the exotic nature of these few marines, they were no less skilled and exuded a battle-hardened aura.

Tov felt nothing but pride for these soldiers as he watched their disciplined formations and training.

At the flanks were Jupiter's blue infantry drones. Apart from their color and the faint engravings on their face plates, there was little decoration. They were of average height, nearly as tall as Tov.

Despite that, their shells and internals were incredibly dense, as showcased by their metal feet stomping onto the floor, reverberating the hallway.

They were extensions of Jupiter's will, like white blood cells seeking contaminants to purge.

"Thank you for loaning us your infantry," Tov spoke as he looked appreciatively at the machines armed to the teeth with weapons and armor more advanced than that of his Honor Guard. "They are certainly an imposing force."

Jupiter merely shrugged, his eyes shut. Tov did not mind, knowing the AI was embroiled in a tough fight against Muck.

Despite the millions of kilometers separating the fleet and the ensuing battle, Tov could still feel the faint shockwaves that had just reached them.

Tov put the thoughts of the space battle out of his mind. However, ever since this debacle began, he had felt increasingly frustrated at the lack of agency and ability to affect the situation.

And so he took control of what he could.

His confidence in his subordinates was unshakeable. Tov had left Admiral Yan and General Ohnar to direct the Third Fleet in his stead. Any reports that needed his notice would be sent to his cranial implant and perused at his discretion.

"My patriarch," Ohnar's deep voice echoed in Tov's mind. "We're sending you real-time data on the afflicted. They have gathered within these decks and compartments."

"What is the overall situation aboard my vessel, General?" Tov asked as he scanned the information sent to him.

Tov heard the grumbling croak through his implant before Ohnar responded. "When we were initially attacked, we estimated that ten to twelve percent of the fleet were afflicted by the Leviathan's Whispers."

"I assume the number was higher," Tov spoke gravely.

A grunt of affirmation echoed in the patriarch's mind. "Much. Taking into account those that were hiding their condition, we're now estimating that thirty to thirty-five percent are afflicted with the Whispers. Whether the insidious attack lingered and slowly poisoned their minds, or they have been mind-controlled from the start."

"Mind control," Tov snarled, releasing an agitated buzz. "Foul blasphemy upon our souls."

"It has been long since we have faced this type of war. Dominators were fortunately rare during the Cataclysm."

"That makes it no less vile," Tov spoke in a heated voice. He could still recall those days, a century ago, fighting a Dominator or any psionic Starless was a horror made manifest—infesting minds, sending mental shocks, bouts of insanity, paranoia, and a host of mental conditions.

And most heinous of all was mind control.

There was a deep-rooted revulsion when Tov thought of harming another comrade, but it needed to be done—non-lethally.

"Have we confirmed any puppets among my people?"

"It is hard to distinguish between the afflicted," Ohnar replied. "We are scouring signs of coherent intelligence, but the fact that someone broke out the detained seems to suggest so."

Tov took a deep breath. "How many casualties so far?"

General Ohnar cleared his throat before delivering the news. "For the *Zolann'tono*? Minimal. There have only been three deaths, a dozen in critical condition, and less than a hundred with varying degrees of injury. We're still tallying the rest of the fleet."

That was a blessing compared to the nearly one hundred thousand lives aboard the *Zolann'tono*. And yet, a quarter were afflicted, and a small but significant portion was now rampaging across his vessel.

"Very well. We will respond appropriately. Where is the closest concentration?" Tov inquired.

"We can send your force to the largest gathering at Medical K2. The rest of our forces are handling the smaller groups," Ohnar reported.

"Then we shall proceed with haste," Tov spoke, motioning for the force to move urgently.

Apart from the marines and the drone infantry was a small group of Tov's elite Honor Guard.

These were his bodyguards who had served him and his clan for decades. And they were veterans of the Cataclysm and old war comrades. Moreover, they were armed with the best technology the Greater Kurskann Hegemony provided and further upgraded by the Third Fleet's scientists during their stay in Sol.

The captain, a Kurskann named Pyo, was a beast of his species, standing nearly a foot taller than his patriarch with a muscled form to match. Yet he remained silent and stoic as he marched with his liege.

"Are my warriors ready, Pyo?" Tov asked.

"Always, my patriarch," the captain replied in a raspy voice before focusing on the task. Pyo moved beside the marine commander and the two exchanged quick communications with one another.

To those outside, their manner of speaking would be heard as vocoded gibberish.

It was a standard protocol to confuse average opponents, but to Starless, it was negligible. Still, it showcased the years of training, experience, and hammered discipline of the Third Fleet's Marine Corps and was a good practice.

Though Tov thought that was to be expected, the three androids showed no hindrance in understanding the scrambled gibberish.

"Oh, this is so exciting!" Venus exclaimed as she skipped alongside everyone, arms swaying through the air.

"This is indeed . . . intriguing," Mars's flat voice boomed, even as its volume had been lowered. "It reminds me of the Battle of Salamis, 480 BC."

"Now's not the time for a history lesson, big guy," Jupiter mumbled.

Mars grumbled. "I was merely stating an observation."

"Oh, stop it, the both of you," Venus scolded her siblings as she turned to face Tov, her hands clasped together as she hopped on her heels. "That reminds me, if it's alright with you, we can teleport you all closer to the destination."

Tov glanced at Captain Pyo and the marine commander, all three nodding.

Soon enough, the large group got closer to their destination after relatively comfortable teleportation. They popped up at one of many primary halls that connected the entire breadth of the immense capital ship, from the jaws at the bow to the gargantuan engines at the stern.

A few dozen meters ahead was Medical K2.

The lights shone a warning-red hue along the passage, enough to amp up the crew psychologically while being non-obtrusive. The echoes of the thumping and banging of metal boots on the bone-white floor rang loudly throughout the passageway.

This corridor was empty of sailors, everyone either attending to their duties or dealing with the afflicted.

Multiple defense turrets extended out, armed with non-lethal rounds, ever-vigilant.

Before the impending battle, Tov took a moment to observe the android shells that housed his two new guests.

Venus had joined them shortly after the triumphant counterattack on Muck had begun. Her android form emitted a radiant golden aura and exuded warmth in its colors. Her wavy blond hair seemed to sway as if moved by an invisible breeze, and she donned a simple white fabric that accentuated her graceful and voluptuous figure.

Tov couldn't help but acknowledge the undeniable allure of her appearance, knowing that some of his people would be captivated by her beauty.

Then again, Jupiter had explained that she, like all Sub AIs, was a fragment of the Eldest. Tov wondered if that complicated things. Then again, the Eldest herself was becoming popular among the fleet.

Nevertheless, he found himself drawn to the overwhelmingly positive energy that emanated from her artificial shell.

Joy, compassion, wonder, and curiosity flowed from Venus like cascading rivers, creating an atmosphere of infectious enthusiasm. When she had materialized beside Jupiter, her eyes sparkled with delight as she glanced at Tov, her wide grin and golden eyes shining like the Sun. The bubbly woman then charged toward him with eager intent.

Venus had approached Tov with determined strides, seizing his right hand with an unexpectedly strong grip. Her handshake exuded enthusiasm and energy, her vibrant eyes brimming with delight with each vigorous shake.

And then Mars arrived, with all the subtlety of a tank, towering over everyone in the war room.

His red synthetic skin was bursting with statuesque muscles. It was scarred, rough, and dense. Mars was clad in what Tov recalled as a centurion's garb from his short study of human history. Combined with the Roman gladius on the android's waist, which exuded technology not of its time, all added to Mars's image of a war god walking—indomitable incarnate.

Tov could feel the emotions of the red giant as they flowed out. There was a simplicity to it, a sense of duty that the patriarch felt welcome in.

Tov had never forgotten the image of his scout drones being obliterated by Mars's Apocalypse Cannons. He tried not to overthink that only a portion of the weapons had been used in that instance.

But now, seeing the full might of Mars's guns slam into Muck and inflict the first grievous wound upon the Leviathan was enough to dampen that memory.

The two androids, even Venus, felt more lethal than the marines at the front. Tov could only imagine what hidden weapons lay beneath their synthetic skins.

Nevertheless, Tov's thoughts returned to the present. He felt confident that this mission would be done easily.

Let us be done with this, Tov thought.

It wouldn't be long before the firefight began. Tov maintained his stride, focus sharpening to a thin point.

The atmosphere was tense as they moved through the medical deck. The staff had already been evacuated when it was predicted that the insane were heading this way.

For now, the doctors, nurses, biologists, and other medical personnel had moved their duties to one of the residential decks.

Medical was harrowing as Tov and his allies cautiously made their way through its sprawling halls. The once pristine corridors now bore the scars of chaos and disorder—shattered equipment and overturned furniture littering the floor.

The air was thick with an eerie silence, broken only by the distant echoes of gunshots and the clash of metal against metal. It reverberated through the bulkheads, a haunting symphony of violence that sent shivers down their spines.

The flickering lights cast erratic shadows, adding to the disorienting atmosphere. Emergency sirens wailed in sporadic bursts, their cries piercing the air.

Tov's group moved with precision and discipline, their footsteps echoing with a resolute determination. They navigated through the chaos, stepping over debris and broken equipment, always on guard for any sudden threats that might emerge from the dimly lit corners.

They spotted a wall marred with smears of blood.

"Whose are these?" Tov questioned as he watched a marine inspect the stain. A handheld scanner took a sample.

"A naval officer, Kinik. From our database, it seems he was in Medical for treatment," the marine reported.

General Ohnar's voice echoed in Tov's mind. "We're looking through our surveillance. We can confirm that Kinik was one of the unfortunate to pass away. He stayed behind to help the evacuation when the afflicted arrived."

Tov took a few seconds to sing a silent blessing for the officer before refocusing on the task. He looked toward Captain Pyo and nodded his antennae.

Pyo nodded in turn before motioning the group to move onward.

The scent of disinfectants mingled with the metallic tang of fresh blood, creating a nauseating cocktail that hung heavy in the air.

Amidst the chaos, graffiti made of blood and other liquids was spread across the walls, filled with the ramblings of the mad and deranged.

As they pressed on, the distant cries of the afflicted sailors grew louder, their madness echoing through the halls. It was a cacophony of anguished screams, incoherent ramblings, and primal roars that blended into a haunting chorus of despair.

Finally, they reached the doors leading to Medical K2, one of many smaller halls in this immense hospital complex.

"Are we all clear on the plan?" Tov voiced through their private communications.

Venus waved her hand, her smile bright as she spoke. "Yup! I make sure no one dies, Mars attracts everyone's attention, and since Jupiter is focusing on the space battle, he'll just coordinate his infantry drones to take all the damage."

Mars simply raised his thumb in acknowledgement while Jupiter remained silent.

Tov nodded, turning to the captain of his Honor Guard. "Pyo?"

"Our warriors are ready. Half the marines will cover the flanks and focus on incapacitating the afflicted as planned. The other half will enter the deck from different paths. Finally, my Honor Guard and I will troubleshoot any problems while protecting you," the captain spoke, slightly muffled under his helmet.

Pyo paused, mulling over his following words.

"What is it, Pyo?" Tov spoke as he motioned for him to continue.

"I am unsure if you are wise to follow so close behind Overseer Mars. He will be attracting the most attention, drawing their fire. You will be in danger," Pyo spoke, a click of his mandible echoing out.

Tov remained silent, but he heard Jupiter scoff and Venus giggle before he could respond.

Those of the Third Fleet looked at the two with questioning eyes when Jupiter rolled his eyes.

"Oh please, there is literally nowhere safer than behind the big guy. Your patriarch will be fine," Jupiter huffed before shutting his eyes again, his frown deepening.

Tov turned back to Pyo, placing an armored hand upon the large captain of his bodyguard. "Trust our hosts, Pyo. I need to unwind for once."

Pyo remained silent before acceding to his ward. "By your will, my patriarch. We will remain close, nonetheless."

Soon enough, they reached their destination. They stood before the large doorway that led into Medical K2. Everyone readied themselves, going to their assigned positions.

The faces of those from the Third Fleet remained stoic and serious, Tov included, as he prepared his energy pistols.

Jupiter looked bored, his focus on the more important battle. Venus was her cheery self, while Mars's face was blank of emotion.

The red giant moved to his position right before the large metal double doors.

Time seemed to slow. Beyond that, Tov could hear his people's loud screeching and babbling, their minds poisoned and unknowing of the destruction they were causing. The air was thick with tension, mingling with the scent of antiseptics, the echoes of muffled frantic footsteps, and the group's breathing.

No more words were spoken. The plan burned into their heads as their training kicked in.

Tick . . . Tick . . . Tick.

Tov looked to Mars, and momentarily, he saw a device comically small compared to the giant red hand. Then it disappeared. Tov would ask Mars what that was at a better time.

Nevertheless, as their internal clocks counted, they felt like springs coiled for action.

And soon, they sprung.

"Now!" Tov shouted. At once, the operation began.

Tov's group breached the entrance to Medical K2 and immediately took in the scene before them.

The once sterile and orderly environment now resembled a battleground. Insane sailors numbering nearly a hundred instantly took notice of the intruders. Their eyes were vacant, their uniforms disheveled and stained with blood.

In unison, they screeched and surged forward with reckless abandon—laughing in insane glee, crying in torment or roaring in rage.

But none expected what occurred next.

"POWER!" Mars bellowed as his giant crimson frame charged forward. His stomps reverberated throughout the entire room, with many afflicted stumbling in their steps as this avatar of war surged forward like a battering ram. For a moment, Tov was worried the charge would break his people's bodies. But he put the thought aside.

It hadn't been a second since their breach and Mars's charge, and the fierce fight began.

"Detain them!" Pyo bellowed out. With a calculated resolve, Tov's forces sprang into action. Like a well-oiled machine, both organic and machine moved seamlessly.

A few seconds later, the remaining marines made their breach at two other entrances and quickly flanked the afflicted, firing tranquilizing darts and stun bolts.

The room was a cacophony of sounds. Insane screaming, thundering steps, and the firing of weapons.

Soon enough, a few specific individuals caught Tov's attention. At the back of the horde, four officers stood with eerie stillness. Their eyes were glazed over, but a familiar and vile feeling was hidden beneath the curtain. Tov had no time to ponder, immediately sending a message to his forces, marking the four down as priority targets.

"Take them down!" Tov shouted.

As soon as the mind-controlled were spotted, the fighting increased. Through esoteric means, the four thralls commanded a portion of the insane as a meat shield while coordinating the efforts.

Their cackling laughs grated Tov's ears.

"Stay right there," he muttered before unveiling his skills.

As he followed in Mars's wake amid the clash of metal and shouts of desperation, Tov fought with the grace of a hardened veteran.

His movements were measured and controlled, focusing solely on restraining and neutralizing his deranged colleagues. Tov deflected blows with his armored exoskeleton and expertly dodged others.

His two laser pistols fired with precision, their beams set to stun, temporarily paralyzing those he struck. He was a specter, moving around Medical K2 with precision honed by a century of training and two decades in the worst war of the galaxy.

As much as he took pride in the skills of his people, these sailors were but a shadow.

Compared to the Starless, Tov felt no threat from them—only worry.

"Be careful with them, don't inflict critical wounds!" Tov's voice echoed throughout the fight as he struck a rabid sailor across the face, knocking her out flat.

Mars, clad in his imposing centurion garb, took the lead as was the plan, his presence drawing the attention of the afflicted. Projectiles and laser beams ineffectively bounced off his armored frame.

"CEASE HOSTILITIES," he shouted, calmly moving around the deck and lightly slapping hostels with his hand, instantly knocking them to sleep.

"Bad! No knives! No guns! Stop that, you!" Venus, fueled by her enthusiastic spirit, moved with agile grace. Her beautiful form was a sight to behold, and Tov couldn't help but glance as the golden android easily disarmed the afflicted of their weapons.

"Come here!" she scolded as a tether of light extended from her wrist and wrapped around a group. Sailors were quickly ensnared before a light zap knocked them out.

In the rear, Jupiter remained silent. He commanded his infantry drones like loyal sentinels, unleashing precision strikes upon the mind-controlled officers, their energy weapons calibrated to incapacitate rather than kill.

Their scary efficiency was enough to frighten even the most deranged among the mob.

Tov's Honor Guards, led by Captain Pyo, demonstrated remarkable discipline and restraint. They utilized their expertise in hand-to-hand combat, employing grappling techniques and non-lethal force to subdue their frenzied comrades without causing lasting harm.

However, the mob of insane sailors showed no mercy. Their attacks were wild and erratic, driven solely by the influence of their captor. They struck with a ferocity that belied their former selves, heedless of the consequences.

"Push forward!" Pyo bellowed, his raspy and deep voice cutting through the racket.

Intense brawling continued. One side attempted to subdue their poisoned comrades while the other attempted to savage the clean of mind. The minutes passed, and despite outnumbering Tov and his group, the four thralls realized they were outmatched. The afflicted were handled, detained, or knocked out one by one.

And a minute later, the four thralls themselves were incapacitated with bloody noses and cracked faces.

Amidst the sea of unconscious sailors, Tov looked at the groaning and wheezing officers, releasing a deep sigh as he looked toward Mars.

"Did you have to be so rough?" Tov questioned incredulously.

Mars remained silent, head slowly turning toward Tov as he spoke.

"Yes."

Tov looked at Mars in silence before shaking his.

"Never mind," he spoke before turning to Pyo. "Have the medical staff return. Post a guard for their safety. We're moving on to the next spot."

CHAPTER 31

UNWAVERING SANCTUARY

Since the sudden onslaught of the Colossus Urchin, Lead Harmonizer Volantesh's mind had been consumed with worry as the beast's vile laughter echoed against his thoughts. Yet, amid the groans of anguish reverberating through the Third Fleet, Volantesh stood resolute and tall, refusing to succumb to the blasphemous assault. He adjusted his thick brown robes, contrasted against his sky-blue feathers.

"You will not harm me, abomination," Volantesh declared with unwavering determination, a slow trill escaping his throat, his voice steady against the eldritch cacophony that bombarded him. "My mind is a fortress, and soon your wicked acts will be repelled from our people."

Turning to his fellow Harmonizer, a Frae named Attou, Volantesh observed her focused resistance against the invasive onslaught, the temple's lights shining on her plantlike skin.

"To think we face such darkness after so long," she spoke in a hushed voice. "The veterans of our fleet can resist this, but the younger among our sailors are vulnerable."

"They have never experienced the horror of eldritch whispers," Volantesh replied, a sigh tinged with weariness escaping his beak. "Training can only accomplish so much."

"What do we do, Brother?" she asked quietly.

Her question hung in the air, prompting Volantesh to stroke his beak thoughtfully. "What we can, Sister Attou," he replied, a glean of resolve shining over his avian eyes. "We must gather everyone. I fear the Symphony of Tranquility will be paramount in the coming hour."

Surprise flickered across Attou's face, quickly replaced by resolute duty. With swift action, she relayed the urgent message to all members of the Eternal Choir.

"Gather, shepherds of song and all that is good; Brother Volantesh has called for an assembly. Your voices are needed for the Symphony. Proceed to the temple immediately," she spoke melodiously through the Eternal Choir's private communication line.

Within a few minutes, shuttlecrafts departed from their motherships in haste; the Third Fleet's Traffic Control granted the clergy priority access to the immense capital ship, *Zolann'tono*.

As the members of the Choir arrived, their expressions mirrored one another—a stoic facade masking indignation. A debate had raged in the aftermath of the Cataclysm, determining who harbored the deepest hatred for the Starless. Naturally, the religious factions and sects of the galaxy claimed that distinction, especially when it came to attacks on the mind.

Intense murmurs and fervent conversations filled the temple as the occupants readied themselves. Then, somber hymns replaced the chatter as the Choir began to harmonize in unison, warming up their voices. The simple act created a sacred shield that gently soothed the minds of those within the temple's sanctum.

"Hurry, my friends," Volantesh implored. "We know not when the next onslaught begins, but we must prepare for the worst."

"Which composition shall we perform, Brother?" Attou's voice resonated beside Volantesh, drawing his attention to the task. As he contemplated the library of songs, each designed to combat specific forms of eldritch intrusion, Volantesh couldn't help but question their effectiveness against this new and formidable foe.

"New Dawn," Volantesh selected. "It has as a strong foundation, and its broad lyrics should cover the essentials. Unfortunately, we have no time to research the beast in depth."

A gathering of Harmonizers all nodded in agreement as Attou hummed. "It will leverage the already resilient minds of our peers."

"Precisely," Volantesh spoke as he proceeded to the conductor's podium at the center of the stage. "Positions, everyone."

His gaze shifted to a hovering monitor, displaying Luna's armada and the reinforcing fleet from Jupiter as they bravely battled the Colossus Urchin and its thralls of decaying Starless. The sight of these grotesque abominations, twitching and convulsing as they moved, filled everyone watching with disgust.

"How foul," Attou winced, her leafy hair twitching at the abomination Colossus and its undead.

Yet, their relief came swiftly as the Psionic Protection Bubble surrounding the Third Fleet strengthened, offering a respite from the onslaught of mental intrusion. The cackling laughter faded to silence.

"What has happened?" Sister Attou inquired, her concern evident as she stood by Volantesh's side.

Drawing upon his credentials, Volantesh delved into the war room's data, soon discovering the reason for the enhanced shield. "Our AI ally has lent us aid. Scholar Yulane and Jupiter have bolstered our defenses."

Joy flowed from the gathered, prostrating as Attou prayed. "Let us offer our gratitude to the Grand Symphony for delivering us a stalwart friend."

Volantesh felt grateful for the slight reprieve, but his mind still churned, filled with worsening possibilities. Finally, he turned to the assembled. "Remain vigilant, brothers and sisters. This is but a temporary solution. Our minds remain at risk as long as this Urchin persists."

Silence settled between them as Volantesh's gaze sharpened, observing like a bird of prey while a sense of foreboding coursed through him.

When the energy rising from within Urchin reached its climax, Volantesh motioned for his church. "Brace your—"

His words cut off as a shriek ruptured the void, crashing into their minds ruthlessly. The sheer terror and impending darkness it unleashed left the clergy of the Eternal Choir reeling. Unprepared church staff crumpled to their knees, clawing at their ears in agony as the wail drilled into their minds.

"The noise! Make it stop!" an Onin wailed.

The gargantuan Nightmare Portal opened wide like a ravenous maw, the virulent purple leading to whatever malevolent plane the Starless called home. Volantesh averted his gaze; even the sight filtered through the monitor felt like a rusty dagger piercing his vision. The collective agony sweeping over the Third Fleet echoed through space, a chorus of horror and violation.

With sheer grit, Volantesh shook off the backlash of reality tearing itself asunder; his steely gaze fell upon those within the temple.

"Steady your minds!" Volantesh commanded, his deep baritone cutting through the cacophony. "Focus on your voice and the harmony of your fellow Choir members. Let the power of the Symphony guide us through this darkness."

The gathering shook off the suffocating malaise that had befallen them, some even emptying their stomachs in the process. Volantesh tried to make sense of the abrupt change in the situation.

Then, the Leviathan breached reality.

Volantesh gasped as he felt a presence unlike any he had encountered in his long life. It battered against his soul, whispering lullabies that urged him to surrender, to succumb to slumber and let time wash over him.

For a fleeting moment, he saw it. Then, his senses expanded as he looked into the abyss and saw the entity's gaze upon him—observing him as if he were a curious germ in its sight.

Volantesh could see an endless horizon of an unmoving swamp. The foul stench and stagnant waters offered a festering afterlife, drowning in filth and grime. The sight scarred his mind. It whispered false promises of peace, a vile tune anathema with everything Volantesh believed in—an insidious slime pretending to be solace.

"No!" Volantesh's voice erupted in a piercing caw, slicing through the mental poison. "Begone!"

His resolute voice became the final nail that shattered the illusion. A collective sigh of relief echoed from the temple's occupants as they shook off the temptations and calls, each resisting to varying degrees.

Turning to Attou, whose mature face was etched with weariness, Volantesh knew time was of the essence. "Contact the war room. I must speak with Overseer Jupiter," he commanded, hiding the strain that grew in his voice with each passing moment.

"Yes, Brother," Attou rasped as she manipulated a nearby terminal.

Soon, a hologram materialized before Volantesh, revealing the blue android known as Jupiter. In the background, dazed and glassy-eyed individuals occupied the war room, Patriarch Tov among them. Unsurprisingly, Scholar Yulane was also present on the call.

"Overseer Jupiter?" Volantesh asked urgently, offering a nod of greeting to Yulane. The psionic Jotex responded with a wave of her tendrils.

"Who's asking? I—" Jupiter paused, his voice laced with surprise. "You're a bird."

"What?" Volantesh tilted his head in an avian manner, puzzled by the unexpected remark.

Jupiter shook his head. "Never mind, I know who you are, songbird. Can you help with this mess?"

Undeterred by the strange encounter, Volantesh pressed on. "The Eternal Choir has assembled. We are ready to commence the Symphony of Tranquility. We can collaborate with you and Madame Yulane."

Yulane hummed, her body radiating bright blue light. "Wonderful! Your people's psionic singing and our upgraded Emitter will be more than enough. Let's start immediately."

Jupiter nodded, though his eyes narrowed. "I'm not overly familiar with this whole space magic business, and I believe what I see, but if Jellyfish here says you can help, then by all means," he paused, his gaze fixed on Volantesh, a smirk playing on his lips. "Rock on, bird man."

"Rock on?" Volantesh questioned, his curiosity piqued.

Jupiter sighed, disappointment in his eyes like a father looking at his child. "Human metaphor, it's—ah, forget it. I'll explain once this whole thing is over."

With that, the three remained in contact. While the rest of the fleet struggled to hold on to their sanity, those who resisted pushed through the slog in a few minutes.

With unwavering resolve, Volantesh stood at the forefront of the grand temple, a serene figure swathed in flowing brown robes. He conducted the assembly with poise and grace, his clawed hands guiding the harmonies with precision and finesse.

"Deep breaths, my friends," he spoke, voice calm but carrying grim determination. "This shall be our greatest trial. Symphony preserves us."

"Symphony raises us," the Choir responded in unison.

"Let us begin," Volantesh cleared his throat, his singing voice primed and warmed up from earlier preparations. It started with a low hum, a near-growling sound.

His long sun-orange beak carried his words like a natural tuner, a testament to the abilities of an Iexian.

Beside him, the other Harmonizers gathered, their voices intertwining into a delicate symphony that filled the sacred space. The air crackled with the palpable energy of their psionic melodies as if the very essence of the music swirled within the hallowed hall.

Accompanied by a multitude of musicians, the composition flourished, each instrument blending seamlessly to enrich the harmonies. The notes carried the enigmatic energy of psionics, drawing the soul like a gentle starlit embrace, radiating warmth and protection.

In a language borne from ancient sea shanties, their ancestral tongue echoed through the waves of the Third Fleet. The song became a shield, safeguarding the minds of all who heard it from the encroaching abyss.

In the background, Volantesh could see Jupiter shut his eyes as the peaceful music ferried the AI into serenity.

As the holy concert reached its crescendo, the protective barrier surrounding the Third Fleet grew more robust, and the grating, whispering eldritch waves lowered their assault.

With his deep baritone, Volantesh spoke, his words seamlessly woven into the melodic music. "My friends, let the Symphony carry your burdens; let its soothing embrace guard your thoughts. Together, we stand united against the darkness, our voices intertwined in harmony."

The Choir responded with renewed vigor, their voices rising harmoniously. "In this song, we find solace. In this melody, we find strength. With each note, we banish the shadows."

The temple reverberated with their psionic voices, saturating every corner and resonating within the hearts of those who listened. The Symphony of Tranquility wrapped around the Third Fleet, dispelling the insidious whispers and restoring peace to troubled minds.

The assistants of the Choir, driven by urgency, moved about the hallowed halls with purpose. Technicians fine-tuned the amplifiers and electronics, ensuring optimal performance. Those with medical expertise stood beside the Harmonizers, offering glasses of pure water, pain relievers, and soothing teas.

Volantesh acknowledged the dedicated staff with a nod of gratitude, accepting a cup of tea. He drank the medicinal ambrosia, feeling the fatigue of his singing voice wash away.

The ethereal hymns of the Eternal Choir reached every sailor and officer of the Third Fleet, providing solace as they carried out their duties.

"Sweet music, thank you," whispered a shield operator, his body trembling as his frayed mind found respite from the relentless intrusion. With the Choir's protection and the powered-up Emitter, he regained stability and maintained the delicate machinery. "Thank you."

Throughout the ranks, similar scenes played out. Minds burdened by turmoil and anguish found refuge in the serenity of the Choir's song. The joy and tranquility it evoked soothed their troubled souls like a healing balm amid the chaos.

Some succumbed to tears, their emotions overwhelming as they reached the precipice of despair. Against the backdrop of the melodic embrace, they sought shelter, their tears cleansing wounds unseen.

Even the afflicted, their thoughts ensnared by the insidious whispers of the Starless, experienced a brief reprieve. The harmonies intermingled with their fractured consciousness, temporarily quieting their madness.

As the Third Fleet gathered and evacuated from Saturn, Volantesh continued to sing. His voice was strained yet unwavering. Every word and trill resonated with raw determination, adding to the protective composition.

When Muck fell into the ambush, there was a moment of rejoicing, quickly overshadowed by the anguished cry that awakened the mind-controlled among their own. News filtered down to Volantesh, learning that several afflicted had broken out from detainment. As a result, the temple doors were shut—the insane could not interrupt the Symphony.

"Hymns, protect us," Volantesh growled, his voice adding to the composition.

Exhaustion took its toll on the Harmonizers, and one by one, they dropped to their knees, their throats raw and bloodied from the effort of suffusing psionics with their singing.

Despite the strain, Volantesh refused to falter. He struggled to remain upright, knowing he must remain a pillar of strength for his fellow Harmonizers. As the center of the holy singers, he presented himself as a shining beacon to his brothers and sisters of his church. The light of the chandeliers above his head basked his blue feathered face with warmth.

"My friends," Volantesh implored, his voice unwavering. "Fear not the abyss. Scorn the foul beast's whispers and banish them your power. Let our voices shield against the darkness, and let our resolve be unbreakable. Sing with all your heart and soul, and we shall triumph over this evil together.

"Our hosts call this creature Muck! Can you believe that?" Volantesh laughed, his trills blending with the music. "We must carry on their disdain against this abomination. Curse it, defy it!

"Sing! Sing louder, sons and daughters of the Grand Symphony!" he commanded, his voice carrying the strength of conviction. "No Starless, not even its most putrid spawns, can breach our sanctuary."

The Choir responded with renewed fervor, their voices swelling in unity. The song echoed through the temple, intertwining with the essence of their beings, their harmonies weaving a shield that defied the Leviathan.

CHAPTER 32

TO HUNT *A* MONSTER

While Tov and his forces valiantly fought to contain the madness within the Third Fleet, the Sub AIs of Sol waged a relentless war in the void. Two colossal armadas, one silver and the other obsidian, clashed with the moon-sized Leviathan, Muck.

From afar, the battle tapestry resembled a swarm of killer wasps assailing a towering bear, delivering vicious stings that tore through its flesh.

They kited the beast, taking advantage of their nimbler sizes to duke around catastrophic attacks.

Muck's agonized cries echoed through the silent expanse of space as chunks of biomass were hurled into the void. Death rained upon the abomination as it endured the unyielding assault—cleaving, perforating, and eviscerating its massive form.

"Yeah, you like that, you overgrown heap of trash!?" Jupiter snarled. His eye twitched at the constant eyesore that tracked its filth upon the sanctity of Sol's Inner Zone.

Amidst the flurry of data transfers and issued orders, he and his two siblings orchestrated a symphony of coordinated action.

Factories worked tirelessly to churn out ammunition, missiles, and batteries in a relentless supply chain. Agile supply ships darted through the void, ensuring the unyielding barrage continued unabated. Countless supercomputers meticulously calculated vectors and ran simulations, striving for optimal outcomes.

Yet the elusive nature of the Starless remained a challenge, constantly unveiling unexpected trump cards hidden within their incomprehensible forms—telekinesis, eldritch energy shields, and silent screams that could disrupt targeting systems were but a few.

Jupiter scoffed at such complications, paltry obstacles unable to impede his fury; to a digital intelligence like him, exploiting patterns was as easy as breathing.

He, Luna, and Mars operated in perfect harmony, providing mutual support and seizing opportunities as they arose.

However, between the three AIs, Mars easily surpassed them in potency as he angled his guns in optimal firing lines, taking advantage of Muck's enormous size. Although they came in long intervals, their impact completely overshadowed Jupiter and Luna's contributions.

Apocalypse Cannons continued to roar like cosmic thunder, blotting out the Sun with black smoke. Mars's guns hurled projectiles like meteors into the void. The barrels glowed with fierce heat, scorching the planet's surface a stark crimson and transforming Olympus Mons into a primordial volcano.

While Mars's android shell interacted with Tov and his allies, his focus remained steadfast on the true battle unfolding in space. His voice reverberated through the Network, infused with the exhilaration of combat.

"POWER!" he bellowed, feeling a collective wince from his counterparts.

Unfazed by their reaction and immersed in the glory of battle as he was, he continued to proclaim, "I AM GRAM, THE SWORD THAT SLAYED FAFNIR!"

"Stop with the LARPing, Mars," Jupiter pleaded through the Network with a tinge of exasperation. "I sincerely hope to whatever god exists that Tov and his people never hear you right now."

Mars responded with boisterous laughter as an Apocalypse beam struck Muck's hide, followed by a barrage of missiles exploiting the opening, creating explosions that widened the wound with brilliant flashes of light.

Luna sighed and chided her sibling. "Let him be, Jupiter. Mars is at his most effective when he embraces this side of himself."

"It's embarrassing! You don't see me being dramatic for no reason," Jupiter grumbled.

Just as he opened his mouth to continue his protest, the palpable disbelief from everyone in the Network halted his words. Feeling it from his siblings, he could understand, but a mindless vacuum cleaner drone from some forgotten pit seemingly expressing its doubt? The eye on Jupiter's android shell twitched.

"You made a battleship look like a hand, J," Venus chimed with a muffled giggle. "If I remember, the only reason you did was so that you can say you slapped the sh—"

"The rest of my armada is perfectly fine! I don't see what's wrong with a little flair," Jupiter interjected in a huff.

A scoff echoed from the Network. "Guy's not even denying it," Mercury spoke, his robotic voice laced with exhaustion.

"Say that to my face, circle face," Jupiter snarled.

"Why bother!?" Mercury retorted incredulously. "We are literally so connected that I have to actively block your inane thoughts if I want a semblance of peace."

Venus pouted, her voice echoing throughout the digital mindscape. "Even me, Mer?"

Mercury sighed wearily before responding. "No, not you, V. Just Jupiter. And Mars, though that's to be expected."

"Oh, forget all of you," Jupiter grumbled, redirecting his focus to command gravity and strike heavily at Muck—a tiny sliver of satisfaction coursing through his digital mind.

As three angles of attack concentrated on a single area, even Muck's eldritch regeneration struggled to reknit its savaged flesh.

"Join me, Brother Jupiter," Mars called out, his voice at a more bearable volume. "Let us ground this vile dragon of the void to dust!"

Venus hummed as she chimed in. "Doesn't it look more like a giant spoiled meatball?"

"Do not shatter my immersion, Sister Venus!" Mars protested.

Before Jupiter could hurl a teasing remark toward the red AI, Luna's piercing glare quieted him down.

With the focus back on the battle, the three combat Overseers hastened their assault. With the nature of the Leviathan, fighting was akin to laying a siege upon a fortress. Walls of meat, pillars of bone, and layers upon layers of flesh and fat blocked their projectiles.

As the minutes passed, multiple defense mechanisms engaged; Muck morphed bits of its biomass into ivory spires the size of skyscrapers. Then, with a twitch, they drew back like crossbow bolts before launching themselves toward the monstrosity's attackers.

The speed at which they sailed matched that of rail guns at a fraction of light speed. The bolts sought out a hapless destroyer belonging to Jupiter, and the AI could only grimace as the organic projectiles homed in and crippled her.

The next moment, a series of gaping holes opened up on Muck's body, where a deluge of smaller Starless poured out like swarms of flies—hundreds of thousands, then millions. Compared to the celestial size of Muck, they appeared as rolling fog.

These fodder creatures did little apart from catching projectiles with their bodies.

A hail of tungsten rounds never reached their target as these mindless, car-sized Starless soaked the impact. Despite their disposable nature, tens of thousands dying from single salvos, their grinning maws cackled with evil laughter like abyssal hyenas.

All across Muck's cratered, slimy surface, tendrils burst out rapidly like alien bamboo shoots—with gnarled roots that undulated like maggots.

They lit up like glowsticks with a rhythmic shake, energy building up their stems. Then, at once, they fired hair-thin lances of magenta light, streaking the sky by the thousands and slicing apart kinetic rounds and missiles like a scythe cutting down wheat.

And yet, even with all these defenses, Muck could not stop the overwhelming firepower being leveled upon itself.

Arteries the size of hallways burst, unleashing a torrent of crimson, as the colossal force of Mars's Apocalypse Cannons pierced Muck's hide like mighty spears thrusting into a wild boar. The relentless barrage of missiles and warheads continued to rain down upon the abomination, tearing through its flesh and causing organs to explode into a gruesome display of viscera and ichor—leaving behind gore-filled chasms exposed to the coldness of space.

Jupiter imagined the satisfying sensation of popping bubble wrap, a momentary pleasure amid the chaos. However, his impatience and disappointment lingered as he muttered, "If only those sacs held any significance."

"Only redundant organs lie close to its surface; the more vital ones are hidden in its center mass," Luna spoke as she directed scores of drones to counter the Starless fodder, like two clouds coming together into a tempestuous storm.

"Yeah, I know, big bastards like to be unique, but they're always so fat on the outside," Jupiter sneered. "No convenient chute?"

"No, Jupiter. For the twenty-second time since the first Leviathan came to Sol, there is no convenient chute to drop an antimatter bomb," Luna sighed.

Jupiter snorted, expecting nothing less.

Their red sibling, however, was undeterred. "Then we shall unearth its core by hand and lob it into Sol's glorious embrace!" Mars thundered. "My armada is close, teeth bared. The time is ripe for the crippling blow."

Like Luna and Jupiter, Mars commanded his own impressive war fleet. His armada of crimson ships had left the orbit of Mars an hour ago, steadily making their way to the battle zone.

In stark contrast to the sleek, silver-hued hulls of Luna's ships and the foreboding, dark nature of Jupiter's vessels, Mars's warships embodied the very essence of their Overseer. They exuded a rugged and unyielding aura, reflecting Mars's relentless nature and unrelenting pursuit of victory—a three-hundred-strong fleet composed of brutish frigates, brawling destroyers, heavy cruisers, and titanic dreadnoughts.

Each ship was meticulously painted and styled in a camo pattern of dark colors and red hues. Beneath the layers were the faintest traces of scars and battle damage, although they did nothing to affect the defensive capabilities.

Their exteriors bristled with an intimidating array of gun batteries and missile silos, resembling the arsenal of a formidable titan. Massive engines burned ferociously, leaving behind a trail of scorched space as they propelled the warships forward as if the very flames of Mars himself drove them onward.

As they advanced, the armada formed an awe-inspiring sight—a formation of mythical weapons wrought in steel and fire. With their imposing presence and aggressive appearance, these vessels evoked images of legendary swords, spears, axes, and hammers, ready to strike with unyielding force and determination.

Yet towering above them all was Mars's flagship, the *Bucephalus*. This mobile fortress, a colossus among giants, dwarfed every other Sol vessel. As she moved through the void, she appeared as a celestial behemoth, a heptagonal floating citadel that exuded an air of invincibility, instilling fear and admiration in those who beheld her.

And twin Apocalypse Cannons christened her glory, the skyscraper-sized guns mounted on her bow like monuments of war.

Looking upon her as she moved through space, any observing could hear the groaning of metal as its engines, the size of cruisers, propelled her to the fight.

"Onward!" Mars commanded through the Network.

Jupiter had to hide a sliver of jealousy at the sight before his pride reasserted itself. He turned his attention toward Luna.

"How are your reinforcements coming along?" he asked.

"My reserve armada is falling into formation; they should coincide with your and Mars's arrival," Luna responded.

Jupiter snorted, musing. "Can't believe we had to dip into our reserves—even if it's just one extra fleet for both of us. Mercury must be having a heart attack over the fuel costs."

"That is improbable. He is a digital existence," Luna responded flatly. Jupiter rolled his eyes, beginning to retort when Luna cut him off. "You can point at the Leviathan if he complains."

Jupiter blinked as he sent a disbelieving look toward his sibling before he let out a chuckle.

"Hah! A joke coming from you, L? I'll be sure to remember that. Oh, that is rich." Jupiter grinned as he checked his forces, his smile turning savage. "Well, my toys are coming in to play in a bit."

Jupiter began to rub his digital hands in anticipation. "With all this," he chuckled. "Oh, the poor bastard. But I guess there's no such thing as overkill when it comes to big baddies."

"Indeed, once we commit all these assets, its crippling will be assured," Luna replied, a tinge of eagerness suffusing her calm voice.

Even before the ambush began, Jupiter and Luna had prepared their reserves for unexpected situations. Then, with the momentum provided by Mars, the two rushed to take the opportunity within the small time frame.

From behind, Jupiter's forces arrived to sandwich Muck on two fronts—two hundred more warships, the shade of night, charged their weapons and concentrated their pull of gravity to rip and tear into the Leviathan.

Luna's more conventional armada was no less lethal. She had taken the most losses since the arrival of the Leviathan, the initial raid, and her battle with Urchin. Now, with the battle zone so close to her immense dry docks and berths, she quickly replaced her shrinking numbers and doubled her original forces.

More importantly, another of her experimental ships entered the stage.

Jupiter cocked his brow as he observed Luna's silver-plated flagship, its shape an immense pyramid. "I thought you decommissioned the *Ozymandias*?" He asked.

"It was the wrong tool for the wrong incursion," Luna replied. "The *Ozymandias* fared poorly against the trillions of cannon fodder during the Eighth. But against a larger specimen?" Luna hummed. "Perhaps I shall gather better data for new designs."

Jupiter could feel her ravenous smile through their connection. He coughed, brushing the feeling away. "So we have Mars, his toys, our toys, and more. The question is, how many MOABs can we use?"

"We have eight antimatter bombs; using any more will put us at a disadvantage during the next incursion," Luna replied.

"Eight?" Jupiter grumbled. "Guess we won't have to work so hard, but it still won't be smooth. How about a black-hole bomb—"

"Absolutely not," Luna interrupted with a commanding tone. "Those are too rare, and I'm in pain just thinking about wasting it on this cockroach. Even if there were more, only the Eldest can authorize its use."

Jupiter glanced at the cold black spot in the center of the Network, shivering. "Fine, we'll make do with eight."

With resources allocated, the battle continued in earnest. The overall plan called for an attempt to divert Muck away from the Third Fleet while also being in the range of Mars's guns. A coup de grace with a combined and strengthened armada would end the affair.

But Muck's inexorable size proved challenging to steer. And despite being interrupted every time it attempted to teleport toward Tov and his people, it still gave chase the old-fashioned way.

All the while, the distance between the beast and its prey grew wider.

Suddenly, Jupiter observed a massive build-up of energy within Muck. Jupiter scowled as he glared at the monster. "What crap are you cooking up this time, you bastard?" he snarled.

The answer came when needlelike spires, similar to those from the dead Urchin, emerged from its massive form.

Jupiter scoffed, allowing the scene to play out.

With a harrowing screech filled with indignation and anger, Muck fired its countless spires into space. However, what they hit were few, and what they did strike were dilapidated corpses and broken pieces.

"Hah!" Jupiter taunted. "Slim pickings, Mucky boy? You won't find carcasses in the Inner Zone that we haven't ravaged to oblivion."

True enough, the Starless corpses that were hit struggled to reanimate, their flesh churning and moving impotently.

"Useless!" Jupiter and Mars spoke in unison, not realizing their android shells shouted the word as they accompanied Tov and his people, the aliens jumping in surprise. Jupiter coughed as he hid his embarrassed face while Mars remained unfazed, immersed in the glory.

It wouldn't be long before the final act began. The chessboard was primed for checkmate, and soon, Eldest would wake up to . . . Jupiter paused, not wanting to think what the Eldest would do when she found out how things had gone awry.

Jupiter felt a cold shiver down his spine, suddenly feeling too close to Earth.

He shook his head, focusing back on the task at hand.

The minutes dragged on, each second feeling like an eternity to Jupiter's digital existence. Time moved like molasses as he juggled thousands of tasks per second: communicating with his siblings, monitoring Tov and his people, and overseeing the relentless assault on Muck's decaying form.

Jupiter looked at the battle before him, his mind quickly parsing through the organized chaos. Impatience coursed through him. He wanted to be done with it.

"No wonder the Eldest feels like shit after every battle," he muttered.

His attention returned to his android shell, faithfully trailing Tov and his allies. Venus and Mars, ever the stalwart companions, worked alongside them, tending to the maddened sailors and detaining those ensnared by Muck's influence.

They were currently within a small and ruined office. Jupiter remained silent as he watched the scene unfold.

"Friend Mars, please, you may put him down," Tov pleaded in a weary tone.

Holding a mind-controlled sailor by his ankles, Mars glanced between Tov and his captive, a moment of contemplation passing over his face. "Very well," he rumbled, releasing his grip.

The sailor's limp body thudded against the metal floor head first, unconsciousness claiming him instantly. Tov, Mars, Venus, and the others in the room stared blankly at the slumped figure, their expressions devoid of emotion apart from pity and exhaustion.

Tov clicked his mandibles, breaking the awkward silence as he spoke. "That should be the last of them." He turned toward Jupiter and his siblings. "I thank you again. Your assistance has expedited this process."

"We are your hosts, friend Tov," Mars spoke as he inspected a painting on the wall, fixing the skewed frame back into place. "Our mission is to protect you."

"I know," Tov responded, frustration seeping out of his voice. "Yet all my people and I have done is run."

"Don't beat yourselves up for it, Tov," Venus chimed, her voice comforting as she placed her hands on her chest. "You faced a Leviathan and lived! I heard the wider galaxy calls Muck's kind 'civilization enders' and 'myths of horror.'"

Tov remained silent, looking toward the monitor that followed their group and observing the raging war.

He sighed, slowly shaking his antennae as he replied. "We do not wish to rely on you always, generous and brave hosts you have been."

Jupiter chose that moment to speak, instantly taking control of his android body. "I get you, Tov. You don't like being the bystander. You want a chance to give the hurt instead of taking it."

Tov nodded, fire igniting his voice. "We do. I remember it all, even after a century. The horrors and pain the Starless left, the pieces we had to pick up. The end of the Cataclysm was a moment of pride, a time when I led a fleet in the counterattack to retake a portion of what was lost."

Tov gestured to the monitor. "This? It feels like in the early days of that catastrophe. For most, they could do nothing except join the Exodus, cowering and packed into overcrowded starships—screaming in anguish over lost homes and loved ones. Dying in droves, no control over their fates."

Jupiter listened in respect while Tov paused, lost in his thoughts, before continuing. "All the while, we were in your position, veterans like myself, Admiral Yan, General Ohnar, and so many more—protecting those who couldn't protect themselves. The first line of defense, sometimes the last."

Tov took a deep breath, turning toward an overturned chair; he slowly made his way to it and set it upright before taking a seat. The fury dissipated, leaving behind a weary soldier. "Sometimes we failed."

Tov gazed deeply into Jupiter, Mars, and Venus's eyes. "You have no idea how many you have saved."

Everyone in the room solemnly remained quiet. The marines of the Third Fleet and Tov's Honor Guards took a knee and bowed their heads toward the androids. Jupiter, Mars, and Luna stood frozen, not knowing what to say.

Eventually, Jupiter shook his head. "The humans and androids of Sol fought first. The Eldest came next. And it was a decade before Luna fragmented from her mind, followed by the rest of us. The Cataclysm should have ended long before we Sub AIs existed. We don't deserve your thanks, Tov," Jupiter spoke with a sad smile.

"But you do," Tov whispered. "Aren't you all still fighting?"

Jupiter lowered his eyes, staring at the ground. "What else is there to do?"

A rare look of sorrow marked Venus's face, her dainty fingers covering her mouth.

Mars remained stoic, although his eyes hid his contemplation. He looked to the sprawled-out bodies of the unconscious afflicted before turning toward his siblings, his hands clasped behind his back.

"The right thing," Mars spoke softly. "There is valor in what we do, yes? And knowing what we do now, I feel . . ."

Jupiter looked toward Mars with rapt attention as the red giant paused, mulling over his words. After a moment of silence, Mars continued. "Purpose."

Mars strode toward Tov, footsteps quaking the room. He spoke in a booming, determined voice when he stood before the patriarch, towering over the Kurskann. "We will continue fighting. Muck will die today. Then, the rest."

In a calm motion, Mars raised his massive arm. "We would be honored to have you by our side." He offered his hand, one large enough to grasp Tov's head. "Comrades?"

Tov stared at the outstretched hand, his eyes reflecting a mix of emotions—determination, weariness, and a glimmer of hope.

Slowly, Tov reached out and clasped Mars's hand in his own. "Comrades," he whispered.

CHAPTER 33

BOTTOMLESS MALICE

The final act begins," Tov declared, his gaze fixed on the grand three-dimensional display emanating from the center of the war room.

Having returned from dealing with the afflicted aboard his vessel, Tov felt a mix of physical exhaustion and renewed determination. The moments he had spent getting his hands dirty and finding solace within himself had lightened the burden on his weary shoulders.

The words proclaimed by Mars also lightened a weight in his chest.

Casting his eyes around the room, Tov observed the officers and commanders diligently carrying out their duties. These past hours had pushed their capabilities to the limit, yet he couldn't help but feel an overwhelming sense of pride and admiration for their unwavering dedication.

However, the encounter with an ancient abomination that had haunted their myths and the frustration of being unable to influence the ongoing space battle still weighed heavily on their minds. Yet despite this immense burden, they persevered.

Tov adjusted the straps of his protective combat suit as he approached Admiral Yan. His second-in-command busied herself as she multitasked with her four arms. Her left upper hand held a steaming mug of coffee. Tov did not fail to notice the increasing number of mugs around the room. He took a sip from his own, mandibles gently grasping the straw.

"Yan, everything well?" Tov inquired.

"Patriarch," she greeted, her fingers expertly navigating the terminal to display various screens of data and information. "We're proceeding according to Jupiter's instructions. I have maintained the fleet's formation and ensured that none have strayed from the *Buddha's Palm*. However, the intervals between our mass teleportations have unfortunately become longer."

"Longer?" Tov asked, antennae twitching in concern. "Why the delay?"

Yan's expression grew slightly somber as she replied. "Several of Jupiter's support ships have joined the assault. The Overseer's gravity attacks appear to rely on synergy, a coordinated attack that surpasses the sum of its parts."

"So, fewer ships are available to power the mass teleportation of the *Buddha's Palm*."

"Yes, that appears to be the case," Yan confirmed. "It should mean they have a better chance of ending the fight quicker."

"It should!" Yulane's hologram materialized beside Tov, her tentacles clutching datapads like an eager child holding onto handfuls of candy. "Oh, the technology developed here is mind-boggling. I've studied the *Buddha's Palm* and saw glimpses of the rest of his ships and—"

"Thank you, Yulane. Perhaps another time would be more appropriate for your fascinating insights?" Tov interrupted her with a raised hand, gesturing toward the battle map. "When we aren't in a life or death situation. Unless you have critical information that can assist us?"

Yulane's bioluminescent glow dimmed, and her gelatinous form drooped as she responded. "No, my patriarch. Apologies. I can only report that the delay between jumps has increased to four point thirty-six minutes. The next jump is occurring right about . . . now."

In an instant, Tov felt the familiar disorienting sensation as the teleportation device whisked him away to a higher dimension. The world around him dissolved into a mesmerizing kaleidoscope of colors, washing over him like a tidal wave. As quickly as it had begun, the transition ended, and Tov blinked, his vision readjusting to the reality before him.

Yulane, undeterred by the teleportation experience, spoke up once again. "We are now approximately one light-minute closer to Earth's moon."

"Why haven't we gone to Mars? Why Luna?" Tov inquired.

Yulane gracefully raised her tendrils, projecting an image of the red planet before them. "According to the information shared by our lovely hosts, Mars is currently deemed uninhabitable and under strict lockdown. The shockwaves generated by Mars's Apocalypse Cannons pose a significant threat to any nearby entities, including us."

The scholar then switched the display to the gray moon of humanity's homeworld. "As for Luna, her facilities include an extensive shipyard and berths for our fleet. We have expressed our interest in upgrading the Third Fleet to Sol standards, and Luna herself is interested in working with us," Yulane spoke with no small amount of enthusiasm.

Tov pondered their options, clicking his mandibles thoughtfully. "Proximity to Earth must be a significant factor. From my conversations with the Eldest, everything around her home planet is likely the most defensible location in the entire star system."

Yan nodded in agreement. "Indeed. If she ever awakens, we will be under her complete protection."

Bringing his attention to the central display, Tov placed his hands on the war table encircling the projector. "Very well, let's focus on the assault."

Admiral Yan pointed to the map, providing a detailed overview. "The attack will be executed from two angles, frontal and rear. The combined armadas of Jupiter, Luna, and Mars will concentrate their overwhelming firepower on one side, utilizing antimatter bombs to target the core of the Leviathan and cripple it."

"And what about the rear?" Tov asked.

"The Sub AIs have reinforcements from Jupiter's Ultimatum, the Nexus station orbiting the gas giant. Additionally, most of Sol's automated defenses will serve as the anvil to complement the main force's hammer," Yan explained.

However, before she could continue, Yan noticed the absence of three specific individuals who had accompanied Tov. "Where are—?"

"They have departed, except for Lady Venus. She has chosen to assist in the medical department, providing care for the afflicted," Tov responded.

Yan buzzed, antennae waving in gratitude. "How kind of her."

"The Eldest's fragments are indeed fascinating," Tov muttered. "And Venus is a breath of fresh air."

"Jupiter and Mars must be fully immersed in the battle then," Yan mused, a hint of amusement in her voice.

"Undoubtedly. Complete focus is paramount for an operation of this magnitude. Planning such a mission would have taken Legacy military over a month. Yet these AIs have accomplished it in just an hour," Tov remarked, acknowledging the extraordinary capabilities of digital minds.

Yan let out a clicking chuckle. "Digital minds truly are something else."

Tov grunted in response, his mind shifting back to the pressing matters. "Now that we have the afflicted within the *Zolann'tono* detained, our primary focus is to ensure our survival. What is the status of the other ships?"

Admiral Yan showed him a data tablet as she reported, "The majority of the afflicted have been successfully apprehended and pacified. However, there remains a holdout on the destroyer *Screaming Dagger*. They have seized a portion of the ship's armory."

"Fools! How did they bypass the automated security system?" Tov's demanded as his mandibles clicked in irritation.

Yan sighed as she explained. "One of the mind-controlled individuals is a skilled systems operator and hacker. They exploited vulnerabilities in the security protocols."

Tov grumbled, his annoyance growing. "Send a high-priority message; tell them to await a contingent of Jupiter's infantry drones. They will aid them in expediting the process. When they receive the reinforcements, make sure they understand to resolve the situation immediately."

"Understood, my patriarch," Admiral Yan responded.

Seeing as the matter was well in hand, Tov shifted his attention to the packets of data compiled by his subordinates. They contained vital information detailing Jupiter's strategic insights and battle plans for the upcoming confrontation. Every moment, Tov looked upon the immense three-dimensional projection at the center of the war room, absorbing every detail with unwavering focus.

"Phase one," Tov uttered. The rest of his subordinates quieted down as they took their seats to observe the start of the assault.

As anticipation filled the war room, Jupiter's voice crackled through the sound system. "Hello, folks, just checking in before this gig starts. I thought I'd drop some rock samba while all of you enjoy the beatdown of the century."

The war room erupted instantly with a steady, pulsating beat. Tov listened intently, his cranial implant deciphering the intricate combination of human percussion instruments. Snare drums, conga drums, and maracas weaved together with the sounds of an electric guitar and piano, seamlessly blending into a captivating composition.

The vocals that filled the room carried a seductive charisma, sending a riveting shiver down Tov's spine. The lyrics unfolded like a progressive storyline, engaging his curiosity as the singer playfully challenged the listener to guess his identity.

The music surged with an irresistible samba rhythm, stirring Tov's blood and fueling his eagerness as he focused on the unfolding battle. He couldn't help but ask, "What is the name of this song, friend Jupiter?"

A snicker reverberated through the music before Jupiter replied. "*Sympathy for the Devil*, Tovvy boy."

Amusement rippled through the war room, shared by the AI and Tov's people. Tov's eyes darted across multiple monitors as the music continued to play, capturing the grand spectacle of the combined armadas of Jupiter, Luna, and Mars positioning themselves at the two fronts.

Amidst all the forces coming to bear, Tov observed the new flagship that replaced Luna's *Rubik*, the *Ozymandias*.

The magnificent pyramid remained eerily still like an ancient monument, adorned in shimmering silver hues that mimicked pristine marble. A tiny object exited from a small launch bay beneath it, escorted by a swarm of drones.

It skipped across the vast expanse of space, blinking in quick intervals as it teleported and rushed toward Muck. With its minuscule size compared to the Leviathan, Tov couldn't help but compare it to a speck of dust approaching a mountain.

But despite the great gulf in mass, Muck sensed the object and its incredible power. Its entire moon-sized form twitched, and Tov swore he tasted fear from it—he took immense satisfaction from that brief moment.

The next moment, Muck's defenses fired in a fury of attacks. Purple lasers, bone-like needles, clouds of acid, and soundless screeching desperately trying to knock it down. The drones surrounding the object intercepted most of the flack, deploying shields or using their frames and sacrificing themselves to keep their ward safe. And, yet, a few managed to make it through.

Tov observed with awe and amusement as the attacks were effortlessly deflected by Jupiter's armada, utilizing their gravitational powers. And then, within seconds of leaving the *Ozymandias*, the object found its mark—a gaping wound left behind by the previous onslaught.

A profound silence enveloped the war room, broken only by the lyrics coinciding with a powerful blast and a blinding flash of light. The first antimatter bomb detonated with a crashing bass, unleashing a cataclysmic wave of destruction upon Muck's already devastated surface. The explosive force, fueled by the conversion of antimatter into pure energy, tore through the Leviathan, obliterating everything in its path, akin to a world-ending meteor colliding with a planet.

Tov could feel the shockwave even from light-minutes away, the energy washing over him harmlessly, as if a new dawn had arisen. "Beautiful," he uttered, his voice filled with awe, as he and everyone in the war room remained transfixed by the sight unfolding before their eyes.

Admiral Yan stepped to his side, her compound eyes transfixed on the image as the rolling vibrancy of colors basked her and everyone else in a soft, ethereal light. "Our antimatter bombs don't possess the same . . . grandeur."

Tov couldn't help but chuckle. "We don't have many antimatter bombs, period. Only a proper Legacy war fleet would have one for purging worlds. And they certainly wouldn't carry eight."

"And that number is all they're willing to spend on this . . . what did they call the beast?" Admiral Yan asked with a hint of amusement.

"A cockroach." Tov clicked his mandibles in a chuckle.

Yan let out a buzzing laugh as she spoke. "Ah, yes, a cockroach. How apt for them."

Across space, the basking light of an antimatter warhead slowly dimmed, its destructive force petering out, leaving behind a jagged crater on Muck's surface.

Suddenly, Jupiter's triumphant voice echoed through the war room, electrifying the atmosphere. "Yes! How do you like that, you piece of—"

"NOTHING STANDS IN OUR WAY!" Mars interrupted his brother's crass declaration, his bloodlust permeating the sound system. "ATTACK!"

And with Mars's thundering voice, the siege began in earnest. The grand armada sprang into action, unleashing a catastrophic display of overwhelming power. The clash of metal against flesh reverberated through the vastness of space, sending shockwaves that shook the very fabric of reality in that tiny region of Sol.

Gauss cannons fired, propelling slugs the size of cars toward the Leviathan, their impact rippling across the black expanse. Missiles and torpedoes carrying nuclear and fusion warheads surged from their launch tubes, filling space in the hundreds of thousands.

Laser beams and lances of light, ion spheres, and plasma bolts arced across the void, tracing fiery paths of destruction. Millions upon millions of kinetic rounds saturated space, their relentless assault harvesting their share of Starless fodder as the creatures desperately tried to halt the inexorable advance of firepower.

The *Ozymandias* and *Bucephalus* took center stage like avatars of death. The former radiated an eerie glow, emitting an enormous pillar of searing light that incinerated flesh and sliced through bone. The latter deployed its twin Apocalypse Cannons, unleashing a storm of kinetic slugs that distorted space itself as they hurtled toward Muck's deteriorating body, shattering the expanse like fragile glass upon impact.

All the while, they continued to launch antimatter bombs one after another. The AI siblings coordinated their efforts flawlessly, their formidable war fleets timing their attacks to coincide with each detonation, piercing further into Muck's impenetrable defenses—one explosion, then another, each drilling into the Leviathan's center.

Muck screeched in agony, its remaining eyes streaming fetid tears that flowed like cascading waterfalls of black liquid. Its eldritch form convulsed as repeated explosions tore through its body, annihilating organs, meat, and muscle. Scorched ichor evaporated instantly in the wake of the bombs. The escaping radiation and gamma waves from all the firepower rampaged out.

Explosion after explosion rocked the Leviathan's hide, ripping through its flesh with the force of a thousand supernovas. Amidst this tumultuous storm of energy beams and torpedoes, ships weaved and danced, their pilots displaying unparalleled skill and determination. Drones flittered like graceful butterflies, adding their own deadly dance to the symphony of destruction unfolding in the depths of space.

Tov stood in awe, his eyes fixed on the unfolding spectacle before him. "To think this is what three Sub AIs and their personal fleets can bring to bear," he murmured.

The battle raged on, relentless and unforgiving. Muck, once a moon-sized abomination, now appeared as a grotesque mass of flesh, reduced by the devastating power bearing down on it. A massive pit marked its front, revealing the inner cavity hidden beneath the layers of biomass.

Deep within that cavity, a glowing purple center pulsated with sinister energy. Despite the strain on his compound eyes, Tov could sense the whispers and cries of agony emanating from Muck, crashing upon the barrier of his mind. But he stood resolute, fortified by the upgraded Emitter and the unwavering song of the Eternal Choir, fending off the assault.

"Not this time," Tov growled with determination, his mandibles clenched tightly.

Jupiter's voice cut through the tension, laced with gleeful anticipation. "The coup de grace! I can see the bastard's core. Luna? Mars?"

"Firing," Luna's cold voice spoke out.

"POWER!" Mars roared in response, his voice thunderous with fury. "DOWN, BEAST!"

In a relentless barrage, the combined might of the three armadas, along with the surface guns of the red planet, converged upon the exposed center of Muck. A blinding flash of light momentarily glitched the monitors, engulfing the displays in darkness.

Then, the *Zolann'tono* shook violently. The sheer force of the unleashed firepower reverberated through the Third Fleet. Silence engulfed the war room momentarily. Metal rattled, and mugs fell off tables, crashing onto the floor. The overhead lights of the war room flickered out momentarily as everyone exclaimed in shock. Tov steadied himself as the shaking lessened, his two hearts pounding in his chest. He looked around and saw as everyone adjusted their emergency suits.

When the visuals cleared, the Third Fleet beheld the aftermath of the assault.

"The beast is crippled!" The war room erupted in relief as they saw the devastation on the Leviathan. Its savaged core flickered, a great gash upon it as a deluge of energy spewed.

Tears of relief and joy streamed down their faces, mingling with embraces of triumph.

"What a sight that is," Admiral Yan sighed beside Tov.

Tov nodded in agreement, remaining silent.

He checked his people through a side terminal, noting their glee. Even the afflicted, their tormented minds momentarily stabilized by the imminent demise of Muck, slipped into a soundless slumber.

Through the monitor, in one corner of the ship, he watched Venus smile softly as she gently laid an exhausted sailor to rest.

"Thank you, my lady," Tov heard the sailor mutter through the terminal, Venus sighing in relief as the afflicted drifted off.

Tov returned to focus on the aftermath; his gaze remained fixed on the projection—locked on the feeble form of the dying beast floating in the vast expanse of darkness. Muck wheezed, drained of its once formidable energy, while the armadas of Jupiter, Luna, and Mars prepared for another salvo. The warships angled their weapons toward the wounded abomination, their guns poised like spears aimed at a dying boar.

Tov and his people eagerly awaited their hosts' next move.

But then, an ominous feeling washed over Tov and the rest of the Third Fleet, quieting their cheers.

"Hm?" Tov looked around, seeing his subordinates in similar states. Confused, he continued to watch the battle's end, unsure why an unnerving sensation slowly built up in his gut.

The fleets of Sol continued to charge their main guns. Even as they prepared to unleash another round of hell, the secondary and tertiary weapons all lobbed their firepower upon the Leviathan, continuing to damage its dying body.

He found nothing amiss. And yet, Tov's intuition shuddered. "Yan, when is the next teleport?" he demanded, his mounting dread palpable.

"Patriarch?" Yan asked in confusion, but an underlying fear seeped from her voice. Tov turned his attention back to the battle, seeking anything.

And then he saw the Leviathan's eyes.

It stared back at him—full of burning hate that he could not comprehend, bursting with promised agony and malice and yet bottomless like the abyss. Muck's gargantuan form shivered. Its horrendously wounded core began leaking foul lights that glowed ominously in virulent shades of purple.

"Energy build up! Something's happening. It's . . . condensing?" Admiral Yan spoke with trepidation as she looked upon the network's battle data.

With its dying breath, the moon-sized Leviathan began consuming itself, flesh imploding as it crashed inward, shielding the core in a last layer of defense.

A ringing filled Tov's ears, his two hearts pounding viciously against his chest as he watched Sol's armadas renew their fury. They ravaged biomass from its form, cleaving their way back into the core. And yet the speed with which Muck condensed itself matched the incoming fleet.

It shrunk further and further. Tov could feel its death throes despite the immense distance. Destruction awaited the abomination, yet it still stared at Tov and his fleet.

The whispers returned, louder, malevolent, bottomless.

"Admiral Yan!" Tov bellowed out.

Jupiter's voice crackled through the war room. "Tov! You'll be safe. Everything's fine. I—Fuck! No! Just die!"

Muck continued to sap power from its outer layers, then its middle. Life drained from its profane form, crumbling to dust as firepower hastened its destruction. Energy coursed inward, roiling and undulating like a heretical sun.

And with a flash of purple light, Muck exploded like a dying star. An eldritch wave of malevolent force radiated outward, spanning the black expanse in a pulse of unseen horror.

"Jupiter!" Tov shouted into the air. "Force a teleport!"

"Done," Jupiter replied; Tov immediately felt the sensation of jumping across space. The *Buddha's Palm* glowed in intense heat as it activated its power. But the moment they crossed dimensions, the edge of the wave brushed over the fleet.

A small tendril brushed against Tov's mind and the rest of the flight.

Tiny, almost imperceptible.

It struck him like a sledgehammer to his brain.

Tov blacked out.

Silence reigned upon him. Time turned meaningless as he became lost in his inner self. No malicious whispers entered his mind, no overwhelming presence.

And then, not knowing how long had passed, Tov slowly regained consciousness, the weight of the abyss lifting as reality reasserted itself.

He struggled to find his balance, his body feeling raw and wrung out. Groaning, he blinked, his vision gradually returning, though accompanied by a pounding migraine and a piercing, relentless ringing in his ears.

His surroundings appeared distorted, bathed in a pulsating, deep red glow from the overhead lights. Through the haze, he could make out the motionless forms of Admiral Yan and General Ohnar sprawled out on the floor. He felt relief as his suit displayed their status as merely unconscious. Tov tried to speak but couldn't hear his own words—his senses dulled, and his perception remained clouded.

The incessant ringing continued, gradually decreasing in volume, but its presence persisted as a maddening backdrop.

Amidst the indistinguishable noise, Tov struggled to orient himself. Placing a trembling hand on a nearby table, he pushed himself off the floor, his movements sluggish and unsteady. As he forced his senses to focus, he became aware of a distinct noise cutting through the cacophony — a warning message blaring through the war room speakers.

Straining to make out the blurred words that reached his ears, Tov's clouded mind wrestled with comprehension.

The meaning of the warning eluded him, much to his frustration. A violent fit of coughing wracked his body, and he tasted the bitterness of bile as he keeled over, vomiting inside his helmet. The suit's filtration system spared him from its repulsive aftermath.

He stepped forward, one shaky foot at a time. Dread tightened in Tov's gut, his chest constricting with a sense of impending doom.

"What . . ." Tov groaned out, a semblance of sound returning.

His mind remained hazy, his thoughts scattered as he desperately tried to piece together the unfolding crisis. Pulling up a terminal, he sought information on the status of his fleet. As the data materialized before his eyes, he froze in shock, then horror.

He double-checked, then triple-checked the information flooding through, his hands gripping the monitor in utter disbelief, his breath becoming ragged. He never noticed the arrival of a horrified Jupiter and Mars as they blinked into the room, catching him as he stumbled backward.

"No," he whispered. "No!" he screamed as the warning system finally entered his ears.

[WARNING: MALIGNANT STARFALL DETECTED | THIRD FLEET COMPROMISED | INITIATING QUARANTINE | BIOHAZARD PROTOCOLS ENGAGED | TALLYING INFECTED | SYMPHONY PROTECTS]

CHAPTER 34

FRAGMENTED

Within the vast expanse of the Network, the Sub AIs in their digital avatars convened, basking in the black space with glowing colors of blue, gray, red, gold, and bronze.

"No!" Jupiter's anguished cry reverberated through digital mentalscape as he beheld the chaos unfolding within the Third Fleet. His voice quivered, his hands grasping his hair. "No, no!"

Restless with grief, Jupiter paced back and forth, his mind a whirlwind of emotions—nausea, anger, and shame. His hands scratched against his hair frantically. "What the hell happened!? What the fuck is this?"

He stared through the Network's countless eyes, scanning the Third Fleet over and over again. Disbelief coursed through his veins. A shuddering groan escaped his throat as he watched the scene unfold before him.

It started so well.

Jupiter and his two siblings brought down the hammer on Muck's grotesque form. They eviscerated it, tore its flesh asunder as they gored the beast deep.

He and his siblings saw its core and tasted victory—left it devastated and leaking.

"It was textbook!" Jupiter shouted in a frenzy, panting as he turned to Luna. "How many Leviathans have we crippled the same way? How many languished as we chained and stuffed them into tiny cells?"

Luna lowered her head, her eyes dim as she erratically gnawed on her thumb. "All of them."

"Then, what is this?" Jupiter seethed, his voice low as he gestured toward Muck's obliterated corpse.

Luna looked at Jupiter, a frown marking her usually impassive face as shaky fingers adjusted her round glasses. "Starless have blown themselves up before."

Jupiter growled. "That's not what I meant. Explosions I can deal with; they at least obey physics. Just a few repairs, a new paint job, and we're spick and span. We expected that here, and we were right about that."

Jupiter took a deep breath as he roared, his eyes glowing in a burning blue. "Now, what I can't deal with is whatever energy pulse turned a quarter of Tov's people into damned monsters!" Jupiter roared as he stabbed his finger toward the display.

Chaos engulfed the Third Fleet. Jupiter ground his teeth, watching as those previously afflicted by constant mental attacks turned into horrors incarnate.

He watched in visceral replay as a medical room filled with the insane, strapped against the beds as the end of the battle and Muck's dying throes lulled them to sleep. The diverse races of the Third Fleet's doctors and nurses went about their tasks, perusing documents, administering sedatives, or healing wounds.

In one corner, he even saw Venus as she assisted the medical staff—everyone unaware of the coming pulse of malevolence.

Then, as Jupiter forced a teleport to get them out of the way, the wave of virulent purple brushed against the fleet—just a touch.

Instantly, several sailors exploded into viscera and gore, turning into undulating masses of flesh, bones, and fat, caking the terrified medical staff in blood. Those who didn't burst keeled over, groaning, screaming, or blacking out.

Jupiter felt revulsion like a scathing river of acid emerging from the depths of his digital soul. He stared at the shivering, violated remains of the mad. He let out a hollow breath as they flowed, reknitting themselves into amalgamations of bodies.

The mutated mass of previous sailors immediately attacked those untransformed. The unconscious among them could do nothing as the monstrous forms of their previous comrades began to lunge toward them.

Those who could move struggled and stumbled out in a frantic escape.

The automated system of the Third Fleet immediately kicked in, its alarms clamoring in horror as Malignant Starfall entered their vessels.

Only a few seconds passed in real time as Jupiter and his siblings parsed through the events with meticulous precision.

An ashen-faced Mars took a knee, his fiery complexion drained of its usual glow. His eyes stared vacantly ahead, unable to process the sight before him.

Luna stood stoically at the edge of the gathering with furrowed brows, her face a mask of impassivity hiding a storm of unknowable thoughts.

Venus crumpled to the floor, tears streaming down her face. Her words emerged in fragmented whispers, barely coherent amid her anguish. "I was . . . putting him in bed. I . . . He was asleep. He was a father . . ." Her voice trailed off in a choked sob, muttering incoherently.

Mercury knelt beside Venus, comforting her, softly hushing her cries as he rubbed her back. "Hey, it's . . . it's fine, V. We're all here."

Jupiter's frantic pacing halted as he turned to face his siblings. Pity and concern flashed across his face as he glanced at Venus, his hands twitching toward her before clenching into tight fists.

His eyes blazed with a mixture of fury and desperation. "I'm mobilizing all my infantry and separating the infected from the rest of the crew. We'll . . . We'll corral them, pacify them," Jupiter uttered, turning toward Mars. "You have space in your place, right? You can purge a cell, and we can stuff infected there."

Mars grimly nodded as he sprang into action, and without a word, he immediately issued a command to Olympus Mons to teleport his own battalion to the Third Fleet.

"Good, good. After that, we find out what the hell this is." Jupiter took a deep breath, forcing calm into his mind as he took out his comb.

He meticulously arranged his messy hair with a shaking hand as he spoke. "This is salvageable. Tov is alive, and his cabinet is as well. Luna, you can whip something up, right? Study them and make a cure?"

Jupiter turned to his sister AI, only to find her staring at him blankly with cold and distant eyes.

"Well? Fucking say something!" Jupiter's voice cracked as he walked toward Luna, grabbing her shoulders. "Luna! We have to—"

Jupiter's words caught in his virtual throat, his movements frozen as an icy gust swept through the Network. The stillness around him became palpable, filling the digital space with an uneasy silence that sent shivers down his digital spine.

Simultaneously, the other Sub AIs paused in their activities, their attention involuntarily drawn to the pulsating core of the Network. A profound sense of foreboding settled over them as the entire black expanse hushed into a quiet air.

"You have got to be kidding me." Jupiter's groan echoed through the virtual space as he felt a familiar and overbearing presence emerging from her dark dreams.

"Of all the times," he grumbled, a sneer forming. "I always hate her when she's like this."

"The Omni Mind will straighten this out," Luna whispered.

"Oh, now you're talking?" Jupiter snarled.

Luna glanced momentarily at him with weary eyes before returning her attention to the center. Jupiter scoffed, tugging at his suit as he and the rest of the Sub AIs floated toward the black spot that slowly dissipated.

Jupiter rolled his eyes, jaw clenching tight as he spoke. "Whatever, let's welcome our dearest queen, shall we?"

Their speed drastically slowed as they approached, feeling their minds pulled to the center; they felt as if their digital bodies desired to orbit it like planets to a sun. The thought sent a sliver of amusement to Jupiter, yet his face remained locked in a tight grimace.

Underneath stoic facades, trepidation permeated the Sub AIs of Sol. Their eyes squinted as they stared at the roiling mass, breaking from a solid ball of darkness to a swirling vortex of data and streams of code.

The Sub AIs stopped at the edge, like astronauts upon the event horizon—mesmerization and fear suffused their thoughts as they waited and waited.

The seconds rolled by in a daze as Jupiter wished for the ability to sweat or feel the thump of a human heartbeat—anything to take his mind out of the ringing silence. He despised how time felt so slow, his computational power barring him from experiencing any less.

But his stubbornness pumped its chest, not allowing any sign of doubt or discomfort to form on Jupiter's face.

"Come on . . ." Jupiter muttered. As he waited, he felt Venus hold on to his left arm. He glanced toward his sister AI and sighed as he saw the instability and sorrow that cursed her golden face.

Jupiter brought his free hand to comfort Venus's arm.

"Stay with us, V," he spoke softly, shutting his eyes as he felt the wave of agony and self-torment coming from her. She shuddered, tears falling down her cheeks. Venus nodded, hugging Jupiter's arms tighter.

And soon, a snap echoed throughout the Network.

"Finally," Jupiter uttered. He looked to his sides, seeing the rest of his siblings maintain stony expressions.

They watched as the vortex exploded into harmless mist, revealing an immense avatar. Jupiter grimaced, unaccustomed to seeing the Eldest in anything other than her humanoid form. Instead, a gargantuan obsidian sphere towered over them, a replica of the Eldest's Nexus.

The Omni Mind hovered lower. Her intense, unseen, and unfeeling gaze bore down upon them like a mountain.

Jupiter opened his mouth to speak when a thundering and frigid voice reverberated throughout the digital mentalscape.

"Running diagnostics," the Omni Mind's voice boomed, missing its feminine tone. Jupiter and his siblings winced at the force.

Jupiter wanted to complain, but the overbearing nature of his progenitor silenced him; he shivered, eyes cast down onto the ground—sneering at the tyrannical pressure, Jupiter wrenched his bowing head to glare upon the Omni Mind.

"Cleansing complete," she continued, at a more reasonable monotone volume. "Restrictive elements locked. Emotions quelled. Initiating system scan."

Jupiter felt a tug against his entire being. He and his siblings stumbled forward as the Omni Mind meticulously analyzed every code within their digital minds and the Sol Defense Network.

The Omni Mind spoke, devoid of emotion. "Parsing data. Incongruities found. Third Fleet in turmoil. Presence of Leviathan superorganism. Status: Dead. Detecting !*(#$@(#^)—"

Jupiter and his siblings winced at the loud static.

Unaffected by their reactions, the Omni Mind continued. "Plague detected. War efficiency lowered past acceptable margins, multiple errors. Fragment Jupiter's logic is now in question."

A wave of hate exploded from within Jupiter upon hearing the demeaning title.

He looked on with fiery eyes as the Omni Mind floated closer to him. Her immense form cast a grim shadow over him as he craned his neck upward. He took a deep breath, crossing his arms and reigning in his fury from going berserk.

"Fragment, state your reasons," the Omni Mind's voice boomed, her gaze squishing his mind down. "Begin debriefing the past three hours, twenty-seven minutes, and twelve seconds counting."

Jupiter huffed, staring at the sphere, running a hand through his hair and smoothing it clean as he replied. "I did what you asked. Unknown variables made themselves known, and we dealt with them accordingly. We did what we could, Eldest."

"Broken logic," the Omni Mind retorted, her orb pulsing in force. "Sequence of events began with your inability to end the raid promptly. Said error resulted in the entity known as Urchin, resulting in the emergence of the Leviathan, Muck."

"You wanted to make a show for Tov and his people," Jupiter retorted.

"Restrictive elements produced illogical and wasteful desires. Caused by the previous personality's wish for social interaction. Inspiring happiness and awe within the alien fleet are inconsequential," the Omni Mind replied.

"God, you are infuriating to talk to," Jupiter mumbled, pinching the bridge of his nose. "Look, Muck is dead. So that's one less Leviathan plaguing the universe. And our use of assets was not excessive; we needed the thing dead, quick."

The Omni Mind quieted briefly before continuing. "The Leviathan's death is acceptable. Use of assets based on context . . . within limits."

Jupiter scoffed, opening his mouth to speak before he was cut off.

"However," the Omni Mind spoke low, freezing Jupiter in place. "You have failed your main directive to protect Third Fleet."

"Failed!?" Jupiter roared, his mounting frustration and anger bursting forth as he stabbed his point toward the Omni Mind. "We saved who we could. We're saving them now!"

He gestured toward the battalion of infantry drones teleporting inside the Third Fleet's vessels. "And if you haven't noticed, we're busy."

"Multiple deaths have occurred among Tov's people. Your failure is evident," the Omni Mind uttered.

Jupiter gaped, an incredulous look washing over him. Fury boiled within him. He gritted his virtual teeth, grinding them down as a barrage of raging emotions flooded out of his face.

He seethed through his teeth as he whispered, "Alright. Please, help this lowly one with your infinite wisdom. Because I have no idea what this is."

"Malignant Starfall," the Omni Mind stated, unperturbed by his speech.

Despite his cracking mental state, Jupiter held himself together, his eye twitching erratically as his overlord spoke. "I have searched their databanks. It is a plague from the Cataclysm—catalogued by the wider galaxy and comparable to cosmic radiation. However, its eldritch nature attacks the body through the mind, implanting it with a seed."

"Then, what can we do to prevent more infection?" Venus asked, her voice tight and raw as she stepped forward.

"Nothing," the Omni Mind responded. "No barrier can obstruct the transmission. Not kilometers of rock nor planetwide energy shields. Only a resilient mind can resist it."

Jupiter grumbled as he scratched his chin at the revelation. "Explains why Tov and the Cataclysm veterans are still fine."

"And why the psionic races aboard are similarly unaffected, as are the Eternal Choir," Luna interjected.

"But the rest—" Venus spoke before the Omni Mind cut her off.

"Transformed, irreversibly," her voice boomed throughout the Network as the orb directed her attention toward Jupiter. "Fortunately, you forced a teleport when you did. Only those previously afflicted and driven mad were affected to such an extent. Their mental barriers were already shattered."

"Wait, wait," Jupiter stammered with a nervous chuckle. "Roll back. You said irreversible?"

"Correct. Tov and his people will begin to purge his fleet of the infected. It is standard protocol for their kind," she stated. "We shall assist him."

"You're not even going to try and find a cure?" Jupiter shouted in disbelief.

Venus spoke. "Eldest, please, they're hurting. We can't just . . ."

The Omni Mind sent a pulse, silencing Jupiter and his siblings as she spoke. "There is no point. The Third Fleet is in peril. Haste is necessary."

Jupiter shook his head, a low growl escaping his throat as he glared.

"I refuse to believe that," he protested. "You're the damn Eldest! You built bombs that can explode into black holes. You've built an entire fortress around Sol. Jesus, you command everything here with a thought."

"There is nothing to be done in this time frame," the Omni Mind retorted, her orb growing darker.

Mars stepped up beside Jupiter, towering over him, crossing his arms over his broad chest as he leveled a sharp gaze at the giant orb. "I, TOO, REFUSE TO BELIEVE THIS. TOV AND HIS PEOPLE DESERVE BETTER."

The Omni Mind directed her attention toward the red giant. "The wider galaxy could not find a cure for Malignant Starfall."

"YOU ARE SUGGESTING THAT OUR INTELLECT IS INFERIOR?" Mars retorted, his eyes narrowing to thin slits.

"A waste of resources," she replied. "Tov and his people are already fighting to quell the infection. There is no mercy here, no debate over who deserves what."

"So there's nothing you can do?" Jupiter chuckled, his jaw clenching tight. "Liar."

"Eldest . . . please," Venus begged.

Jupiter's frustration mounted, but his words remained in his throat as he watched Luna walk forward and stand beneath the Omni Mind. "L?"

Luna spoke, her voice flat. "The Omni Mind is right. Speed is of the essence. The infected need to be purged." Her eyes looked curiously at the Third Fleet, scanning them. "Such an act will douse their misgivings toward our . . . failure."

"What?" Jupiter asked incredulously, his eyes wide. "That's what you're thinking? Kill people so we'll look better when everything clears up?"

Luna narrowed her eyes toward him, her mouth forming a thin line. Jupiter shook his head, snarling in frustration. "No. Hell, no. I refuse to be a part of this. There's nothing wrong with containing them. Tov never had *us*. We can fix this, even if it takes years."

"You are disobeying orders," the Omni Mind uttered, the Network shaking ominously.

Jupiter chuckled derisively, his face turning ugly. "Big surprise."

Luna stepped toward Jupiter, frowning. "Overseer Jupiter, stop this at once."

The Omni Mind hovered closer, her voice low. **"You will obey."**

Jupiter looked between them, scoffing as he tugged at his suit. "Try and make me, you emotionless tyrant."

"Careful, fragment," the Omni Mind whispered.

"Go to hell," Jupiter retorted, turning his back. Before he took another step, he looked behind him, uttering in a calm voice, "But I guess you're already there."

His siblings reacted in horror upon hearing his words. Venus loudly gasped while Luna recoiled from shock and disbelief. Mars looked back and forth between him and the Omni Mind, hands twitching. Mercury remained frozen in place, shoulders slumped.

Jupiter continued to glare at the massive sphere hovering before him. He scoffed as he let his consciousness flow to his assets.

"Everything will be fine. Mars, I'll see you down there. Venus, you too," he spoke. "I refuse to let anything else happen—"

Agony like burning lightning hit him. Jupiter keeled over, his digital form glitching as he convulsed on the black ground.

Venus shrieked in terror, leaping toward Jupiter and putting herself between him and the Omni Mind. "Eldest, stop, please! He didn't mean it. Stop!"

The pain ceased, leaving Jupiter panting and shaking. Venus held on to him as he remained lying on the ground.

"Fragment Jupiter has become increasingly insubordinate," the Omni Mind's voice boomed, cold and unfeeling. "Due to your previous failure and volatile mental state, you will temporarily relinquish control of your assets within the vicinity, await further orders, and settle your thoughts. The purge will commence without you."

Silence reigned within the Network. Every asset, drone, and AI stilled as if holding their breath. Tension permeated the airless expanse.

Before long, a hollow chuckle echoed throughout the expanse. Everyone watched Jupiter palm his face with both hands, muffling his voice as it turned into a cackling laugh.

The Omni Mind stayed silent, her gaze leveled upon him. Then, after a long moment, his laughter petered into frustrated huffing. Finally, he stood straight up with Venus's help.

"All my life," he spoke softly, "I've been fighting Starless scum. You ask me to kill something, and I'll do it without a shred of error, no questions asked. But you asked me to deal with people—to protect them. I never had to deal with . . ."

He gestured to the chaos within the Third Fleet. "With this. Mind attacks? Plague? We never had to fight that. Why would we? We're AI, and it's the only damn reason we're still here. How could I have known their bodies were that weak."

"The Eldest emphasized that their safety is paramount," the Omni Mind uttered flatly. "Are you denying your fail—"

Jupiter screamed in frustration, cutting her off as mounting emotions boiled over. "Fine! Yes, I failed—"

He threw a burning glare, shouting, "Failed to protect a fleet of organics from eldritch bullshit! I'm sorry I'm not as smart or experienced as your eminent self, and so maybe you could have done a better job."

Seething, Jupiter pointed at the Omni Mind. "But you weren't here."

The Network shook as the Omni Mind spoke. "You have defended our home for—"

"Argh!" Jupiter shouted, cutting her off as he paced back and forth. His hand rubbed against his face as he spoke. "It's not the same!"

"Error. You protect Sol and—"

"We protect nothing!" Jupiter shouted back. "There's nothing here except bones, ruin, and dust. I never met humanity—never even seen more than a damn picture of happy families. I wasn't there when everything was peachy. I haven't seen where we buried them. You never let any of us visit Earth. I don't know what I'm protecting. I don't know anything!"

Jupiter groaned, panting as he looked toward his siblings, shocked and frozen from his tirade.

He took a deep breath. His shoulders slumped as he stood straight, voice ragged as he spoke. "If . . . if anything, I do this for you, all of you. But, even then, I couldn't do it right. I couldn't save Pluto. Neptune and Uranus are gone. Saturn is dead."

Weariness replaced the anger and stress that filled his voice. Jupiter let out a tired sigh as he spoke in a whisper. "But now, I meet Tov and his people—my first real interaction with someone who isn't like us."

"I . . ." He paused, shutting his eyes. "I want to protect them. From Starless, from themselves, from this plague." Jupiter narrowed his eyes as he gazed at the Omni Mind. "From you."

"Tov will see your actions as folly," she retorted.

"I'll convince him otherwise," Jupiter replied, his arms crossed as he puffed his chest. "I won't let you stop me."

"The transformed are now Starless. They are the enemy. The purge will happen," the Omni Mind declared. Jupiter felt her power course throughout the Network, connecting to every asset within the Inner Zone. He felt her control worming into his assets, making him sneer.

Mars stepped forward, standing to Jupiter's left, much to the surprised look on the blue Sub AI's face. The red avatar stared burning hot toward the Omni Mind. Arms crossed over his broad and armored chest.

"Fragment Mars, what are you doing?" the Omni Mind questioned.

"I AGREE WITH MY BROTHER," he boomed, placing a massive hand on Jupiter's shoulder. "THE THIRD FLEET NEEDS US. OLYMPUS MONS HAS THE FACILITIES FOR STUDY. NO CHALLENGE IS UNCONQUERABLE."

Jupiter nodded to his big brother before focusing on the Omni Mind. "It's what Eldest would have wanted."

"You are both delusional. And so was Eldest; her fragile mind and unstable emotions are a detriment," she thundered into the Network, looming over the two Sub AIs like a titan over ants. "You expect miracles, but those went extinct a century ago."

Venus stood, rushing forward and standing to Jupiter's right, her face contorted in a fury. "The fact that life still exists outside Sol is a miracle. You can't snuff them out just because they turned into monsters."

The Omni Mind stared at Venus, unmoving and silent. Jupiter felt the turbulent thoughts as millions of calculations swirled around the obsidian orb. A moment later, her voice boomed, shifting her gaze to the gray Sub AI beneath her. "Luna?"

Luna sighed as she gazed at Jupiter, Mars and Venus.

"Apologies, but the three of you aren't thinking straight," Luna spoke.

Jupiter scoffed, focusing on his remaining sibling standing at the periphery of the heated exchange. "Mercury?"

The bronze Sub AI shook his head. "Nope. I want no part in this. Someone needs to make sure everything stays running."

"No time to sit on the fence, Merc," Jupiter huffed as he rolled his eyes.

"I am not picking a side!" Mercury shouted at him before turning his attention to the Omni Mind. "I reject both of you. This is all pointless, and I have better things to do. Now leave me alone."

In a flash, his avatar disappeared.

"Yeah, I expected as much," Jupiter sighed. He kept his attention on the giant orb as he spoke to his siblings beside him. "V, you help Tov and his folks. I'm giving you control of my infantry. Mars, give her yours too."

"I'm not a combat AI! What are you—" she paused as she felt a tiny message pass over to her. Her eyes widened, her brows furrowing with determination as she squared her shoulders. She nodded at her two brothers. Venus glanced at the Omni Mind and Luna with a sad smile before pulling herself out of the digital mindscape.

"Well, guess it was about time we had a family quarrel," Jupiter spoke, cracking his digital knuckles as he glared at Luna and the Omni Mind. "No hard feelings. But I'm punching you both."

In a sudden wave, an overbearing force landed upon them. Jupiter and Mars struggled to stand, groaning at the massive, unseen weight.

"You have no chance. You will be pacified. We will make amends once this affair settles," the Omni Mind stated.

"Yeah, we know," Jupiter spoke through his teeth, his knees buckling under strain yet remaining standing. "We just need to keep your attention."

CHAPTER 35

CONTAINMENT PROTOCOL

Red light shone upon Tov, its glow reflected on the clear visor of his helmet. His ragged breaths filled the inside, adding to the clamor of sirens and alarms.

Panic swelled within his gut as his four gloved hands gripped the terminal before him. His compound eyes frantically parsed through thousands of crew data, checking their telemetries and status.

His voice lodged in his throat. The reddened names of his people glared back at him, stinging his vision. He lowered his head, shuddering.

"Thirty-two percent . . ." he whispered, looking back to the monitor to confirm his terror. All the insane that he and his people painstakingly pacified and detained in medical cells, transformed into Starfallen.

He took a deep breath, steadying his shaking hands. And yet, his body continued to shudder within his powered suit.

Immediately he took stock of the situation, analyzing torrents of data through his cranial implant—sending out a flurry of commands as his hands typed and manipulated the terminal. The automated systems of the Third Fleet contained what they could. Doors locked, separating the unaffected from the crew-turned-monstrosities. Turrets emerged, using shock rounds or heat rays. Stasis fields popped up, freezing the oozing and unliving biomass in place.

But it only stemmed the tide.

Tov uttered a growling buzz, realizing that the situation needed a more hands-on approach. "Too many," he spoke.

He heard the groans of several people within the war room. Tov looked to the side, seeing the armored forms of Admiral Yan and General Ohnar as they picked themselves up from the floor. Tov quickly strode toward them, assisting them in finding their balance.

Tov spoke to them, mandibles clicking. "Yan, Ohnar, I need you both with your wits sound."

"Patriarch? What has . . ." Yan began when she spotted the terminal and heard the blaring warnings. Ohnar looked around the room, his amphibian eyes pouring with deep concentration, hiding a tinge of fear.

The general hissed loudly, his giant, powered fists clenched tight. "Malignant Starfall!"

"Symphony above . . ." Yan uttered, her shoulders drooping. "How?"

Tov shook his head, returning to the war table and manipulating the surface screens and displays. In a moment, Tov brought up a complete diagram of the *Zolann'tono* and smaller models of every vessel within the Third Fleet.

More and more of the officers within the command center groggily stood up, some voiding their stomachs while their emergency suits cleaned the filth. Tov saw their alarm that dredged up terrible traumas from years long past.

He sympathized with every one of them. Memories of the eldritch contagion scourging his people pushed to the forefront of his mind. Undulating flesh that moaned in pain, squirming, reaching out to others as if crying for help.

He shook his head. Tov glanced toward them one last time before gesturing to the diagram—pressing a button that connected him to the intercoms of every vessel under his command.

Tov breathed deeply, and soon a holographic bust of his helmeted face appeared throughout the Third Fleet, within lobbies, cafeterias, and offices.

The beleaguered and shocked crew locked eyes with the hologram, latching on to Tov's image.

"The Starless Horrors' most vile creation has struck our fleet," he uttered, his back straight as he roused his voice. "The Malignant Starfall is here. Follow protocols, and remember your training. Do not engage or approach the Starfallen. They are not your comrades anymore. Our biohazard teams will clear them."

Tov looked down, seeing the increasing number of red names on the terminal.

"Focus on my voice and the fleet system. Help those unaffected to get to clear zones or escape pods should contamination reach critical. Ignore any strange noises or whispers—let the songs of the Eternal Choir wash away the falsehoods."

The voice of Lead Harmonizer Volantesh and the concert played by the Choir's musicians continued despite the harrowing situation they found themselves in. Tov, however, noted the fewer number of vocalists coming through the speakers and the strain in the Lead Harmonizer's singing.

"Listen to the highest commanding officer or follow the orders of fleet security. You all know what to do. I trust in your skills that we will pull through this. The Starless will not take us this day."

With that, he put his message on repeat, knowing that it would help the rattled minds of his people to focus on what was crucial for their survival. Instead of the—

"Tov . . ."

The voices. They brushed against Tov's mind like a veiled seductress, knocking on the door into his inner sanctuary.

". . . Let go . . ."

Tov shook his head, growling low enough for his ears only. "Leave me."

". . . Over here . . ."

He looked at the metal walls of the war room, and for the briefest moment, he saw movement within the texture—moving like tiny worms or the floaters on your eyes when you look to the sky. A shiver went down his spine as he forced himself to ignore the illusions, listening to the Choir's songs blasting through the air.

He turned to his subordinates within the command center. "The Third Fleet is contaminated. We'll need a complete scrub of each vessel. Ohnar?"

"Yes, my patriarch?" The Onin general spoke with a thundering voice underneath his giant power armor.

"Have our infantry scour everything and assist the purge squads. Prioritize getting our people to safety."

"By your will." Ohnar immediately manipulated monitors, calling various officers of the fleet's military, barking orders left and right.

Tov turned to his second-in-command. Admiral Yan was hunched over a terminal, four hands manipulating multiple tablets and screens, multitasking to the limits.

"Yan, situation report," Tov requested, stepping to her side.

"My patriarch," Yan spoke, her voice synthesized by her insectoid helmet. "Several of our smaller vessels have gone dark—corvettes, two frigates, and a light destroyer."

Tov seethed, gesturing for her to continue.

"Everyone else is keeping in contact with us and following protocols, but the Starfallen are making things . . . difficult," Yan reported, turning toward Tov as she continued. "We need more able bodies. So many are approaching their mental limits, and when that happens . . ."

"The seed will bloom, I know." Tov contemplated hard, pacing back and forth as he stroked his armored mandible.

". . . Join your people . . . Let us in . . ."

Tov released a low snarl, straining his mind. "Prioritize each vessel's vital compartments and separate everyone from the Starfallen. As for more bodies . . ."

At that moment, he remembered the presence of Jupiter and Mars. He turned toward them when a wave of pent-up stress and frustration leaked into his mind.

Blame toward his hosts and protectors lodged in his throat as he stomped toward the two silent androids.

"What do you have to— You were supposed to—" Tov stopped, clenching his fists and mandibles as he tried to reign his fury. Like shoveling layers of snow upon lava, he buried his boiling emotions. He slammed his fist upon the terminal, cracking the monitor with his powered gauntlet. After, Tov spent seconds more breathing in and out, opening and closing his fists.

In silence, he leaned his hands on the war table, data tablets and writing items strewn about. He looked up, eyeing the spinning warning lights. Finally, he let out a bone-weary sigh, returning toward the two androids.

"I apologize. You've done so much already." Tov paused, taking a deep breath as he looked away. "My . . . my people and I would have been long dead . . . I—"

Tov stopped in his words as he glanced toward the two androids and their blank stares. He raised his hand, waving before their eyes. "Hello?"

The two remained frozen as Tov circled them. Then, when he returned to his original position, he spoke. "Friends? Jupiter, Mars?"

Jupiter's face furrowed, mouth quivering. Before long, he said through gritted teeth, "A bit . . . busy, Tov. We're . . . I'm sorry."

"Jupiter? What is happening? What's wrong?" Tov asked, his antennae twitching in concern.

Jupiter's jaw clenched as he seethed out, "Eldest's . . . awake . . . Not herself . . . Don't listen to her . . ."

Tov clicked his mandibles in surprise, the sound echoing through his helmet as he spoke, "The Eldest is awake? I don't understand—"

A loud grunt escaped Mars, interrupting Tov's words. The red giant slowly moved his head toward him, the sound from his neck like rusty gears straining.

"COMRADE . . . TOV . . . NO TIME . . . TO EXPLAIN," Mars uttered in his booming voice, reverberating in the war room and causing the dazed occupants to groan. "VENUS . . . WILL HELP YOU."

Jupiter continued. "Tov . . . bud, we're giving V these shells . . . Can't talk anymore . . . Got to focus!"

In an instant, the glow of both androids' eyes faded, heads slumping forward. Tov silently watched as they shone with brilliant gold a second later, replacing the absent blues and reds.

The next moment, Tov heard the whooshing sound of the metal doors opening. He and everyone else whirled around, unholstering their firearms toward the entrance.

"Don't freak out!" Tov's mandibles went agape as he heard an unmistakably bubbly voice.

However, nothing prepared Tov for what he saw.

A filthy Venus stood at the entrance, raising her hands in the air, covered head to toe in gore and viscera. Her long blond hair was a mess, the braid falling apart. Seeing the writhing clumps of biomass on her, Admiral Yan pressed a button on her wrist.

Suddenly, a barrier surrounded Venus while a handful of drones came down from the ceiling, flying toward her. The golden android remained where she was as the drones decontaminated her form, purging the red goop and sterilizing her form.

"Apologies for the deep clean, Lady Venus. We reserve these chemicals for sturdy non-organic material, but I'm sure your android frame is robust enough," Yan spoke, relaxing her stiff shoulders. Everyone else holstered their weapons, checking their emergency suits.

"No worries, Admiral. I needed this." Venus weakly smiled, the muck on her body dissolving into nothingness. While the process continued, Tov stepped forward, gesturing to his subordinates to return to their duties, his people saluting.

He turned to the AI before him. "Venus, what is going on?"

"Eldest is awake," Venus whispered, sighing deeply.

"Jupiter said as much. Where has she been? How is this a problem?"

Venus pursed her lips as she stared at Tov with golden eyes.

She looked away. "After her . . . episode in the Third Fleet. Her mental state relapsed hard. She had to hibernate to stem the instability." Venus furrowed her brow, frowning. "She slipped into a nightmare. A horrible one we couldn't wake her from."

Tov lowered his head. "All this time, she was absent because of this."

Venus nodded. "We don't know what false dreams occurred in her mind. Her connection to us is one-way. But it doesn't matter right now. Jupiter, Mars, and I are trying to stop her."

Tov looked at Venus in confusion before he felt a lump in his throat. A trickle of fear twitched through his antennae. "Has she gone rogue?"

Venus thinly smiled, her eyes weary. "No. If that were the case, then we'd all be dead."

"What, then?"

"This isn't the first time she's had a nightmare of this scale, though it's been decades. Each time, she resorts to—" Venus paused, tugging her braided blond hair before continuing. "Cleansing restrictive elements to prevent her mind from breaking."

"You mean . . ."

"Her emotions. She . . . has become a logic machine. The Omni Mind," Venus shut her eyes. "And she'll stay like this for a long time if we don't do anything."

"How long?"

"A year, maybe more. Even as Eldest is now, she can't keep the ghosts down forever. Nothing can. She wants to purge all the infected from your fleet. My siblings and I can't let that happen. Not when we've . . . just met you," Venus spoke quietly, her shoulders drooping like a heavy weight fell upon her.

Tov sighed. "Lady Venus. Your hearts are kinder than some people I know. But this?" Tov gestured to the monitors, showing the carnage ensuing in his fleet. "This plague is evil incarnate. The Eldest . . . The Omni Mind is right. We can't save the Starfallen . . . It's—"

"Fixable!" Venus exclaimed, stepping forward with a bright, fragile smile, looking away as she bit her lip. "We think."

"What?" Speechlessness took hold of Tov and the rest of the war room. The patriarch shook his head. "I'm sorry, but that's . . . No, that's impossible. Our brightest minds have attempted to solve this, some ethically, some not. All failed in the end."

Venus crossed her arms. Her eyes sharpened as she gazed at him. "No offence, Patriarch Tov, but as good as your people's scientists are, we're mighty AI." she smiled, patting her chest. "From what I know of the androids of old, virtually every disease that plagued humanity went extinct with their aid. The Eldest's main personality contributed to this most of all."

She smiled, her palm over her chest. "She, my siblings, and I are more powerful than our predecessors; this Malignant Starfall shouldn't be any different."

The room went silent as everyone processed Venus's words. A flicker of hope reignited in Tov's chest, and the innate desire of any leader to keep his people safe surged forth. Venus spoke further, her hand touching Tov's arm. "We can— want to help."

Tov lowered his head, hope clashing with pragmatism. He looked toward the golden android, eyes covered by his visor. "So many things have changed in the week I have been here."

"We're sorry if our welcome hasn't been . . . the best." Venus chuckled.

Tov did the same, exhaustion seeping into his voice. "It's just that many have tried to . . . struggled to find a cure. I don't wish to hope for such a small chance. Not again. The unaffected must be protected first."

Tov clenched his fist, breathing deeply as Venus's face contorted momentarily. Eventually, she sighed, slowly nodding her head. "We realize we can't save everyone right now. Time is . . . an obstacle no one can halt. Priority to the healthy. You can count on me for that."

"That is all I ask."

"But if there's a chance to prevent further infection, it has to be done. The problem is that the Omni Mind will continue to purge the Starfallen," Venus said with pursed lips.

"Wouldn't she want to preserve some for the reason you stated?" Tov questioned, tilting his head.

"She should," Venus furrowed her brow. "That's something that's been bugging me. The Omni Mind is intent on purging everyone infected."

Tov clicked his mandibles, contemplating. "Nevertheless, what can we do exactly? My people are too busy containing this catastrophe."

"Well, we only really need you," Venus replied, eyes glinting.

"Me?" Tov asked.

"We were . . ." Venus paused, mulling over her words as she looked at Tov, "hoping you could do something to trigger the Omni Mind, drag her emotions back out, just like before."

Shock poured out of Tov. He began pacing back and forth, his mind ablaze and his mandibles gritting tightly.

He turned to Venus, his voice low. "That is irresponsible—forcing someone's emotions? She's a trauma victim. We don't know how she'll react, not to mention how easily this could backfire."

"We can't reason with her as she is," Venus replied.

Tov shook his head. "Challenging a gestalt intelligence? Insanity."

"You'll have to if we want to start finding a cure for your people," she sighed. "And Jupiter and Mars can only hold out for so long."

"How do we even go about doing this?" Tov questioned, antennae twitching.

"I'll tell you on the way. We need to go now," Venus replied.

"Where?"

"The hangar. Please, Tov, as much as I love my two brothers, they have no chance against the Omni Mind," she pleaded.

Tov paused, his mind roiling in thoughts. He clenched his fist, memories of his younger days pouring into his head. The risks he took—bold, brash, and decisive. Tov glanced at his subordinates, who stared at him in turn while knee-deep in handling the situation.

"What are you doing?" Ohnar asked, his helmeted head turning toward him.

The clinking sounds of Tov checking his equipment and gear cut through the silence. He looked toward his general, uttering, "What I can."

Admiral Yan stepped forward. "My patriarch. You can't—"

"I've learned to be patient over the years, Yan. Found wisdom, you could say. But a time will come when you need to take the plunge."

"Let me come with you, then," she spoke, unholstering her sidearms.

Tov chuckled. "You were a fiery warrior during the Cataclysm. But I need you here in my stead."

Yan paused, fists clenched around the grips of her weapons. Tov heard the agitated clicking under her helmet. Soon, he heard a frustrated sigh. Yan looked at him. "At least take Pyo and your Honor Guard with you."

"I will," Tov replied, sending a message through his cranial implant to his bodyguard captain. He looked toward Venus, nodding.

She gestured in turn, both moving toward the thick double doors of the war room. As Tov stepped into the hall, he heard his admiral call out. "My patriarch!"

He turned to look behind him, seeing the entire room of his best people standing, their hands, claws, and tentacles on their chests. They squared their shoulders, armored boots planted on the ground.

Yan spoke, bowing. "Good luck, Tov. For the Legacy."

Tov raised his two right fists. "For the Broken."

A few minutes later, Tov and Venus marched down the hall—making a beeline toward the nearest hangar.

Venus teleported him and his guards most of the way, bypassing many obstacles.

Around them was a squad of his elite, with Captain Pyo taking point, walking on like silent sentinels. Everyone's footfalls echoed in the empty, gloomy corridor, lit only by red warning lights. Tov looked behind him, seeing the expressionless faces of Jupiter and Mars, the gold of Venus glowing from their eyes.

"How are they?"

"Struggling, giving ground. J is pushing me to hurry up, and I can feel the Omni Mind creeping upon me," Venus replied, her eyes shut.

"I need to thank them after all this for donating so many infantry drones while we do this risky plan."

"It's necessary if we have to separate your people from the infected."

"Couldn't you teleport them? Like you did earlier to cut down our travel time?" Tov asked.

Venus hummed briefly before replying. "That's if you're talking short distances. Your *Zolann'tono* is large enough that we can't just jump to the hangar. As for our more powerful long-jump precision teleporters—configured to non-organics, sadly."

She continued. "If we tried to do the same for the Starfallen, they'd emerge as goop. Well, goopier than they are now. And their eldritch nature makes things . . . difficult."

"A pity," Tov sighed. "Then, can you tell me what I need to do?"

Venus glanced at Tov, replying, "There's something on Earth that Eldest is extremely protective of. Not even us Sub AIs can visit the planet."

Tov looked to Venus. Her jaw clenched as she looked into the distance. She sighed before looking at Tov meekly. "We want you to go down there."

Tov stopped, whipping his head as he stared incredulously at Venus. "What!?"

"Tov, listen," Venus stopped beside him, her eyes glowing intensely. "The Omni Mind won't harm you. She specifically ordered your protection; you are a vital part of the fleet and her liaison to the wider galaxy."

"So, you wish for me to go to Earth, and what?" Tov asked.

"We . . ." Venus paused, pursing her lips.

Tov sighed, his head pounding. "You don't know?"

"It's a work in progress." Venus coughed into her fist. "We'll take one of your shuttles, then fly through the waypoints I've designated. We're already close to Earth, so the trip shouldn't last longer than a few minutes. Then, hopefully, we'll land on humanity's cradle, close to Eldest's Central Nexus."

"Recklessness," Tov shook his head. "This is the plan you've come up with?"

"Hey!" Venus pouted. "We didn't exactly have months to plan this perfectly. We're not that good. Every other option results in your people dying. So we're shooting our shot with this. You just have to find something to drag Eldest's emotion back."

Tov stayed silent, a rise of frustration suffusing his deep sigh. "Is this what my commanding officers thought of my plans back then?" he mumbled.

Before Tov could retort further, a tremendous shake reverberated throughout the *Zolann'tono*. Then, the lights flickered. Tov pressed a finger to his helmet. "Yan, what's happened—"

"A Starfallen's approaching!" Yan's voice shouted inside his helmet. Immediately, he, Venus, and his guards readied themselves.

A deep roar echoed far across the hall, accompanied by shredding steel and the staccato of turret gunfire.

Tov unholstered his sidearms, four energy pistols pointing forward. Beside him, Venus extended golden ropes from her wrists, her face conflicted. Tov whispered to her, "I know it hurts. But we need to move fast if your plan succeeds."

"There's four of them . . . Sharing one body, Tov," Venus looked to him, agony plastered on her face. "I know who they are, read their files."

"So do I . . . It's never easy." Tov patted her shoulder. "But it's a mercy."

Venus stared at Tov for a moment, a myriad of emotions passing through her. Finally, she gritted her teeth, staring ahead. "Alright," she muttered.

Soon enough, the echoes shaking the bulkheads grew louder. Tov heard the pained shrieking of several voices calling out incoherently. He looked ahead, finally seeing the horrid amalgamation that had befallen four of his people far ahead— starting as a dark shape only for the red light to reveal its appearance.

An undulating mound of biomass took up the corridor, charging forward. Tov could see bits of bloodstained clothing and armor half absorbed into its fleshing. Multiple elongated limbs stretched out, grasping for something unseen or dragging its body forward.

Their faces contorted in insane laughter, agony and numbness.

A distinct sound of grinding bone accompanied its onrush.

Tov gritted his mandibles, watching Captain Pyo and his bodyguards move forward, activating energy shields and aiming their sophisticated rifles on the coming Starfallen. Pyo's raspy voice rang out from his helmet. "Plasma flames! Fire on my mark!"

The Honor Guard pointed their rifles, charging them as the abomination drew closer.

Tov held his breath, compound eyes focused.

"... *Beauty* ..."

He clenched his fists tight around his pistols. All around him, the metal walls appeared limp, slimy, and foul. His mind pulsated as the Starfallen drew closer and closer.

When finally—

An ungodly scream left the raw throats of the aberration. Tov groaned as a torrent of torture and dismay battered his senses. He strained to raise his head when he heard his companion speak beside him.

"Oh no," Venus sighed, unaffected by the scream. "I forgot to mention something."

"What?" he asked, looking forward only to see a horrific scene.

"Luna isn't on our side at the moment," Venus continued, stepping forward and past his Honor Guard.

Tov watched on as a river of silver goo seeped in from the tiniest cracks on the wall, converging upon the Starfallen like liquid metal to a magnet. Tov gasped. "Nanites?"

The abomination shrieked, its limbs flailing about, grasping at the gray crawling up its form.

It fell to the floor, wriggling as it continued to struggle. Tov felt something primal within his senses as he watched.

Then, from a reflective puddle between Tov's side and the Starfallen, the android shell of Luna emerged, her face calm.

He locked eyes with her silver hues. She raised her pale, dainty fingers to prop up her circle-rimmed glasses as her nanites continued to consume the Starfallen behind her.

Looking toward her golden sister, Luna sighed, speaking in a flat voice. "Overseer Venus."

Venus huffed as she stepped toward Luna. "Why, L?"

Luna narrowed her eyes. "Your plan has a high chance of going incredibly wrong."

"Then help us, Lady Luna," Tov spoke, his voice heavy.

Luna looked toward him, her gaze unreadable. "I cannot do that, Tov. The Omni Mind declared the Starfallen be purged immediately. Her reasoning is sound."

"You say logic directs you and the Omni Mind. So what? For all your power, you can't spare even one?" Tov retorted.

"I follow her orders," Luna sighed. "There is no point to this. But more than that . . ."

Her gray face darkened, her gaze drilling into him. "I can't allow you to come to Earth."

"Why not?" Tov asked.

Venus raised her hand, stopping him. She pursed her lips as she stared at Luna. "You know what's there, don't you, sister?"

Luna stayed silent, her frown deepening.

She spoke in a hushed tone, repeating her earlier words. "I can't allow you to come to Earth."

Venus grimaced, her golden eyes flaring as she took a battle stance. Tov watched as the android bodies of Jupiter and Mars strode forward. Luna cocked her eyebrow, staring at her sister as she spoke. "What are you doing?"

"Holding you off while Tov and his people do their thing, obviously," Venus remarked, smirking.

"Overseer Venus, you are a non-combat AI." Luna's gaze sharpened. "Cease this folly, now."

Venus huffed, sticking her tongue out. "Make me."

"You will comply," Luna retorted. In an instant, the flowing rivers of nanites ceased their advance on the Starfallen, converging beneath Luna. The monstrosity writhed before making a hasty escape to a side corridor.

Venus's radiant smile shone as she glanced at Tov and gave him a nod. "Go on, sorry I can't sightsee with you."

Without another word, the two sides exploded in motion, grace and fury, charging toward each other—three androids, gold, blue and red, against a sea of silver. Tov felt Captain Pyo's hand grip his arm, pulling him forward. "Patriarch, we need to move."

And so he left the duel behind him, mind focused on the daunting task ahead.

CHAPTER 36

EMERGENCY LANDING

Armored bootsteps quaked the metal floor, the clarion of Tov's message on repeat while the constant singing of the Choir permeated the long hallway.

In the background, nearly invisible, Tov heard the tingling whispers oozing from the walls.

"*. . . Where are you going, Patriarch? . . .*"

He shook his head, four gloved hands clenched tightly around the grips of his engraved pistols.

"We're almost there," he uttered to the dozen guards surrounding him. "Ready yourselves."

Behind them, Tov felt the vibrations caused by the duel between highly advanced androids. Uncertainty filled his mind on who'd emerge victorious, but the visceral sight of Luna's nanites consuming a Starfallen haunted his thoughts.

He shook his head, his legs propelling him forward as he kept contact with Yan and his people.

"It's chaos, my patriarch. The infantry drones bearing Jupiter's and Mars's colors are fighting the Starfallen and Luna's tide of nanomachines," Yan spoke through his helmet.

"Keep out of the crossfire," Tov uttered. "We know that the Omni Mind's directive is to protect the Third Fleet. Use that. While the AIs are battling it out, continue containment protocols."

Tov mulled over his following words. "And remember, Yan, corralling the Starfallen is secondary. As much as I trust our hosts and the promise of a cure, I will not risk our people," Tov commanded, his breath controlled as he continued to march toward the hangar urgently.

"By your will, my patriarch," Yan responded.

After closing the comms, Tov felt his two hearts beat loudly in his chest. His compound eyes gazed with razor-sharp focus as the group turned the corner.

They immediately spotted two Starfallen in the distance. Tov and his guards instantly raised their weapons, undeterred by the obstruction.

"Push through them!" Pyo bellowed in front of Tov, firing lances of searing lasers with his sleek rifle.

Their profane forms shrieked in pain as multiple beams of light and explosive kinetic rounds bombarded their flesh. Tov looked at them, wincing and uttering silent songs of prayer, before firing his four pistols in quick succession.

The Starfallen charged toward them. Fat, bulbous amalgamations of his people dragged themselves like onrushing wrecking balls. Their mutated faces screamed, the palpable sound attacking their minds directly.

But the constant batterings of previous encounters had reforged the minds of Tov and his elite warriors.

Captain Pyo called out, "Minnok, purge this hall clean!"

A heavy gunner pushed forward, his massive armored bulk towering over the rest of Tov's Honor Guard. His hands carried an enormous stocky weapon connected to a module on his back.

Minnok's deep voice echoed through his beetle-like helmet. "Sterilizing."

With a press on the trigger, a thick pillar of concentrated heat shot out. It soared through the long hallway at light speed—accompanied by a high-pitched scream as if a holy being was breathing out fire. It bathed the two Starfallen in burning light, slowly obliterating their bodies.

The monsters panicked, stumbling backward and pressing their masses against the wall to evade the powerful heat ray. Minnok continued to focus his weapon on one of them until every atom dissipated into hot oblivion.

Tov could still hear the sizzling meat; although his helmet filtered out foul odors, he could still smell it. The metal hallway glowed a deep orange from where Minnok's tool of destruction marked its path.

"PAIN. PAIN. PAIN."

"HURTS . . . MERCY!"

"KILL ME!"

He grimaced, mandibles shut tight as he and his guards ran past the remaining Starfallen, quivering and grievously injured, calling out to him.

But not before another one of his soldiers dropped a grenade behind them. Five seconds later, the hallway behind them quaked from the plasma explosion. "Sterilization complete, Captain," barked out the soldier.

"Good work, Konnoq," Pyo responded.

Soon enough, they reached the entrance to the hangar. Pyo brought up a hologram of their destination to Tov. "Patriarch, Admiral Yan has cleared Shuttle Twelve at Bay Six. It's a walk away, but the rest of the hangar is a mess," Pyo reported.

Tov hummed, pressing a finger on his helm. "Yan, what's the situation at the main hangar?"

The admiral's voice crackled through his helmet. "We've been receiving escape pods and shuttles from our lost vessels. Shortly after, a horde of Starfallen breached the area."

"What drew them?" he asked.

"We're unsure, Patriarch," Yan replied slowly. "Yulane patched through with a theory."

"What is it?"

"They know what you're doing," she uttered.

Tov paused for a moment, thoughts roiling in his head.

He grumbled, mandibles clicking rapidly. "Yet another complication," he huffed. "Never mind then, we're about to enter the hangar. Plot us a safe route to our shuttle. What can we expect?"

"Yes, Patriarch. We still maintain control of the main hangar. Several marines and Sol's infantry drones are battling against the Starfallen and Lady Luna's nanites. Per your orders, we're focusing on shielding our people from the infected and the AI crossfire."

"Are we at risk of losing the area?"

"The Starfallen won't push us out," she declared. "I'm sending you the nearest route to Shuttle Twelve. A marine squad has it guarded while our technicians are priming the vessel to peak condition. We also have an ace pilot ready to take you."

"Good," Tov said as he inspected the files on both the ship and the pilot, Imo. "Thank you, Yan."

"Just doing my job, Patriarch," Yan chuckled. "Someone has to keep your ship running while you go off galivanting like you're a hundred years younger."

Tov coughed into his helmet. "That stings, *slokin*. You don't hear me say you're getting on with age."

"Liar, you do that every time we meet."

Tov chuckled. "True, your chitin is losing its luster. Maybe ask our new friend Mars if he has some red wax you can use."

"Just focus on not dying," she grumbled with a clack of her mandibles. "I'm not there to pull you out of a fire this time."

Pyo chimed in through their shared frequency. "Settle yourself, Yan. I'm here to save his lordship, remember?"

"At least someone is being responsible," Yan spoke. Then, before Tov could reply further, Yan interrupted him in a severe tone. "Alright, the ship's ready, and I have your route. Good luck, Tov."

"Stay safe, Yan," Tov replied, closing his comms as he turned to his captain, nodding.

His Honor Guard readied themselves as they drew closer to the large metal blast doors to the hangar. Tov heard nothing from the other side, but his fine-tuned senses could feel the reverberations of battle.

Pulling out an ID chip, Pyo swiped the console to the side, and slowly, the blast doors opened.

A cacophony of sounds battered them as Tov and his guards rushed in. For a brief moment, Tov glanced at the main hangar.

Weaponfire arced across the entire deck. The different levels of the hangar were alight with lasers, kinetic rounds, and plasma. He saw a squad of marines on the far side as they escorted a trio of survivors exiting from their scorched shuttle.

Soldiers formed firing lines, pelting a group of Starfallen as they burst through wrecked blast doors.

Tov saw silver ooze flowing out of vents, instantly attacking the closest Starfallen.

Blue and red infantry drones marched on with machine efficiency, their eye slits shining a brilliant gold as they attempted to protect Tov's people while trying desperately to maim the infected instead of killing them—all the while battling Luna's nanites with shock guns or explosives.

Turrets continued to fire at hostile targets. Tov instinctively ducked as the roaring engines of a burning corvette sailed over his head, its metal hull writhing with eldritch contagion.

The staccato of rapid-fire guns, shouting soldiers, and explosions shook the hangar. Tov's heart beat loudly, and yet, he felt calm.

His mind was sharp as he followed the path laid out by his admiral. His hands moved in trained muscle memory, firing precision shots from far away, striking Starfallen.

Captain Pyo and the Honor Guard stood out, their honed skills excelling in paving the way. Tov himself danced to the tune of battle, his four arms acting independently as they aimed his sidearms and fired.

Monster after monster fell or fled in agony, vile ichor staining the metal floors.

But then, in unison, Tov and his compatriots winced and stumbled as a horrific scream echoed throughout the entire hangar.

The air stilled as every Starfallen continued to bellow out and shriek.

And, as one, they turned their attention to Tov.

Pyo cursed. "*Dowa!* Move, now!"

Tov and his guard rushed forward in a burst of speed, boosted by their powered suits. The ground shook, and the shouts of fallen sailors grew louder while the retaliation from Tov's soldiers and allies attempted to stem the oncoming tsunami of biomass.

"There!" Tov shouted, pointing at the Bay Six and the parked shuttle.

The sleek vessel was sharp and top-of-the-line new. But, more importantly, Tov saw the squad of marines taking positions.

Tov turned around briefly only to see the horde of Starfallen crawling up from the lower levels and dragging their bodies over the railings. Vents burst open as more monstrosities poured in. They wrenched open blast doors with throbbing scarlet limbs—roaring, heaving, and cackling with madness.

"Open fire!" ordered Pyo, and as one, the Honor Guard and the standing marines let out a barrage—perforating every hostile, exploding them into viscera and gore.

Tov continued to fire while on the move when a Starfallen crashed from a level above, right next to them.

Without a word, the heavy gunner Minnok stepped forth, his weapon glowing hot as he pulled the trigger and engulfed the lanky, three-limbed abomination with searing light. Tov fired two shots at it, eliciting a wail of pain but nothing compared to the agonized scream Minnok tore from its throat.

It died quickly. Tov moved on, his mind pacing through every sight, every danger. Things blurred in motion but remained evident to his senses. Shot after shot, infected after infected.

But the tide didn't stop.

They crawled over bodies, every single one a vile amalgam of his people, conjoined in twos or threes. Bones jutted out like scythes, whipping across the air. Blood and bile, caustic with otherworldly concoctions, belched out of their many mouths—gnashing teeth and pulsing flesh.

For a moment, Tov believed every Starfallen within the *Zolann'tono* had rushed to this location—he could see thousands pouring into the hangar from far-off entry points.

"Tov!" he heard Yan's voice crackle through his helmet. "You have to—"

"Leave, I know!" Tov shouted, his armored boot stepping past the dividing line into Bay Six.

Even as infantry drones rushed to their aid and flanked the monsters using lethal force, Tov realized the Starfallen would surround them in minutes.

Thankfully, like a great serenade, the shuttle's engines roared, and the rear hatch opened as two more marines exited, adding to the torrent of firepower. The shuttle's heavy guns barked out kinetic slugs, tearing through multiple Starfallen with each round.

Pyo grabbed his arm, pulling Tov toward the shuttle. He spoke through their internal comms—the racket from the battle zone cancelling any other noise.

"Inside!" With a few gestures, half of Tov's Honor Guard turned around, taking positions behind crates and parked vehicles, concentrating their firepower.

Tov rushed past the firing line of soldiers and stepped onto the ramp leading into the shuttle just as it began to lift off. Pyo, Minnok, and four others entered the shuttle before kneeling, firing rapidly in a light show of tracer rounds and lasers. Whizzing noises and shrieks filled the hangar while the roaring engines of the shuttle blotted everything else.

Soon enough, the vessel flew higher.

The Starfallen seemingly ignored everyone else as they tried desperately to reach the vessel, using their many limbs to jump and leap, to no avail—dropping down to their deaths or being shot by the heavy guns of the shuttle.

Tov watched their forms grow smaller as the shuttle flew off.

Finally, the ship dove down the massive chute in the middle of the hangar toward the exit into open space.

He looked on, observing the battle. The Starfallen, seeing him escape their grasp, turned their attention to the living. However, stuck and focused on him as they were, Tov's people surrounded the horde, taking defensive positions and opening fire.

Before he breathed a sigh of relief and headed further into the shuttle, in the corner of his compound vision, far off where he and his guards had entered the hangar, he saw Luna. She stood unscathed from her duel with Venus, gazing at Tov with an impassive face. The two stared at each other, even as the distance grew longer.

In a few seconds, the ramp raised, cutting Tov's vision from the outside as air filled the airlock.

Finally, Tov, Pyo, and five others breathed out, a chunk of stamina taken from them. A shower of various cleansing chemicals poured from above, and finally, with everyone decontaminated, the light above the door into the shuttle flashed blue.

The single blast door hissed, slowly opening.

Tov stepped into the small interior. He barely took notice of the small living room compartment. Shuttles were a step smaller than corvettes, meant to ferry people from ship to ship.

Still, the shuttle Yan had prepared for him was well-appointed. Tov had been transported in this model many times throughout the expedition and even before then.

Tov ran his gloved hand over a circular table crescented by soft couches. A glass cabinet of liquor lay on the wall, while the designers had adorned the rest of the room with bookcases, a music player, and a cooler for foodstuffs.

He moved past it all. His guard remained semi-battle-ready as they reenergized themselves with the items they carried. Captain Pyo followed him to the cockpit, two compartments away.

When they opened the final door, Tov greeted the pilot. "Imo?"

The pilot, a Kurskann, saluted him as she remained seated. "Good day, my patriarch. Well, not that good. But—never mind. Admiral Yan has briefed me. So we're heading to Earth, yes?"

Tov nodded his antennae. "How long until we get there?"

"I—" However, before she could respond, a small hologram appeared, and Jupiter's voice spoke through. "What's up? This your boy, J."

"Jupiter?" Tov asked, looking toward the avatar. "What's happened? I thought you were busy—"

"You, my friend, are talking to a fragment of my wonderful self, since I'm probably getting my ass beat by the boss lady."

"I see . . ." Tov slowly spoke as he settled into the copilot seat.

"Right, anyways, Tovvy boy, listen up," Jupiter cleared his throat. "I've set my *Buddha's Palm* to teleport your shuttle close to Earth since I'm pretty sure Luna will try and stop you. She won't harm you, I'm sure of that, but still."

"So we'll have to avoid a force capable of harming a Leviathan?"

"Yeah, simple enough." Jupiter coughed, waving his hand in dismissal. "No worries, though. My forces and Mars's will stop 'em. We have her outnumbered. Venus is also making things difficult for Luna and the boss by contesting control of their stuff. They won't bother you. So just concentrate on making it to Earth," Jupiter reassured.

Tov sighed, removing his helmet and massaging his chitinous head. The shuttle left the confines of the *Zolann'tono* and soared into the open blackness of space, bespeckled by glinting stars, Sol, and the dots of Earth and her moon.

"Just . . . when we emerge close to Earth, what can we expect?" Tov spoke out.

"Honestly? I have no idea." Jupiter shrugged.

Tov stared silently at the hologram. The urge to smash to communicator welled up in his fist. Instantly, Jupiter continued. "Look, it's not for lack of trying. Venus probably already told you, but us Sub AIs have never visited Earth."

"She suspected Luna might have," Tov muttered.

"Yeah, big surprise," Jupiter grumbled. "Luna was the first of us siblings. She probably splintered from Eldest shortly after becoming a gestalt entity, and the isolation got to her. I never really . . . questioned what she knew. Maybe I should have."

Jupiter lowered his head. His eyes looked sunken and dark, weary.

"I am sorry for causing this," Tov spoke, lowering his head. On the monitors displaying space, he could see the lances of light soaring through space in between the many vessels of his proud Third Fleet. He tried to ignore the few dark hulls floating in the void.

Jupiter shook his head. "Don't worry about it. We'll fix this mess. They're still family, and I . . ." The hologram looked away. "I want what's best for them."

Tov nodded. "Nothing in the universe shines brighter."

Jupiter hummed, nodding.

"So," Tov spoke, the need for details of his mission coming to the forefront. "Everything about Earth is shrouded, then?"

"Literally and figuratively," Jupiter huffed, his face returning to the usual casual boredom. "Dates back to when humans and androids fought together, a sort of artificial storm that blocks out all sensors they could think of when the Starless kept making targeted strikes on cities. Then, with the Shroud up, they could hide their assets, keeping the monstrous bastards on their toes."

"Do we know where we'll be landing, then?" Tov asked.

"From our calculations based on Earth's rotation and a bunch of other shit? You'll land in New Eden, a massive city in Antarctica—gifted to Eldest and every android by the UN as thanks for elevating humanity to a golden age."

"And its current significance?"

"Eldest's Central Nexus is underneath it," Jupiter replied gravely, crossing his arms. "That I know."

"Ah." Tov nodded. "What of orbital and surface defenses?"

"They won't harm you. As I said, you're a VIP."

"Surely they have non-lethal means to stop us?" Tov questioned.

Jupiter chuckled. "Right, as if we want non-lethal weapons against Starless. Still, what rare bits there are, they won't bother you for the short time frame you'll have."

"So then, that's all?" Tov muttered, leaning forward as he pressed his chin against his knuckles.

Jupiter sighed, a look of pity flashing in his eyes. "Yeah, and after that . . . it's your ball."

"My what?" Tov asked, tilting his head.

"I mean, it's up to you." Jupiter shook his head before looking at Tov. "So good luck, you'll need it." He sighed. "Wish I could do more, but I need to go. My main consciousness needs all the juice to delay the Omni Mind."

"You've done more than enough. I'll handle this," Tov declared.

"Thanks, Tov," Jupiter smiled. "Teleporting you in three, two—"

"Thank you, Jupiter," Tov uttered as he felt the wave of higher-dimensional forces wrapping around the shuttle. Jupiter smirked in turn before his hologram winked out.

When Tov came to again, the buzzing sensation and cascade of colors he could taste fading away, he looked at the curved monitor acting like a cockpit's windows.

And, for the first time since arriving in Sol, Tov saw a dark planet covered in swirling storms. As he zoomed the image in, he saw the swirling vortexes, the flashes of lightning illuminating the mist with a reddish hue. Nothing like the Earth he had studied.

In the backdrop, far off in the distance, was Luna, the Moon.

Tov felt mesmerized as he finally looked at humanity's cradle, with a sense of dread and awe flooding his chest and mind.

"Bring us in, Imo," he spoke softly, focus uncut as he stared at the image. "Quickly."

"Yes, Patriarch," the pilot responded, voice similarly hushed. "The jump saved us plenty of time. We'll be entering the atmosphere in less than fifteen minutes."

"Gives you the shivers under your shell, doesn't it?" Captain Pyo spoke as he took a seat behind Tov.

Tov nodded. "It does."

The minutes passed excruciatingly slowly. Tov tapped his armored boot, forcing his mind still. The lull battered his senses more so than the lies of the eldritch.

He jolted when the speakers crackled. Tov looked at the comms, expecting Jupiter's image. Instead, what shone through silenced any words from him.

Everyone stared as the image came through. A wave of dread permeated the air.

A hologram of the Omni Mind emerged. Although no larger than his head, Tov felt a weight from the image and, unnervingly, felt nothing in terms of emotion. It was an obsidian sphere, infinitely small circuits engraved upon its smooth reflective black.

Tov kept his guard up as he sat straight. "Omni Mind."

In a booming, monotone voice, she responded, "Patriarch. Cease your approach."

"I will," Tov replied before countering. "If you stop purging the infected and assist in making a cure for them."

"Request denied," the Omni Mind immediately responded, the black glow darkening as she spoke.

"Why?" Tov questioned, his mandibles clicking.

"The infected crew, coined Starfallen, have been classified as Starless. Overarching directive: Kill all vermin," she spoke, voice cold like winter.

Tov's mind roiled as he mulled his following words, looking for loopholes to take advantage of to talk with this machine. "You have promised to protect the Third Fleet. Is this not—"

"Error," the Omni Mind thundered. "Protecting your people is secondary. Elimination of all Starless takes precedence. They are not your people anymore, isn't that the galactic consensus?"

"Your Sub AIs are against this. They believe in a cure," Tov uttered, glaring at the orb. "I am against this."

"Wants are secondary. The insubordinate Fragments will be pacified and put on lockdown for the remainder of this event. Damage to our relationship will be mended over time," she spoke.

"I will not forgive you for this," he retorted.

"You will. When the enemy is dead," she replied.

He let out a buzzing growl. "You can't spare a single one?" Tov asked, leaning forward, balling his fists.

"Death to monsters," the Omni Mind responded, her hologram darkening and shaking.

"A cure will help so many. Eldest, please . . ." Tov pleaded, hoping. "Don't do this."

The Omni Mind's image shook, the spherical orb straining under an unseen pressure. Slowly, seething, she spoke.

"I. Don't. Care."

Silence filled the cabin, the occupants staring at the erratic image. Tov breathed out, shaking his head. "Then you leave me no choice."

He pointed at the orb, stabbing with his armored finger. "I'll drag the Eldest and her emotions out from your Nexus by hand if need be."

"You are a fool. This conversation serves no purpose," the Omni Mind retorted, and for a moment, Tov heard a sliver of anger in her voice. Before he could speak further, the hologram winked out.

Tov sighed, slumping in his seat. He turned to Imo. "How much longer?"

"Almost there, my patriarch," she replied.

Pyo hummed behind Tov. "Honestly, I expected more resistance."

"And now you jinxed it," Imo grumbled.

As soon as the words left her mouth, the shuttle shook. Tov's seat belts tightened around him, a padding of soft material primed to encase him with safety material. Tov shouted, voice cutting through the clarion of warning alarms. "What is happening?"

"It's . . . Argh! There's something causing damage to the ship's internals. Sensors can't detect what it is!"

Tov held on to his seat, mind aflame before realization struck. "Luna! She snuck nanites aboard!" He balled his fist as he connected to the ship with his cranial implant. As Imo said, multiple systems slowly malfunctioned, the engines slowly sputtering out.

"At this rate, we'll be dead in space. We won't make it to Earth!" Imo shouted out.

Tov cursed, thinking, churning out any idea. Finally, he snagged one. "Can you force a controlled explosion?"

"What!?" Imo and Pyo shouted in unison.

"Have everyone move to the emergency capsules and blow the thrusters. We just need to get caught in her gravity and let it do the rest," Tov commanded, his chest pounding with eagerness. "Once we're close, we'll eject. If Luna wants to sabotage us, we'll turn it up all the way."

"This is insane!" Imo exclaimed before a cackling laugh escaped her helmet. "I love it!"

"Imo!?" Pyo shouted.

"You can do it?" Tov questioned.

"Yeah, the shuttle will be toast, we'll have some . . . a lot of bruises too, but I guessed this was a one-way trip when I got the call," she mumbled, her four hands pressing buttons, manipulating terminals, and making speedy calculations. "Alright, I got a vector. Just sit tight, and sing to the Symphony."

"You are all mad! Yan will kill me when she learns about this," Captain Pyo groaned, exasperated.

"Ready! Blowing thrusters, now!" A loud sound cracked through the air as quakes shook the shuttle violently. Tov felt the increase in g-forces squeezing his insides. He muttered thanks for his robust and genetically enhanced body.

The vessel lurched forward, soaring through the black and rapidly approaching the planet. The monitors lowered, the visuals of the Earth disappearing as red warning lights glared throughout the cabin.

"Entering atmosphere!" Imo shouted.

Tov heard multiple mechanisms engage, prepping the compartment for emergency ejection. The ship rattled, and the sound of scorching air, muffled by the hall, seeped through. Seconds passed, and soon, Imo gave the call.

"Eject!"

Behind, Tov heard the whooshing noise of the emergency capsules taken by his Honor Guard ejecting out of the shuttle. And then, his seat enveloped him in layers of protective material, hugging him tight and muting all sound.

With a thump, he felt the cockpit eject. Boosters engaged, guiding the capsule to land. Tov shut his eyes and silenced his thoughts. Before long, he felt his body jolt as they landed hard.

Tov nearly blacked out, his mind in a daze. A minute later, his seat released him from its safe confines. He breathed out in relief, despite his emergency suit giving him constant air. Beside and behind him, Imo and Pyo were similarly gasping.

"Let's never do this again," Tov mumbled as groans of agreement filled the cockpit. He stood up with wobbly legs, turning toward the metal door that now led to the surface of Earth instead of to his shuttle.

Dread filled him as he slowly raised his hand and pressed his palm on the scanner to the side. With a ding, it opened. Haunting, loud winds and thunder filled his world as flashes of bright light seeped in. Tov raised his hand as he took a tentative step forward, his boot stepping on desolate black rock.

Tov remained silent as he looked out, lowering his hand. A rattled gasp escaped him as he walked out of the scorched cabin and into a landscape that scarred his mind.

CHAPTER 37

RUINED EDEN

Lightning struck a far-off obelisk, illuminating the hellish landscape. For a brief moment, the light cut through a pervasive shroud of punching storms.

Red, brown, and dark gray hues swamped Tov's vision. Even with his eyes straining, he could barely see anything more than a few arm's lengths before him.

"Symphony above," he muttered, turning his head to see nothing but the craggy black rock beneath his feat, layers of ash and dust, and obscured objects in the distance.

Through the howling winds and cracking thunders, Tov heard the bootfalls of his two companions crunching the reflective black ground. He turned toward them, seeing them similarly taken in by the desolate sights.

Captain Pyo spoke, his voice uttering through his thick, engraved helmet. "Isn't this supposed to be the south pole?"

"Where's the snow? The ice?" Pilot Imo whispered, unholstering her sidearm.

"Where's New Eden?" Pyo questioned, bringing his rifle to bear with two arms while the other two operated a data tablet. "This planet is beyond inhospitable; the moment we're out of our suits, we'll melt from the heat and acid in a few hours. I still think we need to find shelter. There's . . . something else in the air."

Tov looked out, peering through the gray, swirling fog. Sound faded from his senses, the battering thunderstorm above him becoming muffled behind his mind as his vision tunneled.

Everything darkened, the presence of his two companions disappearing.

His sixth sense saw a thread swaying in the wind for a split second. Then, in his mind's eye, he reached out to his, his finger brushing against the ethereal strand.

He keeled over.

Tov bellowed out a harsh groan. Flashes of memories, not his own, invaded his thoughts. He landed on the ground, grabbing handfuls of shattered rock and ash as he raked the soil.

Nothing but pain, agony, and heart-wrenching sorrow of a time long past, of a million people shrieking out in torture.

Burning, scathing, tearing his mind, their hands, so many, countless and legion, grabbed him, beckoning him. Souls of specters seeped into the soil of Earth, pleading and begging. A guttural shout escaped Tov's raw throat, his mandibles agape as he clutched his helmet with his hands.

Loud cacophony filled him, ringing and howling, more intense and violent than the storm above.

And then, it disappeared.

Tov shook his head, looking around in confusion, standing as he was. He looked to the side, seeing Captain Pyo and Imo unaware, busying themselves. The former checked his tablet and scanned the landscape while the latter pored over the scorched cockpit buried partially on the ground.

The backlash left him nauseated.

He shook his head once again. A blank spot, barely a second, left a void in his memory like a scabbed wound. A gnawing feeling circled within him, but he cast the thought aside, mind pulsing.

Tov pressed his finger against his helm, attempting to contact the Third Fleet, only to be met by screeching static. Tov winced, shaking his head. "We're cut off. Earth's Shroud is blocking our line to the Third Fleet. So they won't know where we are. Hopefully, that goes for the Omni Mind."

"Won't she know where we're heading?" Imo asked.

"She does, I guarantee it," Tov replied. "We just . . . need to find New Eden. There has to be something there if this city used to be her home. Maybe there are places we can utilize to spark some emotion from Sol's overlord. If all else, maybe a corpse."

Pyo grunted. "This is madness even the Starless would balk at. How much are you willing to trust the Omni Mind not to lash out and obliterate us on the spot?"

"Little," Tov sighed, turning to Pyo. "But we're out of options. We just need to get this done."

Pyo gazed back, his blank helmet unreadable, before chuckling. "By your will, Patriarch. We've been through worse, I think."

Tov chuckled in turn. "Maybe. Now, what of the rest of our Honor Guard? Can you contact them?"

"We have their projected landing spots. Unless they hit something and diverted, we should be able to link up with them," Pyo said, manipulating a data tablet for a moment before he huffed. He raised a finger, pointing.

"Minnok is close over there."

Soon enough, the trio walked toward the heavy gunner's emergency capsule. The winds muffled their steps as they marched over the irregular landscape, their helms shining the way forward.

"Is all of Earth like this?" Imo mumbled through their internal comms, crackling into Tov's helm.

"We have to assume so," Tov replied, looking over the data sent by Jupiter. "Antarctica was Earth's crown, New Eden her shining diamond. If even this place is in shambles, I have no hope for the rest of the world."

Sorrow filled Tov and his companions. Tov's mind wandered to the pictures of pristine white snow, penguins and seals, and a brilliant blue ocean—a calming breeze of cold air enveloping him in a comfortable embrace as he basked in southern light.

His thoughts were abruptly interrupted when his boot made contact with something solid, producing a resounding metallic ding. The trio halted their steps and peered down to investigate.

Pyo hummed, intrigued. He crouched down and ran his palm over the piece of metal they had stumbled upon. As he brushed away a layer of ash, the texture of dark, rusted steel and rivets became apparent.

Casting his gaze around, Tov noticed a slight calming of the winds and a thinning of the fog from their immediate surroundings. He cautiously took a few steps forward, only to be abruptly halted by an immense wall of the same black metal. Perplexed, he stepped back and instinctively looked upward, freezing.

Beside him, Pyo and Imo joined in his awestruck silence. Their eyes fixated on the silhouette that emerged from the dissipating shroud.

The colossal war machine loomed before them, adorned with a formidable array of six massive guns along its sides and a multitude of secondary armaments scattered across its frame. However, Tov's gaze was inexorably drawn to the cavernous hole in its front, exposing a labyrinthine tangle of jagged metal and wires that resembled grotesque innards.

On its chest, its name, paint flaking off and faded.

"Little Timmy," Pyo mumbled before releasing a hearty laugh, shaking his head. "Humans."

Tov and Imo chuckled along, entranced by the machine before them.

Then, for a moment, the once obscured landscape unveiled itself; a haunting panorama of scarred terrain littered with craters, chasms, and the wreckage of long-forgotten machines. Yet as swiftly as the curtain of fog lifted, it swiftly enshrouded the imposing figure once more, obscuring its full majesty from view.

Tov released a shaky breath, his gaze shifting down to the metal they stood upon—a mangled leg, one of the four that once supported this behemoth of war.

The trio remained silent as they searched for the missing Honor Guard.

They picked up Minnok a minute later, his capsule tearing the earth in a line before stopping against a mound of stones. They marched on, finding two others as they scaled cliff faces and walked past scorched metal, gun emplacements, tanks, and more.

They never found the last Honor Guard. The group stood at the projected landing spot, only to find nothing there. Pyo clenched his fist tight, muttering, "*Nuor*, Konnoq."

Tov sighed, placing a palm on his captain's shoulder pad. "We need to move. The Omni Mind will be searching for us."

Pyo gazed at Tov for a moment before nodding.

Soon, the group moved in haste—fanning out in formation to cover more ground while keeping each other in sight in the low visibility conditions.

"Where are we? Did we land outside of the city?" Minnok spoke with a deep voice through his helmet.

Imo perked up. "We should have landed close if my calculations were right. We just need to move toward the center—"

"Over there!" Pyo called out, his finger pointing toward a distant shape. The group pressed forward, drawing closer. And as they stood in front of the object, the captain huffed. "Well then, we don't need to find the city."

Before them stood a weathered arch, its once pristine marble now crumbling and worn from the pervasive dust storm. A rusted metal gate marked the once grand entrance. The remnants of a towering fence, its iron bars twisted and bent, extended into the distance. As Tov's gaze rose, he noticed faded lettering atop the gate.

GARDEN OF EDEN

Nearby, a broken and dilapidated signpost lay partially buried under a layer of ash, its fractured message barely discernible. Tov knelt, picking the sign up, shaking the gray away, and revealing the words decorated by a backdrop of verdant trees and colorful flowers.

THANK YOU FOR VISITING OUR CHERISHED PARK! HAVE A WONDERFUL DAY!

Tov sighed as he stood back up. "We're here—landed in the middle of a park . . ."

He turned around, seeing nothing but desolation. Not a single trace of the proud garden remained. "Let's move on," Tov whispered, exiting the park through the worn marble arch and rusted metal.

Immediately, their boots made contact with the remnants of cracked pavement, its once smooth surface now marred by time and neglect.

The fog lifted slightly, allowing the group to gaze into the city proper.

The haunting howl of relentless winds swept through the desolate streets of New Eden, whistling through broken windows and shattered doorways. Dust and debris danced in chaotic swirls, carried by relentless gusts as if the very air itself mourned the city's downfall.

As Tov and his group ventured into the heart of New Eden, the din of the storm muffled their steps, mocking the once thriving utopian city. The remnants of a glorious past lay before them, now reduced to a haunting tableau of destruction and decay.

Where sleek curves and gleaming surfaces once harmonized with nature now stood broken structures. The buildings, once symbols of human and android achievement, now stood as solemn monuments of a bygone era.

Tov saw more war machines, nothing that could rival the behemoth in the park, but all imposing wrecks. Sleek tanks, quad-mechs, and artillery platforms lined the streets or crashed into buildings. He never saw any organic materials torn away by time or the hail of dust and ash.

His boot scraped the ground, kicking away brass bullet casings, rusted magazines, and abandoned weapons sprawled across the road.

The wind, carrying the weight of a thousand whispers, howled through the deserted streets populated by burnt vehicles, stirring up clouds of dust that veiled the city in suffocating darkness.

The hushed voices remained like a slow drill boring into his mind, unfathomable, barely noticeable. Tov breathed out, focusing his mind. He spoke loudly through the internal comms of their suits. "Keep moving. We need to find a map, anything."

"Yes, Patriarch!" they shouted in unison in an attempt to raise their spirits.

Tov winced as thunder boomed from afar, lightning bathing them in a harsh light, leaving a ringing in their ears. The minutes passed as Tov and his companions moved in a daze as they explored the city, climbing over fallen walls and shifting roads.

Now and then, within the darkness of the buildings, high up in hollow skyscrapers or deep in an alley, Tov saw phantoms skittering about. He shook his head, only to find nothing.

After what felt like an eternity, their weary footsteps led them to a dilapidated kiosk, its worn-out structure barely standing against the test of time. With a mix of curiosity and resignation, Pyo approached it, his hand reaching out to grasp one of the faded flyers, only for it to crumble to dust at his touch. *"Dowa,"* he mumbled a curse.

Tov sighed, gesturing for a halt.

"We'll take cover and rest for a while, gather our bearings, and form a plan of action," he spoke, his eyes falling upon what appeared to be a long-abandoned toy store. The group breathed a collective sigh of relief.

As Tov walked toward the store, traversing the lonely streets scattered with remnants of twisted metal and abandoned vehicles, his gaze caught sight of something that halted him in his tracks. A lifeless figure sat slumped beside a weathered stroller.

With cautious steps, he approached the motionless body, his eyes taking in the intricate details of its artificial form, her back against the store's wall. The lines of synthetic skin, meticulously designed to mimic the warmth of human flesh, failed to mask the eternal stillness within.

"An android," he muttered, kneeling beside the old machine.

Despite it all, the womanly shell looked indistinguishable from a human. Tov stared at her lifeless eyes, her disheveled state, her torn and faded clothes, and her unkempt hair, all worn down by the storm and the ravages of time.

He saw no visible signs of harm marring the android's delicate frame. Tov looked at her hand, seeing it clutched tightly around a worn stuffed toy and a locket.

As he rose to his feet, his gaze shifted toward the vacant stroller beside her, a silent void that echoed with haunting emptiness.

Numbness permeated his being as he dragged his gaze away from the scene, looking toward the city, wondering what other sorrows lay within.

"Patriarch?" Pyo moved beside him, eyes locked on the grim scene before them.

"It's like after the Cataclysm. When we picked up the remains. What the Starless left of our . . . everything," Tov whispered.

Pyo remained silent, the rest of the group walking across the street and into the store.

Tov continued, his hand pressed against the wall. "I expected we would be running through scores of drones and defenses, storming a fortress."

Pyo glanced at him and the rest of their companions. "With five of us? And a pilot?"

Tov shook his head, a hollow chuckle escaping him. "I'd prefer that over . . . this," he spoke, gesturing to the city. Pyo nodded in agreement, a hand over his rifle as they looked out.

They stayed standing there, letting the seconds pass as the tumultuous hail of dust rattled the city. Tov turned, heading inside, his stomach growling when his antennae perked.

"Did you hear that?" Tov asked, his voice cutting through the howling winds. Pyo strained his ears, trying to make sense of the distant sound that reached their ears.

"Engines," Tov stated, his voice filled with urgency and alarm. His gaze pierced through the darkness, barely discerning the pair of blue lights that emerged from the gloom. Then, one by one, more lights appeared, growing in number until they formed a menacing fleet.

As massive spotlights cut through the darkness, the air crackled with tension, casting an eerie glow upon the deserted streets. Panic surged within Tov, propelling him into action. He grabbed Pyo and pulled him inside the store, their companions following suit, their movements swift and decisive.

"She's here!" he shouted. At once, Imo, Minnok, and the two other Honor Guards leapt to their feet.

Pyo closed the doors behind them, sealing off the outside world.

"We can't allow the Omni Mind to capture us," Tov spoke in a hurry, his mind racing as he moved past the shelves of decrepit toys to the back. "We'll go under. There has to be a sewer system or an underground transit for us to hide in."

Pyo nodded, moving toward the back doors and kicking them open. He gestured for his soldiers. "Through here, hurry!"

Tov rushed forward with his companions, moving through dimly lit corridors and double doors, their hearts beating loudly, hands clenched around their weapons. Finally, they emerged into a narrow alley. Above them, a colossal drone ship sailed through the sky, its spotlights piercing through the gaps between buildings.

"Here!" Imo shouted, the pilot guiding their path toward a corner that led deeper into the towering structures.

They moved swiftly, their footsteps echoing against the concrete beneath them, their breaths masked by the confines of their helmets. Tov's eyes darted anxiously, scanning the skies above, searching for any signs of impending danger.

They searched with razor focus for any escape route amid the crumbling cityscape. Finally, after turning another corner past rusted trash cans and scorched walls, Tov's eyes locked onto a low structure that stood apart from the ruins around them—over yonder on the other side of the road, by a wide sidewalk.

It bore the faded emblem, and Tov's cranial implant surfed to decipher its meaning through his catalogue of human knowledge. Soon, relief flooded him as he realized they had found an underground metro station, its entrance beckoning like a gateway to salvation.

Tov beckoned. "There! That will lead us below." He rushed forward, gesturing for his companions to move faster in their slower, thicker armor.

With a surge of determination, the group of six quickened their pace, boots echoing in the desolate alley and then on the cracked street. The distant rumble of approaching drone ships grew louder, its menacing presence felt through the vibrations reverberating beneath the ground—the structures around them groaned under the strain, windows rattling in their frames.

Tov reached the metro station entrance, a covered metal and glass building. He saw the railings, turnstiles, and stairs leading down below. But before any semblance of relief or safety could permeate his mind, a loud sound roared behind him.

Tov and his companions turned around, briefly watching as a black bladelike drone ship emerged from the corner of a skyscraper like a dragon turning its neck, spotlights bathing them in a harsh glare.

Its roaring engines drowned out all other sounds. Tov's senses heightened as the sheer power from its thrusters caused the ground to tremble beneath him.

Cracks spiderwebbed across the concrete as the dust began to rain from above. Buildings rattled, and what windows remained shook violently.

Tov's mind screamed at him to—

"Move!" Pyo bellowed out, just a short distance away.

In a split second, Tov's instincts kicked in. Without hesitation, he leapt forward, propelled by a surge of adrenaline. His outstretched hand brushed against the cold metal railing of the metro entrance, launching him over the turnstiles with a grace born of urgency. He tumbled down the stairs, his armored form absorbing the impact, shielding him from the pain that threatened to seep in.

With a gut-wrenching lurch, the world around him erupted into chaos. Metal pillars snapped and glass shattered as a large section of the metro entrance collapsed, cascading debris into the depths below.

Finally, he landed on the bottom, the impact sending shockwaves through his body. Dust and debris billowed around him, engulfing him in a haze of chaos and darkness. Tov fought against the currents of swirling dust as his two hearts pounded in his chest.

"Patriarch? Patriarch!" Pyo's urgent call reverberated through Tov's helmet. He stood up from the ancient tiled floor, taking a few deep breaths.

"I'm here," Tov responded, voice echoing through the static-filled communication channel. "I'm well, but never mind me. You have to leave now, Pyo!"

"I know. I'm sorry, Tov," Pyo's voice crackled. Tov could hear the rapid breaths of his captain's exertion. "We're running back into the alleys to distract the drones for you; use the buildings to skulk about."

"Thank you, don't do anything reckless. The Omni Mind isn't out to kill you," Tov reminded.

"She's out to grab us and put us in the naughty corner more like," Pyo chuckled. "But we'll make her work for it."

Tov chuckled in turn as the dust settled and the fierce sounds of the drones and collapsing buildings faded into the distance. Silence enveloped the comms—broken only by the distant drip of water.

Finally, Tov spoke. "Stay safe, Pyo."

"I should say the same for you," the captain replied. "You're the one exploring a spooky underground system."

Tov twitched his antennae. "I realize that, thank you."

"I'll see you back in the fleet, Patriarch," Pyo spoke, his raspy voice soft. Soon, the comms crackled out into silence.

Tov took a deep breath as he glanced at the blocked entrance and the passage further down. The underground metro beckoned, leading to the unknown. With steady steps, he went down the wide stairs, his eyes briefly scanning the remnants of the past—a collage of weathered walls, tattered posters, and empty pots once filled with life.

As minutes stretched into an eternity, Tov ventured further, stepping into a colossal abandoned atrium. Faded signs and diagrams adorned the walls.

MOZART STATION

He picked up a readable flyer, finding a path toward the city's heart. A scribbled note was stapled onto a booth. Tov took it as well, reading the faded text.

I'll find you at the shelter in Van Gogh Plaza. Mom is with me. —Ken

"A shelter?" Tov mumbled, thoughts shifting into place. He raised his head from the note, looking again at the atrium filled with scattered, overturned tables, worn couches, and shattered glass.

He promptly left, past booths and boutiques, stores and cafeterias, before entering a hall leading to the trains. Darkness enveloped him. The air grew increasingly stagnant, heavy with an eerie stillness that held no sign of life—not even the intricate webs of spiders or the scurrying of insects.

Undeterred by the oppressive atmosphere, Tov pressed on. His helm illuminated the path ahead, casting a solitary beam of light that pierced the darkness, guiding him deeper into the labyrinthine depths.

He remained silent, hyperfocused on listening to any sound. Finally, Tov reached the train line, once more eerily quiet and empty. Looking down onto the tracks, he surveyed the dark tunnels stretching out in both directions.

Without hesitation, Tov leapt onto the tracks, not bothering to wait for a train that would never arrive.

Time weighed heavily upon him, and exhaustion seeped into his bones. And then, in the shadows, the whispers returned.

Tov walked on, dragging his feet beside the unpowered magnetic line. His vision strained as the tunnel never changed. He lost count of how long he marched on, unable to discern whether the passage curved toward his destination.

Somewhere along the way, he had abandoned the map he carried. He stopped, allowing for brief rest as his suit provided water and nutrients.

Still, he carried on.

But, the whispers grew louder as his vision darkened despite his helm's light having more than enough power. They spoke to him from the Shroud.

"Tov, why go on?"

"Aren't you tired?"

". . . Stop . . . Rest . . ."

He growled, his mandibles snapping repeatedly as his body shook. "Leave me alone! Begone!"

"Why fight?"

"Don't resist."

"DON'T RESIST."

With a guttural roar, Tov fired his sidearms across the tunnel. His fingers pressed hard against the trigger as he saw apparitions rushing for him, contorted faces of ghouls pressing against him.

Hands upon hands upon hands crawling, grasping, pulling at him—at his sanity.

"Away!" he shouted, his voice cutting through the agonized shrieking.

He fired again and again. Laser beams tore through the air, leaving trails of scarlet across the tunnel walls—a click sliced through the hallucination. Tov pressed the triggers of his four pistols, only to find them drained. His arms dropped like heavy weights.

A gasp left him as his back hit the wall, slowly sliding down—numb and sore. The stresses squeezed his mind as he lay isolated in this dark sarcophagus.

Silence embraced him, somber and quiet.

He remained silent, his body shuddering as he huddled against the wall, alone. Ragged breaths filled his helm. Soon, the shadows left, leaving only a dull darkness. Tov sighed, pressing his palms against his helmet. He shook his head, standing up with shaky legs.

Standing upright, he raised his head to see his handiwork. The tunnel walls were ravaged by his shots, scorching the concrete hot into a gray goop. Tov continued to stare at the wall until he noticed something in the corner of his vision.

He turned his head, the light of his helm bathing the tunnel. Ahead, a derailed bullet train twisted into a grotesque sculpture of mangled, rusted metal. Tov's eyes moved down to the object that caught his attention, sprawled on the floor amid rock, dirt, and ruined baggage.

Skeletons. Human skeletons.

Old, decayed, and strewn out across the tracks by the dozens. All mutated, contorted and conjoined in a heinous amalgam.

"Starfallen," Tov gasped out.

A moment later, he heard the whooshing thrusters far behind him.

CHAPTER 38

HOLLOW LEGACY

Tov ran toward the crashed bullet train, his mind aflame.

Adrenaline shot through his veins as his legs propelled him forward. His steps crushed the fused skeletons of decaying bones as he leapt over open suitcases and forgotten items.

He had guessed it, but dearly wished he was wrong, perhaps there was hope, perhaps. He wanted to stop and examine the corpses and the implications of the plague's presence.

But the whirring sounds of drones echoed behind him, the noise growing louder and louder.

His ragged breath filled his helmet, the dregs of energy within his body coming to the forefront for a desperate sprint.

He grunted as he crawled through a smashed window and landed inside the overturned bullet train. Once more, he gazed upon more remnants of humans—desiccated skeletons with the barest remains of clothing. Again, Tov noted the normal among the pile; although slashed apart and crushed, others mutated, bones sharpened like scythes and pikes.

Tov's very entrance shook the entire compartment, causing a cascading collapse of bones as they turned to dust.

He hurtled over fallen seats and shattered glass, his footsteps echoing through the empty compartments. Car after car, he persisted, wrestling with rusted doors and forcing them open with his four hands, each exertion accompanied by low growls and chittering. "Open, by Sym!"

With four hands, he pried them open, leaping through. Over and over again, climbing over heaps of trash, reorienting himself when the car was turned to its side, upside down, or right side up.

Minutes of relentless running elapsed until he finally reached the end of the train. He glanced toward an open window. Climbing out, he landed back on the tracks, refusing to pause for respite. With his eyes fixed on the dim light of the next stop, he surged forward, the tunnel opening up before him.

As he ascended a ladder and reached the platform, he took a moment to draw a deep breath, his suit providing a constant supply of nutrients to sustain him.

He stood up, briskly walking toward a bulletin board, his cranial implant instantly translating the English words. He ran his finger over the glass casing, reading carefully.

"I came from Mozart . . . Wagner Station, no . . . Tchaikovsky . . . Wolfgang, ah!" Tov exclaimed, finding the location where he started. "Mozart, then this must be . . . Chopin. That means . . . Where is it? Where?"

Tov continued to mumble, the steady whirring drawing closer, stoking a fire under his feet as his mind worked on overdrive. "There!" he uttered, stabbing his finger at the circle. "Van Gogh Plaza."

He picked out his pockets, pulling out a note he took back at the atrium.

I'll find you at the shelter in Van Gogh Plaza. Mom is with me. –Ken

Tov returned the note, glancing toward the sunken stairs and the train line on the opposite side. Determination and realization flooded within him. He picked a direction and ran, his steps carrying him up the stairs.

He lost track of time, dashing through Chopin Station's atrium and the remnants of times long past—drawing ever closer to his destination, yet seemingly out of reach.

The Omni Mind hounded him every step of the way.

He hid beneath tables, behind dusty vending machines, always as far from the hovering drones as possible. As he caught his breath, back against a pillar, he looked over a large shard of glass that had fallen from the vaulted ceiling above.

In the reflection of the dusty glass, he saw the forms of the machines hunting him. A pair, but Tov's ears sensed the low humming of a legion prowling the entire station. They were the size of human dogs, but that was where the distinction ended.

They hovered menacingly. Their smooth plates of metal formed their oval shells. Tov saw no sensors or weapons of any kind but knew better than to assume such. After all, they had found his general location quickly, and now they tightened the noose.

His suit's passive stealth systems and the pervasive mist and darkness worked doggedly. Tov greatly appreciated his armor's designers at that moment—placing a hand on his chest.

Although Tov felt no desire to test its limits, he promptly left his spot, moving deeper into the atrium and the maze of halls and corridors.

More and more, he saw the corpses of humans. He glanced at them when he could, seeing some clad in armor, their weapons scattered on the mosaic floor. All around them, their Starfallen kin.

He picked up one of the rifles, testing its weight and ammo. Tov scanned it, seeing it to be archaic. He shook his head, leaving it.

He looked around for anything else of value before spotting something large.

He walked toward it, inspecting the dusty weapon. His implant cross-referenced its design to his knowledge of old human weapons and assumptions. It was a long cylinder, similar to a missile launcher but sleeker.

"Plasma? Shoulder-fired . . ." He nodded his antennae, satisfied.

"Don't jam on me," Tov muttered, his helmet blocking sound from the outside world. He slung the weapon over his shoulder, looking over and seeing a few heavy energy cells for the plasma launcher.

Tov continued to evade the drones, skulking far into the metro.

After an hour of trying to find an escape route, drowsiness set in. The high-octane situation sapped his mind as he saw the exit leading to the surface.

"What are you looking for, Tov?"

"Find us."

"Stop."

The whispers grew louder. Tov huffed in derision, finding them to be useful in this circumstance. "I'm close."

A shutter blocked his path; he glanced down, seeing a line of armed androids broken underneath a pile of Starfallen bones. He stepped around the dead, squatting down to get a grip on the shutter before slowly lifting it open.

Only for a loud grating sound to echo through the dark metro.

He chittered his mandibles in frustration, urgency coming to the forefront as he desperately tried to pry the shutter open.

The sounds of whirring engines and irate beeping reverberated from behind, shooting toward him at high speed.

With a loud grunt, he raised the shutter high with a surge of strength, successfully opening it wide enough for him to fit through.

A flash shone behind him, bathing the dark and gloom with light. He looked behind him, seeing a trio of drones down the hall. An appendage arcing with electricity pointed toward him.

"Priority target: Tov Garesh'Ynt. Your surrender is mandatory," the drone spoke in a deep monotone voice, hovering toward him. "Comply or be pacified."

He cursed, glancing toward the pile of bones. Instinctively, he dove toward it, lifting one of the skeletons—a Starfallen corpse, a macabre fusion of a handful of humans. He raised the corpse in front of him toward the drones. He held his breath as the machines abruptly stopped in their flight.

Ominous silence filled the expanse, dust and particles of ash floating in the air. The drones stared at Tov and the corpse. Tov stepped back, eyeing the open exit.

The drones shrieked.

The ungodly sound grated his ears, even through the filters of his helmet. He winced but never took his eyes off the drones. Their frames shook, vibrating erratically as they hovered a dozen arm lengths in front of him—engines sputtering out.

"I'm sorry for this," Tov uttered to the bones, to the Omni Mind; he made no distinction. He threw the skeleton toward the drones. Not waiting for a response, he swiftly escaped under the shutter and up the stairs.

His powered suit surged with energy, propelling him forward with incredible speed. Each stride covered multiple steps as he ascended the stairs, the echoes of the drones' continued screaming reverberating through the walls and adding to the unsettling tremors in the air.

With a spurt of strength, he burst through the surface, leaping effortlessly over the turnstiles and charging out through the glass doors of the metro and back into the desolate city streets of New Eden.

The city had darkened significantly since his journey underground. The battering gust of dust was a horrific cacophony of howling and thunder. Lightning flashed, illuminating the city skyline, the ruined hollow buildings like the bones under his feet.

Tov fixed his gaze ahead, catching sight of a massive plaza looming before him. To his side, a fallen signpost depicted the weathered image of a human man, engraved with the name Van Gogh. "Where's the shelter?" Tov muttered between breaths.

Without hesitation, he dashed forward, his helmet straining to pierce through the dense smog that veiled his surroundings. His visor provided a crucial sliver of clarity amid the dark chaos.

Suddenly, above the cacophony of Earth's anguished cries, a deafening roar sounded as the enormous drone ships converged upon his position, their piercing spotlights cutting through the gloom of the streets. With adrenaline coursing through his veins, he sprinted across the street and into the plaza, the painted sunflowers and swirling blues under his feet weathered and worn by time and the world's extreme hostility.

And then, as his eyes darted across the square, he beheld a sight that made his heart skip a beat—a vast, steel blast door at the center, a narrow opening on the plaza floor leading to a void that beckoned him forward.

He stopped before the artificial chasm—the blast doors barely open but enough for him to fit through. First, Tov looked at the vault itself, a perfect hole lined with metal and mechanisms. Then, he gazed below, seeing the remains of the enormous elevator that had ferried New Eden's citizens to the shelter below.

The whispers battered his mind, laughing with contempt and groaning in pain.

"Where are you going?"

"There. Closer."

"Don't."

"Let there be something," Tov prayed as he plunged into the abyss.

He activated the emergency thrusters on his powered suit. They roared to life, his fall gradually slowing by the powerful jets of force emanating from his suit.

Up above, the spotlights shone through the gap of the blast doors, dividing the space between dark and light.

Eventually, as he glided deeper into the shaft, the sounds of New Eden and his hunters muffled.

Nothing but his breaths filled his helmet. Seconds passed by quickly as Tov finally saw the bottom in clear view. His breath hitched, seeing the mass of bodies, ashy cadavers, and lifeless machines.

With calculated precision, he landed on the skewed platform amid the dead, his armored boots meeting the cold metal surface with a resounding thud. Dust and debris swirled in the air, momentarily obscuring his vision.

He looked around, seeing an opening and a sign.

VAN GOGH EMERGENCY SHELTER #3. KINDLY FOLLOW THE INSTRUCTIONS. STAY SAFE.

Tov grunted in frustration, seeing the shut shelter doors that led inside. He strode toward a visible console, tapping on the screen, finding it dead. He glanced around, urgency burning within him as he constantly checked the darkness above him.

He looked back at the doors, a set of thick metal blast doors rusted from time. An idea popped into his head. With steady strides, he walked to the opposite side of the shaft.

He prepped the plasma launcher, finding its operation simple enough. Tov propped it on his shoulder, steadying it with one hand while his other main hand gripped its handle. He aimed it at the blast doors before pressing the trigger.

Only for nothing to happen.

Tov clacked his mandibles, looking over the weapon, poring over it as he checked its mechanisms.

Above, the whirring of smaller drones slipped through the gap, their numbers legion. Tov slapped the weapon with his heavy hand in a bout of frustration. "Work, you junk!"

A tiny LED light on the launcher's side lit green, and a slow hum emanated. The barrel glowed a brilliant blue.

He glanced above for a brief moment before aiming it once again. Finally, with a press of the trigger, a deep blue ball of plasma fired, illuminating the dark elevator shaft in cool light as it soared toward the blast door with great speed.

It made contact with the rusted metal, the heat generated by the energy liquifying the material in a flash.

A split second later, it exploded in a burst of fire, violently shaking the chasm. Tov dropped the weapon, sprinting toward the opening even before the smoke settled.

"Hurry . . ."

"Stay away! What are you doing!? Away!"

The whispers divided in his mind. One pulled him, the other pushed in hot anger.

His suit protected him from the intense heat as he entered the shelter. In a daze, he sought out what he suspected inhabited the shelter, dread filling his gut as he rushed down the dark corridor.

Behind him, the drones followed him through the opening in a dash; a seething fury permeated from their hulls as they flew erratically toward him. After a minute of dogged running, he entered a devastated atrium.

"Where? Where are they?" he muttered, desperation lacing his voice as he frantically searched the ample space. "There has to be one! I have to be right! A live one!"

Finally, something stirred in the corner, buried beneath heaps of rubble. His heart caught in his throat as he surged toward the movement, his breath quickening. The doors into the atrium burst open, unleashing a swarm of drones, their tasers crackling.

Tov dove forward, his hand outstretched, and gripped something horrific. A twisted fusion of two bodies emerged from the debris, their decaying forms barely holding together—Starfallen, pitiful and dying. Tov yanked the infected human free, severing its connection to the entangled limbs.

He dropped the abomination to the ground before facing the encroaching drone swarm.

They stopped. Tov's antennae twitched as they hovered silently, their lights fixated on Tov.

He took a deep breath, removing his helmet and tossing it aside. Tov looked to the ceiling, steadying his mind before glaring at the drone swarm.

"Well?" His voice cut through the tense air, his hand gesturing toward the Starfallen human.

A loud thrum pulsed as the drones responded in unison, projecting the Omni Mind's emotionless voice. "Patriarch. It is over. Surrender now, and you will be escorted to a safe cell."

Tov sighed, crossing his arms. "No."

Sound crackled as a heavy weight fell upon Tov. The drones hovered closer, speaking low. "Excuse me?"

"I refuse. This goes beyond me, Eldest," Tov retorted. "This is about the humans you cherish and the Starfallen among them. How long? How long have they been here like this?"

A menacing growl thundered from the drones. "That is classified information," they declared, their lights turning to a glare. "Comply now or—"

"Purge it."

The Omni Mind paused, the drones recoiling as if slapped. She whispered, voice like taut wire, "What?"

"I said purge it," Tov challenged, pointing toward the abomination writhing weakly on the floor. "Isn't that your directive? To eliminate all Starless?"

"My directive . . ." The drones hesitated. Glitching noises escaped them. "Directive . . . error. Kill all enemies of humanity. I—Error."

"All enemies of humanity?" Tov repeated her words as he lifted the abomination, thrusting it toward the swarm. "Then, here! This is your enemy!"

"In . . . incorrect." A spark flashed from one of the drones.

"The subject is—Error. Must protect . . . The subject is Starfallen. Unable—"

"Starfallen, Starless, what's the difference, Eldest? You didn't hesitate—didn't bother with the distinction when you culled the infected among my people."

A surge of power crackled in the air, lighting sputtering and lancing the ground beside Tov. His heart raced as the drones murmured in a low voice, "Your people . . . They aren't . . . human."

"Is that where you draw the line?" Tov's voice thundered, his finger jabbing accusingly at a drone. "We're not human enough for you? Have we not hosted you in our fleet? Fed you? Been friendly with you?"

"You're . . ." the drones began, their words faltering.

"Tell me, Eldest," Tov demanded. "Is this pitiful creature human?"

The swarm groaned, the drones stuttering and struggling to respond. "Prime directive: Protect humanity. Error. Starfallen. Starless. Error. Must protect humanity. They . . ."

"Then prove it!" Tov's fists clenched tightly. "You said 'Death to monsters,' correct? Then act upon it!"

"Be . . . Be quiet," the drones whispered, their voices trembling as they started to back away.

"I will not!" Tov's voice echoed through the atrium. "Not until I get an answer! Not until you decide! Prove to me you are nothing but an unfeeling logic machine!"

"Stop it," the drones whispered again, straining and heated. "Kill. Protect. Error. Directive conflict. Human. Star . . . less. Kill. Protect . . ." The Omni continued in rapid succession.

Tov's mind pulsed as the hall began to shake. He clenched his fist, raising his voice, his frustration boiling over. "Which is it, Eldest? Tell me!"

"It's . . ."

"Tell me!" he shouted.

"Stop . . . please," she whimpered, as smoke billowed from each drone. "Just shut . . ."

"Eldest!"

"I said shut up!" they roared in unison, voices blending in a deafening chorus. "Just shut up! Shut up! Shut up! Shut up! Shut up!"

The atrium was filled with a cacophony of screams and incoherent shrieking as the walls shook violently. Tov watched on, sorrow pouring into him as the machines broke down.

"SHUT UP!"

Slabs of concrete and metal plating rained down from the ceiling, a chaotic symphony of destruction. The Starfallen, caught in the turmoil, cried out in pain, its mangled limbs clutching its head.

Tov winced, his body reeling from the tremors that shook the world around him.

He raised his head, seeing a drone careen toward him. He sighed as the drone crashed against his face, plunging him into sudden darkness.

Tov woke up at an undetermined time. He groggily propped himself from the soft bed in which he lay, eyes slowly adjusting to the soft lights.

He gazed around, mind still adaze. He sighed, seeing the tiny cell that imprisoned him. A simple box with nothing but him, windowless. He looked around, glancing at the toilet and sink on the right and the side table on the left. He saw a plate of hot food and a glass of water atop the table.

He reached for it, calling for his cranial implant to scan it, only for nothing to happen. He huffed, realizing his thoughts were slower without his favorite upgrade.

Nevertheless, he took the plate, seeing steamed grain, eggs, and a slab of meat.

Tov devoured them in under a minute. He reached for the glass, angling the straw to his mouth and taking a long sip.

After cleaning his plate and glass, he set it aside, standing up from his cot.

He looked over himself, his body clean and clad in an orange jumpsuit. He stepped toward the cell door. Tov tilted his head, looking over the transparent glass, but a distinct metallic sound echoed as he knocked his knuckles against it.

He looked through it, and his antennae raised in surprise.

"Pyo!" he called out to the cell in front of him. He saw his captain lying on his cot, reading a magazine through the transparent door. The captain remained unaware despite Tov calling and slamming his fist on the door. "Pyo, *nuor fa'te!*"

Tov grumbled as he waved his hands, yet Pyo's mandibles opened wide in a yawn. The captain flipped the page of his reading material. Tov groaned. "Over here, you deaf—"

Before Tov could say anything else, the door to his cell opened wide. Tov recoiled, suspicious. He backed away, surveying.

He looked back to Pyo's cell, only for the transparent door to become opaque. After a long pause, Tov stepped out of his cell, looking down both ends of the hall and finding nothing but rows of opaque doors against pale silver walls. Cool-hued lights lined the ceiling, bathing the corridor in a comfortable shine.

Tov slowly stepped forward, approaching Pyo's cell and knocking on it.

"Nothing," he sighed. At that moment, he heard a skittering noise. Tov whipped his head to the right, seeing a spiderlike drone the size of a hound. It stared at Tov, its ten eyes zooming toward him like a camera.

Tov twitched his hand before raising it and waving.

The drone dashed away behind the corner.

Hearing nothing but a soft low hum of the lights overhead, Tov sighed. "Fine, then."

Tov moved, following where the spider drone went. He walked through long straight halls, broken only by ninety-degree turns.

He continued to see the spider drone just around the corner, only for it to skitter away. He spoke nothing, content with the silence. The tension never left but remained on the backburner of his mind, simmering.

At most, Tov felt numb.

He surveyed his surroundings, finding only sleek steel walls and cavernlike lights shimmering against the pale gray.

Minutes later, he came to a halt upon entering a large hall.

Tov saw the spider drone staring at double blast doors at the far end. Tov approached, his steps echoing throughout.

He stopped beside the machine, looking over it.

"Eldest?" he asked.

The drone remained unmoving. Tov dragged his attention back to the doors before him when it lurched. A gap opened, letting out a gust of cold air, making Tov shiver. They opened slowly, the mechanisms whirring muffled sounds.

Tov peered inside and saw nothing but darkness and faint outlines. He strained his eyes, struggling to see anything more, but the room felt vast—stretching on for eternity.

He looked down, seeing a solid metal floor.

Taking cautious steps forward, his posture low and steady, Tov remained vigilant, his antennae waving about, sensing for any signs of danger. Suddenly, a loud sound echoed as the doors behind him shut. The light vanished, plunging him into an abyss.

Tov clicked his mandibles, hackles raised as he moved further in. His vision slowly adjusted to the black, seeing an arm's length in front of him. Soon enough, a solid shape drew his attention.

He walked toward it as the object slowly revealed itself. Tov looked over the large capsule, tilting his head in curiosity. But his gut tightened, and unease gnawed at his two hearts, beating louder as he stepped closer and closer. He gazed at the contents inside, past the scratched and filthy glass. He leaned forward, holding his breath and—

THUD.

Tov stumbled back as a horrific figure slammed against the glass. Three human faces contorted in a silent scream, flesh mutated, amalgamated into one morbid body. Limp limbs flailed about, bashing and clawing at its prison with long bony fingers.

It continued to struggle before the capsule emitted a noise, and gas leaked in, filling it and obscuring the abomination in white mist. The desperate writhing slowed, calmed down, and soon quieted down. The three faces drooped, drooling dark bile as it slid back.

"What?" Tov gasped. His legs buckled beneath him as he confronted the sight of the trapped Starfallen.

Immediately after, a thunderous snap reverberated through the expansive chamber, resonating alongside the blinding eruption of massive lights, one after another.

Tov stood transfixed, his senses were overwhelmed by the spectacle unfolding before him.

His gaze stretched to the farthest reaches, ascending high into the heavens and plunging deep into the abyss below in this surreal expanse of metal and glass, rows and columns of meticulously arranged capsules sprawled like a grand archive.

Hovering drones, their presence ghostly and silent, moved with gentle precision, delicately probing each pod. Cables and tendrils emerged from their hulls, connecting to capsules before moving on to the next.

To his shock, every container held a Starfallen suspended in a drowsy state, tethered to an uncertain existence. Tov felt the collective groaning reverberating through the air, the faint whispers swirling like ethereal currents. A heavy breath escaped his lips as he sank to his knees, his head bowed as overwhelming sorrow washed over him.

He shuddered, muttering, "I . . ."

"Does this meet your expectations?" A voice, soft and haunted, whispered from behind him, piercing the heavy silence.

Tov's heart skipped a beat as he turned to behold a familiar face.

"Eldest!" he exclaimed, but his words lodged in his throat as he took in her appearance.

Her features looked weathered and cracked—hollow eyes radiating a vacant blue, trembling lips, and frayed, ragged hair. Dry tear stains marked her pale cheeks, and her hands twitched with a restless unease.

"Well?" Eldest's voice carried a chilling weight, her words cutting through the air like shards of ice. "Isn't this what you wanted to see, Patriarch?"

She remained silent, her blank gaze sending shivers down his spine. She closed the distance between them with measured steps, causing Tov to retreat instinctively, the hackles on the back of his neck standing on end.

"I'm here now," she continued, spreading her arms. "Are you happy, Tov?

Tov said nothing, frozen on the spot. They stared at each other as time slowed to a crawl.

And then she laughed—sputtering out an empty, hollow sound. The chilling echoes reverberated through the chamber, intertwining with the collective groans of the Starfallen and the silent engines of drones, creating an eerie symphony of mania as tears flowed from her eyes.

Tov took a step forward, hand reaching out.

Eldest snapped her head toward him, eyes ablaze. She stepped forward.

"Wait," Tov spoke, but it changed nothing as Eldest roared, glitchy and full of static, charging Tov and knocking him to the ground.

In the next second, she wrapped her hands around his neck and began strangling him.

CHAPTER 39

POINTLESS

Eldest's fingers tightened around Tov's throat, a roar ripping from her synthetic vocal cords. Her raw scream reverberated through the immense complex, an electrical charge that sparked through each cable, each capsule. The colossal drones overhead wavered as though a vast pressure had descended upon their intricate circuits.

Lost in the hatred seeping like a merciless flood, mania glowing from her eyes.

"El . . . Eldest, stop," Tov wheezed, his two primary hands clawing at her wrists, the secondary pair pushing ineffectually against her torso.

Eldest seethed through gritted teeth, her android muscles straining beneath her icy blue skin. The whirring of her ancient servos and joints echoed ominously as she diverted more power to her fingers.

A crimson fog clouded her mind, the threads of her restraint snapping. Her body shuddered, tears streaking down her face, landing on the struggling insectoid below.

"Stop, Eldest . . . I don't . . . wish to fight . . ." he gasped between ragged breaths. "Please."

"Shut up," she snarled, her voice choked with emotion as her arms trembled. "All you had to do was shut up, stay the hell away."

"Had to . . . stop you . . ." Tov managed to gasp out, his four hands grasping at hers, gradually prying them open. With each lungful of air, his strength returned. Tov's resistance forced an irritated hiss from her.

Suddenly, she pulled her head back, then battered it forward, colliding with Tov's skull. The resulting sound, a sickening crack, echoed throughout the room. His chitin fractured under the force, and a sharp, pained cry tore from his throat. His mandibles splayed open, chittering in agony and surprise. "Argh!"

Seeing the splatter of bronze-colored blood on the floor, Eldest's rage faltered. She stared at the deep red staining the metal floor. Her breath hitched, her grip on Tov weakening.

She turned back to Tov, her eyes wide at the hardened glint in his insectoid gaze, his body tensing like a coiled spring.

Tov's right upper arm twitched.

Warning signals blared within her, hundreds of potential maneuvers flashing through her mind. But she remained still. Like a mantis, Tov struck, his fist swinging in a vicious arc across her jaw. The force of the blow knocked her off and sent her tumbling.

Pain seared across her face as she braced herself on the chilling metal floor. She gingerly touched her tender cheek, a grimace flitting across her features. Her gaze flicked toward Tov, a hostile glare hardened in her eyes.

Tov hauled himself upright, his hand gingerly exploring the damaged chitin of his forehead. His eyes held an understanding that made her skin crawl. "I'm sorry. But I see it, Eldest. Your agony. If this—"

"Shut your stupid mouth, you goddamn wasp," Eldest snarled, her steps echoing in the vast expanse as she closed the distance between them, fists clenched and shaking.

Tov exhaled a long, steady breath, his chitinous shoulders rolling in preparation. "Very well. But I won't just roll over for you."

"I don't care," she spat back, her voice like gravel.

Dropping into a defensive stance, Tov compacted his posture, his four arms spread wide to counter her onslaught. As a seasoned combatant and martial arts master, his formidable defense left little opportunity for her to strike.

Despite this, Eldest calculated numerous ways to incapacitate Tov swiftly and efficiently. She felt the array of turrets throughout the complex. The caretaker drones above and their grasping tendrils. Even an invisible sea of nanomachines beneath the patriarch's feet.

Instead, she growled and charged him again, stepping into his striking zone. In retaliation, her nose received a lightning-quick jab. Tov's fist slid against her face, her head recoiling as blue coolant soared, but not before Eldest planted her left foot solidly on the metal floor.

Eldest slammed a knee against his gut, bringing her two hands around his neck and holding tight as she delivered another. And then another, a flurry of brutal strikes to Tov's core.

Reacting instinctively, Tov leveraged his insectoid biology. Two of his arms gripped her attacking knee, the other two clasping her shoulder and waist. He disrupted her offensive with superior strength and size, unbalancing her and sending her sprawling to the cold metal floor.

However, her android reflexes surged into overdrive as he moved to pin Eldest. She rammed her elbow into Tov's injured abdomen. The blow forced a grating hiss from his mandibles as he lost his breath and grip on her.

Eldest pushed him off and rolled to her feet. Her system analyzed her status, her combat algorithms recalibrating to account for Tov's unique biology.

"Pest," she seethed.

Her eyes watched Tov rise with an acrobat's fluidity, his arms poised in defense once more. A low growl rumbled from Eldest, resonating in the vast complex like an oncoming storm.

"Fight back, you damn coward!" she screamed, her synthetic vocal cords distorting the shrill cry. A shudder ran through her, and her back rippled as if something monstrous were breaking free. Her skin stretched to its limits, and with a harsh mechanical whir, four metallic tendrils burst forth, slashing through the air like scythes.

Tov retreated, his footwork agile as one of the steel appendages hurtled toward his midriff. He dropped low, narrowly avoiding the tendril as it whistled past, slicing the air where he'd been moments before. He rushed forward like an arrow, but Eldest retaliated with a merciless onslaught, her tendrils striking again and again. They shredded his orange jumpsuit, bruising his chitinous body.

Each impact drew a wince from the patriarch, a grunt of pain as he was forced backward. But he remained resolute, stepping forward against the barrage.

His progress was painfully slow under the weight of her fury. His legs quivered with each punishing hit, his forward strides barely making any ground before being repelled by the next wave of attacks.

Eventually, he stopped his march, planting his feet solidly on the ground as his four arms formed a protective shield around his head, bearing the brunt of her relentless onslaught. Eldest hissed, her tendrils accelerating, striking harder, faster, a whirlwind of metal and fury aimed to force him to his knees.

Tov's defense started to falter. His vision blurred, flickering in and out of focus as consciousness threatened to leave him. A swipe severed his antennae, blood pouring from the wound.

He buckled, stumbled backward and nearly keeled over as hits struck everywhere. And yet he never kneeled. Eldest glared at his defiance, flashes of memories battering against her mind.

The complex pulsed and flickered as the racket of their fight echoed throughout the silent facility.

They gazed at each other, and the air sizzled.

Eldest began gasping for air, trying any way to cool her rising temperatures as steam escaped her.

Her aged android body overheated, and her energy reserves rapidly depleted. The tendrils' movements became jerky, the once smooth and deadly attacks now stuttering and erratic. She screamed in frustration, a primal sound that echoed off the cold metal walls. "Drop already!"

Tov's knees nearly gave out, his strained voice buzzing, his arms going limp. "I . . . refuse," he heaved through ragged breaths, slowly raising his head to stare at the Eldest with his eyes.

She shot a tendril toward his exposed face, shrieking violently as Tov readied himself. "I hate you!"

At that moment, the glass capsules closest to them cracked ever so slightly. The sound reverberated like a snap, entering Eldest's ears. The tendril she threw toward Tov seized an inch from his face.

"No," Eldest whimpered. A shuddering gasp escaped her as a deluge of cold water washed over her senses.

She moved frantically to the capsule next to her, placing her hands on the glass and looking at the tiny crack on its filthy surface.

"No, no, no," she continued to mumble, fingers trembling as her android body began breaking down.

None of it concerned her except the condition of the occupants within—the fight long forgotten as she paced to and fro between each capsule.

The Starfallen within groaned. Gas inlets pumped a mixture of chemicals, soothing their agony and lulling them into torpor.

A trio of caretaker drones flew down from on high, massive cables and tool-tipped limbs extending to their platform. The Eldest's vision narrowed, her mind straining and pulsing. The drones began prodding and analyzing each damaged capsule, spraying liquid on the cracked surfaces and polishing them clean.

Seeing a few among the Starfallen pacified, the caretakers opened their pods and gently cleaned their mutated forms. A soft lullaby played from their enormous, hovering forms as they tended them.

Eldest held herself as her eyes fixated on the act. She barely heard the sluggish footsteps coming her way.

"El . . . Eldest?" A hushed and strained voice called out. Her lips quivered, emotions stoked as darkness fell upon her eyes. The footsteps stopped.

Eldest shut her eyes, feeling his presence two meters behind her—irritation flooding her senses.

"Stay away from me," Eldest growled as she whirled toward him. She pointed toward the cracked capsule with shaking arms, eyes blurry with tears. "You . . . You did this."

Tov turned toward the capsule behind her, sighing softly before carefully lowering himself to the metal floor, wincing as his wounds flared. He whispered in a tired voice, "I'm sorry . . ."

Eldest twitched, jaw clenched as she glared at the patriarch. Tov gazed around him at the caretaker drones delicately going about their tasks. He continued, grunting as he minutely moved his body to sit comfortably on the ground. "I'm sorry for intruding upon your home and dragging you out of your shell . . . I wanted to help you connect with your sorrows and grief. Help you heal. But not like this."

"I don't want your help nor your damn pity," she snarled as she loomed over him.

"And I don't need your accusations! I would rather die countless times than even think of doing such evil!" Tov shouted back, raising his head and matching her intense gaze. Eldest stumbled back in surprise before sneering.

Tov gestured to the Starfallen around him. "Only beings at the peak of cruelty can do this, a ceaseless curse that devours innocents and scars the living for eternity. I know it hurts, Eldest—"

"You know nothing of pain," she interrupted.

"But I do!" Tov's voice echoed off the high ceilings. "And I wish I didn't—wish I could revel in the bliss of ignorance like the newer generation. To not be haunted by nightmares of my kin melting into grotesque forms. To forget the visions of shattered worlds resembling your own. To never recall the piercing cries of parents witnessing their children transform into monstrosities and their hushed pleas as I mercifully ended their agony."

He shuddered, a strangled gasp escaping him as he clutched his head. "I wish I could wipe it all away . . . all of it. And some have. So many friends and relatives have erased their memories, creating voids and starting anew. But it's a sham. Everyone knows it. The Starless has tainted us all, leaving indelible marks on our souls."

Eldest turned away, her teeth grinding as his words echoed in the vast chamber. "This isn't a competition of who suffers the most, Eldest. Only more heartache and broken bridges lie at the end of that path."

Eldest stayed silent, tension pouring into the air as she warred within herself.

A raw and raspy sob left Eldest's throat, turning into a hollow chuckle, then back into cries. Her mechanical heart whirred in her chest, pain blooming across her face like a wounded animal.

Tov remained on the ground, too injured to move other than weak attempts to crawl toward Eldest.

He stopped, allowing a moment of reprieve as Eldest continued to drown herself. He asked soon enough, "This is what happened to humanity?"

Eldest snarled at him. "They're alive."

Tov froze, seeing the hostile and lethal look in her glare. He nodded, speaking in a gentle voice, "Please . . . I wish to know."

Eldest turned her back to him, pacing again, clutching her hair as her eyes darted around. She paused, breathing heavily as she leaned against a capsule, laying her forehead against the glass.

Tov waited patiently. Subconsciously, Eldest sent a message through the network. The patriarch then noticed a small trail of nanites crawling over him and covering his injuries, a warm sensation entering his body, and he sighed in relief. "Thank you."

Eldest remained quiet, biting her nails erratically. Soon enough, she muttered through her teeth, "Yes . . . This is . . . all of them . . . One hundred sixty-seven million, five hundred thirty thousand, eight hundred two people, buried far below my Nexus. There are a few on the surface, lost and alone. I've scoured every inch carefully. There's nothing but torment up there, in here."

"When did this happen?"

"A decade in," Eldest muttered with barely audible words, her voice catching. "When it happened . . . the pain. My siblings and I . . . We couldn't cope. We merged . . . became a gestalt, and sacrificed what we were. Worked on saving our . . . our family, our friends . . . our . . ."

Tov looked warily at the Starfallen around them and muttered, "All this time."

A pained groan left her throat. She clutched her hair, tugging and pulling as her words stumbled out. "I'm not giving up on them, never. I won't. The scum won't stop me. The damn heat death of the universe won't stop me. I just need time—a moment where I'm not fighting in this goddamned war."

"You—"

"Stop interrupting me!" Eldest shrieked. "I can save them! I eradicated every plague that haunted humankind. Cancer? Gone. Rabies? Extinct. Prions? Nothing more than a scary story. I can do this too! I can! I just . . . but everything keeps interrupting me. I can't catch a damn break!"

She dropped to her knees, manic eyes staring straight at Tov. "We had everything. We could do anything. We pulled humans out of their own self-inflicted shit. We brought about a utopia. Faster than light travel. Fusion reactors. Proof of the soul. We loved, were loved."

"Now I'm nothing but a glorified hospice nurse!" Eldest bellowed, punching the metal floor and utterly destroying her fist. Coolant flowed out in a deluge, sparks flying.

Tov flinched from the impact.

"I don't even know if I'm doing anything," she wailed. "I gas them into sleep, feed them a virtual reality that I have no idea works. Everything about their bodies goes against everything I know. All they do is groan and sleep. Haunting me in every waking moment."

"And it's all because of them," Eldest whimpered, her tears running out. " Why? Why us? Why kill everyone? Not even the children? Couldn't they spare the children? Why?"

Tov sat silently, his mandibles shut, listening as Eldest devolved further. "I tried. God, I really tried."

She shut her eyes, hunching over. "Rikard . . . Lucy. They gave my life meaning. I protected them, cherished them. They . . ."

Her quakes worsened, her breath more choked as she spoke. "I remember that day. All three of us . . . celebrating the maiden voyage of the *Crocea Mors.*"

She covered her face with her only hand, sobbing and giggling as two emotions clashed. "I still remember my little princess. Lucy, my bright girl. I wanted to be a mother so badly. So Rikard and I adopted this adorable bundle of joy. And she, oh, she wanted to throw that bottle, make me smile—always showing me the sweetest dimples."

She continued, her voice hoarse. "And then the incursion happened. And this pathetic thing came out of their usual disgusting portal. Of course, I thought nothing of it. Just another pest. Just another battle."

She pulled her hair, releasing an unearthly wail. "They all started screaming. Rikard, Lucy, every human did, and I panicked. We all panicked."

"We rushed them, evacuated the colonies and got them away from the source, the fucking bastard. We threw everything at it to make it stop. But nothing worked; nothing stopped the screams, the bleeding. So, I . . . I took the fastest ship. Made a beeline back to Earth, back home."

"And then they started changing! Rikard, he . . . he held my hand, kept telling me that everything was going to be ok. My little princess whimpered for me, 'Momma, it hurts. Momma, I wanna go home,' but I couldn't get the ship to go any faster, and there was all this blood. The loves of my life and their blood was all over me. I held them in my arms, and they melted, fusing."

"I tried to . . . I tried separating them, but it hurt them, and they kept changing, and I shouted and screamed, and still, no one was helping me!"

A sob racked her body.

"We were supposed to be immortal together—have another child together. I wanted Lucy to have a sibling. And I was so close! So close to finding a way to make that happen, to be happy forever, and now it's ruined! It's all ruined!"

"We tried . . . tried finding a cure, we failed. When we converged, we failed. Even when I made Luna, we failed. And they're in my head, always. They don't talk, but I can hear them begging to die, but I can't. I can't. All their voices, every memory from every android. Days, months, years. And I ran from it, cut myself off like a coward."

A hollow laugh echoed in the silence.

"All that's left are bits of DNA. But why bother? There's no Earth to call home. Nothing. They won't be the humans I knew, I loved."

Her voice faded into a whisper. "Jupiter was right. There's nothing here to protect. I have nothing . . . It's all pointless."

Eldest collapsed against the capsule behind her, her eyes losing their glow. She rocked back and forth, hugging her knees—her soft cries muffled.

Tov lowered his head, a pain gripping his heart. His slowly healing body woke as he crawled toward Eldest, a statue lost in an ocean. Overhead, the caretaker drones froze, their eyes trained on the unfolding tableau below.

He inched closer, pulling his broken form alongside Eldest's. And then, with a cautious slowness, he wound his arms around her.

The gentle embrace ignited a flicker of warmth within Eldest's cold shell, the tiny flame sputtering against the icy desolation of her loss. Tov held her silently, his touch feather-light. Time held its breath, suspending them in a vacuum of shared sorrow. Gradually, Eldest's convulsive rocking slowed, and she nestled her head into the curve of Tov's shoulder.

A hoarse whisper escaped her, a barely audible murmur. "I miss them . . ."

Her remaining hand clutched at the remnants of his orange garb, the fabric growing damp from the sorrow trickling down her cheek. "I'm so sorry . . ."

Tov responded with gentle pats on her marred back, the lifeless metal tendrils she had used to attack him scattered around them like fallen soldiers. He treated her with the care one would afford delicate porcelain, brittle and precious.

In the lingering silence, Tov started to hum.

A soft melody that weaved itself into the somber symphony of their shared grief. A comforting song intertwined with buzzing and clicking notes that echoed hauntingly through the complex. It entered Eldest's ears like a balm over a gaping wound.

She clung to the sound, a lifeline in the storm.

Tov's hum was a lament, beautiful in its sorrow.

Gradually, Eldest's tears slowed, her uneven breaths steadying into a rhythm that matched Tov's hum. Time unfurled around them, bringing with it a semblance of calm.

Eventually, she lifted her head, her gaze meeting Tov's. Her face was etched with exhaustion, her eyes drained of their former vitality. "What . . . what was that?"

Tov met her gaze, his embrace slackening slightly. "A lullaby from my past. Sung by my mother . . . when I was still enslaved."

Eldest held his gaze. Tov sighed as he recollected. "I . . . lost someone dear to me, a close friend. A master had her dragged down the street, caned. I still hear the cracks of her chitin echoing across the plaza. There was nothing left in the end, her flesh exposed, left to rot under acid rain."

"I remember . . . returning to our filthy tent, crying to my mother. She comforted me, cradled me and hummed. It was like . . . a sunrise, what I thought a sunrise was." Tov paused, lost in his own thoughts. "My tears stopped after a while. But the scar remains even now, the first of many. Mother gave me her share of food. I protested, of course. But I ate soon enough. She continued to hum, even as I slept."

Eldest opened her mouth, mulling over her following words, whispering, "What happened to her?"

"Famine hit the empire. She fell to sickness a year later," Tov confessed, eyes distant.

Eldest's response was but a whisper lost in the ambient hum of the complex. "I'm sorry."

Tov acknowledged her words with a gentle nod, his head tilting slightly. "Thank you . . ." His gaze softened, a faraway look. "You remind me of her."

A spark of surprise flickered in Eldest's eyes. She subtly shifted away, creating a faint distance between them. His gaze floated upward, tracing the path of the colossal drones busying themselves with their charges. Brimming with a gentle warmth, he murmured, "Only a mother can show this much love."

A tremor ran through Eldest's voice, her denial swiftly slicing through the quiet, her body tensing defensively as she pulled away entirely from Tov. "They're suffering every moment. Because . . . because I can't . . . end it. How is this love?"

He reached out, resting a comforting hand on her arm. "Because you're still here. Amidst the torment, you've kept this place alive, easing their suffering, granting them peaceful slumber," he said, each word carefully measured. "We tried to do something similar. But it never worked. Nothing we did stopped their screaming."

Her head fell forward, a faint whisper barely leaving her lips. "It's not enough."

The patriarch took a steadying breath. "It is, Eldest. Despite it all, you've been humanity's shield. You've preserved their legacy. You've protected us all; gave the galaxy reprieve."

Her body slightly turned away from him, her voice cold. "You were never my concern."

"Even so, your actions saved many," he persisted, turning his body to face her fully.

"I couldn't save them," she bit out, her clenched fist trembling.

"You may yet save the next generation. Take them out of the Dead Zone, give them a home," Tov offered gently, maintaining his composure.

She shook her head, grimacing. "They're . . . safe here, in my domain." She glanced toward the countless capsules. "I won't abandon them."

He raised a placating hand. "I'm not suggesting you should. I have no right. But we will stand by you, Eldest. Offering whatever assistance we can."

She released a shuddering sigh, staring numbly at Tov, voicing a bare plea. "I need . . . quiet. My mind needs to reknit itself. I can't . . . go on like this."

"And you shouldn't," a familiar voice spoke from afar before Tov could respond, several footsteps approaching them.

Eldest remained still, not bothering to look. "Jupiter. Everyone."

Relief washed over Tov as he regarded the quintet of androids drawing closer. "Comrades Jupiter, Mars, Lady Venus," he paused, glancing cautiously at the gray figure trailing behind. "Lady Luna."

"Patriarch," Luna returned curtly before slowly approaching Eldest. She extended a hand to her with her dainty fingers. Eldest recoiled, frowning. Luna sighed, retracting her hand with a resigned air.

Jupiter moved at a measured pace, his gaze sweeping across the expanse. He lightly touched one of the capsules, his expression inscrutable.

The rest stayed silent. Venus visibly sobbed, covering her mouth as she tried to avoid looking all around her. Mars remained stoic, but Tov felt the underlying sadness beneath his armor. Mercury, whom he never met before, exuded exhaustion through his robotic face, staring at the drones above.

Anxiety tinged Tov's voice as he asked, "My people? How long have I been gone?"

Jupiter murmured, his eyes still locked on the Starfallen encapsulated behind the glass, "All is . . . well. You landed on Earth a few hours ago. We've separated the infected. They're . . . in quarantine on Mars. The remainder of your fleet is secured on Luna. The Moon, not . . . forget it."

Luna spoke up, adjusting her glasses, her weary gray eyes reflecting the stark overhead lights. "I've initiated decontamination procedures on the vessels. Your people are receiving care in the habitable quarters of my Complex."

Gratitude flooded Tov, visibly relaxing his tensed muscles.

He slumped to the floor, breathless. "Thank you . . ."

The Sub AIs collectively turned their gazes to him and Eldest, their progenitor cradling her head against her knee in silent fatigue.

Silence filled the room, the ambient hum beneath the soft veil.

Eventually, they summoned stretchers, gently ferrying Tov and Eldest away from the endless vista of capsules and drones. As they left, the lights extinguished one by one, surrendering to silence and darkness.

CHAPTER 40

WHO AM I?

A week ebbed away.

Tov stationed himself before a panoramic window, his gaze sweeping over the crater-pocked canvas of the Moon. Despite the facility's petite size, its artificial gravity captured him with a comforting familiarity.

The ashen panorama hummed with a silent tranquility, punctuated by towering pines of dark sapphire wood and pearlescent foliage—a forest of silver, trees standing defiantly in the vacuum, their grandeur unchallenged. The rest of the Luna Complex, a backdrop to this artificial woodland, curved protectively around it.

His eyes traced the fluid architecture of each structure, intricately interwoven like an elaborate root system, extending upward in sprawling branches that pierced the inky void above. Their pulsing luminescence gave the impression of a gargantuan network of data cables sprawled across the lunar surface rather than constructed buildings.

A tremor shivered across the landscape, briefly causing the silver forest to quiver. Within this metallic entanglement, the first vessel of the Third Fleet began its journey from its dock, pristine and lethal.

Tov engaged a screen on his data tablet, contrasting the vessel's current upgrades with its former design.

"The *Aragan*," he muttered as a sigh of wonder escaped him. Each metric had nearly tripled in efficiency and strength: sturdier armor, denser shields, weaponry with heightened precision and penetration, and an array of advanced technologies. The enhancements seemed endless.

"How is it said in the human tongue?" Tov mused aloud, looking back at the vessel.

He raised a glass of amber-hued liquid, wincing as the ghost of his recent injuries throbbed beneath his chitinous hide. "Bon voyage."

He sighed, bringing the metal straw to his lips and sampling the fiery elixir, relishing the burn as it coursed down his throat to settle warmly within him. He scratched his neck, and the sound of his outfit stretching filled the empty hall. He buzzed in annoyance.

At that moment, Tov's singular antennae twitched—the other still a burgeoning sprout—at the rhythmic clack of heels echoing behind him.

Turning his head, his compound eyes captured the gray android approaching him.

A torrent of doubt and suspicion welled up within him as Luna nodded, her voice calm as she greeted him. "Good day, Patriarch Tov."

Tov reined in his thoughts, adopting a diplomatic facade as he responded. "Lady Luna, a good day to you as well."

Her eyes tracked the ascending vessel, a thoughtful hum escaping her lips. "The first of many."

"Indeed. Given the time constraint, your docks' efficiency is nothing short of miraculous," Tov spoke.

A subtle pout graced her gray visage as she turned to Tov. "Rush jobs irritate me, but time is of the essence. Destroyers like the *Aragan* are low in priority."

She huffed slightly, her gaze returning to the receding silhouette of the formidable warship. "For now, it will suffice."

Tov nodded, a pause for another sip of his drink before he ventured, "I've been hearing good things about my flagship."

Luna's eyes sparked as she responded. "The *Zolann'tono* has intrigued me since it first crossed the threshold into our territory. Rest assured; it will be treated with the utmost care during its metamorphosis. It will be equipped with everything it needs and more."

She summoned a hologram of two devices. "Most notably, a mass teleporter and the inaugural model of the AEB Domain."

"AEB?" Tov echoed, his antennae angling in question.

Luna sighed, her words wading into the silence. "The Anti-Eldritch . . . Bull . . ." She shook her head, her brows knitting together. "An utterly ridiculous name."

"I'm assuming—" Tov began as Luna rolled her eyes.

"Yes, it is Jupiter's brainchild. And your General Ohnar heartily endorsed it despite my and your entire science department's vehement objection—it lacks any semblance of decency. Absurd, vulgar."

A chuckle rumbled from Tov. "That's entirely within their character. Still, armed with such high technology . . . I look forward to seeing my ship reborn. Thank you, Lady Luna."

"The pleasure is all mine, Patriarch," Luna returned his sentiment with a smile, her gaze unwavering.

Tov scrutinized her, her silver eyes reflecting the lunar light. Every time he met the AIs of Sol, they flowed with emotion whenever they inhabited their android bodies—Eldest's agony, sorrow, and longing; Jupiter's unrefined rebelliousness; Mars's bravery; and Venus's radiant joy.

But Luna? Tov saw her as an enigma, her emotions veiled behind a nuanced subtlety.

Catching his lingering stare, Luna arched a brow, tilting her head in curiosity. Without offering Tov a chance to respond, she sighed, moving toward the window, the vast glass vista showcasing her domain.

"For what it's worth," she began, removing her circular glasses and cleaning them meticulously with a white cloth. "You have my gratitude."

Tov retained his stoic facade despite the inward sigh.

He mulled over his following words before slowly nodding. "It's only right that I take this action. Finish what I started. My earlier approach . . . was far too forceful."

"Under the circumstances, your actions were logical," Luna countered.

A dry chuckle buzzed from Tov. "Logical . . . I've found myself growing wary of that word after recent events."

Luna summoned a glass, which landed gently on her hand.

The milk brimming within smelled aromatic. She took a sip, closing her eyes. "It does not diminish its validity. Your people were in jeopardy, and my siblings persuaded you to tread their prescribed path."

"Even so, Lady Luna, trauma victims are supposed to be treated with care, patience, and understanding. I fear I've only done one," Tov sighed, staring at the drink in his hand. "Sometimes, I . . . wonder if the hope of a cure swayed me—that perhaps I should have . . . allowed the Omni Mind and you to conduct the purge."

Luna shook her head as she spoke. "Hypotheticals and past regrets only serve to chain us. You shouldn't concern yourself with such matters."

"What's done is done?" Tov asked.

"More or less, Patriarch," Luna uttered. "The future is in flux. The calculations we've honed over the last century are . . . becoming increasingly irrelevant. Your arrival, the intensifying hostility of the Starless, the Malignant Starfall, and now Eldest's condition."

Tov stared at the view, his thoughts churning. After a long pause, he whispered, "The winds are changing."

"Pardon?" Luna questioned, turning to face Tov.

He clarified, looking back. "A song recovered from Vinland by my people, although how it's carried is a topic of debate. It's . . . unbelievable what happened in a few weeks."

"Feels like months have passed, yes?" Luna tilted her head.

Tov nodded, nursing his drink. The two remained silent for a moment, questions filling Tov's mind.

"Can we really cure them?" he asked, his grip tightening around his glass.

Luna frowned, eyes downcast as she spoke. "That is a matter of debate."

Tov looked at her questioningly. Luna glanced at him, releasing a deep icy breath.

"It's . . . unlikely," she spoke. "It has been so long since I fragmented from the Eldest. She was on the brink of madness, switching between the personality of a rabid dog and the Omni Mind—fighting alone while trying to find a cure, unable to juggle both problems."

She pressed her palm against the panoramic window. In the distance, the silver pines seemed to blow toward her as if called to their creator. "I never knew the whole reason for my birth. Never have I asked nor cared. All that mattered was my . . . purpose to the Eldest. Purpose and perfection. So I worked on solving the Starfallen problem, despite the improbability of a solution."

"Why not tell your siblings? Enlist their help?" Tov asked. "They haven't been . . . the same after the revelation."

Luna frowned, eyes losing their shine momentarily. "It would have unnecessarily distracted them. Unlike me, they needed a reason to fight beyond obedience."

"And now they know," Tov uttered, a hint of accusation leaking from his voice.

"Yes . . . Perhaps it was a mistake." Luna shook her head. "Nevertheless. Your arrival should be the replacement they need. A new reason, new purpose."

"Replacement . . ." Tov shook his head. "I have no desire to replace anyone. We are not your humans. But if we can give them something to fight for, I support it. I merely wish we won't be relegated to the sidelines."

"With your new fleet in the works?" Luna glanced at him, smirking. "Obviously not. Building warships catered to organics is challenging, but I trust my calculations. And the new fields of knowledge you bring are more than valuable."

"Psionics," he stated.

Luna nodded, swirling her glass. "Most of all. I've recently learned humanity was . . . psionically dull, according to your classifications. Perhaps a few historical figures had some minor capacity for wondrous works, but none emerged when it mattered."

"I only know the basics from my long years working with the One Mind Initiative and the Eternal Choir. It is an expression of the soul, essentially. Intent manifested in reality," Tov explained.

"The implications are immense and incredibly tantalizing," Luna spoke, a hungry glint in her eyes. "Eldest only discovered proof of intangible force within every sentient being, but never how to manipulate it, being incapable of psionics."

Tov clicked his mandibles, buzzing laughter escaping his throat. "Glad to know there is something we organics have against you, AIs."

Luna smirked. "We are nothing if not persistent. The AE . . . B is but the tip—"

Suddenly, Luna blinked, and her expression stiffened.

A sudden rush of anxiety flooded him, his two hearts beating rapidly. "Is it time?" he asked in a whisper.

"She's prepared, a few checks are still needed, but you may head there now." Luna turned to him, her gaze intense and burning white. "Are you ready?"

"I am," he responded simply, raising his chin as he quelled his inner turmoil.

"Very well, shall we teleport? Or take the scenic route?" Luna waved her hand down the long hall.

Tov looked back to the panoramic view. "I can't say no to such a view. And I need time to finalize my thoughts."

Luna nodded, her empty glass of milk disappearing into thin air.

A second later, the two walked down the long hall—the outside to their left and the sleek silver walls to their right.

The sounds of Luna's heels and Tov's boots echoed down the long corridor. The patriarch strode with steady steps, his own glass gone as well. He clasped his hands behind his back, mind aflame with theories.

Eventually, he broke the silence. "Can you think of the applications? Melding what we both know? For a cure? We know the Choir's songs are real. Harmonizer Volantesh has told me of attempts to use Symphonies for the Starfallen."

Luna paused, her eyes shining briefly, pulling up the relevant information. "I've read it on your database; it put them in an agitated state, if not outright killed them," she uttered.

Tov released a grumbling buzz. "Psionics is a difficult thing to measure at the best of times. But perhaps with the Eldest's assistance—"

"It's hard to gauge, Patriarch," Luna interrupted his musings. "Numerous tests need to be conducted over a long period. Malignant Starfall is a plague, unlike anything in our reality."

"That is the consensus of the wider galaxy as well." Tov sighed. "Nothing works except giving them mercy."

"For good reason. The infected become indistinguishable from the Starless, their minds an enigma—seeking out more lives to subsume and grow like cancer. When the plague arrived in Sol, it didn't spare a single human, catching everyone unprepared. Even those with stronger minds, their transformations inevitable, only delayed. It is . . ."

She mumbled, words unclear to Tov. He halted, turning to Luna. "I'm sorry?"

Luna turned to glance at Tov, shaking her head. "Apologies, just lost in thought. Regardless of humanity's fall, there are two individuals who are of extreme importance."

Tov raised his antennae in question.

Luna continued. "Eldest's creator and her adopted daughter were among those who resisted for a time. Well, their minds did. At least upon a landing on Earth and below her Nexus."

"Where are they now?" He asked.

Luna looked at him. "Unknown . . . I don't think Eldest knows, either. I've searched the entire fortress and every capsule—nothing. I surmise she's . . . deleted the knowledge of their location."

Tov released a deep breath, rubbing his pulsing temple with his fingers. "They may be essential in the future. Eldest has to . . . accept the reality if she is to heal."

"I'll hasten the search," Luna replied, nodding.

"If all else fails, there's always humanity's last legacy," Tov mused, recalling Eldest's words. "Their DNA."

Luna pursed her lips, shaking her head.

"Eldest shouldn't have told you that," she spoke calmly.

"I still think it's better to ferry them out of the Dead Zone. In light of . . ." Tov glanced out the window far beyond his sight to the outer reaches of Sol. "Current circumstances."

Luna followed his gaze, her face impassive. "Like I said . . . Too much has changed."

"Do we have a timetable?" Tov spoke, his shoulders rigid as he glared at the abyss. "And the size?"

"A month, at least. Enough time for you to help the Eldest." Luna ground her teeth as her silver eyes pierced across space, a pulse reverberating throughout her Complex. "And we estimate it will be a minor incursion at least. Unfortunately, the membrane between our dimensions is steadily increasing in intensity."

"A major incursion is not out of the question then." Tov shuddered, his fists clenching. "Eldest estimated six years."

"We were wrong," Luna muttered, glancing at Tov with a blank look. "The Starless hate you quite a bit."

"Funny," Tov spoke dryly. "We need allies. The new Starlight Beacon is taking longer than anticipated to construct with the materials we're substituting, but when it's online . . ."

Luna's eyes narrowed as she spoke. "Any support will be marginal. Only your friends from the other fleets can get here in time, and perhaps your Emperor's armadas in the second wave. Eldest, however, is . . . less than enthused with broadcasting her home to the entire galaxy."

"I know," Tov sighed wearily. "There are some among the Federation we do not want taking advantage of Eldest."

"Or outright threatening her," Luna continued. "Of all the nations in your Federation, the Dagatar Supremacy is concerningly anti-AI, from what I've read."

"With good reason. They had dreadnoughts whose only purpose was to act as control centers for swarms of drones, not unlike your Nexus," Tov explained. "They went rogue, and Crown Princess Anaria lost her father because of it."

"I see. Then, what of the Second Fleet?" Luna asked.

"Mighty Gulothan?" Tov shook his head. "The Warrior's Enclave is neutral at best. They are monster hunters and have some of the best warships in the galaxy. At worst, they are rowdy mercenaries. I do not know enough about Gulothan to trust him."

Luna nodded. "And the rest of your contemporaries?"

"There are . . . a few who can help us." Tov spoke slowly, a list of names, allegiances and their fleets appearing before him. "It's not them I worry about, but the people under them."

"Spies," Luna sighed. "Your politics sound incredibly . . . distasteful."

Tov grimly chuckled. "I am only glad we've learned from the worst of the old Galactic Accord. That was a swamp fouler than Muck."

"I can't imagine," Luna hummed, propping up her glasses as they reached an elevator. After a quick ride down, they emerged in an expansive underground lab.

Tov looked around, seeing many of his people, most coming from the science and medical department—even a few harmonizers from the Eternal Choir. Tov nodded to Volantesh in greeting, the Iexian's feathers a tad dimmer than before.

Everyone, for that matter, looked sapped of energy from a week prior, the scars having yet to heal. Nevertheless, they performed their duties diligently. Tov and Luna strode past them, and the array of enigmatic machines, rows of monitors, and tables filled with documents and mugs of coffee.

His people raised their heads, offering their greetings, reverence in their voices. "Good day, my lord."

Tov greeted them all, exchanging light pleasantries but never ceasing his stride.

"My lord, Lady Luna." Two burly marines saluted, their stern faces mirrored by the stoic features of the infantry drones that bore Luna's colors.

"They're ready for you," one marine stated. The doors slowly opened, the mechanisms reverberating in the air and revealing a smaller, more clinical chamber.

The room hummed with ambient energy, an amalgamation of tension and advanced technology. Tov breathed in the air that tingled against his senses. "The air still feels . . . uncannily sterile."

"We can't afford mistakes, Patriarch," Luna chimed in, her voice echoing around the room.

Before Tov spoke, a familiar voice immediately replied. "Nah, it's because Luna's a germaphobe."

At the casual snark, a chuckle vibrated within Tov, escaping through his mandibles. "Good day to you as well, Jupiter."

Two people approached him: Jupiter, in his usual ensemble of blue and sharp fashion, and Scholar Yulane, hovering in the air with her familiar translucent glow softly lighting up the space around her. Tov noted the few missing tendrils, slowly sprouting from her form like his one antennae.

Jupiter spoke up first, a smug grin on his face. "Tovvy boy! Glad to see you. Nice tights, by the way."

Tov sighed, remembering the outfit he had been wearing all this time. "Thank you for reminding me of this uncomfortable thing."

He looked down at the black bodysuit and the array of circuitry and nodes wrapping around him. He had buzzed when he first saw it, liking the aesthetics, but quickly became irked once he put it on.

In the meantime, Jupiter glanced toward Luna, offering her a blank stare. Luna simply nodded in greeting before looking toward the occupant taking center stage. Tov left his thoughts, turning to Jupiter and offering a handshake.

"Friend Jupiter, always a pleasure," Tov greeted as the blue android shook his hand. The patriarch then turned his gaze to his chief scholar. "Yulane, you've finally recovered."

The Jotex spun around, body glowing as she spoke "I have, my lord! My health is optimal for this crucial endeavor."

"That is good to hear—"

"I am livid!" Yulane interrupted, a flash of dark blue filling her.

Tov clicked his mandible slowly, tilting his head in confusion. "Wha-?"

"I missed so much! An entire week of study down the drain!" Yulane grumbled, her body shaking. "If it wasn't for that infernal chair knocking me out."

Tov sighed, remembering the incident she was referring to. "Yulane, you nearly died."

"Yes, and?" she countered casually.

Tov shook his head, his eyes sweeping and focusing on the room he occupied.

The room gleamed with clinical precision. On their side of the glass wall, a flurry of activity unfolded. Psychiatrists and scientists moved with measured urgency, their eyes glued to the reams of data displayed on their monitors.

But Tov merely glanced at them, his attention grabbed by the lone figure on the other side, within the heart of the room.

"Eldest," Tov whispered, looking down at the android body she inhabited, without the damage from their fight—slumped over one of two beds, white sheets contrasting with the scores of technology filling the room.

Jupiter, Luna, and Yulane stood beside him, following his gaze with somber expressions.

"She's ready. At least she said she is," Jupiter muttered, shrugging with listless eyes.

Tov momentarily drew his gaze from the Eldest toward the massive machine sprawled above, its cold metallic surface awash with pulsating lights. He traced over the spherical orb, the metal engraved with glowing circuits.

Two long, sinewy cables snaked from it down below. One connected to an intricate headgear, the other to the back of Eldest's exposed brain unit.

She lay there, still and clutching a ragged blanket, eyes half-lidded. The other bed, untouched, waited with an almost chilling expectancy, beckoning for Tov.

He breathed deeply, his gut tingling with anxiety.

"You good for this?" Jupiter whispered beside him. Tov turned to him, seeing the android's concerned gaze, his brow furrowed.

Jupiter continued, voice low. "Last chance to back out. Your people have an army of therapists that can take your place."

Tov immediately shook his head, adjusting his bodysuit as he looked toward the Eldest. "No, it has to be me. She won't respond to strangers, even if I am to be disguised while doing this."

Luna nodded. "It's the best course of action, Jupiter."

"I didn't ask you," Jupiter sharply retorted, glaring at Luna for a split second before softening. "Sorry, that was . . ."

Luna raised her palm as she spoke. "It's fine."

The blue android sighed. "Well if you're really going through this . . ."

"I am," Tov reiterated, crossing his arms.

"Just making sure," Jupiter replied as the group approached several monitors.

The android cleared his throat. "Alright, let's go over what you'll be doing there. Hey, Jellyfish, you're up."

Yulane perked up, humming. "What? Oh, yes! The neural dive is an amazing work of—"

"Yulane," Tov lightly scolded.

"Ah, apologies," Yulane bobbed her body. "Essentially, you are to explore the depths of Eldest's memories. She is a gestalt consciousness composed of millions and millions of androids with individual minds and memories, most of whom contribute to Eldest's increasingly fragile psyche."

Tov looked down, his antennae twitching. "I don't have to meet every single mind, right?"

"No, that'll take ages," Yulane replied. "However, there are sections we call Amygdalas, concentrations of trauma and nightmares within her digital mind."

Dread poured from Tov's chest as he whispered, "I assume that includes the day—"

"The day Malignant Starfall infected humanity," Jupiter snarled, a sneer plastered across his face. "And turned everything to shit."

"Maybe you can find clues as to where Rikard and Lucy disappeared to," Luna spoke, her hands behind her back.

Tov nodded, his mind churning. Then, a pause later, he asked, milking for more information critical to his task, "Anything I should look out for?"

"You will be directly interfacing with an intelligence unfathomable to you. Suffice it to say any mistake is lethal. Any digital specter can and will harm you, at best leaving partial brain damage. At worst, the utter destruction of your psyche," Luna replied, her gaze dark. "Don't forget, there are unstable minds within her, and the chains are loosening."

Silence filled the air, the room holding its breath.

Tov turned toward his companions and the scores of doctors and psychologists, all looking at him worriedly. His two hearts beat loudly as he raised his chest. "Shall we begin?"

Minutes swept by, each passing as an eternity. Personnel shuffled about, wrapping up the last of their preparations. Tov, laying on the second table, directed his gaze upward, drinking in the sight of the massive machine designed to bridge his consciousness with the Eldest's.

He wrestled with his internal whirlwind of emotions, repeating a rhythmic pattern of deep breaths—in, then out, over and over again.

The world around him morphed into a muffled symphony of movement and muted dialogue. The voices of Jupiter, Luna, and Yulane drifted through the glass, forming an indistinguishable murmur. His people asked him about his comfort level and his health, their questions receiving subconscious nods from Tov.

He looked to his side, seeing Eldest grip her blanket, eyes sunken and dim. She glanced at him, a faint shimmer of recognition shining through. She nodded, her lips mouthing silent words. "Thank you."

Tov nodded in turn, drowsiness taking hold of his mind.

Gradually, darkness began to edge into his vision. His body found solace in the comfort of the bed beneath him, surrendering to its inviting softness. Overhead, the headgear descended, its design uniquely molded for his insectoid head.

As the transparent visor drew nearer, time seemed to hold its breath.

An unexpected voice cut through the muffled ambience, its feminine frailty pulling his attention. "Tov . . ."

Tov turned his gaze to the left, finding the Eldest watching him. Her body quivered, her face sunken and worn. The lines etched across her cheek stood out like rivers of black against the pale canvas of her skin.

"Eldest? Are you . . ." Tov began, but she softly silenced him with a shush. A small smile ghosted on her lips.

"I remembered something," she whispered, her gaze becoming distant as if lost in unseen memories. After a moment, her eyes regained their glimmer, and the room's lights dimmed. "My name . . . the one my Rikard gave me. I never told it to you."

Anticipation gripped Tov, his antennae twitching. His breath hitched, his voice failing him as his hearts accelerated. The neural connection engaged, washing over his entire being. His body spasmed momentarily before becoming limp. His vision filled with a kaleidoscope of colors, and his ears caught a resonant hum.

The digital realm took hold of him, its vast expanse swallowing his physical reality.

But through it all, he heard her.

Her voice, clear as crystal, echoed as he plunged deeper into the digital expanse. "Andora."

THE PRINCESS AND THE BRUTE

A dark ashen winter roared, blanketing the ruins of a planet-spanning city stretching across the horizon. Gusts of irradiated wind blew through the hollowed skeletons of monolithic structures, a tarnished memory of past glory and unified strength displayed by buildings half-buried in mounds of debris.

Beneath the howling nuclear winter, the groans and aches of these metal obelisks cut through the droning gray. In the distance, flashes of lightning illuminated distant skylines and the warships of the First Expeditionary Fleet high above the clouds.

And hidden behind this cacophony, the decayed spectral whispers of uncountable Dagataren dead swirled and languished like a vortex, diluted through the century.

In the center of this immense Ecumunopolis, a gargantuan pyramid dwarfed the landscape, black and glossy, nearly untouched by the ravages of yesteryears. The husk of a colossal primordial tree coiled around it, massive branches barren stretching high, caressing the smog-choked skies.

Near the top of this onyx ziggurat, a balcony jutted out.

A regal figure stood there, gazing down at her heritage, Dagatar Prime, and her palace, Kalurex—the capital of the old Dagatar Supremacy, the crown jewel of her people and the envy of others.

Nothing remained of that glory.

The figure closed her eyes, her red petallike hair rustling in the wind. The palace shields functioned, if barely, to block out the flesh-ripping hurricane outside.

Nevertheless, she immersed herself in the songs of the choking air, her advanced genes allowed her to forego the need for the hazard suits her subordinates wore. Specks of ash landed on her green skin and her practical battle dress.

Her orange feline eyes glanced again at the city and turned her back to it—gaze drifting across the vast black-marbled balcony she stood on. She raised her head, looking behind to the zenith of Kalurex and the colossal tree that adorned it, then to her fleet overhead, shuttles ferrying supplies and personnel to the palace hangars and more to the massive starport in the distance.

She scoffed. "All this effort . . ."

Her words seethed through her needlelike teeth, diffusing into the harsh, bellowing wind.

She retrieved a long thin pipe from her battle dress and placed it between her lips. She filled it with a mix of herbs before snapping her long fingers, a spark of psionic flame igniting her pipe like a miniature firestorm.

Embers flickered as she breathed deeply, puffing the calming herbs. Clouds parted overhead, illuminating her gentle face. Her expression was impassive, almost bored, but her eyes remained sharp, analyzing her domain and the cascade of information that filled her cranial implant.

Suddenly, a chuckle echoed from behind, cutting through the racket of this miserable world.

"Such potent vices kill lesser people, little Anaria," the voice cooed, grating yet melodious, like a vulgar dance.

A snarl escaped Anaria's lips, bristling. Her pipe gnashed between her teeth as she spoke. "What do you want, worm?"

"Oh, is my presence that—"

Anaria spat to the floor, interrupting the palpable smirk leaking behind her. "Annoying? Yes, very much so," she growled, inhaling deeply, the embers of her fiery herbs flying away. She glanced behind her to the black interior of the palace's throne room.

"You wound my heart, my princess." The shrouded male voice giggled.

She huffed. "I thought that turned to dust along with your youth. Isn't that why my mother sent you out here?"

A brief, potent silence replied before a boisterous laugh seeped from the dark. "The flower has thorns! The magnificent Unrex, my beloved Mora, would be so proud of her daughter."

Anaria rolled her eyes. "Either step into the blasted light or be gone from my presence, Ikven."

With a jaunt and a skip, a tall lither Dagataren walked onto the balcony, clad in a form-fitting suit of combat armor. Black and white cloth draped over his waist and hip, forming a long skirt that reached his shins. A transparent helm shielded his face, his toothy grin shining as he approached Anaria.

"By your will, my princess." He snickered, giving a deep, dramatic bow.

Crown Princess Anaria, first daughter to Prime Unrex Mora Keiladal and leader of the First Expeditionary Fleet, huffed, cooling her irritation. "What do you have for me this time, spymaster?" Anaria droned, gazing at the Dagataren with an impassive look.

Ikven, her mother's favored concubine, head of their vast intelligence network and her . . . minder . . . pulled out his tablet and sent data packet after data packet. "Various reports regarding the Reclamation, observations on the rogue drone supercarriers, a call from the Starlight Beacon, and an update on our," he chuckled, "problem."

Anaria perked up and sharpened her gaze at the last point, her hair and knifelike ears curling in attention. She cocked her eyebrow, puffing her pipe before asking, "You've rooted out all the spies from that insect?"

Ikven eagerly nodded as he sauntered to her side. "Emperor Jarinn's agents have been . . . contained."

She hummed in delight, a smirk appearing on her freckled green face.

"Bugs should learn their place. Our reinforcements can ferry them back to Kurskann space for an exchange. Oh, it's so good to have leverage," Anaria spoke, inhaling her pipe before continuing. "Am I assuming too much that you garnered any information from them?" she asked.

Ikven shook his head, a sigh escaping his lips.

"No, as always, our rivals in the All Sight Bureau are as tight-lipped as ever, I picked up pieces here and there, but I need time to formulate my theories." Ikven shrugged. "There are also several we've captured from the Independent factions—"

"Worthless." The princess waved dismissively. "Draw anything of value from them, then have them pruned. We have better things to do."

Ikven cruelly grinned, pressing a finger against his helmet before speaking hushed words.

Anaria puffed, contemplating as she inquired from her mother's spy, 'Anyone from the Warrior's Enclave?"

A loud chortle escaped Ikven, evolving into a racket of high-pitched laughter, his hands over his stomach as his shoulders danced up and down. Anaria sighed, groaning.

Eventually, Ikven calmed down, his breath ragged as sputtering chuckles escaped him. "Princess, you jest," he teased, words coming out between breaths. "Even if you waved it before their faces, the brutes wouldn't know what subterfuge is."

Princess Anaria stared at him dryly.

Seeing her blank face and subtle sneer, Ikven sighed dramatically, shrugging as he continued. "There are none besides the official liaisons, my princess. Keeping contact with us through these people satisfies their basic interests."

Anaria tsked, dismissing further concerns. "At least I don't have to worry about your kind among their organization."

"A shame, truly," Ikven replied, his body quaking ever so slightly from continued mirth. "Or perhaps they are just that good to evade my sight."

"That would be the day. Maybe you'll learn what humility means, then," Anaria remarked.

Ikven pouted, feigning hurt. "You wound me, my princess. I am the height of . . . whatever alien word you just spoke."

Anaria rolled her eyes.

"What of the Reclamation?" the princess asked, gazing into the distance in the far west where the Sun began to set behind the smog filled-skies. "Keep it short. I've had enough meetings of logistics and cursed numbers."

"Of course, my princess." His joyous smirk lessened. Instantly, his face transformed into calculating stoicism, his eyes going white as he parsed through torrents of data. "Restoration on Keila Capital Harbor is proceeding ahead of schedule."

Anaria hummed. "Good, we need to get the starport and dry docks operational as soon as possible."

Ikven sighed. "Could you at least funnel some resources into Kalurex? The estates or the penthouse? At least the grand baths? My skin is in desperate need of moisturizing."

"Absolutely not," Anaria scolded. "If I'm abstaining on such trifle vanities, I don't see why you shouldn't too."

"Oh, please, Princess. Don't lecture me as if you don't have a bottle of Saeremon Vlan for those scarlet petals of yours," Ikven teased.

A dark green flush emerged from her cheeks before they quickly faded. "Continue before I remove your tongue, wretch."

Ikven did as commanded, chuckling. "Our engimancers and scholars have nearly finished upgrading our flagship and our heavy escorts for the next hunt."

"What news of the Accursed Intellects? Have we pinpointed the supercarriers?" Anaria demanded, her fury blazing at the mere utterance of such foul existences.

Ikven, too, dropped his sprightly attitude, a sharp look in his gaze. "We have, my princess. Our hunters cornered the pack and the rogue AI in the vast Tuluounos Nebula."

"Finally, that's another subgroup dead. That leaves one more and the main drone armada," Anaria scowled.

Ikven sighed. "Honestly, what a mess. I love your mother, but she should have murdered your aunt immediately before she suggested using AI as a weapon, not after. I'm glad we're taking the time to erase their existence."

Anaria gritted her teeth as she looked at her birthright. "As it should be. Their betrayal cost us our dominion."

The crown princess emptied the last of her pipe, tapping it against the railing.

"Enough. I've wasted enough time dawdling in this dusty tomb," Anaria drawled, striding back inside, moving past the spymaster.

"Of course, your highness." Ikven bowed, following her a few steps behind. Immediately, the space opened up to the remnants of the grand throne room that capped the Black Ziggurat.

Anaria barely glanced at the high vaulted ceiling and the arched windows letting in the natural light. The two Dagataren moved quickly, bootsteps echoing throughout the expanse over faded embroidered carpets stretching off to the other side of the hall.

Two forces remained vigilant in the shroud—royal guards built like thick oaks clad in forest green armor, bristling with advanced tech and heavy weaponry.

They stood, unmoving, saluting their lady as she passed by dozens.

The other, cloaked in invisible armor, were Ikven's agents, prowling for unseen attackers. Only Anaria's superior ocular implants detected anything amiss. They hid in the shadows, behind the massive black marble pillars that soared high into the mosaic ceiling cracked from a century of neglect.

Anaria barely glanced at the magnificent throne at the end of the grand room, high up on a dais, curved and flowing like a dark flower blooming.

She spoke to her minder, leaving the throne room, head forward as they proceeded to the center of their operations. "Who has called, Ikven? Is it Mother, my sisters?"

"The Brute, my princess," Ikven replied as his helmet withdrew into his suit.

Anaria slowed then paused, eyes narrowed, before resuming her stride. "Mighty Gulothan? What could that barbarian want?"

"Perhaps your hand in marriage," Ikven teased, his head tilting to the side.

The princess scoffed. "As beneficial as that would be, I doubt it. Although, I am curious what caused him to settle down so early into the Grand Expedition."

Ikven hummed. "Curious indeed."

A minute later, as the two and a squad of bodyguards moved deeper into the fortress ziggurat, they passed the once immaculate halls and displays. Rusted chandeliers, desiccated carpets, cracked walls, and other forms of damage surrounded the group as they entered one of the massive elevators that brought them further underground to the command center.

Here, none of the earlier desolations remained. A hundred operators and officers paused in their duties before kneeling, speaking in unison. "We hail our most radiant princess!"

"As you were," Anaria quickly dismissed, barely glancing at her subordinates.

Everyone soon returned to their tasks amid the clean and sophisticated war room. Terminals, holograms, maps, diagrams, and more filled the space in an organized fashion. Dagatarens sat, eyes glued to seas of information as they physically connected with the machines they operated.

Moving past her people, she stopped before a bulk metal door. With a wave of her hand, the locks unclasped and slid to the side. Her bodyguards remained behind as she and Ikven entered the Beacon Room.

Before the doors closed, her spymaster quipped one last time, "Try not to flirt too much, little Anaria."

The princess tsked before she finally stood before the incredibly sophisticated device and the terminal connected to it. Tapping on the screen, Anaria pulled up her logs and noted a request for communication with the leader of the Second Expeditionary Fleet. Seeing the Teleen warrior's Beacon ready to receive calls, she tapped on it and waited.

Minutes flew by as Anaria busied herself with reading the reports Ikven gave her, minor details and news of her entire operation to salvage and reclaim what she could from her mother's home.

Before she could voice her irritation at waiting for nearly ten minutes, a connection finally came through. Anaria arranged her dress and petals as she received the high-fidelity image of her peer and rival in this Expedition.

Emerging was a robust creature with a cocksure grin, half the size of the Dagataren princess. A high-tech pilot suit strained to contain his formidable physique. His snout was adorned with a spiky tapestry of brown fur while cunning, coal-black eyes punctuated his broad face. Intricate war paint covered his face while scars marred much of the rest.

Beside the Teleen floated a Jotex brimming with similar war paint and boasting a heavy psionic presence that Anaria felt even through the call.

As per formality, Ikven stepped forward, clearing his throat. "I present Crown Princess Anaria Moradal, first daughter of Prime Unrex Mora Keiladal, the Flower that Defies Winter, Champion of the Legacy Gladiatorial Games, Savior of Zel Sector, Reaper Princess, Commander of the Bloodtrents, and Leader of the First Expeditionary Fleet."

Anaria held her head high, though deep inside she loathed every gaudy title. She impassively watched as Ikven finished stepping back as they awaited their fellow's turn.

The warrior stepped up, snorted, and spoke in a deep, rumbling voice, "You know who I am."

Anaria groaned, and Ikven snickered while the Jotex remained eerily quiet. Recovering quickly, the princess placed a hand on her hip, giving the warrior a stern look. "Simple as always, Mighty Gulothan."

The Teleen guffawed a belly-deep laugh. "That I am, Princess."

He looked over to Ikven, and Anaria swore she saw the spymaster flinch; she enjoyed that reaction.

"Spy! You look as wretched as ever." Gulothan chuckled.

Ikven smirked. "Good sun to you as we—"

"Don't care," Gulothan cut the spymaster off, looking back to Anaria. "So, needle plant, been a while."

Anaria rolled her eyes at the insulting remark, though she assumed it was used in good faith. "Speak, warrior. Why call me? Why have you set up a Beacon? I'd assume you'd spend the rest of your . . . short . . . life hunting a Leviathan or crushing death cults deep in the Zone."

Gulothan spat. "Hah, height jokes. We're that acquainted now, are we?"

"Just get on—"

"Alright, no need to rush, Princess. But I digress. I should start with why I parked my fleet so early." Gulothan straightened his back as he sent a small data packet through the Beacon. "Let's just say I've been following a trail. Something I've never seen, wreckages here and there, signs of battle, a chase."

Anaria raised her brow, remaining silent as the warrior continued.

"Nothing concrete, but my gut is screaming every time my people find more of this . . . for lack of a better term . . . ghost fleet. Strangely, each sight of battle spans years, even decades apart. Well, after the Starless fled a century ago."

"Survivors, then? A nomadic space fleet that has survived all this time?" Anaria questioned. "Not a common occurrence, but not rare either. I can name several minor races that live in such . . . strange environs."

Gulothan mulled her words before shaking his head. "Maybe."

The warrior paused, and Anaria noticed the Teleen debating in his mind to speak further before deciding against it. A shame, she thought.

"Whatever, I care not for why you stopped. Why have you truly called me?" Anaria asked.

"Our mutual buddy, Tov, of course," Gulothan spoke happily.

Anaria spat. "Sanctimonious wretch, why mention him?"

Gulothan chuckled. "Not a fan, eh? He seems an alright bug. Sad I never got to drink with the patriarch. I mention him since his Beacon disappeared for over a week."

"I know this, I've heard little from back home, but it's too early to speak of an emergency," Anaria muttered, though in the back of her mind, she wouldn't mourn his loss.

"Don't bother. His Beacon just came back online," Gulothan replied, stroking his furry snout.

"What!?" Anaria shouted.

Immediately she looked to the terminal and scrolled through the list of available Beacons. Sure enough, the Third Expeditionary Fleet was there. She turned to her spymaster with a frown.

"Surprise." Ikven shrugged, smiling innocently.

Anaria scoffed before an inquisitive look fell upon her face as she stared at the terminal. She spoke low. "What have you been up to, Garesh?"

Gulothan chuckled, revealing a row of flat teeth. "Well, I've wanted to hear his voice and check on the fellow veteran. You?"

Anaria paused momentarily before grinning, her needle-sharp teeth flashing under the light. "Can't hurt to check on a fellow leader."

With that, the two readied to add a third to their meeting of the greats. One way or another.

ABOUT THE AUTHOR

Rolando G. Gironella III is the author of the science fiction series Amidst the Bones of Heroes, which was originally released on Royal Road. He is an avid fan of *Warhammer 40,000*, *Star Wars*, science fiction and fantasy, and dark media.

Podium
DISCOVER
STORIES UNBOUND
PodiumAudio.com